PLOUGHSHARES

Fall 1995 · Vol. 21, Nos. 2 & 3

GUEST EDITOR
Ann Beattie

EDITOR
Don Lee

POETRY EDITOR
David Daniel

ASSOCIATE EDITOR
Jessica Dineen

ASSISTANT EDITOR
Jodee Stanley

FOUNDING EDITOR
DeWitt Henry

FOUNDING PUBLISHER
Peter O'Malley

ADVISORY EDITORS

Russell Banks
Anne Bernays
Frank Bidart
Rosellen Brown
James Carroll
Madeline DeFrees
Rita Dove
Andre Dubus
Carolyn Forché
George Garrett
Lorrie Goldensohn
David Gullette
Marilyn Hacker
Donald Hall
Paul Hannigan
Stratis Haviaras
DeWitt Henry
Fanny Howe

Marie Howe
Justin Kaplan
Bill Knott
Maxine Kumin
Philip Levine
Thomas Lux
Gail Mazur
James Alan McPherson
Leonard Michaels
Sue Miller
Jay Neugeboren
Tim O'Brien
Joyce Peseroff
Jayne Anne Phillips
Robert Pinsky
James Randall
Alberto Alvaro Ríos
M. L. Rosenthal

Lloyd Schwartz
Jane Shore
Charles Simic
Gary Soto
Maura Stanton
Gerald Stern
Christopher Tilghman
Richard Tillinghast
Chase Twichell
Fred Viebahn
Ellen Bryant Voigt
Dan Wakefield
Derek Walcott
James Welch
Alan Williamson
Tobias Wolff
Al Young

PLOUGHSHARES, a journal of new writing, is guest-edited serially by prominent writers who explore different and personal visions, aesthetics, and literary circles. PLOUGHSHARES is published in April, August, and December at Emerson College, 100 Beacon Street, Boston, MA 02116-1596. Telephone: (617) 578-8753.

EDITORIAL ASSISTANT: Maryanne O'Hara. FICTION READERS: Billie Lydia Porter, Michael Rainho, Karen Wise, Robin Troy, Stephanie Booth, Loretta Chen, Barbara Lewis, Will Morton, Joseph Connolly, Kevin Supples, and David Rowell. POETRY READERS: Mathias Regan, Rebecca Lavine, Lisa Sewell, Bethany Daniel, Renee Rooks, Kathryn Maris, Tom Laughlin, Mary-Margaret Mulligan, Leslie Haynes, Brijit Brown, Jenny Miller, Kimberley Reynolds, Chris Alexander, and Karen Voelker. INTERN: Nicole Beland.

SUBSCRIPTIONS (ISSN 0048-4474): $19/domestic and $24/international for individuals; $22/domestic and $27/international for institutions. See last page for order form.

UPCOMING: Winter 1995-96, a fiction and poetry issue edited by Tim O'Brien and Mark Strand, will appear in December 1995. Spring 1996, a poetry and fiction issue edited by Marilyn Hacker, will appear in April 1996. Fall 1996, a fiction issue edited by Richard Ford, will appear in August 1996.

SUBMISSIONS: Please see page 254 for detailed submission policies.

Classroom-adoption, back-issue, and bulk orders may be placed directly through *Ploughshares*. Authorization to photocopy journal pieces may be granted by contacting *Ploughshares* for permission and paying a fee of 2¢ per page, per copy. Microfilms of back issues may be obtained from University Microfilms. *Ploughshares* is also available as CD-ROM and full-text products from EBSCO, H.W. Wilson, Information Access, and UMI.

Indexed in M.L.A. Bibliography, American Humanities Index, Index of American Periodical Verse, Book Review Index. Self-index through Volume 6 available from the publisher; annual supplements appear in the fourth number of each subsequent volume. The views and opinions expressed in this journal are solely those of the authors. All rights for individual works revert to the authors upon publication.

Distributed by Bernhard DeBoer (113 E. Centre St., Nutley, NJ 07110), Fine Print Distributors (500 Pampa Dr., Austin, TX 78752), Ingram Periodicals (1226 Heil Quaker Blvd., La Vergne, TN 37086), and L-S Distributors (436 North Canal St. #7, South San Francisco, CA 94080).

Printed in the United States of America on recycled paper by Edwards Brothers.

© 1995 by Emerson College

CONTENTS

Fall 1995

IN MEMORIAM

JANE KENYON

ANN BEATTIE

Introduction

I admit it: I've written some introductions. Except for not being able to worm out of it with *Best American Short Stories 1987,* though, I've confined my remarks to books of photography. You know: The photographs are right there, easily viewed as fast as your fingertips can turn a page, so I've tended to write about various subtleties I've noticed and found interesting, or to call attention to elements more successfully presented in visual form than with words. I sometimes play a game in which I try to figure out the literary equivalent of a Joel Meyerowitz photograph (maybe Eva Figes?) or of a Diane Arbus photograph (Angela Carter?). I only play this game when I am looking at the photograph itself (or at the reproduction, more often). Yet I'm not very tempted to do the reverse: to think about how stories could also be expressed as visual images.

For one thing—though you may be surprised that I say this— the photographs usually linger in my mind longer than stories do. At least in the moment in which I experience them, they seem so real that I suspend disbelief. I know that ultimately they rely on façade as much as stories do, yet the photographs that fascinate me appear to already imply narratives (or, with some of my favorites, to reinforce my belief that words can be absolutely extraneous), whereas, for me, the written word tends only to be involving when it has done all the work something pictorial can do, and more.

I am drawn to stories that are at once on the page and off it, escaping boundaries just as a good photograph does. I look for a double accomplishment, both a bow to the so-called real world (I am tedious with writing students, begging them to include a telephone ringing at an inopportune moment, or a bird flying by the window), as well as a defamiliarization of that world, all achieved by including the detail or details that reverberate, on which the writer has focused his or her lens, in close-up. In short,

I expect the world of stories, and I expect them, in some way, to acknowledge the world. I'm a sucker for the ostensible immediacy of photographs. I want to believe I'm seeing something in the present tense, whereas with stories, I'm skeptical about an all-pervasive present; I have to be convinced the story would still stand up if put in the past tense. Why, I can't really tell you, but I'm here admitting to a particular—and no doubt self-limiting—proclivity. And I do not at all mean to disparage stories by confessing that I come to them much more slowly and skeptically than I do to a photograph. Like every writer, bits and pieces of stories come back to me at the most unexpected times, though I find that photographs tend to recur in their totality (or at least I think I'm remembering them distinctly).

Some individual sentences just kill me. I am constantly astonished by Joy Williams's ability to be a sort of Zen master of risible misery. To think that Mary Robison had such powerful, perfect spacebreaks in her tour de force "Yours," a story of about two printed pages, I consider a miracle. And the first five words of John Updike's "Separating"—I mean, they are so brilliant, we know they could not portend anything good. Perfect timing, perfect words, perfect spacing (I agree with Joan Didion about the importance of white space), can be incredibly powerful. There have been times when I've been almost hypnotized by the perfection of an author's words. Consider the beginning of Don DeLillo's *Libra*. The first time I read the beginning sentence, I closed the book and did not look at it again until I'd finished the novel I was working on. I sometimes feel like a lost puppy, finding safety in following someone who speaks gently and who seems not to lack compassion. And who also, amazingly, stands upright.

Well, in a sense, I do follow after those I admire, sometimes. Writers have a way of echoing each other, of using each other as springboards, so that critics perceive groups and movements, where there is only the puppy trail, I think.

But I digress. When I spoke of images so powerful they remind me of certain writers' stories—certain writers' worlds—what I wanted to say was that I'm drawn to things that seem vivid, and concrete, but that are also intangible. That texts exist as words, though when you are reading, you have the impression that what you see and hear and touch and smell and feel is the thing itself. This is by way of admitting to what is undoubtedly a particular sensibility—and one that has its limitations: When I write, and also when I read, I assume that when something *looks* right, in my mind's eye, I can place people in that right-looking world. Many writers seem to know how people behave and talk once they have a visual context for the room in which they stand, or when they envision the field in which their people have stretched out, but if the context doesn't reverberate, if the writer hasn't zeroed in on the real bull's-eye, concentric circles won't radiate.

When you read Eudora Welty's astounding "No Place for You, My Love," you're swept away because the physical world she describes is so familiarly unfamiliar that it almost becomes phantasmagoric. When Raymond Carver's character thinks, at the end of "Are These Actual Miles?" about the past, a time in which all miles hadn't yet been traveled (but if they had, he would have driven them in a car he remembers at story's end almost as a quintessential love object), you're spellbound because he's telling you what you couldn't possible have known—or at least known in those exact, stunning *visual* terms. As in Eudora Welty's story, Carver gives you the sense that if you identify with his character, you're everywhere and nowhere; that you are car, driver, used-car salesman, wife, lover, cheat, as well as the system that cheats us all. Both stories draw heavily on the outside world, which exists in both close and distant proximity to the increasingly claustrophobic, nearly hermetically sealed interiors where the action transpires. Both stories are seductions, in which the seduction of the reader parallels the seduction of the characters. And I'm a sucker for that. I'll take that ride any day. When you read the stories I've included here, look for the mile markers; look for the way ordinary scenes and routines are glimpsed, and then glimpsed again, slightly off-kilter, and the way the writer suggests the world's consequent reinvention.

I know I could point out some nice images, some clever turns of phrase, some things amusing and powerful in the stories in this issue. No different than an evocative photograph, they're right here, but they're not exactly quickly turned to and taken in—and I'm not saying a photograph should be approached that way, either, except that, as with all visual art, when you look at a photograph you do get a strong sense of the whole—what unity is there can, at best, register with instant impact—because you have the advantage of seeing it all simultaneously. Then you have to start looking deeper.

With a story or a photograph, I usually wonder the same things: Have I ever been here? Are these people familiar, or unfamiliar? (I always hope the answer is "Both.") Why was it composed this way, as opposed to some other? And—why not be honest?—I wonder: Am I better off, or worse off, than these people? (Landscape photography is a different story. In spite of all those graduate school years studying the Romantic poets, I do not identify with birds, gardens, or with stick configurations.) In the back of my mind, not forgotten as I read and write, is always the day's news, which I get by chance, if somebody calls and actually refers to any world event (not terribly likely), or from *The New York Times,* which is, paradoxically, both unbelievably riveting and narcotizing. The context of what I read on any given day is, of course, something created for me by the writer, but it's also partly determined by events large and small, as reported in the newspaper, or announced by a friend, or narrated—usually glumly and briefly—as my husband, Lincoln, paraphrases what he's just learned on "All Things Considered," whose introductory theme is sometimes his marching music from his upstairs painting studio to the cluttered world of the kitchen.

Like most writers, that is where I'm usually found when not at my desk. I stand around on the pseudo-marble tile and wonder about things, probably somewhat the way a religious person goes to sit in a church pew. I tend to stand, though, in confusion. The kitchen reflects this confusion, of course. Necessary to throw out flowers when petals have fallen? But how interesting the anemone stems are, like old men's crooked canes, once the distracting petals have fallen... Photos on refrigerator—good idea to take down, when babies depicted have started college? Food—any food that could pass for dinner, given husband's liberal ideas about what constitutes a meal? What are other writers doing? Eating excellent restaurant meals? Starving? Starving, I hear. Sometimes, the letters from editors that come with the daily galleys suggest, subtly, that the author is hungry, and someone such as myself—do they correctly imagine the amount of time I spend around the kitchen?—might be so kind as to throw a bone. I don't know about blurbs. Couldn't I as well break a wishbone? Blurb writing is a difficult mode: So many seem like epitaphs that simultaneously flatter the blurb writer. I always slightly distrust them, the way I'm wary of most introductions. They don't seem guides so much as sighs heaved after the fact. They're the OPEN ME FIRST appended to the gift you're about to receive. Oh, all right—but isn't excited ignorance to be trusted? You can always rely, then, on intuition and on trying to make your own order out of chaos.

A kitchenesque digression. By way of showing you that pronouncing on things, as one generally does in an introduction, doesn't come easily to me. I've been in situations when I've had to provide synopses to editors of what I intend to write. When cornered, what I do is write the piece. Then I proceed to write the synopsis. The physical laying on of hands seems necessary. It's true that I don't begin anything, story or novel, or even a letter to my parents, knowing what the plot will be. Like fingers hovering over the Ouija board, I find that I linger longer over some characters than I'd have thought, because of a kind of electrical charge they possess; I find, time and time again, that what seemed a digression I decided to follow after (or, really, a moment that expanded as it exercised a kind of magnetic pull) resolves itself by becoming an important element of the plot I could never have anticipated (or, at least, could not have consciously articulated). I often feel that my fingers get me out of trouble, rather than my brain.

Introductions often inadvertently try to tame or quantify that which follows. In her wonderful book *The Writing Life*, Annie Dillard has written one of the most alarmingly true things I've read about the position the writer finds herself or himself in, vis-à-vis the text: "A work in progress quickly becomes feral. It reverts to a wild state overnight. It is barely domesticated, a mustang on which you one day fastened a halter, but which now you cannot catch. It is a lion you cage in your study. As the work grows, it gets harder to control; it is a lion growing in strength.

You must visit it every day and reassert your mastery over it. If you skip a day, you are, quite rightly, afraid to open the door to its room. You enter its room with bravura, holding a chair at the thing and shouting 'Simba!'" When I think about it, that passage entirely captures the push-pull dynamic that I think lies at the heart of writing: You've brought something so monstrous into being (wonderfully monstrous, one hopes; shaggy; unable to be contained; no high-strung purebred, your unique creature) that it takes on a life of its own, and the more captivated you are by it, and the more the work reflects that, the more the monster has succeeded in capturing you. We know this from *Frankenstein*. There is always the danger that in speaking briefly about this monster, in introducing it, we predispose the audience to think this beast more tame than it really is.

Another problem I have with introductions is the same I have with movie previews: They give away what you're going to see. Also, the soundtrack blares; it's too noisy. They begin to take on a sameness, become a genre unto themselves. Introductions are where the editor lead-foots it out to a square dance and extends her hand, first left, then right, touching everyone to let the reader know that all the writers partaking in the festivities have been quickly, and formally, acknowledged.

Well, please assume that in being selected for this edition of *Ploughshares*, these formalities and festivities have been observed. In reading manuscripts, I discovered more powerful stories by writers I wasn't familiar with than I had expected—stories that made all the reading worthwhile, and that made me optimistic about the original, strong-of-voice, serious writers out there writing.

When they aren't standing around their kitchens.

Or whatever else they are doing when not creating—or avoiding—the beast.

CAROLINE A. LANGSTON

The Dissolution of the World

June 1973

Early on the morning of Alice's wedding, when I was nine, I woke to hear the front door slamming into the quiet, and I got out of my bed and went to the window. Standing on tiptoes, feet bare against floor planks chilled by the air conditioner, the breeze running up my nightgown, I held open a crack in the Venetian blinds and peered through to see my father stepping down the front porch stairs. In one hand he held *The Clarion Ledger*, still in its rubber bands, and with the other he clutched at the banister on account of the polio I knew he'd had as a child: under his trousers one leg was forever crooked, just slightly. He wore a coat and tie, as if he were going to work down at the insurance office, but it was Saturday. It was odd to me that he would be leaving then, only a few hours before the wedding at noon, ambling with a vague limp along the flagstone walk to the iron gate that creaked open onto Franklin Avenue.

Just then, I heard the front door again, and my mother rushed onto the porch after him, the hair she'd had done the day before tied up in a scarf and her jewel-toned caftan billowing. From the angle of my room, I could see her calling to him from the top of the stairs, her chin imploring and forward. I could hear nothing, though, could only see him glance back and mouth a word or two—perhaps her name, "Maybelle"—close the gate behind him, and continue down the sidewalk toward town. For a little while, my mother waited on the porch, arranging the folds of her caftan and looking after him forlornly, as if she thought he'd come back, but he didn't, and suddenly she flew inside again, as quickly as she had come out. Yet I stood still, and watched him growing smaller in the distance as Franklin Avenue bore downhill toward the courthouse and downtown, through an aisle of huge old clapboard houses shrouded in clusters of hydrangea bushes that were bursting forth in clusters of blue and pink blooms. At the bottom of the hill, my father would go to his office, I was sure, and I tried to imagine him behind his desk at the insurance agency on a Saturday, on this Saturday of Saturdays, when Alice was a bride and I was a bridesmaid. I could form a picture of him sitting in the dark there, with the glowing red sign, *Car—Home—Health—Life*, blinking long shadows through the picture window onto the linoleum, and I held that scene in my mind until he disappeared from view, then scuttled out into the hall.

Stillness lay thick over the house, except for tiny voices from the television in the kitchen and the floorboards which creaked as I shuffled down the dark hall, pushing open all the closed doors to see who was about, and finding no one. Not Gill, Alice's fiancé from out in the county. I hadn't seen him since the night after she announced their engagement two weeks before, when he came to dinner and sat confounded and awkward at the table, twisting his long, stringy ponytail in hand and mumbling "yes'm," and "no sir" to all questions. I did not much care for him.

But where was everybody else, I wanted to know, where were all the Memphis cousins who were supposed to be arriving? The year before, one of them had gotten married, one of the Rands, my mother's family. We had all gone up to Memphis, my parents, my brother, Rand, Alice, and I to see her in stiff white satin at the Second Presbyterian Church. At the reception CiCi ran about the country club with her husband carrying her train, exclaiming, "I'm so happy, y'all!" and taking tiny sips of champagne out of glasses passed on trays by waiters. I had thought it brilliant, sneaking round the hundreds of guests and stealing four rice bags wrapped in tulle and ribbon which I fingered in the back seat of the car all the way back down toward home. My cousin had eight attendants who had worn wide-brimmed hats and carried nosegay carnations, which, abandoned on the tables at the reception, I had picked up and admired. "Now you will have one just like them," Mama had assured me over and over; it would match my bridesmaid's dress from Peter Fran's in Jackson that was waiting in plastic. How many bouquets would be in the refrigerator? When would all the raucous day begin?

Light from the dining room chandelier burned down the hall, and I walked into it to find my mother settled now at the head of the long table, bent over addressing announcements. She did not see me, and I could see her teeth chewing upon her lower lip as she dashed off an address in her fine longhand, and put the finished envelope on the tottering pile before her. Announcements had to be sent the day of the wedding, she had explained, to all the people who wouldn't've been able to come in such a hurry. Then she had read out to me the section on them in the new edition of *Emily Post* she had bought on the day after we all found out Alice was getting married. "Mama," I braved the silence, "why come Daddy left?"

She seemed not to hear me, but instead ran a finger from a page of her tapestry address book to a name she was copying out on another envelope. My mother had a tendency to ignore questions that she did not think were appropriate for children to ask, and her children were always asking such questions. I stepped farther into the room and spoke again, this time asking, "Mama? Where're Alice and Rand?"

Again she didn't answer, only looked up, softening her face, and said, "Hallie." She stretched out her arms and drew me into the lap I knew I was too big to sit on anymore. At first I felt comforted, and clutched her around the neck with my bare arms, but then something did not feel right and filled me with unease. I could see in Mama's face how tired she was; she looked pale and veined and she hadn't put on her big eyelashes yet. Her arm was around me tightly. Once again, I tried starting over, "Well, where are all of them?"

Writing out an address, she did not look at me but replied with finality, "Daddy had to go to work for a little while; Alice is still asleep," and then, unsure, "Rand is...out somewhere."

"Then when are the cousins going to get here?" I was getting impatient.

"You know I told you yesterday that they were going to meet us at the church, be easier that way," she sighed over the satiny white box of announcements, then silenced me, "Now just wait on me for a little while and I'll help you get ready."

I fidgeted and caught at one of the announcements, pulling it out of the first envelope with our address embossed on the back, and the second one with its square of tissue beneath it, running my fingers over the engraving and reading:

Mr. and Mrs. William Exum East
have the honour to announce
the marriage of their daughter
Alice Honora
to
Mr. Gill Thrasher
Saturday, the ninth of June
nineteen-hundred and seventy-three
First Presbyterian Church
Anathoth, Mississippi

Then I looked around the dining room to see what Mama had done to it, for it had been off-limits all week. The reception was going to be in here, afterwards, with the table set up as a buffet, because the country club had been booked. Every last leaf had been added, and she had draped the table with her best damask linen cloth, but now this morning all was disorder: the stacks of announcements spilled haphazardly around the three-tier cake. On the sideboard she had stacked silverware brought home from the bank vault, next to the great punch bowl, which was hung round its rim with a dozen tiny cups and had fifths of rum stuffed in its hold for the planter's punch. My parents rarely drank, and so my mother had been excited about it, pulling out the recipe their cook had used when she was little. Mama had also set up card tables draped with lawn along the walls, which displayed the presents Alice had received; there were only a few, for in the short time, Alice had registered neither china pattern nor flatware. And through the open swinging door that led into the kitchen, I could see Vera—the maid who had raised Alice and Rand but by my time had retired to the new convalescent home on the edge of town—wearing the uniform she only wore for special occasions. She was standing at the counter arranging deviled eggs in circles on a tray, one eye on the small black and white television perched on the counter, which resounded loud and hollow through the room. She was older than I could imagine, but watching a dance show broadcast from Jackson called "Black Gold." When she finished the tray, she stepped shakily into the dining room and set it on the table edge, saying, "Here you go, Mrs. East," before she disappeared into the kitchen and the door swung shut behind her.

Every night my family had dinner at the table, my mother bringing our plates in full from the kitchen, and it was here that two things had happened. The first had been six months before, in the gray lull between Christmas and New Year's, when Alice had sat down one night in her usual chair next to the sideboard and announced, right after the blessing, "I don't think I want to go back to school this semester, after all." She smiled apologetically as she said it, as if she knew nothing could be more unexpected than this, and pushed a loose strand of blond hair out of her face. For a moment, everyone sat tense and glazed until Rand remarked shortly, "Well, where're you going to go?" He was only fifteen, but observed an orderly code of rules about what was and was not proper.

And Alice had replied, too easily, "I think I'm going to come home and live for a little while."

Diagonally across the table, my mother blanched and asked, "Is there something wrong, sweetheart?" worrying a napkin ring with her fingers. Alice shook her head slightly, as if only for her to see, and Mama visibly quieted. "All right, then," she pronounced. My father only looked sad; he was the first person in his family to graduate from college, and had all our lives told us if you didn't finish young, you didn't finish at all.

But when I thought about Alice back in town, I only felt horrified: In my mind the greatness of her senior year in high school, *last year,* suddenly crumpled in on itself; I blurted out, "You cain't! You cain't come back here!" while my mother leaned across the table and intoned, "Shh, shh, calm down now." People who had never amounted to much could stay in Anathoth without going to college, girls typing in the offices on Attorneys' Row and boys doing shifts up at the plant or the cotton compress. They were all around, but invisible. My sister, Alice, however, had shone, and was meant to carry her brilliance far before she brought it back to Franklin Avenue again, I thought. Her senior year at the Academy, she had sat in the back of a showroom Cadillac convertible as it wound around the edge of a new football field eked out of an acre of cotton land; it was halftime and she was grinning in my mother's mink stole, carrying a sheaf of roses and wearing a ribbon over her shoulder that spelled out, in glitter, "Demeter." She had been crowned queen of the Harvest Festival, and sat on a dais adorned with fruits and vegetables and cotton, her hair like corn silk. Later she had placed the roses in my arms, bending over and saying, "These are for you, Hallie," and I had glowed. Then after the game she had gone off to a party, and out of the window of the car, I had seen her sailing across the school parking lot with her tiara in hand and holding up the skirt of her brocaded silver dress that was luminous under the streetlights. Mama caught sight of her then, and murmured into the dark well of the Impala, "Isn't she beautiful?" Peering over the top of the back seat, I had seen her give my father a look I don't think I ever saw again, a look completely open and full of pure gratitude. It was only the second class to be graduated from the colonnaded Academy that rose up brick-new on the road to Vicksburg, and here she walked with the authority of an empress.

Then she was graduated and went up to Oxford like my mother and father many years before, where she pledged the same sorority as my mother had. Every day during rush, she had called home and described for Mama the parties to which she had been, which houses she had liked and who she had met, as I listened in on the extension. "This boy is pouring champagne for me and I've never been so happy," she crowed to her on Bid Day, speaking of unfathomable knowledge I would have to wait to know.

But then something happened. All fall after that, whenever the phone rang, I ran into the hall from my television program to answer it, but only rarely was it Alice. As the months progressed, she had less and less to say, and there came into her voice an impatient edge: she was just fine, there were more parties than ever, could she speak to Mama, and was I behaving, anyway?

But in January, Alice did stay home, after the letter from the sorority arrived de-pledging her for such a low average, and a note from the housemother of the dormitory expressing doubts about the crowd she had gotten involved with. After I heard my parents whispering about the letter, I found it in my mother's secretary and read it, but could not relate it to the sister I knew: There had been evenings when she disappeared for hours and had to be let in the door by campus security in the small hours of the morning, and she had been visited by boys "who did not appear to attend the University."

"Now what do you suppose that means?" I heard my mother say to Daddy one evening. Nights, they sat in bed and read, the light from the nightstand shining down through the open door into my room; they were reading the letter again, I knew, but my father never answered her. It, like everything else, was passed over in perfect silence.

So the next Saturday, my parents hauled her belongings back from Oxford in Daddy's truck, and she took a job at the public library next to the courthouse, where there was nothing to do but stand behind the great oak reception desk all day long, reading magazines or propping her elbows on the counter and staring out the Palladian windows onto Main Street. A couple of times, I dropped by there with Mama to visit, and one day Alice was not at her post. "She always takes too long a break, Miz East," the librarian, Miss Eloise, complained.

"It's 'cause that job is a drag," Alice replied when my mother timidly confronted her, but she kept on working. As winter passed she began to seem withdrawn, curiously dulled. She began to wear clothes I had not before seen, Empire dresses that trailed the floor and brown leather sandals with bells that jingled as she walked, wandering about the house aimlessly as if she were imprisoned, and smoking cigarettes at the kitchen table against Mama's raised brow. Sometimes after dinner she would escape in the Impala, and in the morning when my mother drove me to school, the car would smell of lake water. Rand was in tenth grade, and I had heard him mention once that there were parties, out on the levee, crowds of wild people camping against the dusk. These were the hippie rednecks with long hair who also hung out in the parking lot of the Big Barn Minit Mart that people said smoked drugs.

"You wouldn't believe who I've heard goes out there," he told Mama one day after school when they were watching *Somerset* in the sitting room, after he had told me to go away and I had lingered on the other side of the door. "Which ones your friends' children," he added, but then she turned up the volume.

Often that spring my mother had Junior Auxiliary meetings,

and Alice picked me up from fourth grade. One day close to Easter, when red buds were beginning to bloom, Alice drove up to the Academy with all four windows down, humming to herself, and when I got in the front and tossed my books into the back seat, she turned and said, "I have to go do something before we go home, okay?" She was barefooted and pressed her toes against the gas pedal, steering the wheel in the flat palms of her hands, and the wind blowing through the car smelled of sweet olive. She drove through town, climbing into the hills under trees hung with kudzu, heading for the fertilizer plant that burst forth at the top, overlooking all the delta. Silvery smokestacks thrust against the sky pouring white smoke and yellow sulfur. In the middle, an aluminum tower rose for a dozen stories, laced with pipes and threaded with stairs. A cooling tower, Daddy had once told me. Getting out, Alice went toward it, shouting up, "I'm here, come on!"

High on a catwalk was a man, with a blond ponytail sticking out of his hard hat, who leaned out over a rail. "Hang on jus' a minute, Alice!" he called out, and when I heard his unfamiliar voice speak her name, I became awakened and suspicious. He disappeared and I knew he was coming down; his footsteps rang on the metal staircase rungs. Then he emerged from the entrance, with his hard hat in one hand, and with the other he suddenly clasped her on the shoulder.

"Get in the back, Hallie, please?" she asked, and they got in the car and slammed the doors. "Oh, this is Gill," she said as she backed out onto the road.

He turned and gave me a look that was too immediately friendly, what my mother would call "familiar," and I mumbled hello.

"Guess your sister don't want to talk to me none," he said, and turned back around. Coming down from the hills, Alice took the bypass that rounded town toward the delta and then went over the river bridge.

"We're going to take Gill home. His car is broken," she explained, and turned on the FM rock station from Jackson. On the other side of the river, she turned onto a county road that meandered along the levee, past a country store or two and a rusty, long-defunct gin. Then she pulled off onto a gravel driveway that ran in a long straight line back to a tiny frame house and a single cottonwood tree, where she cut the motor.

"Y'all'gn come in a while," he said, and I followed behind them with arms crossed as they went inside through the unlocked door. The house was filled with gray, empty light because there were no curtains on any of the windows except one, over which was tacked an old bedspread. "Y'all sit down," he said, and Alice smiled at him, but there was hardly any furniture, only an armchair placed directly in front of a television set into which Alice plopped, a couple of side tables, and a chair that looked as if it were part of a dinette set which I didn't want to sit in because it looked dirty.

"You want a Coke?" he called at me from the kitchen doorway, to which I answered no. Then he came back in bearing two beers, one of which he gave to Alice, who did not, I noticed, ask for a glass. You were always supposed to ask for a glass.

He saw that I was still standing. "She don't want to sit down, eh?"

"Oh, Hallie," Alice said dismissively. My sister was transforming before my eyes; she had already metamorphosed into something different than the dreamy princess who moped around our house on Franklin Avenue. Now she was serenely expectant, leaning back languidly in the armchair so that her short sundress came above her knees. The sweat from the beer can was running down her fingers in rivulets, and she was looking up at him. "Well, now," she pronounced. I sensed that they were waiting for something, and acquiesced, sitting down in the kitchen chair with my feet dangling stupidly above the floor.

He picked up a strange pipe off one of the side tables and began to pack something down in it with an index finger, then lit a sparking lighter to it and inhaled. Don't burn yourself, I thought, or maybe you should. Then Alice took the pipe from him and also inhaled as the scent like incense curled again into the room. Bewildered, I stared at an unplugged electric guitar leaning idle against an amplifier, whose silver logo I began to spell out to myself, trying to tune everything else out: *Fender*.

He saw me looking at it, picked up the guitar, and ran his fingers along the strings so that they made soft faint twangs. All of a sudden, he got down in my face, leaning toward me with the guitar in his arms, and said, "Aren't you going to smile at me?" At first I felt embarrassed, then stole a glance at him and saw he had the clearest green eyes, and for an instant before he turned away, I allowed myself to realize they were beautiful.

"Well," Alice said again into the silence, and got up from the chair. "We better go."

"I talk to you," he called from the open doorway as we walked back out to the car. "Thanks for the ride." All the way home, Alice said nothing, she had not even asked me not to tell, but I never would, anyhow, because no one would believe.

That afternoon became like an illusion, half-forgotten, and I had not thought of him at all until two weeks before, on a day that Alice came home late from the library. This was the second thing that had happened at the dining room table. Mama had entrusted me with collecting plates and Rand was asking could he be excused when Alice appeared in the doorway, her long, pale hands clasping the door jamb. For a second she stood very still, then announced, "Mama, Daddy, I'm going to get married to Gill Thrasher." He was coming over to meet them the very next night. The whole picture of him, that house and those green eyes, came crashing into my mind, and I yelled out, "Hunh? Hunh?" until I fell quiet when I heard my father's tone, "Be quiet, Hallie."

"Who Thrasher?" Daddy demanded, turning around in the chair at his end of the table to face her, while Mama clattered a spoon through her coffee.

There were a thousand Thrashers that farmed on parts and parcels of rented land, and he was one of them. "Gill Thrasher," Alice repeated hopefully, coloring, "from out in the county. He works at Chemical. I knew him," she paused for a second, "when I still went to the public schools."

Flushing red, Daddy glared wordless at her until my mother finally waved Rand and me out of the dining room and slid shut the heavy rosewood doors against us. We waited, not saying anything, sitting on the bottom of the staircase to see if it would truly happen, and in the quiet, I heard through the doors an awful, strangulated sound. It was my father crying. Then I could hear my father asking her questions, questions that began with her name, Alice, and trailed off, inaudible. Her voice would answer, a constant soft murmur, and I heard the clink of china, Mama sitting there nervously arranging the plates I had not finished stacking. When the doors reopened, Mama emerged briskly, and I could see my father stroking Alice's hand with his own, imploring, "You don't want another sin before God, do you? You think you can live with this Thrasher for the rest of your life in some shack back on a field?" then leaned close to her and whispered so I could barely hear, "Can't I just take you away for a while?"

"Daddy, really," she said impatiently, rising to follow my mother into the hall. She stopped to kneel before me and ask, "You'll be my bridesmaid, Hallie, won't you?" Yes, I mouthed nervously, just as Mama returned from the hall closet struggling under a powder-blue box uplifted in her arms. She set it on the hall table, pulling off the top that smelled of mothballs and unfolding a cloud of pastel tissue. Exhilarated, she drew out her wedding dress carefully, fingering seed pearls that sprinkled down the bodice and fluffing out a crinoline that rustled taffeta under the skirt. "Now if we can only let out the waistline a little, it will be perfect. And what should we do for Hallie?"

Through the doorway I saw that my father had laid his head down on the table, but Mama was smiling and excited. Rand sat listlessly beside me, and all I felt was confused. "Oh, don't make it such a bother, Mama," Alice cried out. "You always have to make everything a big deal." She ran up the stairs to her attic room, leaving my mother thinking furiously: two weeks for preparations.

Mama was finally finishing her preparations, writing out the last announcements and pulling them into a neat stack so that Vera could add more dishes to the table. I watched as she brought in crystal bowls of nuts, silver salvers of pink mint roses, ordering them around the great icing-festooned cake in the center, until the table was filled. "Thank you so much, Vera. Now go on and take you a rest for a while until we're ready," my mother said, dismissing her back through the swinging door. Then she hoisted me off her lap and stood. "Now you. We have got to get you dressed and get your hair fixed." She was hurrying me to my room when footsteps fell behind us in the hall, and she called, "William?"

When she saw it was only Rand, swatting a tennis racket idly against his knee and holding the Impala keys in his other hand, she demanded, "Where have you been?"

"Been up at the Club," he shrugged. "Where'd Daddy go?"

She didn't answer but countered stiffly, "I had things for you to do. What came over you to run off today?"

I waited as he pointed up at the ceiling, indicating Alice's room, then spoke soft and volcanic, "She doesn't care, does she?"

My mother stood straight. "Alice was up late last night. As were you. You ought to know," she accused. Alice and Rand had come in late the night before from a rehearsal party that Gill's friends were giving them, even though there had been no rehearsal. It was at the Motel, I heard Alice tell Rand as they left, when they didn't know I was listening. I had fallen asleep visualizing it, the swimming pool glowing blue with underwater bulbs and all the doors around the motor court that winked a haze of pink, then green neon, filled with faceless friends. Later I woke hearing when the front door cracked open into the dark, hearing thudding steps and stifled giggles, knowing it was way after midnight, and now I peered at Rand to inspect him. "Mama, it wasn't all that late, all right?" he protested.

"Go get ready, you hear?" she answered, hustling me into my room by the shoulders and raising my nightgown over my head when I could have done it myself, but all I did was stand quiet. Mama pulled my dress from the chifforobe and buttoned me into it, dotted Swiss that fell to my ankles and a sash with ends that hung down my back, then I found stockings, new shoes from Vicksburg. In my parents' room I sat before Mama's dressing table as she coaxed my hair through her big silver brush, parting it sharply and plaiting it to the ends, which she tied with pink ribbon. Last, a single drop of Shalimar on my neck, and I sat while she stepped into a linen suit, took off her hair scarf, and spruced up the French twist with White Rain. At the dressing table, she put on eyelashes and liner, pinned on a tiny circlet of hat like no one did anymore, collected her pumps and handbag, then padded off into the hall in stocking feet, calling, "Rand? Rand?"

"Mama." I followed her. "Doesn't Alice got to get up now?" But she was not listening.

Rand returned with a loud green tie and his hair wet, which my mother combed to the sides with her fingers as I looked on. Except for his longish hair that brushed against the starched collar of his shirt in curly tendrils, he already looked older, polished, as neat and grave as my father's picture in the Phi Delt composite that hung in the hall, Daddy one tiny black and white square lost in the middle. As she arranged him, he frowned helplessly, resisting her hands, toeing his white bucks into the grooves between the long cypress floorboards. "This isn't going to take long, is it? There better not be a lot of people there, is what I say. I don't feel too well." So they had been drinking, I thought; that must have been the only reason he had gone.

"Listen," Mama stopped, her manicured hands outstretched and imperative, "we are all going to make the best of this."

Just then I saw my father on the porch, his features distorted into pieces by the panes of leaded glass in the front door, and he came inside with a look on his face as if he'd been dreaming. Mama focused on him, "Finally you are back! Your things are all laid out on the bed—" but he disregarded her, interrupting.

"I saw all your people down to the café, Maybelle." These were the Memphis cousins. "Drinking coffee and waiting all dressed up."

"William, they're going to meet us there."

"That's what they said." He looked at the floor.

I hung back in the hollow of the staircase curve, wondering how we were supposed to act: everyone was apart somehow, sunk in themselves. Alice. I held up my hem so as not to tread on it, and edged slowly and unnoticed up the stairs. The curiosity of our old family house was that the stairs didn't go anywhere, only to an attic under the roof peak. Our great-great-grandfather on the Rand side had built the house, and put them there "for decoration," Mama always said. But when Alice came home from Ole Miss, she moved into the attic, dragged up her things, and hung a motel "Do Not Disturb" sign on the knob of the battered door that closed shut at the top of the landing.

Slowly I pushed the door open, whispering, "Alice!" feeling for once older than she, getting her up on her own wedding day with everyone acting so strange. Alice had been very secretive about her room, and though I had been here a couple of times, today it seemed as if I were seeing it for the first time. Bare boards ran steep walls fifteen feet up into ceilings, and only two dormer windows shone thin bands of light across the floor. The windows were open because there was no air conditioner up here, only a huge box fan that droned noisily and swirled the stifling air into waves, which licked under the edges of wrinkled posters she had tacked all along the walls. On the floor, album covers were scattered next to a record player still spinning at the end of a side, its needle rasping in the run-out groove, over and over. And in the middle of the room stood Alice's bed, heaped high with clothes and covers. Alice lay lost among them.

I walked toward the bed and saw her asleep, tangled blond hair across bright paisley sheets, the wild pattern winding under and around her. Against the heat she had slept naked, and the covers and bedclothes trailed down to her waist. I felt embarrassed, thinking I should avert my eyes, but I was stunned still, seeing her tanned shoulders disappear into the whiteness of breasts that seemed swollen, more pendulous. Suddenly it came to me I knew what Mama, Daddy, Rand knew, the knowledge that I now saw had run like a current under the surface of the house. I stepped back, breathless and filled with shame, feeling myself an ignorant child. But I managed, piping up, "Alice, you got to get up now."

She stirred and, when she saw me, pulled up the sheet over her like it was nothing, smelling of smoke and spirits, mascara smudging her lashes. "Hallie Day," she said, pronouncing my full name as I stood rigid, not sure what to say.

At that moment Mama came yelling up the stairs, "Let's get you ready," and Alice stood up, draping the sheet around her like a robe, and loped off to the shower. Freed, I ran downstairs, took my bouquet from the refrigerator, and idled in the hall, picking restlessly at the tight knot of carnations and greenery. I remembered things I had heard adults say, of shotguns, and people counting up on their fingers how many months since the wedding to see if it was nine, and Alice seemed vulnerable to me now, as vulnerable as I, who could only wait for her to come down.

She appeared at the top of the staircase with Mama hovering behind her, crowing, "Here she is!" as Daddy and Rand walked in from the sitting room. Her hair hung across her shoulders like a curtain of light and her dress tumbled loose to the floor in yards and yards of white cotton gauze, its wide angel sleeves fluttering as she descended. She hesitated for a second, and in the silence I heard my father's foot heavy on the cypress planks, saw him limp slowly up the stairs in his seersucker suit to meet her, his face fallen and sad but his eyes fixed on her as he took her hand and led her down, saying, "Well, come on now, we're late."

Rand jingled the keys to the Impala and opened the front door to step out, the humid air rushing in, then Mama murmured, "Your flowers, Alice. They're in the refrigerator."

But Alice said, "No, I want these," and walked out with a train of gauze behind her into the bright heat of June that spirited through the trees. Looping the gauze over an arm, she broke off a stem of hydrangeas from our bush and cradled it in her arms, even as the petals fell on her dress, scattered in her hair.

Mama called out, "Vera," who came out the door wearing an orchid corsage and got in the back seat of the car on the other side of Alice from me. Mama was in the front, squeezed up between Daddy and Rand, so that her elbow was in my face. The car seemed to move in slow motion down the hill, and I felt faintly ill.

"It's hot in here," Rand complained, but no one replied, because Daddy soon pulled the Impala up to the vestibule of the church, where a small crowd of people was waiting under the Gothic arches against the sun because we were late. The minute we opened the doors, my mother's friend Ticey Williamson clambered rapidly toward us, the panels of her long aqua chiffon dress shaking back and forth. My mother had asked her to "direct" the wedding. "Y'all hurry up," she ordered, marching us through all the people toward the sanctuary. "I have had Estelle playing the organ for half an hour." As we moved through the cloister behind her, I noticed the piteous looks on the faces of the Memphis cousins and looked away, but beyond them was only a throng of unfamiliar people, loud and fidgeting, the Thrashers upon Thrashers I had imagined.

While we waited for everyone to resume their seats, we stood in the foyer, listening for the muddy chords of organ to swell. For a small moment, we seemed to share some kind of understanding, of having something to get done, but then Mrs. Williamson said,

"Here," crooking Rand's arm around Mama's and pushing them through the doorway. "Now go."

Then it was my turn, and I trod down the aisle towards the giant, unadorned cross that hung over the altar, then turned my back as I had been told. All too soon, my father and Alice were following as everyone rose to their feet and admired, as her hair caught the light from the tinted windows and hydrangea petals fluttered to the floor in the wake of her billowing white hem. In front of us all, Gill took her hand from Daddy, and as I looked again at his green eyes, I realized that it was not him, that he was not the reason we were sad. The reverend began speaking then, but though his words sounded urgent, they were unintelligible; they fell like soft rain on the ears of the people, who did not seem to be listening. Rand was inspecting all the Thrashers across the aisle, while my mother sat with her face perfectly composed, beaming at no one. It appeared as if my father might start crying again. Right then, I closed my eyes and, behind them, saw what I was feeling: the dull, empty dark that was bearing us away, each from one another.

The Big Room

Jen and I were driving through New Mexico with her father, who was a retired insurance guy just a few years older than me, a tall, thin guy with a swatch of white hair that slipped across his scalp as if it had fallen there from a tree. Jen thought this trip would be a good way to introduce me to her father, but on the second day things remained a little stiff, and Jen was still interpreting.

It had been raining most of the day, and when we drove into Carlsbad, New Mexico, late in the afternoon, the streets were flooded. It turned out we were some distance from the caverns, which I thought were right outside of town, but which were actually twenty-five miles south. The sun was nearly down, but there was still light buried in the thick clouds patrolling above us. The water washing over the curbs in town was metallic copper, reflecting clouds and sky together. We stopped at a four-way, then took a left onto a road that headed toward the caverns. We didn't get far. Jen signaled and pulled into the Holiday Inn, then went inside and registered for two rooms side by side on the second floor. We parked and carried the bags up, then stood for a couple minutes on the concrete balcony, talking about dinner. Jen wanted room service, and that was fine with me, but Mike wanted to go for Chinese.

"Not me," Jen said, going into our room. "You guys go ahead. I'm resting. I'm taking a shower and watching TV."

"What about it, Del?" Mike said.

"Sure," I said.

Jen gave her father a little kiss on the cheek, only the second time I'd seen her do that, and went into our room.

Mike gestured for me to follow him into his room. I didn't want to go, of course. I wanted to go in with Jen and relax and flip through TV channels, but these moments when you're supposed to have the conversation with the girlfriend's father always arrive, even at my age.

Mike tossed his suitcase on one of his beds and sat in the wonderfully generic chair next to the generic table, slapping the arm of the second chair. "Take a seat," he said. "I've been looking forward to having a chance to get with you one-on-one, know what I mean? Know what I mean, Del?"

"Sure," I said.

"So you're teaching at the college over there in Biloxi? And teaching is something you like to do, is that right?" Mike said.

"I don't mind it," I said. "It's good work. It's worthwhile work, sort of. In a small way. It's interesting, pays the bills."

"It's a fine career, teaching," Mike said. "It's a real commitment to society, to giving something back. You shouldn't short yourself about this."

"I'm not shorting myself," I said.

"Well, I mean, it's important," he said.

"Yes, I guess it is," I said.

"These kids need to be educated. Even Jen needs to be educated—she's got her degree, but she could use another one. Another degree never hurt anybody."

"We talked about that," I said. "About her going back to school, getting a graduate degree. Maybe art, we were thinking."

"You talked about it?"

"Yep. Sure did."

"Huh," he said. "Think of that."

I noticed there was a spot on the arm of the chair where somebody must've stuck gum or something, and then somebody else had come along and scraped it off, leaving a little around-the-edges residue.

"Well, we can't all be tycoons, Mike," I said. "Some of us just stay in the shadows, sneak by. Skirt the edges, economically speaking."

"It's not economics I'm worried about, Del," Mike said. "I don't know how to get into this, but perhaps I'll just come out and say it, okay? As I understand it, you're about—"

"Forty-seven," I said. "But I think young."

Mike did a polite laugh. "Anyway, what I was wondering was, see, I'm fifty-three, and there you are with my daughter, and she's twenty-six or twenty-seven—"

"Seven," I said.

"Right. So, doesn't that seem a little odd to you? I don't want to be forward about this, and I don't want to cause trouble, but it worries me, I don't mind telling you. I mean, I figured it would be best to tell you straight out like this, man to man."

"That's kind of you," I said.

"What?" he said.

"Not beating around the bush," I said. "So many people these days beat around the bush, the poor bush doesn't have a prayer, know what I mean, Mike?"

He yanked at the leg of his pants. "Not me, not my style at all, but I'm already retired, so I guess I wouldn't. Know, I mean."

"Well, Jen was a surprise to me, too," I said. "I'm divorced, and at first it was just a friendly thing, and then—"

"That's not the way Jennifer said it was," he said.

"What's that?" I said.

"A friendly thing," he said.

"Well, I meant it wasn't serious. I didn't know it was serious," I said.

"Nooner?" he said. He winked at me then, one of those winks where the message is "Know what this means?" I was not doing as well as I would have liked.

"No, no—not what I meant. I just didn't know what was going on. Now that we've been together a couple of years, well, we're comfortable together."

"Well, the both of you are comfortable, then," Mike said. "That's worth something."

He was around behind the chair now, leaning on its back, his arms folded. He was picking at his teeth with the nail of his thumb. "Comfortable. I like to see that, but I'm not sure. I mean, I'm wondering if you might—I don't want to be pushy here—sort of stand to one side, or try that, so Jennifer can go on with her life. Unless you see yourself as, well, you know—"

"Permanent?" I said.

"Right," he said.

"Well, I see that, yes. She sees that, I think. So that's why I don't get off to one side, as you say. We're sort of keeping company in a serious way."

"Keeping company. Now I haven't heard that since I was a kid, when my pappy used to talk about that. I think he used to talk about keeping company. That's nice, the way you use that," he said.

"Well, thank you," I said.

There was a long pause while he picked his teeth and looked down into the seat of the chair, which was beige. Then he straightened his arms and looked at the TV. The TV wasn't on.

"That Simpson thing's a mess out there, I'm telling you. I don't like it. You think he did it?" he said. "The police seem to think he did it."

"Yeah, that's right," I said.

"I don't know—you know that dog and everything, that dog found them," he said.

"Yep," I said.

"I don't know," Mike said, doing a little tight stretch with his shoulders, trying to move them forward. "I guess I'd better jump over and say good night to Jen. But I'm glad we had this talk. I mean, it didn't go all that far, but I feel better, anyway. We've had a little talk and maybe we could have another one later, you know? Build up to something."

"Sure," I said. "That'd be good for me."

"Let's schedule that. Let's pencil that in. After golf. You play golf?"

"No, I don't, really," I said. "I played golf when I was a kid, as Jen may have told you. I was on the golf team in high school. We were pretty fair golfers there in Houston at high school. But since then, I haven't played much. Golf's not my game, really."

"So what is your game?" he said.

"Well, I don't really have a game," I said. "When I was younger, I liked various games. I liked archery."

He gave me a look when I said archery.

"Well, I can't help it. I liked it," I said. "Shooting those arrows, that was fun. They shot across and hit those targets. Football and baseball, of course. I played Little League. Played grade school football."

"You didn't play high school?" he said. "You're a big guy— probably a big kid, weren't you?"

"Well, yeah, I was, but I didn't," I said.

"Why didn't you?" he said.

"I didn't want to," I said. "I decided in eighth grade that I didn't want to play football. I had an idiot coach."

"Everybody has an idiot coach in eighth grade," Mike said.

"This guy was sort of Vince Lombardi with that gay-jock conflict thing going. He had us line up and smack each other in the face before games—that sort of thing. Slug each other in the stomach as hard as we could. Get one kid to jump on another kid. That was always me, the one getting jumped. So I quit."

"Bet he didn't like that," he said.

"He told the other kids I was scared. Called me names. I saw him once a few years ago in a surplus store with his friend. I'm bigger than he is now, so I don't expect he'd call me anything if he recognized me. It was the Catholic school deal. This guy was still closeted. Liked to watch the little boys shower."

"So that's when you turned to archery?" Mike said.

"I didn't *turn to* archery. I was just interested in archery," I said.

"Were you any good at it?" Mike said.

"No," I said. "Bowling. I was pretty good at bowling. Now, there you go. That's my sport, bowling."

"I always hated bowling," Mike said.

We went to our room together, and after Mike said good night to Jen, he gave up the Chinese food idea and decided to get a sandwich in the restaurant. I said I'd pass and Mike didn't seem to mind, so I let him out of the room and locked up after him.

The comforters on the beds were abnormally plump. The television was a brand-new bottom-of-the-line RCA. I popped through the channels while Jen went into the bathroom and turned on the shower, then came out and started to undress. I liked to watch her dress and undress because she always acted like she was alone. That made it sexier, as if I was watching her strip on television, or I wasn't there at all and she was just changing, getting ready for bed, or for a date—as if she were completely vulnerable. And I liked how she handled the clothes when she took them off. She was neither too casual nor too precious with them. She put them down carefully but not too carefully. She folded her jeans, then folded them again. She draped her shirt over the back of a chair. She put her socks and shoes at attention at the foot of the chair. She looked good in her underpants. She looked healthy and young and a tiny bit awkward. Her skin was only lightly freckled. Her back curved in a pretty way. Her breasts were small and delicate, suggesting adolescence, just hinting that way. Her knees had pretty little wrinkles.

She slid her hands through her hair to freshen it, then stretched out for a minute on the second bed, her hands by her sides, her eyes shut. I got up and went into the bath to turn off the shower for her, and stopped to kiss her forehead when I came back, then sat down and started going soundlessly through the channels again.

"Thank you," Jen said, without opening her eyes. She reached down and pulled the flap of the comforter up on the side of the bed and over her chest and legs.

"Do you want me to wake you?" I said.

"Yes," she said. "Forty-five minutes. No more than that."

I switched to CNN and watched various muted lawyers in studios talk about the Simpson case. Earnest questions were asked by the news anchor (his face gave him away), and earnest answers were given by the consultants. In the courtroom replays, I spent a lot of time staring at Marcia Clark and the thing on her lip, the mole. I was glad I didn't have to listen to her shrill, officious, self-righteous version of justice.

I must have come in late on the Simpson report, because soon after they were on to Rwanda. The most horrifying pictures imaginable, thousands of people in a burned-out, mud-caked landscape with diseased water seeping in dark pools, the kind you see animals wallowing in, flies and bugs and people on the ground curled up suffering, wrapped in rags, smoke rising on the horizon, trees stripped of limbs and leaves, sagging huts, tents, people on stretchers, people being pulled by mules, ghastly, freakish, grotesquely maimed people wandering through the filth. Six one-armed boys in matching brown shorts. I wondered why we weren't more active in Rwanda. People all over the country, all over the world, were thinking exactly that thought, but none of us were doing much—we were going to wonder and wait for the next news story. I rattled through the usual arguments about going over there and not going, and all of them seemed designed to make me feel more guilty or less guilty. Only the simple *go* made any sense, so I took credit for being able to recognize that, but then decided the recognition was another rationalization, another trick. Then I figured I was too hard on myself, I couldn't be expected to do everything, or even any particular thing, and that all the guilt was itself an easy out—learned in Catholic boyhood.

There was nowhere to go with the cycle of guilt and relief, so I started wondering why the country hadn't done something about Rwanda. The massacre had been going on for months and months. I'd read about it in the papers, seen it on the news, it seemed like four or five months before. Eight months. How was it that a country, a powerful country, a country committed to decency, compassion, and kindness, routinely sat on its hands while tragedies unfolded? Again and again.

The pattern was the same. First a few little stories in the press, then more stories, and pretty soon earnest concern, and then grave concern, and then elaborate grave concern while many things were thought of and many people died. And then the crisis took a turn for the worse, and there was even graver concern, and there were more deaths and more stories. And then the crisis took an additional turn for the worse, and perhaps a third, and the process was repeated until what we were fed on the nightly news was a scene of incomprehensible agony. That's when the camera people did their lovely, lingering close-ups of the survivors, the new pictures matched with the hugely solemn voice-overs of the announcers.

I wondered what they thought of the camera people.

The eyes of these survivors always showed an inexplicable determination to live. I looked at them on television and thought, Why aren't you dead? How do you manage to want *not* to die? In that hotel room in Carlsbad, I wondered what I would want in their shoes.

Then it struck me that if they were in *my* shoes they would be sitting in a swanky Rwanda hotel watching me on their big screen TVs as I slogged through a urine-and-feces-strewn America, and they'd be thinking how bad they felt for not helping me out, they'd be wondering why their country didn't do something.

They'd consider doing something ineffective and insufficient themselves, like TV news reporting of the tragedy in America, or gathering medical supplies, or writing torrid op-ed pieces in *The Rwanda Times*, or just feeling guilty about not doing anything— the usual tricks we play on ourselves so we feel less guilty about good fortune. I figured they wouldn't lift a finger and they'd wonder about that look in my eyes.

"He's a really nice man," Jen said. "He feels he's missed something. He hasn't, as far as I can tell, but he thinks it, anyway. He's so cut off from everything."

We were in the Big Room at Carlsbad Caverns, a space the size of several Astrodomes, as the literature was eager to point out, seven hundred feet underground. Mike had gone on ahead of us. Jen couldn't see too well, so she was holding on to my arm as we walked the path. It was cold in there, too cold to be comfortable.

The other cavernites were running around taking snapshots of every weird-shaped chunk of rock they could find, using their point-and-shoots to good advantage, so there were flashes everywhere. Curious formations dropped out of the ceiling, grew out of the floor. The path, lined with a foot-high pipe railing, rose and sank as it weaved through the cave.

"What'd he miss?" I said to Jen. "What does he think he missed?"

"By my reckoning, it's Sting, mostly," she said. "He got married thirty years ago and lived the right life as long as he could. After the divorce he lived more of it. He's been in it all this time. And here you come along with his little girl."

"So?" I said.

"Produces doubts," she said. She grabbed my arm as we went up over a rise next to a rock formation that looked like a giant breast. The room was full of echoes. We could see the silhouettes of people on the other side of the cave coming back along the end of the same trail we had just started on—it looped around the perimeter of the Big Room. Every word spoken in the cave rippled around the rocks. It sounded like nighttime, flooded with delicate echoes and little bits of laughter and the odd drop of water into a standing pool, the footsteps fast and slow, children running on the path, people talking in foreign languages explaining the sights to one another, the wheezing of thirty-five millimeter autowinders.

"So what do you want me to do?" I said. "You want me to apologize for being older?"

"Oh, are we *older*?" Jen said. "Is that how we think of ourselves today?"

"Okay, forget I said it," I said.

"Does all this stuff look phony to you?" she said, waving at the rock structures growing out of the ceiling and out of the floor. "Does it look a little bit like papier-mâché in here, or is that my imagination?"

This had been bothering me, too. Maybe it was just because we were in the Big Room, the one easily accessible by elevator seventy stories below the visitors center, and that we hadn't walked in through the natural entrance, down through the Bat Cave, Whale's Mouth, Devil's Den, Iceberg, Green Lake, Queen's Chamber, and the other evocatively named rooms and halls of the natural path down to the Big Room. Or maybe it was that they'd over-cleaned the place, what with the lamps and pathways and signs and the little multilingual hand-held, tape-recorded personal guides that rented at the visitors center for four and a half dollars. Whatever it was, the cavern looked too well groomed for me, too much like a life-size model of a real cavern that might be somewhere else, hidden away, out of public view, inaccessible save to government scientists, leaving this cleaned, polished, carefully manicured national park service engineer's idea of Carlsbad Caverns.

"Yeah, looks phony," I said. "But these big guys do look like walruses, don't they?" I was pointing to walrus-shaped rock formations.

"Some do," she said.

We were just then passing a place on our right called Mirror Lake. The cavern keepers had put an upside-down lighted sign just above this tiny puddle, so that when you looked into the puddle the words Mirror Lake appeared right-side-up and rippling on the surface of this bit of water. The pool couldn't have been more than eight feet across, two feet deep, but in the Big Room of this putative Carlsbad, it was *Mirror Lake*.

"This is what you mean, right?" I said.

"Yep. I could do that in my tub."

"Well, so much for silent chambers and timeless beauty," I said.

"I think we've been deeply injured by our time," Jen said. "I really wanted this to be wonderful. If you repeat this, I'll deny it, but this morning when I got up, I was excited about coming down here. Maybe if there were a little more dirt around, if we tripped on rocks and stuff?"

"That would help," I said. "Maybe you should go down into the unexplored part. If you're young and energetic, and you are, and you pay the ten dollars or whatever it takes, you get to see an unspoiled, un-dioramatized version of a cavern."

"Do you suppose they've got all this dramatic lighting down there?" Jen said.

"Go back two spaces," I said. "Excessive ridicule."

"Sorry," she said.

"After you factor out the trails and the lights and garden-club beautification, it's still okay, isn't it?" I said. "It really is kind of remarkable."

"Yes, of course it is," Jen said. "You didn't think I was saying it was *un*, did you?"

"Who knew?" I said.

"I'm saying I wish it were a little more undisturbed. And I don't think the theatrical lighting helps much. In fact, it kind of hurts. It's hard to see anything down here. Ordinary lighting would be better."

"You're the matter-of-fact kid, aren't you?" I said.

"So what if I am?" she said.

"You can't blame them. It's a precious national resource. All precious national resources are lighted this way. Have you ever seen the Washington Monument? The Lincoln Memorial?"

"We live to decorate," she said.

Jen sat down to rest on a stone bench in the middle of the cavern. I sat down beside her. The bench was cold. A Chinese family was there with us, speaking in hushed but rapid Chinese. A plump mother, a diminutive father, and two gorgeous, lanky, silk-haired Chinese girls in their teens. The parents were eagerly discussing the scenery. One of the kids was staring at her hand, and the second was reading what appeared to be a comic book, using a flashlight the size of a Pez dispenser. A tall guy, an American, came up behind us and was talking to the people he was with, telling them all about the cavern, explaining everything, challenging the people in his party to answer questions: When was the cavern discovered? What was its principal value then? When did it become a national park? What is the role of water in the formation of the rock structures? How many million years ago did the mesa out of which the canyon carved itself come into being?

Jen poked me in the ribs with her elbow. "Quit staring," she whispered. "He's going to call on us."

We got up and walked along the trail past some kind of wire ladder that dropped out of sight into a hole in the cavern floor, then past another hole called the Jumping Off Place, then past a hole called the Bottomless Pit.

"Throw yourself in," I heard somebody say.

"This pit isn't bottomless at all," somebody else said. "Look. It's only one hundred fifty feet deep or something."

"Is not," somebody else said.

"Read the sign," somebody said.

It was much darker and colder in this part of the cave. We hurried along the trail, arm in arm.

"How is it you know so much about what Mike's thinking?" I said.

"He talks to me," Jen said. "In dad language. He's my dad."

The smart guy had come up behind us again, and he was doing a quiz on bats. "So how do they manage to hang upside down?" he asked his kids. "When they're sleeping?"

"Yeah," one of the kids said. "How do they do that?"

"Magnets," another one of the kids said.

"Don't be smart, Junior," the father said. "The answer is that when a bat hangs upside down with its feet closed onto something, its feet are in their natural condition, just as our hands are when they are open. See? When our hands are open, they're relaxed, and when a bat's feet are closed, *they're* relaxed. It's as if our hands were closed when they were at rest, but for the bat, relaxed is closed and open is working, like our hands would be if we were grabbing onto something. Do you see? When the bat relaxes, its feet close."

"You mean bat feet are like clothespins?" one of the kids said.

"Like clothespins," the father said, obviously a bit flustered. "Well, I guess so. Yes."

We stood aside on the trail and let them pass. We were looking at a small tableau, draperies of stalagmites and other formations called soda straws, which made up an attractive altar-sized indentation off the main path.

"Those little ones look like prairie dogs," Jen said. "See that one there?" She pointed to a little knot of rock that looked like a prairie dog standing on its hind legs. "They're just gathered around listening to Prairie Dog's Home Companion."

"We've got to get out of here," I said.

"What? You're not having fun?" she said.

"I'm freezing," I said.

"What about all these wonderful national rocks and these crystal growths and all these astonishingly beautiful and delicate objects?"

"I'm buying the video," I said. "Let's speed it up, okay?"

And that's what we did, taking the rest of the trail at a near trot, passing up the smart guy and his kids, the Chinese family, some other people we'd seen along the way. We even passed Mike, who was leaning against some rocks, looking up at the ceiling of the Big Room.

"We'll be in the lunch area," Jen said, as we went by him.

"Okay, great," Mike said. "I'm going at my own pace, and I think I'm going to be all right—you kids enjoy yourselves."

"We may be topside," I said, pointing up with a thumb.

He gave me a thump on the shoulder, and Jen kissed him loud on the cheek, and then we moved on fast. The lunch area was a hollowed-out part of the cavern with a fifties-looking concrete concession stand at the bottom of it, the architecture reminiscent of Frank Lloyd Wright's Johnson's Wax office building. We shared a quick Coke and a candy bar and then got in line at the elevator, waiting to go up.

"This is like the minus seventy-fifth floor, right?" Jen said, as we were waiting.

A bald guy in front of us turned around with his video camera,

videoed us. Jen made some faces for him and introduced me as
Jack Ruby.

"You remember Jack Ruby, don't you?" she said to the video
camera.

The bald guy stopped shooting and stood up. "Sure. I saw the
movie, kind of a mob intermezzo."

"You look a lot like Tom Noonan," Jen said.

"You should see how I feel," the guy said.

When we got back up to the visitors center, we stopped at a
trinket shop, and I bought a transparent red comb with Carlsbad
Caverns engraved in its spine. Jen bought a chrome and red and
white decal. Then we went outside and sat on a stone fence in the
warm and gentle sun. It was perfect up there. This little breeze
was around.

STEVEN RINEHART

The Order of the Arrow

Heitman, the queerbait, the insane, is my tentmate. Again. Porter, the fat kid who cries a lot, cried again this morning, saying he didn't want to tent with Heitman ever again. Last night Heitman put ticks on Porter's eyelashes while he slept. This morning our Scoutmaster, Casper, had to pluck them off with tweezers, since the hot match trick was too dangerous that close to his eyeball. The ticks came away with tiny chunks of Porter's eyelid clasped in their jaws, like grains of sand. Casper said this was good; if the head stayed in, Porter could lose the eye. He told Heitman one more time and he was out. As soon as he left the tent, Heitman dropped his pants and pretended to masturbate violently in Casper's direction.

Two nights ago Heitman leapt off his cot in the middle of the night and onto my back, bucking frantically. "Bergie," he cried. "Oh, Bergie, Bergie, Bergie, you hunk of man." I tried to twist out from underneath him, but he knew where to put his knees.

"You bastard," I cried, "get off me," but Heitman was laughing and slapping the back of my head.

"We're buddies, aren't we?" Heitman said. "Say we're hunch buddies, Bergman. Hunch buddies forever." He stopped suddenly, before I could say anything, and got off me. I turned over and saw that the moon was out and shining through the fabric of the roof. Heitman was half-dressed. He stood bent over, peering out the front flap of the tent. His shoelaces were untied, and his shirt was off. He had his Scout neckerchief tucked in the back pocket of his jeans. He turned around, his black hair in his eyes, and said, loud over the crickets, "Let's go out, Bergman. Let's go explore."

"Heitman," I tell him, "you can't catch fish with your hands. It's impossible." He ignores me and wades out farther into the stream in his underwear, the moonlight reflecting around where his knees disappear into the current. He rises up and sinks down, stepping on hidden shelves and rock formations, not seeming to worry about his balance. He stops on a high spot and squats down, his hands in front of him.

"They're sleeping," he says. "You sneak up on them while they're sleeping." I can see his rounded back and the row of tiny knobs that runs up to his neck. The rippling water of the stream makes his back look strange. It looks striped like a trout, or maybe like he's been whipped.

I settle back and look up at the sky, listening to the screaming of the frogs and crickets. My eyes are just starting to close when something cold and spiny hits me on the throat, falls to the ground, and lies there flipping in the dirt. Heitman sloshes back to the bank and climbs out. He squats next to the fish. It has stopped moving, its upturned eye brilliantly white against the dark ground. It arches its tail and lets it fall. Its gills open and close, and its mouth flexes, the moon reflecting off the edges of its scales. Heitman picks it up and walks over to the water.

"Don't hold it tight," I tell him. "Just let it go easy. If you hold it tight then its scales will rot away." It's something my grandfather told me. He never touched the fish he threw back; he cut his best hooks apart with wire trimmers rather than tear up their mouths. He tried to save the small ones, but still when he let them go, some just arced over slow and slid away.

Heitman turns and bends sideways at the waist and launches the fish straight up into the sky. It disappears, and for a second there is no sound, just the crickets and the rustling water, then the fish hits the ground next to me like a dropped stone. Its body doesn't move, but its mouth opens and closes, slower than before. Its eye is now dark and may be gone, I can't tell. I pick it up and walk over to the edge of the stream. The fish is bone-rigid in my hand, frozen in an arc. I bend down and wash the dirt off. But the eye is still black, and I toss it up gently over the water. Seconds later it hits with a small splash, shattering the reflection of the moon, and disappears.

Heitman is furious. "That's fine," he says, shaking water from his arms. "That's just great. Now what do I have to show?" He grabs his pants and starts up the path. He doesn't say a word to me all the way back to camp.

. . .

The next day around the steam tables, everyone talks about Friday night, the Order of the Arrow ceremony, and if they'll be Tapped Out. The generator is on, and Old Willy is watching television under the bus tarp. Old Willy is Casper's father, and he invented the steam tables and the water heater and fixed up the old school bus that takes us around. We know that no other Scout troop has an electrical generator, no other troop gets to wear jeans and not wear shirts and smoke cigarettes just about whenever they please. We are lucky. Casper has always preferred a more natural, Indian-style philosophy. According to Casper, the old army scouts were just half-ass Indians at best, and he considers most of the standard Boy Scout stuff silly. Summer camp is the only organized camp he lets his troop attend, because of the Order of the Arrow ceremony, where each troop selects a few of its boys to be transformed into men, the way the Indians used to.

"Merit badges are for pussies," Casper says. "Uniforms are for mailmen. I should make you all get tattoos instead." Casper has tattoos, up and down both arms. He wears boots with metal toes. He is a Korean veteran, the seniors say. He has a medal for valor against the enemy, and a scar on his shoulder from a Chinese bayonet. He's tough, but fair, he likes to say. Every kid gets a fair shake.

Casper's right-hand men are the senior troop leaders. They're in high school, and they don't eat with the rest of us, the small ones. The only one of us they can tolerate is Heitman, who they get a charge out of. They've learned that Heitman will do almost anything anyone dares him to do; he eats small animals raw, sets his hair on fire, that kind of thing. He eats at their fire, but they won't let him sleep with them in their canopy tent. Heitman has been known to howl at night; an unearthly cry, like rutting hyenas at a fire drill, Casper says. The only time Heitman can be sure not to howl is in my tent, so he mostly sleeps with me. He tells everyone I'm his official Hunch Buddy, and whatever they think, everybody pretty much leaves me alone. When I walk by, they whisper to each other. I know what I am called. I am Heitman's girlfriend.

The seniors spend most of their time sitting around their own fire, smoking cigarettes and telling stories about women they've

molested. Chadwell is the biggest. He has removable front teeth
and long, black hair parted in the middle. In camp he wears feathers in it, two of them that dangle just next to his ear. Sometimes
he soots the area under his eyes. Garcia is only slightly smaller, but
with bigger shoulders. He sits next to Chadwell and breaks the
wood that goes into the fire with his bare hands, sometimes using
the arch of his shoulders for leverage. He once hit me in the back
of the head for leaving grease in one of the big pots I was cleaning.
The next day he came up to me and told me a sex joke which I
didn't really get, and I've been friends with him ever since. I give
him the cigarettes I steal from my mother but don't smoke.

Heitman has gotten ahold of some Mace from somewhere. His
father is a mailman, he says, but I know he's lying. Heitman lives
on the street behind mine, and everybody on the block knows
that his father stays home all day, looking after his chinchillas. Mr.
Heitman has a patent on a chinchilla-killing machine that hooks
up to a car battery. He calls it the Chilla-Killa. You clamp one
electrode to the chinchilla's ear and the other to its tail, then
throw the switch before they tear themselves loose. They stiffen
right up, Mr. Heitman told me, right up like a big furry dick. It's
not the volts, he said, it's the amps. He shook a dead chinchilla in
my face and laughed when I screamed.

We sit on a stone wall by the front gate to the camp, and Heitman hides the Mace behind the wall from a line of Scouts who are
marching in to use the lake. They're from the rich kids' troop.
We're out of uniform, so their Scoutmaster doesn't even acknowledge us. He knows what troop we're from, and he hates Casper.
Earlier in the week, he tried to get us kicked out of the camp, on
account of our conduct at Taps, but nobody did anything. They
were too afraid of us. Every night, the other troop stands at attention while the flag is lowered, while we put our hands in our
pockets and whistle over the pathetic hooting of their fat-faced
bugler. The Scoutmaster closes his eyes in fury, and when the
sound dies, he marches his kids quickly down the hill to his own
camp.

The troop passes the stone wall, and Heitman Maces the last
kid in line as he marches by, eyes forward. It's quick, and the kid

doesn't seem to know what it is, he just wipes his neck and marches on. They tromp out of sight around the corner of the pool, the kid shaking his head, and Heitman stashes the Mace under a loose stone that had fallen from the wall. "Crap doesn't work," he says. "Wouldn't you know?" We walk the long way back to camp, and Heitman traps a black rat snake next to the path. Back in the tent, we put it in a box and collect tree toads. The snake swallows four toads before Heitman throws it into the hot water tank. It boils and turns gray and hard as a spring, its eyes completely white.

The seniors are grimly practicing being Indians for the ceremony when the Scoutmaster from the other troop marches in, red-faced. He walks up to Casper, his forefinger shaking, and wants to see all of the troop. One of his boys got sent to the hospital after being shot in the face with something. It might have been acid, he says. He'll know the boys who did it when he sees them. He knows they're here.

I come out of the tent in full uniform, more or less, trying to disguise myself. Heitman is nowhere to be found. Casper lines us up, and the Scoutmaster starts at one end, looking each of us up and down for a long time, then moving on to the next. His face is still red, and his mouth set, but after a few kids, it's clear he's not cut out for this sort of thing. He's starting to lose his nerve; he's too soft for this kind of thing. Even fat Porter senses it and seems to sneer at him. Casper follows next to him and tries to keep him moving along the line. He's on our side.

There is a noise behind me, and Heitman moves in next to me, naked except for his gray underpants. He stands rigid, almost not breathing, perfectly at attention. His bony chest is thrust out, and the hollows above his collarbone are so deep they're shadowed. The Scoutmaster gets even with me, takes one look, and taps Casper on the shoulder. "That's one of them," he says, pointing at me. I look at Casper, and his face is stone.

"Which was he?" he says. "The one with the can or the other one?"

"The other one," says the Scoutmaster, already moving on. He stops and squints at Heitman. He looks at Heitman's face but not at the rest of him. Heitman's face is cold, reptilian. His eyes don't blink and don't focus. The Scoutmaster draws away for a second, then leans forward, close to Heitman's face. "Have you got a problem, young man, standing here in your underpants?" Heitman smiles softly, then looks the Scoutmaster in the eye. Up close, the Scoutmaster's face is soft and freckled, and his eyelashes are just wisps of white above his eyes. He has a sparse mustache that sticks out slightly, trying to hide a harelip. The mustache quivers, like a rabbit, and it is a second before I realize that it is something the Scoutmaster can't control. He stands there, staring at Heitman, and everyone knows after a couple of seconds he doesn't have the courage to call him out.

Sure enough, he moves on and finishes the line. Under the bus tarp, the seniors have quit being Indians and sit around a table, playing cards loud and smoking cigarettes. When they notice the Scoutmaster looking at them, they lower their cards and stare at him. The Scoutmaster looks for a moment as if he might go over, but thinks the better of it and turns around. He sees Casper walk up to me and slap me hard across the face.

"Who was it?" Casper says. "Talk to me, and I won't kick the living shit out of you."

"Hey," says the Scoutmaster, "there's no need for that." I hold my face and start to cry. The Scoutmaster shoves in front of Casper and bends down at the waist, his hand on my shoulder. "No one's going to hurt you," he says. He's breathing hard, and his hand shakes on my shoulder. "I have a boy in the hospital," he says. "You understand?" I shake my head, and my throat snags when I breathe in.

The Scoutmaster turns to Casper. "I mean, he's going to be all right and everything. It's just the *idea*." Casper looks at him without saying anything. The Scoutmaster shakes his head, his face is terrible to look at. "I mean," he says, "I mean, the boy is *hurt*." He looks at all of us, but nobody says a word, and after a moment he just walks off the way he came. Casper watches him go, and when the Scoutmaster is out of sight, he sighs. He puts his hand on my shoulder, but I can tell he doesn't like touching me.

"Show me the can, you stupid shit," he says, his voice almost gentle. I look up at him with gratitude, but he's not looking at me. He stands with his hand on my neck but looks at Heitman, who is still at attention, his underwear sagging in front.

"Heitman," he says, "one more time and that's it."

Casper walks me back along the path to the stone wall, and I point out the can, under its rock. He picks it up, hefts it, and puts it in his pocket. After a moment he sits down on the wall and I sit next to him. He picks up his legs and crosses them under him, his elbows on his thighs, his metal-toed boot tips tucked behind his knees.

"Heitman's crazy, you know," he says. He stares down the road where the other troop came from. "I used to never think kids could be crazy, but that kid's crazy."

He looks at me like I should explain, and I know I have to say something. I think of Heitman at the river in the moonlight and say the first thing I think of.

"He's got scars," I whisper.

Casper is quiet for a second. "Where?"

I tell him, and he sighs softly. His shoulders sag, and he closes his eyes, just for a moment.

"You know," he says, "I was thinking of tapping him out tomorrow night. I thought it might be just the thing for him."

"Maybe," I say.

His voice drops low, and his face gets dreamy. "The Indians used to make their boys go out into the wilderness for months, just living off the land. When they came back, they were men. That's what the Order of the Arrow ceremony is based on."

"Alone?" I say.

He looks at me sharply. "They look for their spirit guide," he says. "An animal, like an eagle or a mountain lion, to lead them. Then they become one."

I want to correct him. He doesn't know Heitman the way I do. I know what Heitman would do to any animal that tried to lead him anywhere, or become one with him. Instead I say nothing, and Casper shakes his head and looks away from me. A second later he gets up and walks back up the path to camp. I follow him, not too far behind.

When we get back to the camp, Heitman is sitting with the seniors, smoking, looking pleased with himself. Casper walks up and takes his cigarette away and throws it into the cooking fire.

He walks behind him and looks at his back. I know what he's looking for, and I can't remember for the life of me why I told him that. Casper shoots me a dark look and goes inside his tent and pulls the flaps shut. Chadwell hands Heitman another cigarette, and Heitman lights it directly from the fire, his face nearly in the flames, impressing the hell out of the seniors. When I go to get some wood, I pass close to them, and hear them invite Heitman to spend the night in their tent. He smokes his cigarette and smiles at them all, one at a time.

Some time that night, he parts the flaps to my tent. His underwear is gone. I have been awake, expecting him, lying on my back and gripping the sides of my cot. I've been expecting him because I did not hear him howl.

"Come on out, Bergman," he says. "Let's go explore."

I say nothing. I lie stiff, not moving, watching him under my eyelids. He crouches in the doorway, one knee up and the other down.

"Berrr-gie," he whispers, "Bergie, Bergie, Bergie . . ." I hold my chest tight, trying not to breathe. After a moment the tent flaps fall closed, and Heitman is gone. His footsteps blend into the crickets and the bullfrogs and the sound of Old Willy's television. I lie awake and listen for him, but he doesn't come back.

When I wake up Friday morning, Heitman is still gone. Disappeared. He is still missing at breakfast. By lunch Casper is cussing, and Old Willy is passing out trail maps to the seniors. Chadwell tosses his in the breakfast fire and laughs, but stops when Casper sticks another one in his chest. "Find him," he says, "or don't come back." He snatches the feathers from Chadwell's hair. "And get that shit out of here."

The seniors take me with them, almost running down the trail. A quarter mile from camp, they stop as if on a signal and sit on some rocks, begin smoking cigarettes. Garcia offers me one of my own, but I say no. After about ten minutes, they set off again, slower, and tromp as much around the path as on it. Nobody makes any effort to call out Heitman's name, or look away from the path. Chadwell walks along breaking off branches, and Garcia strips leaves from everything he touches. What did you dare him to do this time? I wonder. Did you send him off into the wilderness alone, looking for himself as a man? Their backs don't answer me, and we walk on and on.

Two hours later we're back, running the last few hundred yards into the camp. It is abandoned except for Old Willy, who is asleep under the TV tarp. When Casper returns with a ranger, he is bone-rigid with anger; throughout dinner he is dead silent. Some whisper that the seniors took Heitman out into the woods during the night and abandoned him; others think he just ran away. By nightfall it becomes possible to believe the boy is dead. We wait in our tents for the call to the Indian ceremony; I leave the flap open for Heitman, but he doesn't come.

The woods are black beyond the light thrown by the line of torches. There is no moon, and the wind makes the trees brush up against each other in waves. Our line marches down the side of a ravine. The path is pebbly, and some of the boys slip, reaching out to the man in front, sometimes bringing them both down. On the ground they are kicked by the Indians until they get up. If they try to brush their clothes, they are struck on the shoulders with wooden lances. Porter starts to cry, and two Indians whisk him out of line. Nobody turns to see what happens to him.

At the end of the path, at the bottom of the ravine, is a bonfire, and in front of it stands a lone Indian, his arms folded. It is obviously Casper, in leather pants and striped makeup. In the light of the fire, his tattoos seem to dance up one arm and down the other. His eyes are closed. We line up in front of him and the bonfire. The other troop is lined up on the far side of the fire, standing quietly. Unlike us they are in full uniform—their Scoutmaster is also in uniform, and stands to the right of them. They blink and their eyes shift; one of them raises a hand to wipe his nose. I expect an Indian to rush up and knock the boy to the ground, but nothing happens. Suddenly my head is grabbed from behind and jerked side to side. "Eyes front," someone hisses in my ear. I smell cigarettes; I know it's Garcia, and I stand as still as I can.

Casper opens his eyes. He picks up a feathered pole and walks the line of the other troop. He stops and shakes the pole in front of a boy, and one of the other Indians steps up and taps the boy on the chest with his flattened hand, once, then twice. The boy steps forward, and the Indian leads him up to the fire, hands him an arrow. The boy's face is cold, and he stands with his arms folded, facing his old friends across the clearing, the arrow held diagonally across his chest.

Casper has two more boys tapped from the other troop, then starts with us, at the far side from me. My heart begins throbbing, and my body starts to itch, but I can hear the crunch of footsteps behind me, and I can smell Garcia as he passes. I feel my pulse in my fingertips and in my shrunken stomach, and I want to race back to camp where Old Willy is running the generator and watching television. I listen to the progress of Garcia from one end and Casper from the other, one in back and the other in front.

Casper shakes his pole, and one of our own is tapped out, one of the older boys. The Indian hits him hard in the chest, much harder than the other troop, but he is ready, one foot slightly back, and the sound of flesh on flesh is so loud it echoes off the trees around us. The troop across the clearing sways in line at the sound, their eyes widening. Our boy walks forward and stands in front of us, his back to the fire. He stares over our heads.

Casper taps out one more, then two. He moves down the line and then stops dead in front of me. My heart clenches in my chest, and my breath starts to catch in my throat. I am sure he sees me crying. He looks me in the eye, and his face is too dark to see clearly, but I can see his eyes. They look crazy; the moisture in them reflects the beating of the bonfire. He stands there, staring at me, his chest rising and falling. He seems to stand there forever. *Please,* I say to myself, *please. I want you to.* Then he smiles, but in a bad way, the way Heitman smiles at fat Porter. I close my hot eyes when his feet crunch away from me.

He reaches the end of the line without again shaking the pole. The Indian behind him takes his place next to the three boys, and Casper walks to the bonfire and turns to face the rest of us—the small ones, the ones left over. He raises his arms high up from his sides, eyes squeezed nearly shut, and his chest starts to swell, getting ready to shout at the treetops. Because he is like this, he doesn't see Heitman walk slowly into the light of the clearing. When he opens his eyes and sees him, whatever he was thinking of shouting comes out instead as a kind of twisted yelp. His arms fall to his sides like shot birds.

Heitman is naked, smeared with mud in streaks across his sides. There is blood on his legs and what looks like shit in his hair. He carries something in his arms: a big mess of blood and bone and feathers sticking out this way and that. He is naked, but he walks with his skinny shoulders back, up on the balls of his feet. The way he moves makes the Indians look like school kids lost in the woods in their pajamas. They stare at him—next to them, one of the chosen boys drops his arrow in the dirt. Casper, like a deflating balloon, sits down right where he was standing.

Heitman has caught a wild turkey, and killed it. Heitman has caught a wild turkey with his bare hands. He doesn't say anything, he just stands and faces us, the turkey in his arms. He looks exhausted; he looks done in. We glance at each other, and we start to move and shuffle in our places, and just then fat Porter goes and does it. He starts in, and after a second everybody joins him. We stand there, the small ones, all in a line in front of Heitman and the bonfire and the Indians, and we howl. We howl, and we howl, and Heitman smiles down the line at us all, one at a time. When he gets to me, his eyes rest only for a second, then drift on past to the next boy. My heart clenches again, but it is too late; now we are all Heitman's girlfriend.

Braid

In the late winter of 1985, John Rogan had been a surgeon for almost thirty-five years, and though still active and vital, a tall, erect, white-haired man, with a reputation for audacity matched by success, he was thinking of retiring. His older brother, also a surgeon, had apparently committed suicide the year before. He had fallen or jumped from the turret of a castle he was visiting in Ireland, and Rogan, who had always pursued life as though sighting a rifle, suddenly found he was losing his aim.

It seemed possible that if his brother could destroy himself, then suicide might overtake Rogan as well. He struggled with this thought and concealed it. Now he was on his morning rounds, and Nina Hendersen passing in the hall caught sight of him and on an impulse stopped him, placing herself in front of him, blocking his way. She had heard other women talk about him and liked his looks but didn't know what she wanted with him.

She was plain, and not long ago Rogan wouldn't have given her a second glance, but now he did. She was young-looking to be near forty. The tag on her smock said she was a physical therapist. She gazed up with an odd look of determination and then, remembering herself, smiled. Excuse me. I need some advice, she began in a small voice and then gathered strength and went on in an exacting way as though making a diagnosis. I have a patient with an injury to the adductor longus. It separated from the pubis in a skiing accident. She wants to know when she can have sex again. The words spilled almost without Nina's awareness. She scanned Rogan's face, thinking he looked like Paul Newman. He had the same blue eyes.

Rogan understood she was trying to flirt. Well, how long has it been?

Nina pulled an answer from the air. Weeks.

Anytime, then, Rogan said with a trace of humor, as long as she keeps the leg straight and holds still.

But then it seemed Nina's nerve failed. She blushed deeply, saying she would give the patient his advice, and then hurried off, her thick braid flicking at her waist, putting Rogan in mind of a girl he had once known who spent all her time riding horses, a small, angular, and oddly attractive girl who had little to say, at least to him. He watched her to the end of the hall. At the last instant, she looked back in panic—she didn't believe what she'd said—and turned the corner and was gone. He smiled wryly and dismissed the event, yet at odd moments found himself thinking about her. The braid looked as thick as a man's wrist.

Late that same day, Nina's husband, Johnny Hendersen, arrived home from Cleveland, where he'd been on business for Pharmikon, one of the drug companies that employed him as a PR consultant. She had not expected him that afternoon or any particular time at all, since in the past months his trips had become more frequent, his delays unconvincingly explained in long distance calls from hotel rooms.

She had been vaguely waiting for him to call again from wherever he was, and now when she was startled by the familiar sounds of his movements—the cautious turning of the key in the lock and the surreptitious whisk of his door across the carpeting—as he came in through his office instead of the family entrance, she knew he had been with another woman this trip and could already see the dishonest grin that would greet her. She felt exhausted, her anger banked down to hatred. If she didn't act glad to see him, he would frown and go back in his office until Eric and Ian came home from school and he could avoid her by paying attention to them. If she confronted him, they would argue. But she knew what was true without asking. It was a year since they last made love. She wouldn't lower herself to accuse him. Yet a silent, unthinking part of her wanted to believe he was faithful.

That night, after the children were in bed, Nina sat at the vanity and carefully unbraided and brushed her hair. It made static and sparks. When she was a girl, adults at parties often gathered around her and took turns touching her hair, holding her braid and exclaiming over its softness and weight. Hendersen, lying in bed, watched her over the top of his book. He loved her hair, and the sight of her brushing it, her arms raised so that her nightgown pulled against her chest and ribs, aroused him. Her eyes caught his in the mirror, and he glanced away. Soon, she came to bed, and they lay side by side, he with his book and she with hers. He was a former football player and lay under the blanket like an escarpment under snow. After a time, he closed his book and turned toward her. It's not what you think.

How do you know what I think?

We've been through it before, he said.

She turned a look on him. What else can I think? The way you act, the way you treat me.

I've haven't been cheating on you, he said firmly. I've just been going to see Polly for the past few months—whenever I travel, that's all. I stop off and spend an afternoon or two with her. I didn't mention it because I knew it would upset you.

Polly was their teenage daughter institutionalized with severe cerebral palsy. They seldom talked about her, and it seemed to Nina that he was using Polly as an excuse. Why would you start going to see her again all of a sudden?

I had a feeling.

A feeling, Nina said flatly.

That I should go, he said.

Her frustration with him was becoming unbearable to her. She marked her place in her book and put it on her chest, folding her hands on it. What do you do there? What could you possibly be doing there for days at a time?

I just visit. Hendersen lifted a hand, and his fingers made a small gesture caressing the air. I hold her. I talk to her. Sometimes I take her outside in a wheelchair and put her on a blanket in the leaves. She's getting better.

Nina's voice rose with fear. Better? How is she getting better?

It's just small things. She's stronger, more alert. Sometimes she squeezes my fingers. I think she recognizes me.

You always think that, Nina said.

Hendersen was offended. No I don't.

Yes you do. You just don't remember. Anyway, the doctors have told us over and over: there's no way to reach her.

How do we know that? Hendersen sat up, dragging all the covers with him. If she's aware, then everything we do reaches her, and if she's only a little aware, then *something* reaches her, and even if she can't respond, what difference does that make? It's not about her recognizing us, it's about *us* recognizing her.

I don't believe this, Nina said tensely. Give me back the covers. I thought we'd been over this all a long time ago. I thought we agreed. You have no idea how cruel it is to bring it all up again. Nina was seething. You have no idea—none!—what it's like to be the mother.

A minute passed and then another.

His weight shifted toward her. Listen to me. Will you just listen to me. You don't have to do anything, just listen. He reached for the book on her chest. May I put this away?

She shook her head. I'm going to read some more.

He lay down and closed his eyes, but it was hard to keep silent. He needed to talk it out. He wanted to know what Nina really thought. Unanswerable questions percolated in him. Was there a meaning to Polly's life? If she was given life, wasn't she also given love? But if she couldn't express love, what happened to it? What was love? What was *their* love? His thoughts circulated until at last he said, You know, I get lonely.

Nina eyed him bitterly. Maybe you should stay home more.

Maybe I should, he said.

Later, she lay awake, and a troubling memory came to her. She saw the unborn child, like a small, beautiful darkling god, folded upside down waiting to be delivered. But afterward, the infant, whose injury showed in small indentations of forceps on the sides of her skull, seemed like a punishment for the unwed pregnancy, an atonement she was meant to embrace but could not. It was too ugly, and now it seemed to her she never would have married Johnny Hendersen if she hadn't been pregnant. People said he was nice, but if you listened to him, if you let his words in, they were cold and confusing, coiling around your heart to trick you into admitting something when there was nothing to admit. There was a name for his trick, but what was it? She tried to think until her mind grew weary and blank, and then as she was falling asleep, it came to her that the word she wanted was deceit, and she drifted off with the satisfaction of at least having named the thing.

The next morning, he was up early and out of the house, and Nina, feeling alone and defiant, picked up the phone and called John Rogan's office. She invented an ailment and dropped the name of a well-known internist that would get her in sooner. An appointment was made for the next day. Nina felt herself expanding, pressing outward, filling space so there was no separation between herself and the things around her. She had a mad desire to tell someone, to shout, to break things. The inside of her face felt tight and unfamiliar. She thought the difference must show. But in the mirror in her closet, she looked the same. It was like being two people at once. She parted her robe and drew a line down along her breastbone, over her abdomen, and smoothed her hand onto her pubis. She struck a pose, raising one foot on its toes. Her stomach was flat. She didn't look like she'd had children. There were no stretch marks. She slid the robe off and leaned her forehead against the glass, imagining the other person was him.

When she arrived, a small woman, looking hurried and flushed, and dressed in an odd, plain brown dress as clumsy as a monk's robe, Rogan greeted her with a slight smile. His memory of her didn't quite coincide with the reality. When she was seated, they grew silent until at last he said, What brings you?

The color rose vividly in Nina's face. She had imagined he would make everything easy. I'm worried about arrhythmia, she said. It runs in my family. Her chin strained upward in defended pride, revealing strong chords and vessels in her neck. She looked quite healthy. My heart makes a noise in my ears, sometimes fast, sometimes slow, like the wings of a bug trapped inside my ear. I have pains in my chest. She made a face as if none of it mattered.

The surgeon nodded. I see. And what did your doctor say?

Nina made a small, indifferent noise. He didn't say much of anything.

Rogan thumbed up the corner of Nina's folder and let it drop. It was empty except for the pink sheet she had filled out in the waiting room. I suppose, he said, we could order some tests. That hasn't been done yet. He made an upward turning motion of his hand.

Aren't you going to examine me? She was afraid she was about to be dismissed.

Rogan leaned back, pressing his fingertips together, and gazed at her. I'm a general surgeon, not a cardiologist, assuming that's what you need? His eyebrow twitched up in query.

She seemed to draw back a little into herself. You have a good reputation, and I didn't know where else to go.

Rogan wasn't sure why he was reluctant. The situation seemed clear, and in the past he wouldn't have hesitated. He swiveled his chair and stood up. Her eyes followed him, and she moved to rise, her hands closing like bird beaks on the flat gray purse sliding from her lap.

Rogan cleared his throat. I'll go out while you undress. When you're ready, have a seat on the table. He gestured toward it and smiled musingly. But I guess you know the drill since you have patients of your own.

Nina had been holding her breath and now exhaled. She wondered how much to take off. Her dress was two pieces, a skirt and top.

Rogan went out, pulling the door behind him. His nurse glanced up and thought, I might as well take lunch early.

You look serious as a stone, she teased. I guess I know what that means.

She enjoyed his embarrassment. What's the complaint?

Heart, Rogan said.

Infectious?

Hardly.

Then you'll be safe enough. She fished her wallet out of her purse and touched his arm as she went out.

He was surprised to find himself alone. He went out into the hall, toward the men's room, his heart quickening, which amused him because it would seem that at sixty-one—But I'm young enough, he thought—and as many times as he had done what he was about to do—I'm going to, aren't I . . . yes, I think I am—he should not be particularly nervous, yet there it was, a quickening that would scare the wits out of a heart patient. He paused to take a drink from the water fountain. The arc of water crossed his lips and swirled into the silvery bowl. Could he trust her?

He walked with his hands clasped behind his back, the posture he assumed when talking with the next of kin. By long practice, he approached questions in terms of their underlying statements: Ultimately, the woman in his office was not interested in him personally but in him as a means to an end.

Another doctor rushing by spoke out in passing, Hey, that was a nice piece of work in the ER. Looks like you're back in the game.

Rogan nodded. So everyone thought he was flagging. His brother had once told him that being a surgeon was simply an extreme form of life. You oppose death, and you have to be strong. It was a question of will, and ego.

As he stepped into the men's room, he glanced at his watch. He had an hour and a half free. Perhaps she had figured out his routine and planned her visit to fall before the lunch hour. Perhaps she believed she had thought it all out and understood everything. Or, perhaps she was acting impulsively. In any case, she was bold. But later, if she went home and realized she was more than ever alone, she would be inclined to come back. He would have to be clear with her, so they'd make no mistake.

Glancing in the mirror, straightening a strand of his hair, he thought of his nurse. She had been with him twenty years. Longer than most marriages, and like a married couple, they had grown alike. Their separate lovers came and went, and they remained each other's longest companion. She had an aunt in Iowa and went once a year to visit. When the aunt died, she would have an inheritance. If anything happened to him, she could retire if she wanted or go to work for someone else. But what could happen?

He washed and then dried his hands, holding them up in the mirror. They were smooth from many washings. The lines of his fingerprints barely showed.

Meanwhile, Nina was seated on the end of the examining table in the bay window. The furniture in the room was heavy wood, which recalled childhood visits to the doctor. She liked going because there was comfort in being told you were well, or in having an illness named and being told what to do. She recalled how good it was to be young and strong and growing, and suddenly that sensation went cold. She put her hand on her chest and rubbed the cloth of the dressing gown.

The door opened, and the surgeon came in, drawing his stethoscope from his pocket and placing the earpieces around his neck. He closed the door, and Nina heard the click of the bolt.

He stepped forward, a single, narrow line pinching his brow. Are you all right?

Her hand fell to her lap, and she gazed down. The top of her head seemed round and small. He worried he had misjudged her. Is it your heart? Is it hurting you now?

Nina glanced up impatiently. It seemed to her he should already know what was going on. Her body ached. She wanted to stretch.

He saw it was up to him and cleared his throat. Usually I'd have my nurse in, but it's her lunch hour, and since you're in the profession, too—he made a dismissive gesture with his hand—I thought we could get along without her. It's a risk we can take, don't you think?

Nina spoke as if amused. I'm not going to sue you.

So you say, Rogan said lightly, but patients are notoriously ungrateful, you know that?

She smiled. I won't be ungrateful.

Good. He warmed the head of his stethoscope in his palm. Let's listen to your heart.

He put the earpieces into his ears, and for a moment he and Nina watched each other. He saw the hooded anger in her eyes and knew she was scared. Why don't you turn around? he said.

He opened the vent in the back of her gown and auscultated her. His left hand rested on her shoulder, his thumb at the nape of her neck. Her braid was in the way, and she reached over her shoulder to free it, and their hands touched, sending a hollow sensation into her knees.

Cough, he said. And again.

You're listening to my lungs, not my heart, she said.

That's true, he said, but all we know is that you have a pain in the chest. Does it hurt when you breathe?

Sometimes.

His hand tightened on her shoulder and then released. All right, he said, the other side now.

She slipped her arms from the sleeves of the gown and let it fall to her waist. She was muscular, the collarbones curving cleanly into angular shoulders, the sternum like a deep thumbprint between shallow breasts, the ribs and abdomen well-defined. She turned her face away, a tense smile on her lips.

He placed a hand on her shoulder and brought the stethoscope to her heart and looked down as he listened.

She saw white hair sprouting in his ear and the shaven slickness of his cheek and the starched texture of his white smock, the weave of the cotton minutely clear. She felt dizzy. She wished he would say something.

He listened to the few small ounces of blood moving from auricle to ventricle. Your heart is normal, he said, though I think you're nervous about being here. His hand tightened on her shoulder. Would you like to listen to your heart?

She made a reflexive noise in the back of her throat, half yes and half no, raising an arm to cover herself. He placed the head of the stethoscope in her hand and moved it to her heart. Her eyes trembled with a sudden tenderness. He put the earpieces in her ears and turned and walked a little away to give her a moment's privacy. Perhaps she would change her mind, perhaps not. If life was blocked, wouldn't the heart rebel? Wouldn't it ache?

Nina tried to catch the sound. It came pulsing through the stethoscope, and faintly from inside her.

What she wanted—his back was turned; he would face her in a moment, and she knew she would have to be ready...to lie down with him?—was something she had always believed was wrong. But there was already so much wrong that the old rules no longer held, and something new had to be found. The colliding beats of her heart grew sharp. She pulled the earpieces from her ears.

The surgeon came to her and took hold of the stethoscope, which Nina started to let go of and then held on to, her hands folding in, his hand on the earpiece moving toward her so that neither of them knew how it happened—did she mean to? did he? The back of his hand rested against her breast. His thumb moved across it and paused. They watched the stillness of their hands. You have a husband, he said.

Her hand closed tightly on the earpiece. It won't matter.

Everything matters, he said.

She pushed herself against him, putting an arm over his shoulder. The paper on the examining table crinkled. Her mouth bumped his, and her tongue darted against his teeth. His hands were on her hips. You're determined, he said. But you ought—

Stop it, she said. She pulled the gown from around her waist. Take off your clothes. I want to see you. She tugged the ends of his bow tie loose.

Wait, he said. I'll do it.

He folded his clothes over the back of his chair. She waited, crossing her arms, watching his freckled backside. And then he turned, and she saw he was attractive after all, lean and white-haired. He took her hand, and they lay on the carpet.

As he kissed her, he toyed with the end of her braid, brushing it against her cheek. His fingers tugged the red elastic band. Let me undo it, he said.

No, she said.

Why? I'd love to see it down. It's so thick. He brushed the end against his lips.

It's too much trouble, she said. I'd have to braid it back.

I'll do it, he said.

No, she said and drew it out of his hand, leaning forward to kiss him.

After a while, their breathing grew fast. Rogan got up and went to the desk.

Nina watched, propped on an elbow. You don't need that.

Nevertheless, he said.

He looked ridiculous, the penis arching upward, armored for love, the nipple tip drooping, his testicles hanging like an old valise.

Her expression went unconsciously wry with the comedy of sex, and lying there propped on her side, one leg drawn up, she seemed at once deliberate and innocent. Rogan reflected that people who didn't know any better thought seduction was romantic, but it was usually complex, involving endless strategies. You're beautiful, he said, like a girl standing up on horseback in a circus. Nina saw herself and was amazed.

He knelt, and she gravely drew him down.

For a time, it seemed the pair might exhaust themselves before they reached the end. She watched sidelong, with slit eyes, her head turning in small, rhythmic circles, Rogan raised on his fists, as if pushing up. He varied his tactic and began touching her, and his touches reached her like urgings in a dream. He was a stranger. What they were doing could not be undone. They would do it again and again. Nina came suddenly, dully; and Rogan, a while after. As it rippled away, she saw her apartment, the rooms sunlit and still, the floors tilted yet everything in place. She thought of going there, and the distance seemed too great, her will insufficient to carry her.

His fingers brushed her lips. He was watching. What are you thinking? he said.

Nothing. My mind was wandering. She gave him a little push to get off her, and he rose and went to the sink and brought a small white towel.

Nina laughed abruptly.

What? he said.

You're a doctor— Her voice wavered and broke off.

It occurred to him that she was unstable and might make a scene. He wanted to end things gracefully but would end them abruptly if he had to. He offered a hand to help her up.

She made show of ignoring him, stretching her arms over her head, and then got up on her own. She did a little dance step. She was amused because she was supposed to be uncertain of what was next, yet she knew. All she had to do was whatever she wanted- ed. She went to the window and lifted an edge of the shade and peered out. Cars were parked bumper to bumper. The metal gleamed. I have a child, she said.

Rogan was buttoning his shirt. You have two, I think.

She spoke as though repeating something everyone knew. No, another one . . . in a hospital . . . she's dying.

I'm sorry, Rogan said automatically. Maybe that's what's been causing you pain.

Nina laughed. Didn't you know? I made that up.

She turned from the window and walked toward him, raising her head. Let him look, she thought.

He saw that he had trapped himself. If he refused her, she

would hate him. For both of them, it was a question of getting from one moment to the next.

She came to him with the soft impact of a small, dense body jostling a large, light one. He steadied himself against her. She took him into her hand and circled his waist caressingly. They lowered themselves to the floor, Rogan wondering if he could manage a second time.

After a while, he rose and went back to his desk. Nina studied him. Take off your shirt.

Of course, he said.

He moved to her, and at the last instant, she held him off, a hand on his pelvis, and stared into his eyes. They were deep blue, the pupils narrowed to points of lust in which she felt her power. His hips trembled, her hand sliding off. They joined, and some of her heaviness of soul went over into the emptiness of his. Then, they were nothing more than the act itself.

They scooted, inching across the carpet, and knocked into a sofa. Nina broke out laughing while Rogan plunged on.

She saw the blank ceiling and thought of Johnny who wouldn't love her, Johnny who did this with others. She held on to the surgeon and lifted her hips, and when they came—Rogan, in big, round pulses, and Nina, in sharp, high beats that opened and closed around him—she wanted to say I love you. She felt her heart going out to him and held it back.

Rogan touched her ear, traced the line of her jaw, and kissed her, covering the moment with decorum.

When she was gone, Rogan tidied up and glanced at his date book. He had one more patient to see, a call to make to his broker, and then a tennis match at his club. Afterward, he would go home to dinner. He would turn in early and read from a journal. His habits defined him. He leaned back in his chair and thought about the past, about other women, what they'd said and done, but it was an odd thing about sex that before long it left no memory of the feeling itself. Each new episode replaced the last, *or, no,* Rogan thought, *it's something else.* Each episode was replaced by desire, so that what he remembered was desire rather than love itself. And it came to Rogan that in a life of desire, all that might be left to desire was death. He turned back a page of his date book and then another, as if looking for something.

In the hall outside her apartment, Nina heard laughter. She pushed open the door and saw Johnny and the children and the new au pair lying in a circle on the floor with their heads in each other's laps. When they saw Nina, they stopped laughing, and the room seemed sharply divided. Each of them saw it. Her eyes met Hendersen's with a look of triumph. His face was red from laughing. It's a game, he said and began struggling to his feet.

Nina motioned to the boys. Go get cleaned up, and I'll be there in a minute.

The au pair hesitated and then followed the little boys.

Why do you keep trying to hurt me? Nina said.

That's unfair, Hendersen said. We were only playing.

It's inappropriate, she said.

You make things so ugly, Hendersen said.

I know what I see, Nina said.

That night, Hendersen read a good-night story to Eric and Ian. Tucking them in, he kissed each boy's forehead just below the hairline and inhaled their simple smell, which was dizzying in its reminder of how easily happiness was lost, and as if sensing his father's worry, Ian, the younger child, put his arms around his father's neck and wouldn't let go. Hendersen took the boy into his arms and silently hugged him, their two hearts—Hendersen's big, middle-aged heart bumping with cares and the boy's small, light one—beating together until father and son were contained in each other, and Ian let go of his father's neck and, placing his small hands on Hendersen's cheeks, said, I see where it hurts.

A rush of shame filled Hendersen. I know you do, he said.

It was something of a miracle, Hendersen reflected, that no matter what else, Ian seemed to know what was right.

The older boy, Eric, lay watching them from his bed. I'm trying to sleep, he complained. Above the lip of the blanket, his eyes were full of suspicion and seemed to take in everything for an accounting to be made in the future.

As Hendersen went out, he glanced in perplexity from one

child to the other. That his children looked on him with sorrow and reproach touched his conscience, and passing through the hallway toward the living room, he summoned his resolve to humble himself and try again to put things right.

Nina was in her chair reading, her feet under her, the lamp sending a pool of warm light onto the crown of her head and over her, as though she were in a world of her own. It was a sight that made Hendersen veer. He scarcely knew he was afraid of her, but paced quietly around the room, trying to compose his mind, hesitating to speak. He stopped at the stereo and turned on a jazz station.

Nina spoke to his back, I'm trying to read.

Hendersen lowered the volume and went partway to her. I've been thinking, he said, and maybe it's true: I've been trying to hurt you. He gave a small, sad laugh, and Nina looked up alertly.

I think I'm angry, he said, that I have to go see Polly alone and that you can't really talk to me about her. He knew he was on thin ice and hurried on. But that's no excuse. I owe you an apology. I should have let you know where I was and what I was doing instead of leaving you to wonder. Or, I should have kept it to myself and handled it in a way that wouldn't have mistreated you. I don't know, maybe I wanted you to think I was staying away to see someone else, but I didn't think that. I just thought I was saving you from worry. I'm sorry, he said. I don't want to act with resentment.

He stood there looking uncertain, and her heart wavered. She thought he would say something more to make up for her misery, but nothing came. Instead, he held his arms open and made a little motion of his hands for her to come to him. It was too clever. She couldn't trust him. You only want to feel better about yourself, she said.

But Nina, Hendersen implored, if we don't make up, what else can we do?

I don't know. All I know is you're going away again...aren't you?

It's for work, he said.

It's always for work, she said.

The conversation continued, and they were like two sides of a sharply pitched roof, though neither of them quite saw it. Each counted on the tension provided by the other. Between them were twenty years of marriage, the bonds of familiarity, the hopes and promises begun in youth. It passed through them like nostalgia: if they separated, their life so far would be wasted. They sensed it for the first time and fell silent.

What do you expect from me? Hendersen said.

It seemed to her he was trying to take something away. Nothing, she said. Can't you just let me read?

Hendersen turned and left the room.

The piece playing on the radio was ending. Nina listened. A trumpet cried and faded, the string bass flurried and descended, disappearing, while the piano sent footsteps strolling, someone not ready to go home, rain beginning lightly to fall, and a car passing on the wet street, the last bright notes sounding like dawn and the promise of sleep while others wake. Nina wished for a different life than her own, a life of freedom and choices and exciting people and love.

She didn't owe Johnny anything. She was sick of feeling an obligation. She thought of Rogan and then of Ian's swimming teacher at the Y and how his genitals pressed against his tank suit when he got out of the pool.

Hendersen sat in his office and stared at mail and papers stacked on his desk. He thought miserably of forgiveness and how it was a simple matter of yielding to one's better nature, but it was impossible to forgive someone who wouldn't forgive herself, and equally impossible to live with her if she wouldn't forgive him. He thought of how he had taken care of Nina after Polly's birth, how he had made it all right for Nina to stop seeing the child, but now it seemed that all he'd done was help her hide a pain that was worse for being hidden. There was no relief, and the interior of life was closed to them. He reflected that this misfortune was what their sons would learn from them, and he thought of taking Eric and Ian and raising them on his own. It seemed to him that he could manage it, but as soon as he thought it, the idea of taking the boys from her seemed cruel and impractical. She would never let go. They were what protected her from the fear of being a bad mother, having rejected one child. It occurred to him then that he had everything backwards: She was punishing herself but somehow she had tricked him, or he had tricked himself, into acting like the one who was punishing her. No matter what he did, it would never be good enough. Anger rose in him and quickly grew stale. He reflected that he was responsible for his part in their affairs. But why he had taken on such a role mystified him. It was extremely disheartening, and Hendersen, who was a romantic, sat for a while longer, sentimentally recalling the past and resisting an ultimate conclusion. Finally, he took himself to bed.

Nina was curled under the covers in a fetal posture of sleep, her hair spilled on the pillow. He lay beside her, afraid to disturb her, but he ached with a longing for which he had no name—his own need to be taken care of and loved. He took a thick strand of her hair in his fingers and rubbed it, as if it were all of her, and all of him.

In the morning, she looked so peaceful and rosy, he wanted to let her sleep. He got the boys off to school and was eating toast and reading the paper when she came in the kitchen barefoot, wearing a robe. He noticed the slimness of her ankles and calves and the straightness of her back.

She moved silently around him, fixing herself some tea. She poured water from the kettle, and somehow it slipped and fell, splashing water on her feet. She cried out, and Hendersen jumped up and gripped her shoulders, thinking to help.

Let go, she cried, I'm all right.

Your feet, you've burned them.

She wrenched from his grasp and rushed to the bathroom and ran cold water in the tub. She sat on the edge, thinking he was an idiot who could never make her happy. He appeared in the door with an anxious look and an ice tray, which he cracked methodically into the tub, and then he stood there waiting.

What? she said. What do you want?

He looked surprised. What's going on with you? What happened in the kitchen?

I had a cramp.

He nodded, pursing his lips. Do you want to take a Motrin or something?

She waved him away. The medicine cabinet was full of his pharmaceutical samples. I'm not an addict, she said.

Hendersen frowned. What does that mean?

I'm not— And then she cried out in exasperation, Ohhh God!, and leaned over clutching her knees.

Hendersen put his arms around her. Water was thundering into the tub.

She breathed as if sobbing. Please, he said, what is it? They stayed like that until Nina calmed down and sat up and cut off the tap. Hendersen stepped away. Cramps? he said.

Nina gave a minuscule nod.

Maybe you should see a doctor.

I already have, Nina said, and there's nothing wrong.

There was a noise in the hall, and they looked up to see the au pair. It was as if they had been caught in a guilty act. Hendersen made an open gesture of his hand. Everything all right?

The girl smiled glumly and continued down the hall.

Nina stood up, and Hendersen reached for a towel. He had an impulse to bend down and dry her feet. The idea frightened him. He had no idea where it might lead.

Nina, he said, I'm worried about you.

What exactly are you worried about? She took the towel and began to dry her feet. They were red and bony, and it occurred to Hendersen that he hadn't done anything wrong and there was no reason to keep standing there. In his mind, he began packing to leave town the next day.

Nina's heart was racing all the time. It was bursting out of her chest, and to keep up, she had to move fast. She discovered that certain kinds of shy and deceptively quiet men were drawn to her without her doing anything in particular to attract them. They liked her, and that was all.

A month went by. Late one afternoon she ran into Rogan on the sidewalk outside the hospital. You cut your hair, he said.

Her hand reached up to the blunt edge. Do you like it?

Yes, he said. I miss the girl, but now I see the woman. It was exactly the kind of thing Nina wanted to hear but from him suddenly felt too personal. He looked older than before, slightly stooped. She couldn't imagine him touching her.

There was an awkward pause, and Nina said she had to go. A moment later, Rogan found himself looking back over his shoulder, thinking she had called his name—John. He was sure he heard her, but there was no one there except a group of teenage boys crossing the street, and one of them, a tall, skinny fellow, trailing behind on a skateboard, pushing it with hard kicks, hurrying to catch up with his friends. The first rush of evening traffic was coming up the avenue, and the cars seemed to bear down on the boy with irresistible intent. Rogan wanted to tell him not to be careless, not to be fooled into thinking life would keep pouring onto him like a gift. The boy skated safely out of the street, and the cars rushed by, creating a hot wind.

DEVON JERSILD

Eggs

The Andersons' house perched on the corner of our block like a dinosaur, with wings and a tail that spread into the lot behind it, growing in sections as the family increased. Mrs. Anderson had five children by her first husband, who died in bed of a heart attack the morning of their tenth anniversary. The couple had taken a trip to the Caribbean as a sort of second honeymoon, and to escape the Illinois winter. When Mrs. Anderson awoke one morning, she turned to her husband to embrace him. Feeling his inert body, she almost cried out for help. Then she had a vision of the dreary days ahead of her, the years with no one at her side, and she thought that perhaps she was wrong—he wasn't dead after all. So she lay her head in the crook of his arm and treasured the scent of his body. Finally, at lunchtime, she rose and showered and dressed and called the hotel manager.

Mrs. Anderson liked to repeat this story and to tell us, the neighborhood children, that except for her five babies, she would have thought her life had ended. Who could have known that she would meet Dr. Anderson, a man so beautiful, so loving and refined, and that he would have the power to resurrect her? He came to her with three children of his own; his wife had gone crazy, and the Catholic church agreed to annul his marriage so that he could marry Andrew Scannell's widow. (The annulment scandalized the Protestants on our street and provoked another round of stories about secret passageways between convents and monasteries, where the bones of babies fertilized the soil.) The first three years of the Anderson marriage produced no children at all, and Mrs. Anderson said that it broke her heart to imagine she might never carry the child of this beloved husband. But then she had two more babies in a row, and one or the other was always riding on her hip. All the children from her first marriage had golden blond hair, while Dr. Anderson's first three had hair pitch-black. The two they produced together had nut-brown

69

hair; it was almost too neat to be believed.

Dr. Anderson, the object of all this affection, was the oddest man I had ever met. Something of a dandy, he combed his hair straight back from his narrow forehead and was only ever seen in checkered flannel suits. Every few minutes, he consulted a gold watch he kept in an inner pocket. He never said anything but always looked as if he were about to ask a question. Once, when I was sure a question was forthcoming, I said, "What is it, Dr. Anderson?" and he said, "Nothing, nothing," with a nervous turn of his head. He walked twice around the block after he got home every evening. He was so tall and thin, his shadow sliced across the street like a pencil or a knife.

The entire family adored him and stood in awe of his genius. Every night after dinner, Mrs. Anderson handed him a Bible in which she had marked a passage, and he, seated at the head of the table, would read laboriously. When he was finished, Mrs. Anderson would say, "Thank you *so* much," and the children would nod their heads at their father, as if he himself had written the psalms. Then he would retire to his study. Once, I sneaked into this study and discovered, in his bottom drawer, a *Penthouse* and a bag of jelly beans.

I was part of a neighborhood gang that included Sally, Dr. Anderson's daughter; Christa, from Mrs. Anderson's first marriage; and Sam Button and Jack Cartwright, boys from down the street whom we sometimes fought and sometimes kissed. My sister, Anna, tagged along when I couldn't shake her off. There were other kids, too, and although every fall we were buttoned and scarfed and sent to separate schools, every summer we reassembled our motley group, various in height and age and wit. Evenings, we congregated at unspecified places and times, as if our meetings were preordained. Our games of baseball and "Mother May I" began and ended inconspicuously, with little discussion and no fuss. Always there was the sense of possibility—of what we might do if an adventurous mood overtook us. We encouraged the traits we knew each other by: Jack was a generous show-off, I was bossy and gregarious, Christa was whimsical and stubborn, Sam was fat and cunning. Sometimes a week would pass without our seeing each other, but we would come together again, and take up where we had left off. We were like a family of our own; sometimes I imagined I would marry Jack, and we would have babies together.

The Andersons' house was open to us, as it was to any children. Train sets, art projects, and half-finished jigsaw puzzles covered their living room floor. There was a drawer in the kitchen for us to rummage in, stocked with peanuts and raisins and potato chips. In spite of a three-car garage, the Andersons' cars stayed out on the driveway, because one of the boys raised chickens and used the garage as a coop.

Mrs. Anderson had an otherworldly quality which dignified the confusion of her household. Utterly occupied with cleaning, cooking, and caring for children, she had the air of understanding a larger significance for all her undertakings, so much so that, watching her shake out her linen and pin it on the line, I half expected her to levitate, to lift off with a breeze into the sky. Her spiritual air enhanced her maternal authority, and it was to visit her as much as her offspring that we came knocking at the door. Aware of this, she would say to one fortunate soul, "Darling, would you be so good as to help me grate the carrots?" If you were chosen, you would follow her, the kitchen door rocking into place behind you. She would set you up with carrots and a grater or cereal to feed one of the babies. As she moved about the kitchen, she asked you all the right questions, until you confided the secrets of your heart: how jealous you were of your baby sister, that you'd cheated on a science test at school. As you spoke, you felt yourself relaxing, and it slowly became clear what course of action you should take. I don't know what gave her the mysterious power of absolution; perhaps as you sat there in that kitchen chair, aware of your friends who had sat there before you and would sit there again, you began to see that what you faced were the customary hurdles, and your pain no longer seemed so personal. When you finished talking, she would reassure you, "I won't tell anyone. Except Dr. Anderson, of course. I share everything with him." I didn't mind if the two of them shared my secrets. Odd as he was, I was fond of Dr. Anderson; unlike my own father, who terrorized my family with bouts of violence, he seemed harmless enough.

I tried to stay away from Mrs. Anderson. She was always kind, but I suspected that she secretly disapproved of me, that my confessions were not of the sort to stir her generosity. Whenever I visited her house, I felt the lure of that paneled kitchen, the smell of chicken stew, a baby groggy in the high chair. More often than not, my reserve would melt away, and I would slip in to visit her. Spurred on by a perverse instinct, I would relate the sins I imagined she would least like to hear—how I mocked Mr. Gregory, my history teacher, whenever he turned his back, how the class laughed until his ears turned red—until I'd convinced us both of my spitefulness. That night I would sleep fitfully, for the worst of it was that I longed for Mrs. Anderson's approval. I would return to her house the following day, determined to talk myself out of my ill position, but something would come over me, and instead of referring to Mr. Gregory's vast store of knowledge, as I had intended, I would find myself describing how his voice squeaked out of his ears.

Jack Cartwright was in love with Mrs. Anderson. Before ringing her bell, he combed his hair and tucked in his T-shirt; after peeing at her house, he lowered the toilet seat. He made the rest of us shut up while the babies took their naps, though our silence worried them more than our noise. When Sally Anderson opened the door to Jack, she'd run her hand down her black ponytail and say, "Oh, look, it's Joseph come to visit the Virgin Mary," but neither she nor I could ruffle him nor disturb his sense of sacred mission. Inside, he was a pilgrim; outside, he swore and sneered like the rest of us.

Jack transferred some of his ardor to Mrs. Anderson's oldest daughter, who lived at home and attended a two-year Catholic college. Then one May morning, Maria held up a finger decorated with a small but glistening stone and announced her engagement. It was a traumatic summer for all of us. The Andersons' living room became a sewing center as mother and daughter hovered over folds of lace and chenille. Jack had to watch as Maria grew more pink and breathless every day with love for another man. A mere eight years his senior, now she, too, was slipping from his grasp. To top it off, Mrs. Anderson neglected him, occupied with the transformation her daughter was about to undergo, from Maria to Mrs. White.

Even Mrs. Anderson was flustered that summer. Maria was her first child, the daughter she and Andrew had cherished, and she wished she could impart to her what she had learned in all her years of marriage. Maria's naïveté touched her. She longed to preserve her innocence, to wish upon her an idyll of married life. Yet she had to relinquish her to the painful accretion of experience.

Maria, moved by her mother's turmoil, watched her with new appreciation. Once, when both babies were whining and the teapot screamed on the stove, she cried, "Mother, *how* do you do it?" Mrs. Anderson grasped Maria's hands, and tears came to her eyes. "Sweetheart," she said, her voice wrinkling with emotion, "you'll do it, too! You'll grow as your duties grow, and you'll get pleasure, such pleasure from your husband and children."

I hovered at the borders of these scenes, taking it all in. Maria was the oldest among us, and I looked to her for clues about my fate. Mrs. Anderson could see this, and she encouraged me—she even let me help her pin the wedding dress. She said you never knew, maybe somewhere in the wedding party would be a boy who would grow into the man who would answer my dreams. I didn't tell her about my fears that something terrible would happen the day of the wedding: an uninvited aunt materializing out of an explosion of dust, hurling a curse on the bride and groom. I was also terrified that I would get the chicken pox and have to be quarantined. Every morning, I stood in front of the mirror and searched for little red spots. Sometimes I imagined the boy I would marry looking in the mirror, too.

One evening Maria brought her fiancé back to the house, and Dr. Anderson brought out a bottle of champagne. He must have drunk a little something before the celebration, because after he toasted Maria and Frank, he kissed all the girls in the room, and Mrs. Anderson forced a laugh. When it came my turn, he stuck his whole tongue in my mouth. It felt like a mouse trying to get down my throat, and I tried to pull back, but he wrenched me closer. I think he did the same thing to Christa, because she, too, tried to jerk away. But her mother shot her a look that said "Don't make a scene." Frank said, "You think I'm not a fast learner?" He emptied his glass, and he, too, kissed us all in turn.

Later, I said to Christa that I thought the kissing was pretty gross. She glanced at me as if she could not believe what I had said, as if I were vulgar beyond belief. Her pretty, oily skin turned red, and she said, "God, what's the big deal?" And so I dropped the subject, but I wondered what else she had to put up with in that household, in the name of not making a scene.

The wedding was set for the fifteenth of July. As the date approached, we watched for signs of rain. The reception would be in the Andersons' backyard, manicured that summer like never before. Sculpted shrubbery and potted flowers awaited the appointed day, while sprinklers spun arms of water as far as they could reach. Frank flew to California the week before the ceremony; a great-aunt had left him some property there, and he wanted to sell it and be free of the responsibility. He said his great-aunt was the meanest old bitch he'd ever seen, and he didn't want to be reminded of her. He said she was a shriveled-up old spinster who needed a fuck, only she was so ugly no man could ever get his rocks off.

Maria blushed when he talked like that. Already thin, she grew waif-like in those final days. She made all of us nervous as she pined away, waiting for her love's return.

Because of the commotion at the house, the older Anderson kids found themselves on a new leash of freedom that summer, and Sally and Christa took to sleeping in the treehouse at the bottom of their property. They cushioned the floor with sleeping bags bought at the army surplus and stored their drinking water in 7-Up bottles. If they had to pee in the middle of the night, they went in a tennis ball can. The treehouse hung in a branching oak on the lower slope of a ravine, the site of our happiest childhood play. There was a ditch at the bottom that flooded up to our waists in spring, and sometimes, when it stormed, we put on rain gear, pulled old washtubs out of the cellar, and went rafting down the ditch, using broken tree limbs to guide us. In winter we'd toboggan down the slope. On the other side of the ravine, there used to be a cornfield where we played cops and robbers, sliding on our bellies through the dirt, trying to stalk like Blackhawk Indians, without rustling the corn.

Now a line of identical colonial houses hung on that slope, part of a new development called Hillcrest. The tree line had become strangely regular. The whole row of houses seemed hardly deeper than a stage set, presided over by telephone poles with endless parallel wires. I couldn't believe that real people lived in those houses, but Sally said Maria might move into that development.

The week before the wedding, I wanted to join Sally and Christa in the treehouse. We planned to get Sam and Jack to camp out, too, and for all of us to sneak out in the middle of the night to cause some trouble.

My mother's permission was never a problem. I waited until she lay down after lunch and gave her a kiss, her lips cool and minty from the gin-soaked ice cube she'd been sucking. "Do as you like," she said to me, with a weak pat on my behind. "You're a good girl, Maggie."

"*Such* a good girl," I teased. I fiddled with her fingers.

"You are," she said, shutting her eyelids. Her skin was like mine: so thin you could see the blue underneath. She added, "I've never had to worry about you."

I bent to kiss her again, but she was already asleep. She lay there with her mouth slightly open, her arms winding down to little wrists. I shook out an afghan to cover her, raising a cloud of cat hair. My mother was allergic to cats, but that didn't stop her from keeping them. I tucked the blanket around her neck and kissed her on the forehead. Her skin felt so cool that I looked around for another cover, but there was only the one afghan.

I found my father in his den in his leather chair, smoking a Camel and reading the Sunday paper, his cowboy boots propped on the table. Though last year he had built us a nice sun deck, he preferred to sit alone in his musty room, in the company of the stuffed bear head on the wall, its red tongue and toothy snarl. A low-watt lamp sent his shadow sprawling over the carpet. I hesitated at the door.

"It's okay by me," he answered amiably enough, when I had made my request. "If you take Anna with you, and your mother agrees." He always verbally deferred to my mother, the more so now that my mother spent her afternoons on the couch. But we knew better than to bypass his permission.

"Thanks, Pa," I said.

His hand flashed out to tickle me. I jumped back automatically, quicker than him by now. He liked it best when I called him "Pa." But I wouldn't go so far as to play the tickling game. That game belonged to the past.

My father meant for Anna to serve as our moral guardian, for she could be counted on to report violations to the nearest adult in sight. When Sally heard about this problem, she took the situation into her own hands. From the moment we pushed our sleeping bags up through the trapdoor of the treehouse, she fussed over Anna like she'd just discovered her.

"What a nice bag," she said. It was orange and blue and rolled up like a snail, a wormy head poking out the end. I had just told Anna how revolting it was.

She beamed up at Sally. "You get them at the Globe Store. They come with six Richie Rich comic books."

Sally kissed it on the nose. "What a good deal," she said.

The oak trunk ran through the middle of the treehouse, which was just wide enough for a sleeping bag to fit along each of the four screened walls. I put the head of my bag next to Sally's, clearing a space to roll it out.

Anna began to whimper. "I was going to sleep there," she said, rubbing her nose. She looked like she was about to fall asleep that second, but that was nothing new for her. She liked to get her fourteen hours a night, and sometimes she napped in the afternoon as well. She was so greedy for sleep, I was sure when I had insomnia, it was because she had taken my share.

"Shut up, Anna," I said.

"I had my bag there first. I don't want to sleep over the trap-door."

Sally popped a Sweet Tart into her mouth and held out a fistful to Anna. Anna sniffled and plucked out the mint green ones.

"Look," said Sally. "There's room over here by me."

I didn't treasure the prospect of Anna's smelly little breath next to my head all night, and I thought that Sally was laying it on too thick, but by the time we got around to revealing our plans, Anna was completely won over; her eyes fairly gleamed with the excitement of being included. I had to hand it to Sally: she had mastered her stepmother's techniques and learned to apply them to her own ends.

After dinner, when it began to get dark, the four of us gathered to catch lightning bugs. They were easy targets, spotting the ravine with light. If you stood at the top of the slope and ran down the hill with your arms at your sides, like a swooping bird, you could catch them in your hands without even trying. Then you let them rattle around inside your fist. If you dug out the light-maker with your thumbnail just as the bug lit up, it would stay luminous. We stuck one on each fingernail and waved our glittering hands through the dark. "We're society ladies," said Sally. Christa studded a string of the lighters around her neck, making a brilliant choker, and the rest of us copied her. As it grew later, our features dissolved until we couldn't see each other at all, but only the light-beads, glowing chains floating through the night four feet off the ground.

We climbed up into the treehouse and lay on our bellies in the sleeping bags, our newly sensitive breasts pressed into the plank floor. The crickets ticked away, *reek, reek, reek*. I stuck my face up to the screen and looked at the world through the miniscule squares of netting. A light breeze swished the leaves; we were up in the tree world, up with the squirrels and the birds. Christa let a fart, and all of us giggled. Sally tried to let a bigger one, but she only made a squeak, and that made us laugh harder. Anna chimed in with a pathetic burp.

Sally passed around a bag of red licorice, which we chewed on as the lights went off along the hill and the neighborhood sank into sleep. As soon as it was safe, Jack would come with Sam.

"This licorice reminds me of something," said Sally. "Christa started her period last week." She and I giggled, but my heart jumped inside me. Christa was only ten—two years younger than Sally and me—and she was the first to start.

"Shut up," said Christa. "You're gross."

"Not as gross as Billy Shawgo," said Sally. "Someone told Billy that Christa had started, and when we were walking home from Mr. Fresh, Billy and Sam were right behind us, and Billy said, 'Christa, you're looking really *ripe*. Mmm, you're looking like a cherry tart.'"

"I was so embarrassed," said Christa.

Anna stared unabashedly at us.

"Are you still going?" I asked. "I mean, are you still bleeding?"

"Gross, no," said Christa. "It only lasted a couple days. But Mom said they'll get longer."

"What are you using for it?"

"Pads. Mom gave me pads."

"Yeah," said Sally, "and she left a bloody one in the wastebasket and Mom had a fit."

"What are you supposed to do?" I asked.

"Wrap it up," said Christa. "Stick it in a box. I don't know, but keep it out of sight."

We contemplated this for a while.

"You know what else?" said Sally. "I think Jack is getting a crush on Christa. Now that she's a woman, I mean."

"Shut up," said Christa.

I said, "You're crazy, Sally. Jack does not have a crush on Christa, so leave her alone."

Sally was twirling her ponytail around her wrist. "What are you so touchy about?" she said. "Don't tell me you have the hots for Jack."

I said, "That'll be the day," but I was glad it was dark and she couldn't see me.

"Shh," said Sally. "Listen."

There was a rustle in the bushes.

Christa whispered furiously, "How long have they been there?"

"Shh," said Sally.

It wasn't Sam and Jack. The noise came from up the hill, and it was female voices: Maria and Mrs. Anderson walking in the garden. The night was still enough that we could almost make out what they were saying. Mrs. Anderson's voice was low and purposeful; Maria's sounded excited. The two women talked for a long time, their voices dipping and rising, falling to a murmur, then rising again with new emotion. They walked in a circle around the yard, and when they approached the corner nearest us, where, with the moon's illumination, we saw them emerge from the line of rhododendrons, Maria started crying. She was

wearing a white blouse that caught the light; the rest of her reced-
ed in the dusk, but the blouse shook and trembled and swayed:
for a moment I thought it was a ghost. The cries were silent at
first, just breaking through the crickets, but they kept on building
until Maria couldn't support herself, and she fell to the grass, out
of our view. "He doesn't love me," she was saying. "He doesn't
love me, Mother."

Mrs. Anderson dropped down, too, and then we saw nothing,
just the line of rhododendrons and the neighbor cat slipping into
the bushes. Then the two heads appeared again, Maria's blond
one drooping on her mother's shoulder. She was quiet now; I
didn't know where her sobs had disappeared to. Mrs. Anderson
made her stand up straight and continue walking. She wouldn't
let her rest; she kept her moving, gripping her arm above the
elbow and proceeding around the path. Finally, the porch door
snapped behind them.

In the treehouse, all of us lay still. Nobody sighed; nobody
whispered. I turned my face to the trunk of the oak tree and studied the dents and ledges, the dark, dark bark that got even darker
in the rain. We were all perfectly quiet. As far as I could tell, no
one was even breathing.

I woke up to Jack's low whistle and a pebble glancing off the
screen. The next stone came harder; it split right through a tear in
the screen and ricocheted off the trunk.

"Jesus," said Sally.

I pulled my sneakers on and followed Christa down the ladder.
Anna was snoring in a little ball and grinding her teeth; I was all
for letting her sleep through our escapade, but Sally said if she
woke up while we were gone, she'd tell on us for sure. She whispered in her ear and led her away from the treehouse like a sleep-
walker, up the hill and into the cobble street. Jack and Sam went
ahead of us, veering away from each other then back together
again, grinning, kicking a piece of concrete chipped off from the
curb.

I caught up to them. "Jack," I whispered. "What's the plan?" He
had a bag slung over his shoulder, carrying something heavy.

He shrugged, feigning nonchalance, but I could read excitement in his features; the soft pug nose, the lively forehead, expressed a barely suppressed hilarity that often spurred me on to acts of daring. I wrapped my palms around the smooth eggs I'd hidden in my pockets, and squeezed them as hard as I dared.

The streets were empty. The houses looked remarkably tame, moonlight yellowing the cropped grass, cars sleeping in the driveways. We passed Colonials, a Dutch-like brick, a modern ranch. We knew most of our neighbors by name, but now they were in bed, and we imagined them in nightcaps and gowns, an anonymous crew of sleepers—dentists and secretaries and housewives and accountants who would, when their alarm clocks rang, plug back into their lives. Yet if any one of them woke up now, the trouble they would cause! Walking through the neighborhood, we felt an odd exhilaration; we were a tribe apart, and we had tricks up our sleeves.

Christa did a cartwheel in the middle of the street, showing off. Next she tried a back walkover, but she was hampered by several rolls of toilet paper under her T-shirt, which was tucked into her cutoffs. Jack veered close to her and punched at the false paunch. "Don't hurt my little baby," she said.

"Leave her alone," I said. I hated it when he got rough—it made me want to sock him.

He scowled at me.

"I mean it," I said. "Just don't be an asshole, Jack."

He said, "Just don't be a bitch, Mother."

We entered Valley Court, which sloped down and around a gentle hill, lined with newish houses. We were looking for the perfect target: a place isolated enough to provide protection, but close to the road so we could get away fast if we had to.

One lot in the development was still open; Christa took out the toilet paper and began to wrap it around a tree. Jack took the roll from her and looped it around another low-hanging branch. Sally scrambled up a little maple; she had acrobatic talent, too, and she did a little tree dance. She twisted the toilet paper through the upper branches with her long arms, her long, lean torso stretching, her ponytail swishing on her shoulders. Anna looked on with stupefaction, and I grinned to myself: my little sister couldn't back out now. Sam was too lazy to help, but he stood by Anna, nodding his appreciation. "This neighborhood will wipe its ass for free for an entire month," he said.

We wove a maze of white, and when Sally got down out of the trees, she and I wrapped Christa up in toilet paper, too, with several long tails streaming out behind, like the train of a wedding gown. "Here comes the bride," we sang, as she paraded through the makeshift cathedral. Suddenly Jack lunged like a bear out of the shadows, grabbed Christa by the shoulders, and kissed her hard on the mouth.

"Gross!" she spluttered, pushing him away. Anna was grinning like an idiot. Jack lunged at Christa again, only this time she tried to fight him off. When he tackled her to the ground, Sally and I came running to help. We each took a boot and started pulling him off of her. He giggled madly and grabbed at Christa's hair. She screamed. A shot of fear went through me. I dropped Jack's leg and unpeeled his hand while Sally pulled him away.

He lay on the ground still giggling. Christa sat up and rubbed her scalp, scowling.

"It's not funny," I said to Jack. My heart was still pounding hard.

Sally said, "You didn't have to scream, Christa." She looked past the lot at the low-lying houses, where no lights, at least, had come on. "We'd better get out of here."

"You try talking politely when he's pulling your hair," said Christa.

"Wedding celebration," said Jack, and as if nothing had happened, he went to his bag and pulled out a jackknife and a Pepsi bottle, only the bottle was half-filled with a clear liquid. He used the tip of the knife to knock the cap off of the bottle, raised it to his lips, and choked. I didn't need to taste it to know that it was gin. He passed it around to all of us. I let it wash around my mouth until my head filled up with steam, and then I spit it out in Jack's face. From the hurt look in his eyes, once he dried them off, you'd have thought he'd offered me his kingdom and I'd scorned it.

Wordlessly, I headed for the street. Everyone followed me but Jack. A few steps on, I turned to wait, but Jack was headed in the other direction.

Sally touched me on the arm. "Let him go," she said.

"That's right," I said. "We're better off."

We were quiet now, following the curve of the road. Each footstep made a skidding noise against the pavement. All thoughts slipped from my mind, and I let the night seep into my skin, the smell of grass giving up its store of heat, the distant barking of a dog, the resting cars, the shimmering pool of light beneath the corner streetlight. I would have liked living at night forever, sleeping out the day and coming alive when the rest of the world blinked out. At night there were no clear rules for how to be; you had to make it up. People didn't go to school or to the bank in the middle of the night; they didn't get married then, either. In the nighttime, people loved and hated and kissed and fought; they robbed grocery stores and started revolutions. All the real stuff happened in the dead of night.

We'd walked in a loop around the town, and now we were heading into Hillcrest. At the bend of the road was a pale green house with a pale green car in the yard. It belonged to a family by the name of Hedquist; Kim and Nancy went to the Catholic school with Sally and Christa; Mrs. Hedquist and Mrs. Anderson were friendly. I didn't know them well; I only knew that the two girls were tall and overweight, and they dressed alike in frilly clothes that their mother sewed. The shrubs in their yard were perfectly trimmed. The grass was level; the ugly green paint had been reapplied that year. The whole place was spic and span, as if awaiting some pathetic version of a stately visit—some knight come to court the princess daughters.

As I stared at that house, a kind of disgust came over me and filled me with a sense of purpose.

"Let's hit it," I said. We stood in a group in the middle of the road, our arms dangling loosely at our sides. When we were quiet like this, I could hear each person breathing: Sam in his wheezy asthmatic spurts; Christa emphatically, as if with each breath she were making a statement; Sally in measured, careful time; Anna trying to hold it in.

Christa pulled down on the legs of her jean shorts—her hips were getting wider and the jeans kept shifting up. "No way," she said. "We'll get caught."

"You're crazy," said Sam.

It was true that this house lacked all the qualities we were looking for. Yet its enormous picture window inspired me with
hatred, and I wanted to strike now.

"Mrs. Hedquist has been to our house," protested Sally.

I was silent.

She tried again. "They go to church with us. We go to cate-
chism with their kids."

"It's the perfect target," I said.

One thing I liked about Sally was that she knew when to give
up. She and I had four eggs between us; we gave one to Christa
and one to Sam, and we all took cover behind trees in the opposite lot. Sam went first. He ran into the Hedquists' yard and
pitched his egg at the window. He had the pleasure of being the
first to spoil its pristine look and also the knowledge that the
Hedquists were unlikely to jump from their beds before he made
it back to his tree. Christa ran next, but she stopped short in the
middle of the street. She threw with admirable force; her yolk hit
the bottom corner of the window.

I ran out next, and Sally followed right behind me. We threw
our eggs together, and they hit at the same time. The noise startled us; we looked at each other with mutual fright and ran back
down the street. The other three fled from their trees to follow us.
Sam was so heavy, he waddled when he ran, but I never saw a
waddler move so fast. He headed straight for his basement door
and disappeared like a possum into its hole. The rest of us mon-
keyed into the treehouse and, in spite of our excitement, fell
asleep. We didn't wake up until ten o'clock the next morning.

It had been a beautiful sight, the four eggs dribbling down the
picture window, the splattered shells sticking for a moment then
slipping into the bushes. What started out as a little adventure
became an obsession with me. I couldn't get the Hedquists out of
my mind, and the more I thought of them, the more I hated
them. I thought of the girls' pointed, pale faces, pursed in disap-
proval. I thought of the reticent parents and their moral outrage
when faced with their bespattered house. I thought of Nancy and
Kim growing up and marrying men like their father and produc-

ing more overweight Nancys and Kims. I pictured them at a double wedding, in fussy white dresses that their mother sewed, and everyone beaming at them. Nine months later they'd be pregnant and cow-like, and they'd think they were in heaven. I made a trip to the grocery store and bought a whole carton of eggs.

Anna found them in the corner of the treehouse, tucked under my sleeping bag. Her eyes grew wide, and for once, I thought, she looked fully awake.

"Where are we going tonight?" she asked.

I couldn't help smiling. "I'm going to the Hedquists'. You might not want to come."

Anna considered this, looking no more shocked than if the eggs were for french toast. "Is Sally coming?"

I avoided her gaze. Sally and Christa had refused to hit the same house twice—especially the Hedquists'. I was alone in this.

Anna said, "I'll go. And Sam will come, too."

That night, Anna and I climbed over two sleeping bodies when Sam gave us his call.

Each of us took two eggs, one to a palm. Sam and Anna lagged behind me, and none of us talked. We walked straight to the lot across from the Hedquist house. Their window was wiped clean. We took up our positions.

Tonight was a big occasion for Anna—her first shot—and she ventured out ahead of Sam and me. She was so afraid of missing the window that she ran up within a few yards of it. Even then, her egg crashed on the sill. She slipped in the grass trying to run back fast. Sam and I bent over to keep from laughing out loud. Embarrassed but grinning, she resumed her post behind a tree. Sam and I made bull's-eye shots, and we ran back home again.

I walked by the Hedquist house at noon the next day, and already the window was scraped clean. You'd have thought there had never been a moment's trouble there: no nasty eggs, no vandalism, nothing but two proud parents and two sweet girls in matching dresses.

That night, I left the treehouse with all the remaining eggs, six smooth weapons in a jacket pocket. I meant to go alone, but Anna followed me, inspired by a strange new fidelity. The house was dark as we approached; each night, it had looked exactly the same, the pale green split-level home, no hint of the sleepers within. But this time, as I reached the curb in front of the yard, a light went on, and a man's deep voice hollered. My knees went loose. Anna started running. I took an egg from my pocket and ran forward to pitch it, a murderous fastball. I was beating my retreat before it even hit the glass. I kept my eyes on the pavement as it flowed beneath me, like water slipping under a boat. My skin stung as I imagined falling forward, banging my head on the concrete, stripping the skin off my cheeks and hands. When I reached a garage around the corner, I hid behind it and peeked back. There were people in the yard, angry voices, but they weren't following me. I caught my breath and ran back to the treehouse. Anna was in her bag, her eyes open, clutching the zippered corner. I tried to look casual, but my hands shook, and I shivered as if I were cold.

Soon enough, my father appeared at the top of the hill. You might have thought he was a tree trunk lopped off at a strange height, he looked so thick and dark. "Maggie," he called. His voice was soft—he didn't want to wake the neighbors—but he was angry. I had known what was coming all along.

Sally and Christa were awake now. They lay still and passive as I crawled over them, climbed down the ladder, and walked up the hill to the line of rhododendrons where my father stood. He opened and closed his fists. His eyes jerked in his head.

I said weakly, "Sorry, Pa," and my knees buckled. I tried to skirt around him.

The snag in my walk must have got to him. His leg shot out, and his boot was in my stomach, knocking the wind out of me. I fell, and before I even caught my breath, I tried to crawl away, but his leg shot out and took me to the ground again. My mouth filled with grass and the toothy taste of blood. One more time I raised my knee to my chest and tried to get up. Then all I could see was his boots, the cowboy boots he put on after work, the ones with the pointed toes and the swirls etched into the side. I don't know how I would have seen his boots, for his kicks were aimed at my stomach and my back, as he rolled me over and over.

I didn't cry; I knew that would infuriate him. And yet, as he came toward me again, I heard gasps and sobs. Could I be crying after all? Or were the sounds from farther off? Of course, I thought—they watched from the treehouse, and Anna, she was crying.

My father whispered, "Get back to the house."

I could feel him behind my back, the way I always felt my father, a shadow looming after me, even when he wasn't there. I crawled a little farther, and then I got up and ran.

I missed the wedding two days later because I was grounded for three weeks. By all accounts the bride was ravishing, the weather couldn't have been more perfect, the wedding just gorgeous. My mother brought me back a piece of snow-white cake. She said Mrs. Anderson literally wept with joy. She said the Hedquist family also attended the wedding, and she was ashamed to see them there. My father said he still couldn't believe I would do such a thing, and *three times in a row.* What kind of woman would I grow up to be? Anna told me all the good stuff, how the hens in the garage started squawking whenever the music started up, and a squealing cat nearly tripped the groom, and Jack got blitzed by draining the last drops of champagne from a hundred glasses. Maria herself could hardly walk, she was so far gone. "Too bad you couldn't be there," she said.

She had brought a tray of cookies and chocolate milk up to the room we shared. Downstairs, no doubt, my mother was pouring her afternoon gin. My father would be settling back into his den, smoking a Camel. Mrs. Anderson would be tucking the babies in for a nap while Dr. Anderson slobbered over the very last guests. I stirred the chocolate milk fast to make a tornado in the glass.

Anna went to the window, pulled up the screen, and leaned halfway out. Her blond head caught the sun. "You getting bored up here?" she asked.

"The wallpaper's giving me a headache."

"You chose it."

The bright yellow flowers and pink bows had seemed cheerful and sweet, but now the walls looked like a slaughter of canaries.

Anna leaned farther out the window. "I don't know how you could sneak out of here," she said. "Unless you pulled a Rapunzel."

I stuffed a cookie in my mouth and leaned out the window next to her. Down at the Andersons' corner, streams of toilet paper littered the grass. Someone must have wrapped up the newlyweds' car.

"Screw Rapunzel," I said. "I'd rather fly out of here on a broomstick."

I'd fly to a city well beyond these repetitive rooftops and puffball clouds, a city with sleek gray spires and steamy streets, with angry posters being slapped on walls, excited crowds gathering in public places, and in the air, circling all around, hundreds of other witches.

TONY EPRILE

A True History of the Notorious Mr. Edward Hyde

'Yde's the name. Edward 'yde...or Hyde, as educated folk like yourself would have it. That's my real name, although for the past fifty years, Hyde has stayed hidden under the moniker of Edward Layman. To the good people here in the West Midlands, I'm just Layman or Ed, no different from nobody else, a stand-up bloke, a hard-worker but no boss's tool, fond of his pint of bitter and mild and always ready for a joke or sing-along. Only my cousin Vic—and now *you*—knows my real name, the one that sends chills up the world's spine. As Hyde, I've been called a deformed and depraved creature of Hell, a vicious human Juggernaut. "Edward Hyde, alone in the ranks of mankind, was pure evil." Nice words, I must say. Courtesy of none other than the ultimate toffee nose, Dr. Jekyll, Harley Street specialist and a man noted for his good works. Where's the charity in such talk? I ask. And yet, because he went to the right schools and said things in such a reasonable, sophisticated way, you believe him. Funny, how people can be educated but not smart, i'n' it?

Jekyll. Even today I can't hear his name without the hair on my neck rising in pure animal rage. And to think I used to admire the man. I wanted to be like him, to talk posh and live in a house filled with elegant appurtenances instead of mere furniture. Even when it finally penetrated the great Roman wall of my thick prole's head that I was hopelessly trapped in Dr. Jekyll's rotten web (while *he* grew bloated and fat on my helpless struggles), I still wanted what he had. You see, Jekyll—let him rot in Hell, appurtenances and all—had class. And that, as Cousin Vic would say, is what it's all about.

I was just recently turned twenty when I met the illustrious Dr. Jekyll, and of all the days in my life, that one stands out clearest in memory. It was a spring morning of sharp brightness, sunlight pouring in like newly minted sovereigns. Not at all the usual pewter-gray skies of London, and I was cocksure and full of myself that day. My luck was up, or so I thought. There's something about being young that makes you feel undefeatable: I had a nice chunk of money weighing down my pockets and raw pleasure in the unfettered, wiry roll of my youthful muscles as I strolled the streets of London. The evening before, I had landed an unexpected five guineas. I'd gone with some of my mates to one of Jimmy Wilshire's fighting cellars. This was not one of your Marquis of Queensbury bouts of fisticuffs, but the aptly called "Big Knuckle"—where it's bare knuckles and bare feet and you fight on until you or your opponent are knocked senseless. It was strictly out of the bounds of The Law, of course, but any night of the week, if you knew where to look, you could find yourself in a small ill-lit room in which two brawny boyos were laying into each other on the roped-off mats in the center to the cheers of a crowd of red-faced men yelling themselves hoarse. And it wasn't just commoners who frequented Jimmy Wilshire's cellars, but toffs putting down pound bets on their favorites and standing close enough to the action to get blood on their evening jackets or to catch the occasional flying molar for a souvenir.

Hard Anthony had just knocked his opponent cold in mere minutes of combat, and the barker was now offering a purse of five guineas to anyone in the audience game enough to spend ten minutes in the ring with him. I had been an occasional stevedore on the London docks and taken part in my share of pub brawls, where the stake was your own skin and the weapons included knives, if you had one, and anything else that came to hand if you did not. So, with my friends' raucous encouragement, I took on the bet. Hard Anthony came up to me with a friendly grin and a hand extended for a gentlemanly shake. I'd been caught by just such a bit of commonplace treachery in one of the few street tussles I'd lost, so I pretended to let myself be pulled off-balance but quickly ducked under the flying fist that was following up fast behind the handshake. It was Hard Anthony's turn to be off-guard, and I took the wind out of his sails with a lightning-quick knee to the groin, the good old Ringsend uppercut. He was knackered good and proper, and though he was a tough berk, practiced in a range of dirty tricks—like greasing himself all over with oil so you couldn't get a purchase—I'm no sluggard when it comes to a barney, and it didn't take all that long before I tossed his unconscious carcass into a pile of chairs that seemed to have been placed there for just that purpose. My only injuries were a few scratches—Hard Anthony clawed like a woman—and a bruise under my eye from a vicious head butt.

That is how on a bright morning, with my head still cottony from the rounds of Jimmy Wilshire's home-brewed gin and porter that I had treated and been treated to, I happened to be walking along Harley Street and paused for a moment next to a brass shingle announcing the name Henry Jekyll, M.D., D.C.L., LL.D., F.R.S., and enough other initials to show that the inhabitant could split himself in half and open two medical practices. It recalled to me a condition which was a cause of some embarrassment, the results of a few moments of friendliness with a comely scullery maid. Just thinking about it brought on the discomfort, a burning exaggerated by the quantity of liquor I had consumed the night before. Jingling the still half-full purse in my trouser pocket, I clambered up the stairs and pounded the fateful knocker.

I found myself quite humbled by my surroundings: grim Poole the manservant in his somber duds, the unobtrusively expensive furnishings, and the resounding church-like quiet of the high-ceilinged chambers. Jekyll, a tall man with wispy hair combed back from his forehead, was equally imposing in his fine-tailored clothing, but he knew what he was about and had me quickly stripped and diagnosed...a salve administered and injunctions to use more salve at regular intervals and to drink large quantities of water, only water. "For the next two weeks, you will just have to be satisfied with the fact that the City of London rocks gently upon an artesian well and not a brewery," he said with mocking seriousness. "And, of course, abstinence of another kind for the same period is a definite must."

All this was something I could easily live with, and I was relieved to have taken care of the problem so easily. A quite different shock was in store for me. The bill Jekyll presented me with was for five guineas. I now eyed the gracious furniture with bitterness, having seen how it came to be purchased. This was more than I earned in two weeks of stevedoring and, unfortunately, more than remained to me in the little purse that I now emptied onto the tabletop. Three pounds six was all that was left after the previous night's generosity.

"That's all I've got, governor. And for me that's a tidy sum of money."

"I've no doubt. But I'm not so sure the police would see it in that light." Jekyll looked at me thoughtfully, murmuring to himself: "A fine example of the unconscious brute side of human nature. Enters here without a thought to payment and consequences...a certain animal magnetism...the beast happy in its ignorant cavern..."

He grew contemplative, studying me for a while. Then he began to question me closely as to how I had come about the bruise under my eye and other particulars. When I balked at telling him at length of the source of my little illness, he gazed at me coldly and offered to dispatch Poole to seek out the nearest policeman. But when I told him the details of my rendezvous with the scullion in the small alcove behind the coal shuttle of her employers' house, his friendliness returned, and he smiled delightedly while he drank in the details like a navvy confronted with his first pint of shoretime ale.

"Marvelous," he said, examining his own plump, manicured hand with manifest satisfaction. "It's an ill wind that brings no good, Mr. Hyde. I think we can come to an arrangement that will be of benefit to both of us.

"You see before you," he continued, "a man who is known and respected throughout all London—a doer of good deeds, a pillar of society. My stature, nay, my very upbringing...the air I breathe in these luxurious chambers constrains me to act always in a civilized manner. Not for me the brute spontaneity of a quick dalliance behind the coal scuttle, the thump on the head for the fool who dares look at me cross-eyed. No, I *must* comport myself with decency at all times, fettered by my higher place in the scale of evolution as surely as the gallows thief is prevented from fleeing to freedom by his leg irons..."

Jekyll continued in this manner for some time. I did not understand all of what he was saying at that instant, but I gathered that I was to be his proxy. My work was to indulge in my animal lusts, and all I had to do was report my doings to Dr. Jekyll in order to be forgiven my debt and receive a handsome retainer besides.

"Go forth and be *wicked*, Hyde," Jekyll intoned as he let me out the back door of his building, the entrance I was to use from now on in any communication with him.

At first, I thought that Dr. Jekyll was either cracked or just plain having me on, but the following Friday—the date he had set for our next encounter—curiosity took my feet down the back lane on the far side of Harley Street. On my way there, an odd incident occurred. A small girl dressed in a striped pinafore was so intent on chasing a child's hoop, which she kept balanced by tapping it with a light cane, that she ran full-tilt into me. I lifted her up, helped her retrieve the hoop, and gave her a halfpenny to bring back the smile to her limpid, innocent face.

Approaching the cellar door, I rapped once on its thick oak paneling, thinking that if there was no response, I could chalk the whole thing off to a moment's eccentricity on the doctor's part. To my surprise, the door swung open immediately, and Jekyll ushered me inside with every sign of having eagerly been awaiting my arrival.

"So, my good Hyde, what acts of gross turpitude have you committed since last we met?" he demanded.

Since I had been obeying his orders to stay clear of intoxicating beverages, my time had passed slowly and with little opportunity for mischief. Racking my brains, I thought of a little trick I had played some months before on a certain fishmonger in the Haymarket. The man was a fussy sort, always checking the balance of his weighing scales to make quite sure some poor old missis wasn't getting away with a free sliver of fin or tail. While my best butty, Townsend, distracted the man—"What's this, then? A grouper? Never heard of it. Got any eels? I could go for a nice eel"—I quickly nicked a couple of the weights that served to balance out the scale in graded half ounces. Pretending it had happened just days before, I narrated this history, much to Dr. Jekyll's delight.

"Capital, Hyde, capital. A little rough justice, if you will. And what else? What other means has Satan found to tempt you?"

I was forced to plunder my memory's storehouse—surely I had not done only good deeds in the interval?—when, suddenly, inspiration struck. I told Jekyll the story of the child and her hoop...

only, this time there was no stopping to help her up and dust her off. Instead, I joyously trod the helpless infant into the ground with my heavy work boots, indifferent to her terrified screams. Jekyll shivered as I described how the little hoop cracked under-foot like a chicken bone.

"And you didn't look back at all, Hyde?" he asked, rubbing his hands with glee.

"Not even once, Dr. Jekyll. Not once."

Jekyll gave me ten pounds and said he looked forward to our meeting the following week. As I was leaving, he called me back. "It's almost noon now. If you walk towards Cavendish Square, you'll be sure to encounter a stout gentleman dressed in a finely tailored charcoal-gray overcoat complete with beaver-skin top hat. In all likelihood, he'll have in his hands an ebony cane that is the very twin of this one. The man's name is Utterson, and he has an appointment with me. Spatter some mud on him for me—hey, Hyde? Or, better yet, smear some chalk on the back of his overcoat."

For all his sophistication, Dr. Jekyll's notion of evil-doing was still that of a schoolboy.

For about six months, the arrangement between Jekyll and my-self was useful for us both. For Jekyll, it was a chance to experience vicariously a lifestyle at complete odds with his habitual one. For me, it was a steady source of good money . . . but more than that, it was an opportunity to live outside the limits of my ilk and income. I valued the time spent with Jekyll, and I even borrowed some of his books to go through afterwards in my own time. Jekyll had a command of the Queen's English that I frankly envied, and I would find myself assuming some of his mannerisms and using some of his more eloquent locutions. See?—"locutions," that's a Jekyll word. His influence is with me even now.

Of course, there were difficulties. One day, I wore to our cellar meeting a fancy singlet modeled on Jekyll's own that I had bought with some of the money I had saved up. When he saw me in it, far from being flattered, he was furious.

"I pay you because you bring me the stink of the gutter, Hyde, not the scent of Savile Row," he railed. "Don't try to turn yourself into a gentleman, my boy. It would be a ridiculous sight: like a bullock laying eggs!"

He softened a little under my injured glare. "Come now, don't look at me like that. I suppose we all have a right to play at being what we're not—I, to be a brute, and you, to be a fine gentleman—but we need to keep some perspective, not let it go to our heads."

I suppose if that had been the only problem, I could have borne with it without too much complaint. What did it matter if Jekyll mocked at my lack of education, and even more so at my desire to make up for it? Let him be superior and condescending. It didn't stop me from learning what I wanted to learn. As Vic says about me, I can talk management, and I can talk mates.

No, the real problem was a certain universal fact of human nature: yesterday's vice is worth about as much as yesterday's daily paper. The wine of *my* evil deeds soon stopped intoxicating Jekyll; he must have stronger stuff! From being content to hear about my misdeeds, he went to being an observer... then observer became participant, and the downfall of us both was assured.

It started off with Jekyll having me stage a bare-fist bout in his capacious cellar. The audience was "a select few" of Jekyll's friends, men whom he trusted, classmates and old boys from Jekyll's public school. Among them was Utterson, who chose not to recognize in me the churl who had befouled his greatcoat with a hearty slap on the back. Another was a spry, white-haired gentleman named Sir Danvers Carew, an MP and a peer of the realm, no less. We put on a good show for the fine gentlemen. Too good a show, in fact, for I got carried away one day and beat my opponent, a young ruffian I'd known from the docks, into an insensate pulp.

You see, as Jekyll became more depraved in his desires, so I became more corrupt. I came to revel in the role into which he had cast me, like a music hall performer who forgets that it's all a mickey-take. With the money Jekyll gave me, I found I could buy the downtrodden, attractive youth of London. There was not a young household maid or messenger lad that I could not entice into Jekyll's cellar, where the practice of vice had achieved a rare pitch of refinement. These are memories I prefer not to call to mind, the times I spent swaggering around the city bullying my peers with my own physical strength and Jekyll's pecuniary wherewithal. My encounters with women ceased to be a jolly lark, a moment's warm reprieve from the cares of daily life. Instead, they were a transaction.

Things began to heat up for me, dangers that were the result of my new life. Jimmy Wilshire was out to get me for intruding on his territory, or so it was rumored. Hard Anthony himself was supposed to be waiting for me in some dark lane or courtyard, armed with cosh and shiv. At first I didn't care. I borrowed Jekyll's tough ebony cane and let it be known on the street that Hard Anthony had better stay out of *my* way. But there were other things that did begin to bother me: the way my former mates avoided me or only sought me out when the need for lucre grew overpowering. The hard-edged way the girls now looked at me... how they let me debauch them with my five- and ten-pound notes. People had become afraid of me. The drubbing I'd given to my youthful sparring partner (it had cost me a tidy sum to mollify him while he recovered from his injuries) had become part of city lore and was much exaggerated in the telling. Even Townsend, the jokester who had grown up just two houses away from me and who as long as I knew him was always up for a lark... he only came to me when he needed money, acted sullen and fearful, let me push him around without answering back. I was coming to know Jekyll's loneliness, the knowledge that no one gives a hoot for you yourself but only for the bit of silver that might fall their way. Not to say I didn't take pride in my newfound power—in the very independence Jekyll's money bought me—but it was slowly, much too slowly, beginning to sink in that all this was playacting. I had given up my own soul to become another man's thrall.

I will not bore you, dear Reader, with a lengthy account of my downward spiral in the ensuing months. Jekyll himself berated me for "opening the gates of Hell" to him, while simultaneously charging me with the arrangement of ever more wanton acts of dissipation. One moment he would threaten to bring in The Law on the grounds that I was extorting money from him, the next moment he would beg me not to disrupt his only true moments of pleasure. Many times I thought of simply disappearing, of leaving without a word, but always the lure of Jekyll's fascinating character—along with the sense of invincibility brought on by a steady supply of cash and the protecting shield of the doctor's reputation—brought me back. The truth is that I, too, was addicted to the heady fumes of unbridled wickedness, the gratifying crunch of cartilage beneath knuckle, the wild debauches in the cellar. And yet I was racked by the twin goads of conscience and fear. As Jekyll one day said, we were "like man's twin demons of good and evil locked in mortal embrace while our worldly bark teeters on the edge of the waterfall."

Late one night, as all things must, the whole charade came to an end. It was one of those dark, brooding nights when all but the friendless are home in a warm bed beside the pale embers of a dying fire. Patches of mist floated hither and yon like untethered wraiths, and I wandered alone like them, lost in embittered reflection. All of a sudden, a slender, white-haired figure appeared in front of me. It was Sir Danvers Carew, who seemed both surprised and delighted to see me here. Carew was a quiet sort, with the distinguished air of a man who knows his own importance. He kept himself aloof during our mad carousals, but he was always there to the last minute, smiling to himself, sitting a little to one side.

"Ah, it's Henry Jekyll's hired bravo," Carew remarked in his melodious voice, and began to inquire earnestly and sympathetically after my health. In the next moment, he made a proposal to me of such audacious indecency that my mind reeled. Suddenly, the Spirit of Justice, of right and wrong, that had been until now bottled up inside me as in a pressure boiler, rose up with irresistible force. With a shout, I sprang upon Carew and knocked him to the ground, where I dealt out my answer to his disgusting suggestion with Jekyll's ebony cane. A moment later I came to my senses, and tossing the shattered cudgel aside, I fled.

I wandered away from the city on foot, my mind cast loose from its moorings. For several days I walked, stopping only occasionally to rest or buy some food, and eventually I found myself in the West Midlands, the industrial heart of our fabled isle. It was late afternoon, but it might as well have been night, the way the clouds of factory smoke blotted out the pallid sun. The clang of machinery was almost deafening, and here and there flames shot out to silhouette a human figure as a boiler door was opened to feed the mechanical beast. The place uncannily resembled an oil painting of Hell that had hung in Jekyll's office, but for me it was an honest spot, one where I could preserve my anonymity in the midst of other rough, working folks like myself. I remembered that a favorite cousin lived here, Vic Goodston, and by dint of asking in various local pubs, I was soon able to locate him. Vic helped me get a job at a local foundry, where the softened pads of my fingers and palms soon acquired the callouses of forthright toil. It was work that brought me back to myself. No thought was required, none of the fancy words I had learned while hanging about with the upper crust . . . just a steady hand and muscles that could endure a full day of shoveling coal into a giant, blasting furnace.

As my mind healed itself, the fear that I would be discovered and hauled off to the gallows became ever stronger. Vic's discrete inquiries helped allay my fears as we gradually pieced together the story of why Scotland Yard was no longer searching for the violent madman and killer, Edward Hyde. The first shock was that Dr. Henry Jekyll himself was dead, and by his own hand. Before downing the deadly draught of prussic acid, he had written out a lengthy manuscript, detailing the fiction you all know so well.

Don't believe for a moment that Jekyll was motivated by any desire to aid the man he had so grievously injured. No, Jekyll was simply being true to his race—avoiding the scandal that would bring down not only himself, but his friend Utterson and the rest of the select crowd who frequented Jekyll's cellar. The world could not be allowed to think that its most elite denizens harbored tastes that can charitably be called unsavory. No, far better if society should think that by taking a few salt compounds, the noble Jekyll was turned into a beast, a mere day laborer, a stinking, odious hand-for-hire controlled not by his brain but his brute instincts. It was a fabrication that would not have taken in a child, but the bonded word of aristocrats like Utterson and of the police detectives, whose nests were feathered by a limitless supply of pound notes, was enough to convince a gullible public. I suppose I should be grateful to Jekyll for providing me with a way out, a substantial grant on my lease in this vale of tears, but I'm not. There's no reason to believe he did it for me. There's no reason to believe he ever saw me as his fellow. He took no more notice of the man who carried out the whims of his lowest self than he would have of the bootblack who put shine to his shoes.

There have been many times, though, when I've lain sleepless at night harried by the knowledge that my safety was illusory...that perhaps I didn't disappear into the anonymity of the working world, but my whereabouts were known to Jekyll's friends, to be revealed or not as it suited them. Lately, it has come to me that I'd been gulled more than I knew. All those learned treatises about the duality of man and the thin veneer of civilization that appeared after Jekyll's "revelations" came to light, they're all a load of bollocks. I sense Jekyll's hand in this somewhere, his love of deceit and subterfuge. How can we be sure it was his body in that casket borne by grim procession to Highgate Cemetery? London's morgue is full of happy dossers who have shucked off this mortal coil without friend or relation to mourn or identify them. Would it not be like Dr. Henry Jekyll to get another—some unknown, some anonymous roustabout, whose passing has left not a ripple on the surface of the London "that matters"—to take his place on that final journey while he sequesters himself at a friend's country estate or sojourns on the continent? It amazes me that I did not consider this possibility before, but blithely and blindly pursued my rounds of honest toil while Jekyll—my tormentor, my gilded double—remained alive, chuckling to himself at the stupidity of the inferior classes. How easily we are fooled. How unfailingly we accept even the most obvious fictions. How avidly we seize on the story that confirms our prejudice while the unpalatable truth goes begging. Dupes, all of us. And you, too, Reader. Wot'cher.

MARC VASSALLO

The Three-Legged Man

The summer I was fourteen, I went to stay in a small house in
Connecticut with my grandmother and grandfather. My
mother sent me there, she told me years later, because I was
driving her crazy, coming home late, shirking my chores, smoking my father's cigarettes. She wanted me out of the house, she
said, out of her life, at least for a while. What she told me at the
time, and what I see now as the better reason after all, was that
she wanted me to know my father's parents before it was too late.
She especially wanted me to know my grandfather: to know him
as something other than a three-legged man. I had seen him only
once before, when we traveled to Connecticut for the funeral of a
family member who must have been important, because ordinar-
ily my father did not speak about his parents, much less take us to
visit them.

A curious thing happened during that first visit. I stood in a
long, dark hallway beside a closed door, looking up at the doorknob. My grandfather was in the dining room sweeping the floor
because I had spilled a bowl of cracked nutshells. As I lifted my
hand to open the door, I felt a stinging at my knees, and I fell
backward to the floor. I looked up and saw my grandfather with
the sweeping end of the broom in his hand. The handle of the
broom rested between my legs, where he had jerked it to twist me
away from the door. The rest was a blur of tears.

The incident meant little to me at the time; his legs left the
more lasting impression. "My name is Peter, and I'm in the first
grade, and my grandfather has three legs," was how I introduced
myself to a house guest, a colleague of my father's, a few days after
we came home. My father called my mother aside and told her to
speak to me. She pulled me into the kitchen and said, "Your
grandfather has three legs where other people have two; excepting
that, he's no different from anyone else. He is, in fact, quite unre-
markable. Your father would rather that you didn't speak of him."

I never said another word about him, nor, of course, did my father, nor my mother.

Not until the year I turned twelve, when, on the way home from my father's funeral, driving through the November rain, my mother began to talk about my grandfather, who had not attended the funeral because my grandmother was too ill with pneumonia to travel. "They think he was supposed to have been twins," my mother said. "But something happened in the womb." My mother told me about the woman who delivered him, how she went hysterical and dropped him on the floor and ran screaming out of the house and never practiced midwifery again. This was in a small hill town somewhere in Sicily. My mother said that people came from miles around to see the boy with three legs, and that some of them stuck his third leg with a pin, to watch it bleed, to satisfy themselves that it was real. The leg could not be removed, she said, because an operation would result in paralysis or death. The business with the pins upset me deeply, but I asked her to tell me more. "I've told you as much as your father told me," she said.

She put me on a train that took six hours to get to Connecticut. I bought a girlie magazine in Union Station to help pass the time on the trip, and a tabloid newspaper to wrap around the magazine in case I should sit next to an old lady. I sat next to a businessman, and still I was embarrassed; but when I had finished the newspaper, and the backsides of Philadelphia row houses and everybody's trash and laundry no longer held my attention, I began to sneak peaks at the naked women. The flashes of tanned skin and pink nipples, like the fleeting views into other people's backyards through the train window, were somehow more enticing than a long look would have been. I stepped off the train dizzy from hours on the verge, feeling as if I had spent the day sitting in a fine mist that never quite became a rain.

My grandfather met me at the station, dressed in a starched white shirt, a pink tie, and a pair of dark gray trousers with three pant legs. I had forgotten how his third leg was attached, so I lingered behind him as we walked to his car, pretending I was having trouble lifting my suitcase. The third leg, which was shorter than the other two by some eighteen inches, attached at the back and protruded toward his right. The leg hung in midair and swung gently from side to side as he walked, reminding me of a sailboat's rudder. On his third foot was a polished black shoe that matched the two on his walking feet, but was smaller.

We said little in the car during the ride to the house; I felt like a stranger, which, in essence, I was. My grandfather drove with his third leg resting between us on the front seat of the Buick, the sole of his shoe almost touching my leg. I looked straight ahead and gripped my thigh with my left hand to avoid touching his third foot.

My grandmother greeted us in the kitchen. She sat beside the screen door, turning red peppers on an electric coil burner. She seemed shorter and thinner than I had remembered, the skin on her face cracked and wrinkled like the roasting peppers. She kissed my grandfather as though he had been away for weeks and then stood slowly and kissed me on each cheek; I had to bend over because I was taller than she was now. The house, too, was smaller than I remembered, and all on one floor. Through the kitchen window, I could see a sprawling backyard garden, and beyond a steep brushy hillside that disappeared into woods, and then a wide valley, with smokestacks and long brick factory buildings and a river that looked like a thin line of silver. There didn't seem much to do for a week; I was glad I had the magazine.

"Take your bag back to your room," my grandfather said. "The door at the end of the hall." The two of them stood with their arms around each other as I left the kitchen, studying me, perhaps remembering the many times my father had passed through the same doorway. I walked by the bathroom, and then by the open door to their bedroom. Opposite their door was a closed door I recognized at once as the one I had tried to open as a young child. I decided to take a peek inside, to see why my grandfather had knocked me over with the broom. I thought that perhaps the door opened into my father's old room. But as I reached for the knob, I felt eyes watching me, and, looking back, I saw my grandfather, a three-legged silhouette in the arched opening to the dining room. He said nothing, so I turned back around and went to my room.

The first thing I did was slip the magazine between the mattress and the box spring of the Harvard bed, all the way to the middle, in case my grandmother tried to remake the bed. The room was just big enough for the bed and a dresser, on top of which was a mason jar of fresh-cut flowers. In the center of one wall was an opened window that made the small herb garden outside seem part of the room. The herb garden was terraced above the main vegetable garden, contained by a stone wall, and when the wind stirred, even a little, the room filled with the aroma of sweet basil and lemon balm. After unpacking my clothes, I stashed my matches and cigarettes—the last of my father's cartons—in with the magazine.

I was surprised to find my grandfather still standing at the entrance to the hallway when I came out of the bedroom. He laid a bony hand on my shoulder. "I believe I told you once before to stay out of that room," he said.

"Yes, sir," I said, although I couldn't remember anything he had told me, only the sting of the broom. I felt tall beside my grandfather, out of place; I had no idea what I should do or say next. The smell of the peppers drifted in from the kitchen.

"Come," he said. "You and I, we'll garden while your grandmother finishes supper." He nudged me into the kitchen. As I stepped out the door, I smiled at my grandmother, though I couldn't say why, and she smiled back through her horn-rimmed glasses, her eyes the size and color of worn pennies.

My grandfather handed me a metal tool that looked like a miniature stirrup, but with razor-sharp edges. Ahead of me, he bent over a leafy row, so that his third leg stuck stiffly in the air and seemed to remain suspended there, like a cat's tail, the foot tipped downward. "This is a carrot top," he said, gathering a handful of thin-leafed stalks. "The rest is weeds." He slipped the shoes off all three of his feet, removed his knee-high black socks, and then rolled up his three pant legs. I kneeled down on the damp black soil and began chopping at weeds with the tool. Now and again, I pulled up a carrot, to hear its roots tear loose from the earth, to feel it break free. Then I would clean the dirt off it as best I could and eat it. I yanked out a carrot that forked in two. This one I threw into the woods behind me; its two knobby shanks and hairy roots seemed too strange to eat. I looked up to make sure my grandfather hadn't seen me waste what was, after all, a perfectly good carrot. He sat several rows away, tying a tomato vine to a bamboo stake, leaning back on his third leg so that his three legs formed a tripod.

He caught me staring at his legs, and I expected him to chastise me, but instead, he asked me to tell him about Washington. He wanted to know if his money had been well spent. So I told him about monuments and museums and wide streets. And then he told me about Waterbury, about the floods, especially about the big one in '38, when he was trapped in the basement of his cousin's warehouse, down along the railroad tracks by the river, and we talked some about baseball, which we both loved, and about steam trains and sports cars and wars. Only once, when talking about the big flood, did he mention his legs, and that was to say that, when swimming, he used his third leg to steer. We both smiled at this, he studied my face curiously for a moment, and then he changed the subject back to trains.

After supper I helped wash the dishes—something my mother had insisted I do. As we worked, my grandmother explained all about the opera, so I had braced myself by the time we sat down in the living room to listen to the radio. My grandfather positioned himself on the crushed velvet couch with his third leg propped on his right thigh, so that he was both sitting cross-legged and sitting with two feet on the floor. My grandmother sat to his left. As we listened to *La Traviata,* they patted each other's hands and looked into each other's eyes like this was a first date, mouthing the words in Italian and gently tilting back their heads, as though they were sniffing the bouquet of flowers on the coffee table. I listened in a dreamy sort of way, and when Violetta sang, I closed my eyes and imagined I was rolling her nipples between my fingers and running my tongue up her thighs. When the opera was over, my grandmother struggled to her feet, kissed us both good night, and left the room.

"Now would be a good time for a snack," my grandfather said. He turned on the television to the Mets game, then retired to the kitchen. When he returned, he handed me a bowl of ice cream. "This is for helping in the garden," he said. He sat down again on the sofa. On the coffee table in front of him, he arranged a tall glass of ice water and two enormous bowls, one full of mixed nuts, the other empty, awaiting shells. We watched the first inning in silence, my grandfather working almost feverishly at cracking and eating the nuts.

When he saw that I was watching, he picked up two walnuts, held them together in his left hand, and squeezed until one of them cracked cleanly in two. "I eat fourteen percent more than the average man of my size and build," he said as he ate the walnut, "on account of my extra leg."

I smiled. "Fourteen percent," I said, "and not fifteen or sixteen?"

"Fourteen percent," he said. "Doctor's orders." He winked at me, the amber light from the Tiffany lamp glinting in his eye.

He handed me two walnuts. "Give it a try," he said. I squeezed the nuts together until my fingers ached. Nothing. Not a crack. My grandfather laughed and scooped up two walnuts in each hand. "Put your hands on mine," he said. I leaned forward and placed my hands over his, my palms against his knuckles. His hands tightened at the same time, cracking all four walnut shells.

I let out a breath as if I had done the work. "You must be fourteen percent stronger than the average man," I said.

"Strength has nothing to do with it." He began picking the meat out of the shells. "Practice," he said. "Practice and desire."

In the bottom of the eighth, I noticed that he had fallen asleep with his mouth open. His thick tongue fluttered with each exhale. Both he and my grandmother were now asleep. I saw my chance to slip into the room—I could always call back to him as if from the bathroom.

When I reached the door, I glanced across the hall, expecting to see the closed door to their bedroom. But their door was open, a night light of some sort was on, and my grandmother was sitting upright against the headboard, staring straight at me. I stood still a moment and tried to decide, without fully looking at her, whether she was awake or asleep with her eyes open, or if something had happened. I decided to wait until the middle of the night to try the door, and as soon as I was certain that my grandmother was alive, I walked back to my bedroom.

A warm night breeze blew in from the opened window, bringing with it the now familiar mix of basil and lemon balm. I retrieved my cigarettes, climbed out the window, and sat on the corner of the stone wall, beside a bush that had been manicured in the shape of an owl. As I smoked, adding my own piquant aroma to the air, I watched the lights in the valley, flickering like earth stars, like the fireflies dancing in the woods. I couldn't keep my mind on any one thing: not on the room, not on baseball, not on the fireflies, not on girls, although eventually, when I reached the end of my third cigarette, I could not get girls out of my mind, the way their breasts attached to their bodies, a place I had never touched before, nor seen even, except in pictures.

I climbed back inside and took out the magazine and studied Miss July by flashlight and thought about how her skin would feel where her breasts curved back into her body toward her underarms, and how her nipples would feel, and the hair between her legs, the lips between her legs.

When I had finished my business, I lay on top of the sheets and let the warm scented air wash over me. I lay there a long while before I fell asleep, savoring the heaviness in my head and the limpness in my legs, and wondering, now that I could think again about something other than women, what was inside the room.

My plans to sneak into the room during the night were foiled by my grandfather, who turned out to be a fitful sleeper. I would hear him fussing with the radio in his room, or flushing the toilet, or watching television in the living room, where I found him once, peeling an apple, the peel corkscrewing onto the floor, no wider than a stick of linguine and perhaps ten feet long. One night, while heading for the room on the off-chance that he was asleep, I stumbled into him in the darkened hallway. I had my hand out in front of me to help me find the way, and when we collided, my hand pressed against the hair on his bare chest, which made me shudder and him stiffen. He muttered something at me softly in Sicilian, with breath that smelled of anchovies. I hurried to the bathroom, where I sat in the dark for a while, wondering whether he had been wearing a bathrobe or had been naked. I resolved to find a way into the room during broad daylight. But over the next four days, the chance never came.

We were picking greens for our dinner salad when my grandfather turned to me and said, "I'm sorry about the broom." He rubbed the knee of his third leg as he spoke.

"It's all right," I said. "Pass me the basket, I've got more arugula than I can hold."

"I said some things about you to your mother that I regret," he said. "You're a good boy. A smart boy." I wanted to feel pleased with what he said, but all I could think about was the magazine and the cigarettes and my plan to sneak into the room.

In the garden on my second to last morning, we dug up garlic bulbs my grandfather had planted the previous fall. We worked side by side while my grandmother scurried about her flower garden, singing Italian songs and keeping time with her pruning shears. She sang loud enough for us to hear her as we harvested the garlic, but when the air heated up and the sun began to bake our skin, she grew silent and then returned to the house.

My grandfather, who, as always, was dressed in a white shirt, a tie, and trousers, wiped his brow with a handkerchief. "When I was some years younger than you are now," he said to me, "I went to visit a state institution for children. A friend of my father's took me there." He cleared his throat and put the handkerchief back in his shirt pocket. I sat back on the straw mulch, and he looked down at me, squinting in the sun, his dark face and gray hair in shadow against the sky.

"I saw all kinds of children that day," he continued, "children lying in beds, sitting in the sun, wandering along a stone terrace, writhing on the floor so that we had to step over them. Children with no eyes, children who couldn't hear or walk or talk. Children who screamed as if they had demons in their head. Children with misshapen bodies, stunted hands, no arms, no legs. Children covered with scabs, one little boy without a jaw." He was making me sick. The slug creeping through the straw on the path between us was making me sick. My grandfather raised his hoe and brought it down on the slug, slicing it in two. "I am a lucky man," he said. I didn't know how to respond. I beat a bulb of garlic on the ground to knock off the clods of dirt.

We carried baskets of garlic over to a wooden shed my grandfather had built along one end of the garden, next to his fruit trees. Inside the shed, on tables with wire-mesh tops, bulbs of garlic had been laid out to dry. My grandfather gathered some of the dried garlic and showed me how to make a garlic braid by twisting the tops together, using a piece of wire to give it strength. We braided garlic for several hours. While we worked, he told me stories about his days in the brass business. His cousin owned a company that distributed brass fittings; my grandfather had worked in the office, as a bookkeeper. He seemed prepared to braid garlic clear until supper. Thinking that I would have a chance at the room if my grandmother was busy in the kitchen, I told my grandfather that I needed to use the bathroom.

"You go on inside," he said. "And then you do whatever you like. Read a comic book or go down to the corner store." He took his wallet from his front pants pocket—he had no back pocket because his third leg was in the way—and pulled out a dollar bill. "Here," he said, handing me the bill, "buy yourself an ice cream." I thanked him and ran inside, where I found my grandmother in the living room, sitting on the velvet sofa.

Her head was tilted back, and her eyes were closed. I looked real hard at her, until I was certain I had seen her chest rise. She wore tennis shoes, and appeared twenty years younger in the bright sunlight, and had her legs spread apart in a way I was sure she would have considered unladylike. I thought to myself, looking at her legs where they disappeared under her apron and blue-checked housedress: This is the woman who made love to a three-legged man. And then, feeling ashamed of myself, and sorry for her because she looked so tired, and because it struck me that she and my grandfather didn't have too much longer together, I thought: This is the woman whose only son, my father, suffered and died before her. I walked up to her and put a pillow behind her head, careful not to disturb her bun, and then I went straight for the door to the room and opened it.

The first thing I saw, on the wall to my left, was a huge circus poster, ten feet long and as tall as the room, with swirling gold-leaf ornamentation and the words, "WALTER L. MAIN'S CIRCUS—Home of the World's Only Three-Legged Man," and then, set off in quotations, "King of the Freaks." The date on the poster was 1903; my grandfather could not have been more than thirteen at the time.

The room was filled with circus memorabilia, most of it having to do with my grandfather. On the wall to my right hung framed circus programs and sepia photographs. A picture of my grandfather as a young boy, wearing a checkered jacket, shorts, and striped knee socks on all three legs, standing with a man who must have been his father, my great-grandfather. Pictures of my grandfather sitting in chairs, standing with his right foot on a stool, his left foot on a stool, his third foot on a stool. My grandfather wearing satin shirts and circus tights and polished pointy-toed boots. My grandfather in photographs with silver script: "*Only Three-Legged Man in the World & The Bearded Lady,*" "*Only Three-Legged Man in the World & The Sheep-Headed Man,*" "*Only Three-Legged Man in the World & The Tiny Midgets.*" In this one, he is in a three-legged kneel, with the Tiny Woman sitting on his right leg and the Tiny Man sitting on his left, their tiny legs dangling in the air, ropes to a circus tent crisscrossing behind them. My grandfather is smiling, but the Tiny Man has a stern, joyless expression, a tiny cigar in his mouth. On the far wall, to either side of a window, were posters from Ringling Bros. Circus, from Barnum & Bailey Circus, even from Buffalo Bill's Wild West Show, all with paintings of my grandfather. Behind me were autographed pictures of clowns, friends of his.

I stepped slowly to the window, careful to stay to one side, and peered out to check on my grandfather. He was coming toward the door to the root cellar beneath me, his arms by his sides, each hand holding a cabbage, upside down by the stem. He was whistling a tune like nothing in this room had ever happened. As I backed away from the window, I bumped a table, knocking over a stack of cards. I knew I still had some time while he fussed about in the root cellar, culling bad fruit from last fall or wrapping the cabbages in newspaper. I knelt down and picked up the cards. Each one had a picture of my grandfather in an old-fashioned striped swimsuit, the kind with a tank top and skin-tight, knee-length legs. The cards had his signature on them and a message:

THE ONLY MAN IN THE WORLD WITH 3 LEGS, 4 FEET, 16 TOES,
2 BODIES FROM THE WAIST DOWN. OPERATION IMPOSSIBLE.
3RD LIMB CONNECTED AT THE SPINE.
THANK YOU.
PLEASE SHOW THIS PHOTO TO YOUR FRIEND.

I put two cards in my pocket and the others back on the table, next to a book called *The Giant Book of Freaks*. The book was laid out like a high school yearbook, page after page of photographs and descriptions of people with every imaginable and unimaginable deformity, and wherever it seemed useful, the people were photographed nude. I knew I had to hurry, but I stopped to study a woman with breasts the size of watermelons, bigger than watermelons, they drooped down past her waist, and a woman twisted up like a pretzel, also nude, but with no breasts at all, and another with pubic hair that hung to the floor. It occurred to me that my grandfather must be in the book, perhaps naked. But before I could find him in the index—and even as I looked I wasn't sure I wanted to see his picture—I heard the screen door to the kitchen swing open. I let go of the book and ran back to my room.

I lay on the bed in the heat of the afternoon, dizzy, my cheeks flushed, the way I felt once after looking at one of my father's anatomy books. I had to shake my head to forget the woman with pubic hair that curled down around her toes. My grandfather: King of the Freaks. Perhaps the woman with watermelon tits was the queen. I sat up, afraid I would faint, and stared out the window, past the herbs, past the tops of tomato stakes and bean poles and pea trellises, off into the blank sky.

I got out the magazine and, tired already of the centerfold, found another woman to look at, a blonde stretched out on a pink chaise longue beside a turquoise swimming pool. The room was hot, sunlight pouring in through the big window. I took forever to get hard, but I kept working at it, mostly to keep my hands busy, my mind occupied. When I was through, I lit a cigarette and smoked it with my head out the window, sending smoke into the sky in measured puffs, like smoke signals.

At supper my grandfather and grandmother were more quiet than usual. I wondered if they were sad because this was my last night with them, or if they were tired from their day of gardening and housework, from their long lives, or if somehow one or both of them knew I had been in the room. The kitchen was hot from my grandmother's cooking and from the heat outside, which didn't seem to be going away with the sun as it had on previous nights. My grandmother had fixed fresh grilled tuna steak with roasted red peppers and a thin, brothy tomato sauce. It was as I bit into a pepper that I realized I had left open *The Giant Book of Freaks*. A sinking feeling came over me. I would have to sneak back into the room at night somehow and close the book. I began to sweat, imagining my grandfather finding the open book after I was gone and calling my mother.

"Poor boy," my grandmother said. "Too hot in the kitchen or did you bite into one of your grandfather's peppers?"

"Both," I said. "Water. More water, please." My grandfather passed me the water pitcher. I filled my glass, drank it, and filled it again. As I drank the second glass, it came to me that I should drink and drink and complain bitterly about the heat. Then they would believe that I had to keep going to the bathroom at night. And on one of my trips, surely my grandfather would be asleep and I could slip into the room and close the book.

On my first trip to the bathroom that night, I found my grandfather coming down the hall on his way back from the kitchen, a glass of ice water clinking in his unsteady hand.

"Careful," he said, "watch your step." I could see that he had on his bathrobe this time, the moonlight was so bright, even in the hallway.

On my second trip, I saw a blue flickering light from the television and heard him fanning himself with the newspaper. I left the door ajar and stood on the side of the bathtub, so that the sound of my pee hitting the toilet water would echo down the hall. I wanted to be sure he understood why I was up.

At four o'clock, I scanned the hall and then walked slowly toward the room. Their door was shut, and no lights were on in the rest of the house. Here was my chance. I opened the door.

My grandfather stood at the far end of the room, to the right of the open window, stark naked in the full light of the moon, his back to me. He was flipping through the pages of the book. His bathrobe lay draped over a chair.

"Take a good look," he said, "so you'll never forget." He stayed with his back to me. "Go ahead, it's all right." My hand was still on the doorknob. I should have turned and run, but instead I stayed to have a look. His shoulders drooped naturally enough, his torso curving down toward his waist, but his buttocks were formed by his left leg and his third leg; I could not see how his right leg was attached. I noticed that his two front legs were sized and shaped somewhat differently; he had three legs but not a pair. I thought I was going to vomit or cry or maybe even collapse from the heat and the strangeness of it, his wrinkled, splotchy skin and sagging buttocks, the limpness of his third leg, pale and shriveled in the moonlight, and the tiny club-shaped fourth foot springing from the thigh of the third leg, its toes curled, the whole of it no bigger than a dog's paw.

"I'm sorry," I said, looking away.

"Never mind that now," he said. "Close the door so your grandmother will not be disturbed." I thought he might put on his bathrobe and tell me about his circus days. I wished he would at least put on the robe.

As soon as I closed the door behind me, my grandfather turned around. I caught his eye and then looked down. That's when I saw the area between his legs. My grandfather had, protruding from his tangled, still-black pubic hair, two scrotums and two penises. I took a quick look at them, hating myself for doing so, and then I looked down at my bare feet.

"I was going to show you this room tomorrow," my grandfather said, "before you left. I am proud of this room—I only show it to my closest friends." He slammed his hand on the table, and I jerked my head and looked him straight in the eyes. "I am a lucky man," he said. "Your father never understood me when I said this. He never liked hand work, either. He was not one to help in the garden like you."

He talked for ten minutes, naked the whole time—he would not reach for his robe—and I stood with my hand on the doorknob and listened as best I could and prayed he would finish soon. I stared into his eyes until it was clear to me that he stood there because he wanted me to see him, and then I lowered my gaze to between his legs and took a good long look.

Fugitives

Traveling alone, Martin Grant came to a place on the coast in the rain. A place much as he had imagined—green and balmy, with bright splashes of winter flowers and fruit trees and tall palms that rustled in the wind. A place so far from the frozen cornfields of central Iowa that it made him smile, and imagine that his memories of what had happened there might one day melt and evaporate in this subtropical air.

The job he had been offered—on the basis of an editing test, two phone interviews, and several strong recommendations—was that of city editor for a mid-sized daily. It was a lateral move, at best, although these days Martin Grant was less interested in advancement than he was in change. He needed, at age forty, a new headline in his life.

The sights and sounds and smells of newspapers being made varied little, he had found, and as he toured the building, Martin caught glints everywhere of people he knew, of work he understood. He had a quiet and affable manner that plugged in easily to this new job. His only difficulty during those first several days was one of will: maintaining the faith that had kept him sober for more than two months.

Each afternoon, as Martin set up the next morning's Metro section, the urge to drink at times dazzled him, like the sun sequins that glittered on the green, palm-lined bay outside the newsroom window, and quickly dimmed. In the evenings, he took walks to quiet this craving, making paths from the plush townhouse the publisher had found him, marveling at the lush neighborhoods full of moss-draped oaks and banana magnolias, where air conditioners hummed and birds sang and lawn sprinklers clicked in the Bermuda grass. He thought, during these walks, of his wife, Katie, knowing that she had a warm fire of vodka going inside her, and that she was happy with this new man she had found in snowy Iowa, who liked bourbon, with beer chasers, and sold antiques.

After the sun dropped behind the Spanish roofs, interiors seemed to sharpen, like Polaroid pictures; the scenes of people sitting around dinner tables and in living rooms on these warm December evenings seemed not quite real to Martin, like the mechanical figures he had seen on his only other trip to Florida, at Disney World.

Nearly everyone at the newspaper, Martin found, had also come to this town from somewhere else, and they quickly made him feel welcome. Thomas Persons, a florid-faced political columnist from Wisconsin, with wispy curls of white hair, sat closest to Martin's office, and informed him, on his third day, "You know, Grant, I have to tell you, you're a far better editor than the monkey they had in here before." Lora Lee Moonshower, a tiny Pennsylvanian from the production department, with remarkable posture and wavy brown hair that reached to the backs of her knees, introduced herself on Martin's first day and let her eyes flirt with his. She wore tight jeans, a Harley-Davidson top, and he noticed a green serpent tattooed on one arm. Martin was cheerful, and she returned several times over the next few days, sitting on the edge of his desk and swinging her leg, as if they were courting.

But it wasn't until China Rinaldi invited him for dinner that Martin Grant felt anything had happened—that there was some news in his life, and, thus, that his new life in this new town had begun. Nothing about China Rinaldi glinted quite the way he expected. She looked to him more like a fashion model than the advertising director, tall and slender with long legs and black hair and an alluring upward tug at the corners of her mouth. Yet a fashion model wouldn't possess such earthy politeness. He was surprised by other things: to discover, after their first conversation, that her geniality echoed so hollowly off several other staff members. That some in the newsroom, in their rush to deadline, seemed to step around China when she came in with her odd urgencies, wearing scarf belts and boots and antique bracelets, as if she were some exotic creature they had gotten used to and, then, tired of. It surprised him when she grabbed his arm one morning in the hallway, feigned a laugh, and said, conspiratorially, "This fricking place," without explaining. The "Let Go Let God" sticker on the back of her red Mustang was another twist; as was her remark, "You know what my favorite activity is? Painting." What surprised Martin most, though, was when, on his fifth day in town, China Rinaldi used the ease of their shared politeness to say: "It must be tough moving to a new place and not knowing anybody. Why don't you come over tonight and I'll make you some supper?"

She lived six blocks from Martin's townhouse, so he decided to walk, enjoying the cooling breezes as lightning bugs began to glow in the live oaks. The apartment was on a canal, in a development called the Venetian Village. He rapped three times on unit 423, waited, and tried again.

Moonlight shifted in the tops of the tall, bent coconut palms; he wondered how it looked right now in Iowa, shining out across the fields of snow behind the farmhouse where Katie was living.

"Welcome!"

China, in the doorway with a wineglass raised, seemed to be toasting him.

"Greetings," he replied.

The apartment's smell was warm and spicy, of seafood and bay leaf and burning incense; it drew him in, through the vestibule and the hallway to the main room, where candlelight cast jumping shadows on the walls and wicker furniture. He saw, as they stood beside the dining room table, smiling at each other, that she had dressed up slightly, in a low-cut black caftan, while he had dressed down, changing from a suit to khakis and a sport shirt. A gold chain and small cross hung between her breasts.

"Very nice," he said, meaning everything.

China's face tightened; she held her right hand in the "Stop" position, like Diana Ross.

"Please," she said. "Stay right there."

Martin wondered, as she set her glass on the kitchen counter and hurried to an adjoining bedroom, if she was going to take his picture.

He saw television images changing on the dark bedroom walls through the door, and then she was back.

"These," she announced proudly, her hands on the backs of two small children, "are the famous munchkins."

"The pleasure's mine," Martin said, gazing at eyes glazed with
TV images.

"This"—she placed her right hand on the head of a sullen, tou-
sle-haired boy, who immediately tried to wriggle free—"is Jamie.
And this"—the other hand rested on hair that was silky and
black, like China's—"is Justine. This is Mr. Martin."

Justine went behind her mother's leg and held on, peeking out
at him. Jamie looked down, as if he had done something wrong.

"Mr. Martin just moved here from Iowa. Iowa? Or Idaho?"

"Iowa," Martin said.

As soon as she let go and lifted her glass—again, oddly, in the
gesture of a toast—the children hurried to the bedroom.

"Wine?" she said.

Her brown eyes seemed to moisten with the reflection of the
candle flame. Martin saw colored lights on the boles of the
coconut palms by the swimming pool. He conjured up his number and held on, as if to a talisman in his pocket, a winning lottery ticket in his hand: sixty-seven days. "I'll have soda," he said.
"If you have any."

Her seafood marinara was thick with Gulf shrimp and clams
and scallops, spicy with basil and onion. They talked easily across
the table, with the same ping-pong of politeness they had played
in the office, both sipping 7-Ups, reporting the events of their
lives and careers in capsule summaries. And then, after dishing
him a second helping of marinara, China began to reveal, matter-
of-factly, the secrets of the men and women Martin was getting to
know.

"I see Tom Persons in your office all the time. He's a very nice
man. But I feel sorry for him. Did you know he's been married
four times, and has his salary attached?"

Martin's eyes grew larger. "Is that right?"

She raised and lowered her head, with a flat, knowing smile.
"Drinking."

There was more: Lora Lee Moonshower was arrested last year
for shoplifting frozen french fries in the Winn-Dixie; Hobart
Brice, the sports editor, enjoyed young boys in his Saab, and was
on the verge of declaring bankruptcy, again; the art director was

having an affair with the entertainment editor, and both were married women.

"Sounds livelier than I'd have imagined," he smiled. "You must like it there."

"Are you kidding?" A faint mustache of 7-Up shone below her straight, perfect nose as she shook her head, leaning toward the candlelight. "I quit once before. Six months ago. Fricking Elmer didn't know what to do. He said, 'Listen, China, what would you want to go and do that for?' I think he likes me." The corners of her mouth curled momentarily. Elmer, Martin realized, must be Peter Fudd, the managing editor. "And I said, 'I have to look out for the munchkins.' My children. Which is true. He says, 'Let me see what I can do.'

"So he goes down the hall, right? Closes his office door, comes back twenty minutes later, makes me an offer. I say, 'That's almost what they're offering me at this other job'—of course, he thinks it's the other newspaper. The *Banner*. I claim I'm not at liberty to divulge just where it is. And, sure enough, he comes back the next day, I'm starting to pack my things in a box. Like, a big cardboard box?" She moved her hands as if shoveling sand into a bucket. "Elmer comes up and offers what I want. Asks me if I want to be ad director."

Martin chuckled politely. "Guess that didn't sit too well with the previous ad director," he said.

China's eyes flickered; he saw an earlier version of her gaze momentarily, dark and vulnerable. "Well. I mean, I don't like to operate that way. But that's how the world works."

The telephone rang. China looked at Martin as if her stomach had growled. "Excuse me."

He heard her answer in the kitchen—"Yes?" she said, suspiciously. She turned her back to him, blocking the view of the wine bottle on the counter. Outside, he noticed, looking at the swimming pool, it had begun to rain. As clearly as he remembered Katie's little half-cough, he recalled the sound of vodka pouring into her glass in late afternoon, followed by the softer splash of orange juice, and the way it looked in the morning on the bedstand, the color of thin urine. He wondered if the man, the antiques dealer, had awakened this morning to that smell.

Without saying another word, China replaced the telephone receiver in its cradle, so delicately he didn't hear it.

"So." She sat at the table and laced her fingers together. Martin saw a new energy on the edges of her eyes. She licked her lips once. "I understand you're going through a divorce."

"Yes," Martin said. "I am." His thoughts stuck, though; the events were still like notes in his mind, stories to write. "Thirteen years," he said. "We were as in love as two people can be. And grew apart. It was very hard for me to stay in the same town, the way things turned out." He added, "Drinking had a lot to do with it."

China looked to the side and blinked at unseen thoughts. The long lashes made her seem far away.

"I was married to a very abusive man," she said. "There was no growing apart, it was more like a shattering. A series of shatterings." Her face went blank for a moment, like a television that is turned off and quickly on again. "I came down here from New York to start over, because my sister was here. And, of course, I didn't want the munchkins to be near their father. But I've been here four years now, and nothing's happened. I think we've had enough of this fricking place."

"Where would you go?" he said, holding his fork above the food.

She shrugged, as if she hadn't really thought about it. He saw the reflection of the candles across the room in the sliding glass door and burning absently in her eyes. She looked back at her food, and they finished the meal talking easily about the news of the town and the people at the office. Together they cleared the table.

As she excused herself, to put the children to bed, Martin admired the easy way her hips moved leaving the room. He saw three canvases leaning against a wall by the bookcase, and crouched to look. All were signed "China" in childlike black print. One was of a crumbling barn, with withered fields of corn in the background; it might have been Iowa, the land behind the man's farmhouse in late June. Another was of a sailboat, tilted dangerously on a bright blue sea. The third was of four men disembarking from a train, grim-faced, onto a flat brown terrain, as a storm gathered in the sky behind them. It awakened an old image: Not of kissing Katie Truitt the first time—fourteen years ago, in the gravel parking lot at St. Matthew's church on West Street in Cedar Rapids—but of what happened beforehand. These were the same expressions he had seen in that church, worn by the older neighbor men he had known for years. As the congregation prayed, kneeling, he had glanced across and suddenly not known them, any of them; it was like looking at a familiar landscape from an unfamiliar vantage point and not recognizing it. The grown-ups prayed, the children fidgeted, and he touched Katie's arm, watched her freckled face and clear blue eyes; afterward, without warning, in a wonderful sparkle of spring sunlight through the elm leaves, he kissed her, leaning against the blue Volvo, and it changed their lives.

Martin went to the back door and slid it open. A fine warm rain was falling, and the air smelled of wet bark and chlorine and magnolias. A good fresh scent. Something exciting was going to happen. Hibiscus dripped through the slats of the redwood fence, and the green pool lights quivered distantly beneath the rain-dimpled surface.

He walked along three stepping stones beside the pool and stopped, hearing her voice. Behind drawn curtains, a partially opened window, China was admonishing her children, in Italian: "Daviola! Basta! No! Basta!" A door slammed.

He stared at the glistening bark and thought of drops on a whiskey glass, the sound of ice, remembering just how the first drink of the day felt, going down. Their troubles had begun as evening arguments, over what she repeatedly called "moving in separate directions." As Katie, the talkative high school English teacher, drank more, he drank less, and privately winced each time she had to "freshen" hers—as if it was really just one great big drink she was having. Seven days ago, he had left her there, still drinking it, he'd been unable to take it away. As the wind gusted up through the rain in the sabal palms, tearing at the fronds, he felt something shake loose in himself also.

China was standing on one of the stepping stones, staring at him as if he were modern art.

"What are you doing?" she said. "Let's sit under the awning."

She pushed two plastic pipe chairs together on the terrace right outside of the living room. The candles still glowed inside through the glass.

"The munchkins," she said, "were bad tonight. I think they're just tired. They're usually much more sociable."

"I really enjoyed the dinner," he said, tasting steamed seafood in the air. "I saw your paintings in there. Quite nice. The one of the train—"

"Fugitives?" She pushed her hair back over her shoulders, and he saw that her lashes were tipped now with moisture. "It's my father and his three brothers, actually. They all had that same expression on their faces, all their lives. Like someone had just chewed them out about something. My husband had it, too. Although for some reason, I never saw it until after we were married."

"Fugitives."

"That's what I called it. 'People who travel are always fugitives.' I was reading Daphne du Maurier at the time."

Martin, wanting to say, "What does that mean?" instead asked, "Do you believe that?"

"Mmm-hmm." She seemed to be staring at a memory, just above the redwood fence. "My father moved around, my husband moved around. And, I mean, I tell everybody how fricking awful my husband was. But, I was there, too, wasn't I? I made myself available for it."

He understood then, breathing boiled shrimp in the warm, rain-scented air. Most of the big stories in our lives, regrettably, aren't written by us, he had learned. It was hard to explain, though, even to himself.

"You've probably heard some of the things said at the office about me by now," China said, smiling dimly; she looked off to the side, a place he couldn't see. The cross between her breasts gleamed momentarily with the lights above the swimming pool.

"No," he said. "What things?"

"It doesn't matter."

She looked at his face, her brown eyes glowing again around the edges with an urgent energy.

Martin smiled back.

Her hair felt good on his arm in the wet breeze.

Using the same tone with which she might have asked, "Do you want another 7-Up?" China said, "Do you want to kiss?"

He felt her fingers taking his, and the warmth of her breath in the damp air as she leaned against him. Her lips were sticky at first, and then she pulled away, and her mouth tried different angles. Later, her fingers tightened among his, with the surprise of a perfect jazz riff, and she led him inside, to the bedroom, and pulled him easily onto a thick, clean-smelling quilt, where they held each other, fitting together, as pieces of moonlight slid in drops on the upper window and the shadows of magnolia and jacaranda jockeyed on the walls. She was slender and sinewy, so different from Katie's softness, wearing a light flowery perfume. They undressed with the ease of conversation and began to kiss again, as if starting over, kissing for a long time as the curtain on the lower window filled with the warm, damp taste of outdoors, then she put him inside her, and as she sat up, he saw her dark eyes watching, not smiling, telling him to follow, to go where she was going. She flattened herself on top of him, touched her hands to his face, and moved, slowly, back and forth, watching, biting him gently on the lips, kissing with her mouth closed. He felt her breath hot on his face, as they turned over like one body now, and he began to feel himself returning, going back to places where the breeze spoke of passion and possibilities. He saw her eyes watching, seeing he was with her, and then she closed them, and her face filled for a moment with a private pleasure; she breathed roughly against his face, pulling his head down as her thighs clenched. He, following, felt for an instant the magic of surrender to the way things really are. When he looked at her afterward, she was staring at him comfortably, her eyes still not smiling. It was the first time, he realized, he had broken his vow.

In the morning, shiny fan-shaped palmetto leaves rustled against the screen windows at Martin's townhouse. The pieces of blue sky were bright, promising, among the oak branches. He woke to tell himself the news, comparing the events at China's apartment to the kiss in a parking lot fourteen years earlier, a kiss that had been easy, wordless, wonderful, life-changing. The door to their marriage and, he supposed, to this. Wind made a steady sound like running water in the trees as he drove through the eight o'clock shadows to his new job, where he would write head-lines and edit the news that could be told. It felt good.

Above the clicking of keyboards, as morning sun made prisms in ashtrays and pop bottles, Martin heard Q. V. Robertson, the paper's police reporter, explain what happened: At 7:05 this morning, a seventy-two-year-old tourist had been shot dead in the Holiday Inn parking lot by a seventeen-year-old local boy. The teen, apprehended several blocks away, still carrying the gun, at first denied it. He later claimed the man had provoked him. Martin and Q.V. shook their heads familiarly, sadly. Most crimi-nals, Martin knew, found this instinct early, and carried it through life: insisting innocence, even to themselves, so they never had to look too closely at what they'd done, or who they were. Sometimes, he envied them.

The day began bright, and turned breezy, gray. It surprised him not to see China Rinaldi all morning.

Thomas Persons came back from lunch with his vest buttoned wrong and a glow of alcohol on his face.

"You missed a good one," he said, leaning in the doorway.

Martin smiled agreeably, remembering the way China's arms and back and butt had felt, her breath panting against his ear.

"Next time," he said, and winked.

Thunderheads moved quickly in the afternoon sky, like hands on a clock, and gusts of wind broke pieces of palm frond off into the parking lot. He looked up frequently from his terminal, from the Metro copy he was editing, out at the newsroom, at the bottle of Jovan musk Q. V. Robertson kept on his desk. Sixty-eight days.

When she came in, he had dummied all but the lead story for Metro. The Holiday Inn shooting. They were waiting on a color photo. His clock said 3:49.

"Guess what?" she said, with strained cheer. Martin waited. Her expression wouldn't meet his. He looked at the newsroom and saw Thomas Persons blinking in at them, as if he'd just put on new glasses.

"You quit?"

She raised and lowered her head.

"Why?"

"I told you," she said.

"Two weeks?"

The alluring tug showed briefly in the corners of her mouth, like sun sequins on the bay. "He's going to give me two weeks' severance pay, yeah." With the pleasant tone he'd heard her use in the newsroom, she said, "I'd really like to stay friends," and then he watched her escape, her hips moving with the same ease he had seen the night before, though now in faded jeans.

Putting the Metro section to bed, Martin kept looking at the same thoughts: he was glad it had happened; he should have known better. The green cursor pulsed on his computer screen. More and more he wanted to pull things back, as miscast fishing lines, but you can't; you can only cast new ones. He finished his work and walked out into the windy air behind the building. Lora Lee Moonshower was smoking a cigarette, staring up into an oak tree as if, maybe, an owl were perched on it. Seeing him, she lost all interest.

"Hey!"

"Hi!"

Martin, smiling, narrowed the distance, looking at the trembling trees, feeling something shake loose again, like the leafstalks of the sabal palms.

"Strange, isn't it?" she said. "For this time of year."

Her eyes locked on his with an interest he couldn't ignore. He saw in her face life as it was: news. He had to respond. The wind pulled through the trees again, and they both looked up, together, into the sky, as if waiting for the same thing.

DAVID WIEGAND

Buffalo Safety

Aman walks into the gallery on a sunny afternoon carrying a fistful of golf clubs. I'm aware that there's been some kind of traffic thing going on outside for the last few minutes, but I haven't gone to the window to check it out—happens all the time around here. The softening silence of the gallery is protective that way, I guess. Anyway, the guy walks in with these golf clubs, maybe four of them, looking like some kind of whacked-out classical god with thunderbolts when he steps out of the elevator.

It's around four-thirty or so, maybe later—you lose a sense of time keeping watch over an art gallery; Keats notwithstanding, this stuff isn't eternally on the move. Anyway, I'm paying only scant attention because in this part of town, we get all kinds. Some you keep an eye on, to be sure, but the guy seems harmless enough, and I've seen him around the streets.

The gallery is located in downtown San Francisco, the last resort of the rich and the homeless alike, the edge of all kinds of worlds. No, that's too poetic. It's just San Francisco. I suppose a lot of people have this sort of other-world, romantic idea of San Francisco, but after you live here for a while, you realize it's just another city. Maybe we do have more than our share of crazies, people who haven't come down from that last great acid trip of '68, or drifters figuring it's warmer here and you don't have to spend half your life looking for a heating grate. I don't know. There was a time I probably ascribed more meaning to the place than there is, but that was a long time ago. Maybe the only thing left to say about San Francisco is that it's a good place to get used to most things. Some say it's tolerance. I think it's probably closer to indifference. Or maybe that's the same thing but not worth thinking further about.

The place I work is called the Gallery of Western Realism. Yes, we get our fair share of tourists wandering in looking for Remington statues, but that's not what we mean by western. It's contemporary realism that celebrates the culture of the western U.S., but we stop short of bronzed horseback riders. Over the years, I've made a habit of tracing trends from one group show to the next, and I've found that disaster seems to play a leading role. Lots of paintings of the Golden Gate snapped in the middle or a high-arched bridge on U.S. 1 ending in midair, freeways coiled like DNA and men kissing against a backdrop of crashing trains. A sense of anticipated, if not invited, disaster. I don't know many people who sit around out here worrying about the Big One, but that's the general impression, I guess. Mostly, we sell stuff to people from the East, and I figure it's because it probably makes them feel comfortable thinking they live in a safer place.

So, anyway, I'm behind the desk, lost in mindless thought trying not to think about Nick and, of course, thinking about nothing else, and the elevator door opens, and this guy walks into the room with the golf clubs in one hand, and he's got a shoulder bag on the other side, sort of a Navajo tapestry thing with ratty fringe, overflowing with papers and leaflets and God knows what. The only reason I recognize him as one of the regulars among the army of homeless who work this part of the city is that his thing when you pass by is to ask for "home for the changeless." The first time I heard that, I actually dug down and handed him a buck.

I'd say he's around thirty or thirty-five, maybe younger, kind of wild, sticky-looking hair, wire-rims on the point of his nose, but they're pretty bent up, so they slice across his face on an angle. He's wearing the same thing he always wears: baggy red-plaid pants and an aquamarine bowling shirt with the name "Sal" stitched in white over the pocket.

The elevator door closes behind him, and he stands there a minute and then launches himself into the gallery, marches right past the desk without even looking at me, and keeps on going until he reaches the other end of the room. He stands there a second or two, then pivots like he's on guard duty or whatever, and strides back to the elevator.

I'm watching closely now and for once really not thinking about Nick, because even though this banana seems harmless enough, he's got those golf clubs and might all of a sudden start slashing away at the paintings with his four-iron, or whatever. But he just pushes the down button and stands there waiting, and all the time I'm watching but trying to be a little careful about it, too—subtle, I mean—because you never know what's going to set them off. I hear the elevator make its usual slow, groaning ascent, and then, just as the door slides open, Changeless Sal picks up one of our brochures from the Lucite holder on the wall, looks at it a minute, and then turns to me and says, without even a trace of a smile, "So, I guess realism is the theme of the day. Right?"

At first, I want to chuckle, like it's a joke or something some rich airhead might say at an opening to be clever, but then I figure we're not chatting up Robert Hughes here, you know? So I just smile and say, very politely, "That's right. Realism is the theme of the day."

And he nods, real serious, like he just learned something important, something momentous, and scrunches up his face like he's thinking very carefully about what I've said. And he gets into the elevator, and the door closes, and that's it.

I sit there for a minute or two, wanting to laugh at first, but I don't because I almost expect the doors to open again and Changeless Sal to reappear for an update on realism. But he doesn't come back, and after a while it's almost like he was never there, like the whole scene was just something I imagined or dreamed.

As usual on a slow afternoon, the gallery seems more empty now than before. You get used to the solitude, then people come in and you have to interact, smile, answer questions, try not to look as though you're listening to their whispered comments— and it's a blip on the screen. So when they go, you feel the emptiness more acutely for a minute or two until you readjust to the silence.

I can still hear the traffic on the street, horns honking more frequently because rush hour is starting. But the sounds are soft, muffled, like they're coming from far away. I look around at the triangles of light descending from the ceiling over the paintings, forming a row of almost-touching semicircles on the floor along each wall. Now I'm thinking of Nick again, and it's all mixed up with Changeless Sal and the golf clubs, and for a second or two, nothing makes any sense. It's as if the order of things, the stuff you take for granted, has just gone haywire. I wish there were other people here right now, or that at least the phone would ring. I glance toward the elevator door, as if I can make it open just by looking at it. I almost expect the figures in the paintings to start whispering the way they would in some old *Twilight Zone* episode, telling me everything's going to be okay again, that things will all float back down to where they belong.

I am thirty-one and have worked at the gallery for two years. Before that, I lived in Seattle and then in Portland. Sometimes I figure I'm working my way down the coast, but until recently, I've felt more settled in San Francisco than anywhere else. Now, I don't know. Nothing feels settled at all.

I am attractive enough, I guess—dark-haired, black-eyed by virtue of my father's Armenian-born grandparents, and I work out regularly at a gym in Hayes Gulch, which is on my way home. My life is very patterned, but I like order to things. I broke up with a boyfriend I'd been living with for three months in Portland because he never bothered to close the doors to the kitchen cabinets. No joke. Well, it did start out as a joke between us, and he'd sometimes leave them open on purpose, just to get to me, and it did. Of course, there was a lot more to why things didn't work out, but the open cabinet doors became a symbol of everything else that was wrong. On the day he moved out, I came home to find every cabinet door in the kitchen wide open. I remember thinking there was something obscene-looking about all those gaping cabinets.

Now, I admit if you're looking for order to your life, San Francisco wouldn't be the first place to come to mind. This is a city that thrives on chaos; because people have come here to get away from so many things, there's this kind of universal empowerment against getting locked into anything again. But what can I say? I moved here with Nick, and now he's not here, but I am, and I do the best I can to keep things together. We met in Portland, after the kitchen-cabinet boy moved out, and I needed a roommate, put an ad in the local gay paper, and he answered it. Simple. To the point. We were roommates—I almost said "only" roommates, but of course there was always more to the story.

Maybe I was always in love with Nick because being in love

with Nick meant I didn't have to be in love with anyone else. I never told him, but came close enough that he probably knew. If he did, he was at least kind enough not to acknowledge it, I guess. I don't know.

Anyway, Nick was the kind of guy everybody falls in love with. Yes, part of that had to do with his looks. Greek on his father's side, Czech on his mother's, he had dark blond hair that seemed somehow black and gold at the same time, olive skin, and pale green eyes. Everything made him smile, it seemed, and whenever he smiled, you did, too. He wasn't tall, but he was one of those guys who seem taller than they are, who seem to occupy more space. A presence, I guess you'd say. I remember every feature of his face, of course, but mostly the strange delicacy of his hands, delicacy that somehow always surprised you. More than once, I watched someone talking to him, and they'd be held for a minute or two by the smile, but then, invariably, they'd see the hands. Perfect hands, like Rodin once carved and somehow made more alive in marble than they ever could have been in life.

Okay. More now. I'm afraid to get involved with other men unless I really know them for a while. No, that isn't true, although it's what I've told myself from time to time as an excuse. It would be easy enough to say that in recent years I have learned to be very cautious about dating, and I'm sure that would make perfect sense, given what's going on out there, what we all know—our common Fear of the Great Known in the nineties. But still, it would be misleading if I said that: It wouldn't be the whole truth or even a very significant part of it. Death isn't what I'm afraid of. It's something else, something I always thought I was searching for, but I'm not sure that's true anymore.

I have said and thought and almost convinced myself in the past that the goal here is to surrender the heart, because love is all that counts and all that really lasts. How many times did I say that to Nick, aching for him to agree but secretly relieved, I suppose, when he changed the subject? I thought I never wanted to be one of his flings, one of his one-night stands, and the fact is that I never was.

I've made love, yes, and surrendered myself to another person, and of course everyone practices safe sex, but lately, I can't help wondering if there's another kind of safety going on, a kind that isn't safety at all but something that keeps us too safe. If so, Nick didn't believe in it. Nick took square aim at life without the slightest hesitation or doubt, and if he fucked up, certainly there were never apologies or regrets. I don't mean to imply that he was a callous person, just that he didn't believe the point of it all was to think too much about anything in advance or pick over what had already moved into the past tense, wondering if he did the right thing or if he could have made another choice. Of course, he practiced safe sex, too, but that's not what I'm talking about: What I'm saying is that it never occurred to him to play it safe with life. If you didn't really know him, you might say that Nick was reckless, or that he used sex as an excuse for not falling in love and somehow missed out on something, but I don't think I could agree with that. I think he was always in love. You can fill in the object of that sentence yourself.

I would ask, "Are you dating anyone special these days?" And he'd laugh and invariably answer, "Baby, I'm always dating, and they're always special."

We'd say that all the time to each other, like a private knock-knock joke. And I'd laugh, of course, but there was often enough truth in Nick's answer to cause a secret pain to snake through my stomach. He'd have relationships of a sort that would last several weeks or even a couple of months, and he'd be gone from the apartment a lot more then. After a while, I stopped feeling like I'd been kicked in the gut, praying that they would end soon and not turn into something permanent that might crowd me out of Nick's life. Maybe if there had been more time, that would have happened eventually. Hard to say.

Anyway, in between, the briefer flings came and went, and I didn't mind them as much, believe it or not, because I never figured those men had much interest in the part of Nick I wanted, the part I was always sure would one day be mine, if I could just get through, if I could just wait it out until Nick finally understood that temporary intimacy with visiting strangers was nothing compared to the kind that came with trust and abiding loyalty. I really believed that then.

Sometimes we'd be out on the street when he'd catch sight of a former trick walking toward him, and it would make me feel oddly secure, somehow, almost smug, the way they'd look at each other at a distance, maybe trying to place the face atop a clothed body. And then they'd get close enough to greet each other, maybe still not sure of the "where" or "when" but willing enough to concede the "what." They'd talk a minute or two about nothing at all, and I'd be introduced but then left to stand there to study the other guy. And I'd be thinking the two of them sounded like a couple of salesmen who met casually at a business convention in another city. Nick always called these encounters "the street dance of the one-night stands."

But of course I would be the one walking away with Nick. The other might even take me as Nick's lover. They'd be wrong, of course, but it didn't matter, because I'd tell myself I had something none of them ever could have, something that would last beyond the next morning.

I don't mean to imply that I didn't have flings of my own, but sometimes I have to admit I'd get interested in someone else only as a defense against waiting for Nick, or maybe to gauge his reaction when I told him about the really hot guy I'd met at Badlands the night before. I would have given anything then to have seen even the slightest flicker of jealousy or regret in his face, but he'd just laugh and clap me on the back, thrust his fist into the air, and shout, "He scores!" like a hockey announcer.

Even before I or anyone else knew about Nick, I would read the paper every day and get choked up over death notices of total strangers. Yes, I would see that some had achieved certain things in their abbreviated lives, others showed promise of one kind or another, and it would hit me particularly hard if they were young. I should be ashamed to admit that, because death is sad at any age, but it's human nature, I guess, to feel it's particularly cruel when it comes too early. Well, we should be used to that by now, especially in this city, but I always figured it kept me human, so I'd put myself through the daily exercise.

I would study the bare facts in the obits and try to use them to flesh out a real life, kind of like those paint-by-numbers kits you'd get as a kid. I'd try to imagine that certain awkwardness growing up, the feeling of not fitting in somehow, then the emergence and realization, followed by a kind of explosive defiance and energy. If the obit listed a lover among the survivors, I'd think kindly about the dead man's family for accepting their son or brother, at least in part, for who he was. It doesn't always happen that way. I've heard so many stories of surviving lovers who've been cut off and kept away from the grieving process, as if it was all their fault somehow.

Now I could tell you that I went through this daily ritual in order to grieve for the injustice of it all, for life cut off at the stem, but that would only be part of it. Sure, I'd feel sad about the obvious irony of love being the eventual cause of death, but then in my mind, I would see them couple, open to each other, these lives I had created out of the agate type on newsprint. All shame and doubt would be cast aside, all hesitation, and there was no time then, no past or future, just the bellowing, split-second now of it, and of two bodies and lives, slamming into another, leaping dancers crossing in midair, forming a connecting arc that could never be duplicated in just the same way and therefore could never be broken again, either.

Imagining those moments of crossing, it wasn't the possibility or even the certainty of death that broke my heart, but the understanding that even though at least one of them was dead now, they had been more alive than I had ever been or maybe ever could be. I envied the dead for having lived, but my safe heart slept on while I kept telling myself I was waiting for Nick.

Nick told me he was sick on a September afternoon in Golden Gate Park while we stood by a wire fence, watching sleepy-eyed buffaloes munching grass and lifting their tails to piss from time to time. I don't know why he picked that time or place. Knowing Nick, he probably didn't give it much thought.

Maybe I shouldn't have been surprised at the news, but of course you always are. I felt my body give way and my forehead press into the fence, my eyes pinch shut against the damned, irretractable fact of it. I almost wished the fence wire would cut into the skin of my forehead, as if real physical pain could somehow block out the silent scream I felt in my chest.

I turned to hold him, but I could feel his body tense up, so I stepped back. And I remember taking a very deep breath and then trying to say some hopeful things, but they all sounded lame. I was trying hard to be what I thought Nick wanted me to be, but then I lost it, and it was Nick's turn to hold me and tell me it was okay, that it was just the luck of the draw or some such. I suppose, for him, it was okay, in a way, because he'd never been afraid of living, so why should he be unduly afraid of dying?

We sat down on the bench facing the buffalo pen and talked or didn't. In time, we even found a few funny, macabre things to say. And then there were these long silences with words swirling in my mind, but they wouldn't settle down into sentences the way I wanted them to. At some point, I guess I must have assured him I'd stick by him, because I remember him saying, "I know." Finally, it was getting dark and too cold to stay there anymore, so we got up and started back to the car.

I remember how Nick laughed a little as we set out and said something about how he always used to think as a kid that all the buffaloes had been killed off. It was something he believed growing up in the East, that they were almost extinct except for a very few that he'd seen once in the zoo in Buffalo, New York. Of course, he'd learned otherwise somewhere down the line, but still he said he'd been surprised when he first moved to San Francisco to find a small herd of them calmly grazing and pissing in Golden Gate Park.

"Reports of their demise were greatly exaggerated," I remember him saying in a phony Mark Twain Southern accent. I think he was trying to break the tension—Nick was good at that. I probably laughed out of habit, but I don't remember.

Nick died last month. You wouldn't say it was a peaceful or noble death if you had been there and didn't know him. And yet, because of the way he lived his life, I guess it was both of those things for those of us who loved him. No, he did not go gently, even when there was so little of him left to keep fighting. Pictures of every hour and minute are burned into my memory, and I don't think they'll ever fade. I thought I would be haunted by them above all, but if you've ever lost someone from your life, you know that something much worse takes over, a hole in the middle of you deeper and darker than anything you could have imagined. There are even times when you'd give anything just to relive that last second together, no matter how awful it was, because even the worst moment is better than knowing there will never be any others.

I spent as much time with him as I could, and finally near the end, they just gave me a leave from the gallery because I wasn't doing much good there anyway. I'd take care of the medical stuff, attach the new IV bags when it was time, make sure the refrigerator was well-stocked with syringes, change the bedding several times a day. It helped to have visitors, if only because there'd be someone else to share waiting for him to wake up for a while. And Nick knew everybody in town, so thank God there were a lot of visitors. At last, I wasn't jealous of sharing my time with him.

If I had to be out of the apartment for any period of time, Nick would write notes for me and leave them scattered among the pill bottles next to the bed—sometimes just reminders of things that needed doing, people who had to be contacted, silly things he'd seen on a talk show that afternoon. Other times, he'd just write down things he was thinking, so when I came home later, and he'd be asleep, it was almost like we were having a conversation.

The other thing he had, on the table next to the bed, was this stupid poetry box someone had given him a long time ago. It's a long wooden box with eight cubes in it and a separate word in different typefaces on each side of the cube, so you can make up sentences depending on how you arrange the cubes. Sometimes, Nick would leave me a message, usually suggestive, before he went to sleep at night, so I'd find it when I came in later to check on him. At other times, visitors would play with it while they sat there waiting for Nick to wake up.

I didn't pay attention to it over the final weeks, but then, when it was over, and we were cleaning things up, I noticed it: "GOD— *%#,?—*please*—do—everything—to—TRUST—*love*." Like I said, other people used to play with the poetry box when they came to visit, so I don't even know for sure that it was Nick's arrangement, but obviously I like to think it was.

I wish I could say now that I learned what Nick tried to teach me by the example of his life. I wish I could say I so envied him for having truly lived that I have finally broken free of this half-life safety, that I have finally stopped waiting, or that I think I can at least try to break free as time goes on.

Mostly, since Nick died, I've tried to get through from one day to the next. I don't read the paper every morning anymore and cry over strangers, so maybe that's a good thing. I have a real loss to try to make sense of, I guess. I go to the gallery, I work out, I see people, but I'm still waiting—at least for the time when I'm not always thinking about Nick.

Sometimes I do think about moving, to another apartment at least, another job, another city, but it's too soon to make those kinds of decisions. I guess I'd think about the job thing first, because the real problem with the one I have now is that I have too much time to think about things. It's not as though I spend all day smothering in a cloud of grief. Actually, I sometimes feel very pissed off at Nick, because wishing he'd never come into my life in the first place is easier than wishing he'd never left it.

Is that bad? Maybe, but it's how I feel.

Anyway, at the end of the day, I do the close-up routine at the gallery—answering machine set, security system activated, lights dimmed on my way out.

I did go back to the park a couple of weeks ago, just that one time, maybe in an attempt to focus or something. I stood for a few minutes and watched the buffaloes, still there. Maybe I thought I'd find some comfort in knowing they aren't extinct after all, that life goes on, or that I would look at the high fence that keeps the buffaloes safe and remember Nick and the feel of the wire pressing into my forehead that day. I sat for a while on the bench where we'd sat, wondering things like how long a fingerprint lasts on painted wood, but I didn't focus anything or feel anything I haven't felt every minute since Nick died. And the fact is that right now, at least, I don't give a shit that life goes on and the buffaloes are still safe in their pen.

There's still a trace of daylight when I leave the gallery and start walking toward the subway. I know I should go to the gym, but there's time for that later. There are so many people on the sidewalks, it's hard to move, but I'm in no hurry. I remember one other time, leaving the gallery with Nick at the end of the day, not too long after we'd moved here, how he'd laughed and said, "Imagine if all these people were insects with silk threads coming out of their butts. How long do you think it would take to sew up the whole city like a cocoon?" It was just some silly, throwaway thing he said, but I often seem to remember it when I leave the gallery at night and the sidewalks are crowded. When you lose someone from your life, you want to remember some big important thing they said, but sometimes all you come up with are throwaway lines.

What I am also thinking about now, walking along, is the banana with the golf clubs, wondering if I'll run into him at his usual spot on the corner. Good old Changeless Sal. I look, but he isn't there, and I find myself wondering where he's gone, how he lives when he's not asking for "home for the changeless." And the more I think about him and how he looked when I assured him that realism was the theme of the day, I can't help feeling a little envious. It's not like how I used to feel about Nick's life or even the lives I used to make up to go along with the obit data in the morning paper. But still, there's this odd connection in my head somehow. Maybe it's hard to see the point, but at this moment, at least, I think about the crazy guy and how his head is all mixed up, how he lives on some separate plane from the rest of us where nothing we probably think of as "normal" ever registers or is acknowledged. And one day he comes into an art gallery with his golf clubs, asks a simple question, gets an answer, and leaves. Bingo. His day is made. And when he's outside again, the world might still seem pretty mixed up to him, but maybe not entirely. It may make no sense to anyone else, but at least that poor son of a bitch has been given one small answer, one tiny truth, and no matter how crazy it gets for him later on, maybe he can hold on to that just for a while.

I'd give anything for that.

The Apprentice

Deborah set about making herself useful from the minute she woke up, and most mornings she was first in the household to rise. She pushed off the bedcovers, slipped into her robe, and washed in the bathroom, dressing cautiously and wincing if a zipper or button clanked against the closet door; her bed was in the attic, above where Quentin slept, and his wife and baby. Deborah slipped down the back stairs to the kitchen. Her goal was to be like water, without stop or start, a useful presence that Quentin wouldn't notice except to be vaguely grateful and admiring. Certainly not to ask how long she had been there and how long she planned to remain.

In the morning before her first day off, she pressed the orange switch on the coffee maker and kept vigil while it wheezed and crackled and steamed, and the coffee formed, drip by viscous drip, in the glass pot. The manufacturer, she learned when she replaced the broken one, called it a *carafe*. It was not her fault that the carafe had broken, only her bad luck. She'd noticed the crack but hadn't liked to call attention to it. Once the machine was finished, she transferred the coffee into two thermoses, one a thin stainless-steel rocket with a black strap, the other a homely blue plastic with stripes. Most of the household's items fell into two categories: imported for him; domestic for everyone else. Coffee steam rose from the carafe as she poured and from the thermoses as she rushed to screw on the tops, to capture the genii of the coffee before the morning air diluted it. Milk for her own coffee, she heated in a heavy saucepan, and into this, she dumped the last of the coffee. She washed pot and carafe quickly, before the milk skin dried on the pot, before the coffee stained the glass and the smell of detergent cut through the acrid meaty coffee odor. Then and only then did she settle at the table to drink her milky coffee, almost tasting in it the milk and honey solutions her mother insisted she drink on childhood nights when

Deborah would not fall asleep.

It was the time she liked best in the Quentin household, and it didn't last very long. Either her noises or the smell of coffee brought the rest of them to the kitchen.

Her mother had had an awful time of it, married young to a madman who lived now by the sea and was said not to recognize a soul from his past. This was Deborah's father, and she had never met him.

The only father she'd ever had was Tony, her stepfather, who had the best manners of anyone she'd ever met. Even in situations that made her mother blow up, Tony never forgot to say "Please" and "Thank you." He always thought of his guests' comfort. He remembered birthdays and even anniversaries. He was fond of Deborah, her mother had assured her, and now that she was adult, Deborah could judge that for herself. He had a special set of manners for Deborah that included warm smiles when she was all the way at the end of the dinner table and their house was crowded with guests.

Tony had gone to the same prep school and college as Deborah's father and claimed not to have known him sufficiently to answer questions. Her mother always answered the same: "It was a crazy time, Deborah. He just never came out of it." Her mother had come out of it and so had Tony, but even her father's name, Standish, spoke of being stuck in another time. Her mother had divorced Standish before his final madness and, in exchange for the house, her freedom, and custody of Deborah, had signed away all of Deborah's rights to his fortune, a decision she still debated, sometimes admiring herself, and at other times cursing her stupidity. Then she'd say, "Never look back! Pillars of salt!" She had whispered once to Deborah that she'd bargained with fate, that if Deborah never touched Standish's fortune, then his madness would not touch Deborah; though she denied saying this when Deborah questioned her. Dreaming, she must have been dreaming, her mother said. There were books in the library at home with Standish's name scrawled inside, a careless, skinny signature. Deborah imagined him walking along a sea wall in his town, followed by an attendant—his books, house, wife, and daughter forgotten in the dream where he now lived. Once, in a beach house that Tony and Deborah's mother rented for August, Deborah had opened the door of an upstairs bedroom whose bright blue floor was covered with dead bees, the shells of bees, really. They lay in groups, so many that at first she thought there was a yellow and black rug whose background matched the blue-painted floor. She'd had the sense to tell no one about it. Her father's mind was one of the bees, perfectly formed and hollow, supposed to be dead but perhaps only sleeping. They had tried everything: shock therapy, hydrotherapy, Lithium, antidepressants, antipsychotics, talking. A hot breath could blow him away. She had never met him.

That generation had all been divorced—even her stepfather twice—and at eighteen Deborah had given up on marriage for herself. Now that she was twenty-seven, she had also given up the idea of becoming a great artist. She'd gone to art school and moved into a studio, but decided that though she liked to work with her hands and had thirsty eyes, she would never be any better than a good student.

She gave up the lease on her studio and moved back into her room at her mother's, for how long she couldn't say. Deborah needed something that would never leave her, she needed serious work, and for this she had come to the Quentin household, to be an apprentice to Quentin himself, whom everyone called by that name alone, even his young wife, who was only six years older than Deborah. He was the best in his field, and when Deborah told her mother that she had discovered his latest work one afternoon in a shop on Madison that was more like a gallery, her mother said that Deborah had been looking at Quentin's work all her life but hadn't noticed it. A screen in her mother's bedroom, always half-covered by clothing and robes, was an early example. Quentin was an old friend, her mother said, he'd even lived with them for a time when lots of people were in Standish's big house on the Cape that Deborah had never seen, all living together and, as her mother let her know now that Deborah was grown up, all together for a time and then parting. That's how it was then. Perhaps Quentin might be willing to take Deborah on. Then her mother reported back to Deborah that she had made an arrangement with Quentin, and that Deborah would move there the next week. Deborah had been at Quentin's for a month. She had been entrusted with only a few simple tasks in the studio, but she was learning things all the time.

"Waffles! What a breakfast!" Ellen said. She sat in the chair Quentin usually took, the baby in her lap, so that Deborah had two pairs of wide eyes on her. It was the babysitter's day off, Ellen's weekly chance to concentrate her full attention on the baby, and she was glad for it, she told Deborah. The baby's eyes were wise and knowing, which meant good digestion, Ellen said. Ellen's eyes were wise and knowing but also satirical, as though Ellen knew a few things she wasn't saying. Every word she did say sounded chosen to Deborah, not rehearsed but pronounced with care and forethought. "You won't be here tomorrow, and I'll have to make the coffee and something for breakfast. Cheerios. Nothing special. We'll miss you."

"It's only a day trip. I'll make the coffee before I go."

"That would be so sweet of you."

Deborah had seen pictures of the farmhouse before Quentin married Ellen. He'd been five years or more between wives, and the place was stark, its plaster walls and rough trim the same gray-white, the pine floors beat up and dull. His furniture was simple wood, the one sagging couch the only piece of softness. Now the floors were waxed, the fieldstone fireplace sported a shining copper bucket for kindling, and tiger-striped curtains hung at the windows. The walls were stained a pale yellow, and there was a fat couch with sausage arms dressed in a floral linen that looked as if it had faded over years of use. Black, yellow, copper: all variations and distortions of color blended perfectly. Deborah had come upon a magazine story on Ellen's redecoration shortly after she'd discovered Quentin's work, and took the coincidence as a sign that Quentin would help her find her métier. The equation was completed when her mother arranged so easily for her visit. She had wondered, looking at the pictures, where Ellen had learned to decorate, and if she were born knowing which fabric houses to go to. Deborah, if it had been she, would have left Quentin's house just as it was. Maybe she would have added an armchair. In her mother's living room, there was an invariable group: couch, two armchairs, and a big ottoman that doubled as a table, tweed in the winter, chintz in the summer.

"Will you be going far?" Ellen asked. "Where does this old school friend live exactly?"

"Near Gloucester." But "near Gloucester" was too near the truth. She should have said Stockbridge, at the opposite end of the state. She might have gone to Gloucester anytime in the years since art school, or even when she was at boarding school. But she'd felt timid with the past and had been waiting for her father to call for her at school, the way other parents did sometimes, surprising their boarded children. Her mother's visits were planned long in advance and Deborah's schedule cleared so that not a moment of her mother's time would be wasted waiting for Deborah to finish class or change from her gym clothes. In her last year of art school, she'd studied a map of Massachusetts and located Gloucester, which became her true north, the place she would go when she was ready.

"I've never gone to Gloucester. Have I, baby?"

"I probably won't go there, to Gloucester itself," Deborah said. "She's out in the country, near Gloucester." She'd never been good at lying but was doing all right so far.

"Roommates! It's wonderful you've kept up. I haven't had the time."

Deborah had known girls like Ellen at school, pretty and accomplished, girls for whom things went smoothly. Except Ellen had married a man old enough to be her father and had a baby who looked like the man's grandchild, so that strangers looked around for the missing young husband. Just what Ellen would do in time, predicted Deborah's mother. She said that Quentin never kept wives for long. Ellen looked as though she'd stay as long as she liked. Certainly Deborah was no threat to her, newly unpresentable in baggy work clothes and her bad haircut. Deborah had always been her mother's creature, dressed in her mother's severe, expensive style, her hair cut by her mother's reliable haircutter, who knew how to soften Deborah's features and make her look more feminine, more like her mother. On the way up to Quentin's, Deborah stopped at a mall and got a haircut as a sign of her new life, a different look to go with the work clothes she'd bought used downtown. She was on her way to an apprenticeship, she told the girl at the fast-cut shop, and didn't want her hair to get in the way. A month later it was barely an inch long all over her head, making her look less like a gamine than a newly released convict.

"Is your roommate an apprentice, too? What does she do?"

Deborah glanced at the clock. She was usually in the studio by now, safe from Ellen's questions. Ellen liked to chat while Deborah made the studio lunch or breakfast, planting herself where she and the baby could watch Deborah's every move. Deborah liked Ellen more than she had expected to when they first met. Ellen knew how to make herself cozy with Deborah, and Deborah found that throughout the day she tried to remember interesting thoughts or observations to share with her.

"She's a broker for Merrill Lynch," Deborah said firmly.

"Out in the country near Gloucester?"

"Computers," Deborah said. "There's lots of widows who only trust a woman with their money."

"Funny. As a rule, women like to trust men with their money, not younger women. Of course, she's not so young. Your age."

"Younger than you," Deborah said.

"Not by much. The years mean something when you're a child, most when you're an adolescent. Then it fades. Or it all rolls together."

"Maybe that's why she's so successful at what she does," Deborah said. "The old ladies don't mind."

"Interesting," Ellen said. "When I'm a widow, I might have a younger woman take care of my money. Something I never considered before. If there is any money."

"Of course there'll be money. Why shouldn't there be?"

Ellen laughed. "The golden goose will be dead. Gander."

Deborah widened her eyes in imitation of the baby. "He's not all that old. My mother's age. Younger than my stepfather. He doesn't seem at all old to me."

Ellen loved to speculate about her widowhood and did so often with Deborah as an audience. Deborah would take part only in wondering about Ellen's emotional future, how she would cope without Quentin, and what the baby would do without him. When Quentin held the baby, as he did each night religiously, he turned the child toward him and gave the baby his most serious concentration. Would the baby remember? Probably not. Ellen liked to calculate how young she might be at the break of widowhood, if she'd be young enough to marry again or if she'd even want to (exhausted by Quentin). She knew a great deal about Quentin's ex-wives. Like everyone else from the crazy time, Quentin had married a lot, and some wives did better than others, depending on the market value of his work at the time of the divorce. In gloomy moods, Ellen feared the return of the ex-wives to make ex post facto claims, however outlandish, on Quentin's estate. One thing Ellen didn't have to fear was her status as the mother of Quentin's only heir. Though he'd married carelessly, she said, he must have been cautious about something, because until her baby, there had been no offspring, "legal or otherwise," she always said. They lived as high on the hog as they did because Quentin believed that living in the moment was the only practical thing to do, but Ellen had ticked off several times for Deborah the annuities and mutual funds she had set up in the baby's name whenever Quentin let loose some cash.

Deborah watched him from the foyer outside the studio door, through what he called the observation glass. She thought it odd that a man who prized his privacy would keep unveiled the clear glass panel in the studio door, and she'd offered to cover it with tracing paper. Of course, there weren't very many people on the place to peep through the glass.

Quentin was not very tall, taller than Picasso, and dressed like a super in khaki pants and a matching shirt, or blue pants and a blue shirt, his work uniform. Deborah never saw him in anything else. He usually came directly from the studio to the dinner table and disappeared after the meal with Ellen and the baby into their end of the house. So what he wore for relaxing, Deborah didn't know.

Quentin was famous for his lacquer work, and he had a niche creating furniture, objects, and screens. He was so famous that he had become invisible, and when Deborah had discovered his work, she was surprised not so much that he was still alive as that he existed at all; his name was synonymous with his work, and his work had taken his name away from him, as the Eames chair had from its designer. His latest work went beyond his old, beyond the decorative, and was garnering him new attention. He was applying brilliant technique to pure art with freedom and magisterial imagination. Some said it was a mistake, but Quentin said that it was so hard to know about your own mistakes, how could those fools be sure of his? At first he did not allow Deborah to spend many hours in the studio with him. She worked in the foyer, a kind of anteroom, preparing his materials in small quantities. Because of the glass door into the studio, she called her foyer the glass booth, as if she were Eichmann on trial. While she waited for Quentin to call her, she read Trollope, her stepfather's favorite novelist.

Quentin's studio had been a surprise to Deborah. It was more like a storeroom than a workspace, big enough to accommodate the mess and the work, the boxes piled on boxes (each box stuffed and labeled—*materials, clippings, old photographs, bills*), the platform on which a model might once have stood, now piled with file storage boxes. Quentin's studio was the densest place she'd ever been. Her mother's rooms were paper-thin, decorated, and orderly. Deborah had offered to go through Quentin's boxes for him and to file everything. Perhaps among the old photos were some of her mother and father, when they and Quentin had been on the Cape. He'd laughed at the idea of organizing the boxes. *They're for the bonfire,* he'd said. *Who the hell would care to go through that junk? I never look at it, why should anyone else?* His biographer would care, if no one else, and Quentin must have realized that. He was at an age when biographies of his contemporaries, dead and alive, were emerging. Why keep the boxes at all? Deborah wondered. He was not so careless of posterity's opinion as he claimed, because, after a week, he let Deborah alphabetize and file business letters and reviews. He gave her a corner of the studio for her own, clearing away a stack of art magazines. She valued the hours when they worked in silence and listened to the classical radio station Quentin liked. His work was, of course, beautiful, but so was his concentration, and she found herself imitating his slight hunch as he stood before a piece. He watched her, too. Sometimes Deborah looked up and found him staring at her.

Her mother had asked her if Quentin was still attractive, and she had answered yes without hesitation. Ellen joked about the flesh on his chin and neck that was ceding to gravity; about his farts one terrible Sunday when he stayed in bed with a cold and took Vitamin C in quantity. Deborah's mother told her that Ellen was probably threatened and playing down his magnetism. "You're younger than she," her mother said. "Quentin's wives are always jealous, usually with cause." At night and sometimes in the early morning, Deborah heard Ellen moaning for a long time and then one gasp from Quentin. She heard the baby cry and laugh, and Quentin and Ellen talking in low tones and sometimes arguing. She couldn't make out the words. She wished she had a room far away from theirs, but the babysitter was established in the guest cottage. She couldn't help hearing the sounds and listened for them.

When she reached Gloucester, she would walk along the sea wall and meet her father.

The story she'd overheard her mother telling was that their old friend Grace had gone to Gloucester to visit a cousin, and there, walking by the sea, she'd come upon Standish and his attendant. (I am an attendant lord, thought Deborah, nobody important.) At one time Grace and Standish were an item, then, when Deborah's mother and Standish fell madly in love and were married, she became their dear friend, she and her husband, now dead in a single-car accident that Deborah's mother referred to, though not in front of Grace, as a suicide.

By the sea, Grace had approached Standish. She said that he was wooden-faced, erect as ever, with his head held at an odd, fixed angle, a difference only someone who knew him well would notice. He and the attendant were walking very slowly, and they did not stop at Grace's approach. Grace finally put herself in their path. (Later, a shopkeeper told Grace they walked that same way every day.) *Standish,* Grace said, *it's me, darling. How are you?* He didn't recognize her. He looked at her through eyes she did not recognize. A stranger lived within, Deborah's mother said Grace had said. Grace had retreated. Deborah imagined Grace stepping backward like a Graham dancer, in flowing black dress, the lift of her leg creating a pie slice of fabric. Standish and the attendant moved on as if there had been no interruption to their routine. *He's mad,* Deborah's mother sighed into the telephone, *he's gone.*

When Deborah got to Gloucester, she would find the shopkeeper and the road by the sea where her father walked daily with his attendant. To ground herself in reality, she recited: He is old and has been ill, and he has not seen me since I was an infant. Nevertheless: They walked in their usual direction, eastward, perhaps, the sun to their backs, and moved slowly, in a stately fashion or perhaps a shuffle, but they moved. And she, waiting, saw them coming, and moved onto the road, deliberately, carefully, not stirring the air to alarm them. They paused, or rather her father did, and the attendant, surprised, stumbled. Her father, stony-faced and stony-eyed, recognized Deborah, through all the years and the long absence of physical image, and he said: *Deborah?* Or, *Daughter?* Or, *It's you. I've waited so long.* He saw her and was surprised back into the world. And then? To his house for hot chocolate? She could not imagine any further and would rather have died than have anyone know what she imagined, which contradicted everything she had heard of him in particular and of fathers in general except in fairy tales. Still, she believed or wanted to believe enough so that she always came to the same place after wrangling with herself to be sensible: *What do you have to lose, you who have nothing? And everything to gain. Your father.*

How do you do this? How do you do that? She asked Quentin endless technical questions. "Didn't they teach you anything in your fancy art school?" He was bald on top of his head and kept his white hair cut short and neat, accentuating the strong bones of his skull and his black eyes. He looked like the china bust her mother kept in the library, a man perfectly formed. When he bent over his drawing table, Deborah could almost see the dotted lines and small print labeling the regions of his brain. At first he explained his process patiently, but he must have caught on that she couldn't listen. She could understand but not listen. Her eyes overpowered her ears and her unlabeled brain, and she let them roam over his broad muscled shoulders and his workman's fingers. In early photographs of him—her mother had one tucked in a volume of Pound's poems that she had never read—he had a mustache that concealed the thin meanness of his lips. Deborah's questions stopped him from working, and he commanded her to be there and not to be there. Her apprenticeship would be silent, or at least nonverbal. He kept music on all the time in the studio and, unlike her stepfather, didn't care what it was: Berlioz or Bach or "Carnival of the Animals." But she needed talk. Quentin had a secret that Deborah needed, knowledge of her mother and father when they were young and in love. He wouldn't answer direct questions. He gave her unhappy looks and shrugs and turned away when she compromised her dignity and asked what her father was like.

Quentin looked up for the first time that morning and said to her, "I have a job of work for you, if you're willing to work."

"I always am." If he needed her, she would stay tomorrow, too, go to Gloucester another day or week.

He said, "I'm tired of this mess. Sweep the floor, if you can find it."

"Is there anything you want to save that's on the floor?"

"Of course not," he roared. "Are you deaf? I just asked you to sweep it."

She was trying to be thorough. She was trying to let him know that whatever he wanted from her, she was willing to do it. She saw herself with his sparkling black eyes, a lumpy, overgrown girl with very little hair, good only for sweeping. She turned and got the broom. When she finished an hour later, having swept slowly and carefully, he glanced up from his drawing table and looked at her over his bifocals. "Good work," he said. "I won't need you anymore. Maybe Ellen needs a hand. That girl's off today, isn't she?"

"Yes. I'll be off tomorrow."

"Will you?"

She thought he looked relieved. Two months, he'd promised her mother, a two-month apprenticeship.

When there was company, Ellen cooked French food—a piece of meat or poultry with sauce (wine or cream), rice or noodles, a vegetable. Quentin loved sweetbreads, brains, and liver, and the local butcher saved them for Ellen, along with what he called veal, grass-eating calf. "It will do in the country," Quentin said. He'd lived in the country for twenty years, and his trips to the city were few and far between. Ellen complained that she never got to wear her city clothes. One afternoon while Deborah was supposed to be looking after the baby, Ellen showed her all the jackets and trousers, skirts and silk blouses, creamy cashmere sweaters she'd bought in the last year, covering the bed with them. In the clothes, Ellen looked like another person, oddly like Deborah's mother in her daytime outfits.

Tonight, for the second time in a month, there was fried chicken for dinner. Deborah had walked the baby in the stroller up and down the long winding driveway while Ellen dipped, dredged, and fried. Deborah would feel greedy for it the next day at lunch, not now when it was disagreeably warm. Conversation was sparse when they ate together like this, more so without the babysitter, who kept up a running inquisition of the baby—was he hot or cold, did the food disagree with him, was he a sweet baby?

"I heard," Deborah said, "I was told once, that Standish was genuinely talented. As an artist. And that's what made his madness an even greater shame. The loss—"

Quentin laughed. "Who in the world told you that? Your mother? I thought even she knew better than that. Standish was no genius. Nothing of the sort. First he was a dabbler, and then he was a promoter."

"Quentin," Ellen said.

"A collector but not in any big way. Not enough to really help anyone. He was a succubus. He had just enough of an eye to pick out your best work and then snatch it for pennies when a fellow was down and out."

Deborah stopped chewing the drumstick and stared. No one had ever talked about her father that way, using any but the one note of pity. She had been right to come here. If she learned nothing else, she learned that when her father, her own father, was young and not mad, he had the capacity to annoy someone like Quentin. A vein stood out on Quentin's forehead.

"Your work?" Deborah asked. "Your wonderful early work?"

"Hah! You look just like your wicked mother when you say that."

"For God's sake, Quentin, what is the point of telling Deborah any of this? And keep your voice down." Ellen looked at the baby, who was sculpting mashed potatoes. "Baby doesn't like cross noises."

"Honesty. That's the point."

Ellen rolled her eyes and said, "Someone always gets hurt when you start talking about honesty. It's an overrated quality."

There was a thin layer of grease around Quentin's lips, like a clown's red mouth.

"Didn't they teach you anything in your fancy art school?" His schedule was like her mother's—drinks starting at six and on through the night—so Deborah was used to emotion at meals. "There have always been people like Standish. Auxiliaries, hand-maidens of the arts, patrons, agents, people who oil the market machinery. But are not artists themselves. You've heard of Vasari?"

"I know who Vasari is," Deborah said.

"Your mother. Another handmaiden. Another apprentice! She and Standish fed the artists, let them have a room, a room and a studio. And food and drink. They were generous with food and drink, all right. All for their good hearts. Not so generous. Not so selfless. No one is selfless except the boring dead. All the art! We used to joke about the second-rate drawings we gave to Standish and your mother to pay for room and board. All gifts! Never asked for. Of course not. All gratitude. Some of it first-rate, inevitably. I've wondered over the years. What happened to the art?"

"Some of it's there," Deborah said. "She has a lot of art. Some she sold before she married Tony, but I have no way of knowing what. I mean, there are drawings and paintings in the house, and those are all I've ever known. One of everything, my mother says."

"My screen."

"It's been there all this time. In her bedroom. The first time I knew it was your work was—"

"When she called, called about you, she said it was in perfect shape. That's how we made the arrangement, of course. Room and board for the screen. Very fitting, I thought." He wiped his mouth.

"She never cared about anything but herself. Stupid of me to be surprised she never told you. I wanted to meet you, of course."

"Quentin," Ellen said.

"When did you actually know them?" Deborah asked, to move the conversation along. "What years?" She didn't want to cause a fight between Ellen and Quentin and then hear about it all the next week.

"You must know," he said. "Didn't your mother tell you anything?"

"If Deborah knew, she wouldn't ask," Ellen said. "Would you like some fried chicken for the road, Deborah? Unless you're worried about making the steering wheel greasy. I'll pack a napkin. Deborah's going to Gloucester tomorrow, Quentin. To see an old friend."

"Near Gloucester. Outside Gloucester."

"Will you go to see Standish?" Quentin asked.

"Oh, no," she said. "I've never met him. And he doesn't recognize anyone anymore."

Ellen stood and began clearing the dishes, and Deborah helped her. When she reached for Quentin's plate, he clamped her arm, and she was surprised by the strength and warmth of his grip.

"Deborah," he said in the voice he got at the third drink.

"Why did you say that my mother was wicked?" she asked. *Playful*, Tony said, *your mother is being playful.*

"You don't look much like her. A beautiful woman. Is she still beautiful?"

"Yes. Do I look like my father?"

He was stroking the inside of her arm.

"The eyes are," he said. "The mouth. The shape of your head. Your hands."

"But—"

"Dessert?" Ellen asked.

Deborah broke away from Quentin and took the plate into the kitchen.

She leaned toward the dappled mirror that hung crooked over the attic sink. Her dark ovals and the pale rounds in the blurry photo that she liked best of Standish were nothing alike, her dash of a mouth and his Cupid pout. But maybe the photograph lied. She undressed in a hurry and put on her old flannel gown that Ellen laughed at, calling Deborah a marvel for keeping a night-gown so long.

Quentin and Ellen quarreled that night, and Deborah did her best not to hear. The attic had two dormer windows, and she couldn't stand in most of the room. The baby's room was just below the attic door; Quentin's bed below Deborah's. She pushed aside the worn rug that Ellen said fit nowhere else in the house so perfectly as the attic, and she took to the floor with a glass, which worked only medium well on the bumpy floor. "Original," Ellen had said, unsanded and rough. *Baby's* something. Baby's nights? Baby's right? *Baby, baby, baby*—the only word Deborah could make out in a blur of words. She might have been dreaming one of her annoying dreams with lots of talking, Tony kind of talking, background noise, when she couldn't make out the words in the dream or when she woke, yet she heard it throughout the day, a buzz in her ear.

The music of their quarrel came to an end. Deborah waited until it was as quiet as the morning, then searched in the dark for her socks and robe, and descended the bare wooden stairs, her hand on the wall for support. In the darkened living room, the tiger curtains—the perfect balance of yellow and black—hummed like bees on a summer afternoon, and she glided past the sound without making a sound herself. The baby's room was on the other side of the door, and she paused at the crib. Baby had a night light shaped like a fat bumblebee, its black stripes shadows, its yellow hills glowing. Baby slept on his stomach, his mouth a little open, his wide eyes closed. She ran her palm over his little vertebrae, no bigger than peanuts. In and out, and Debo-rah counted his little warm breaths until he stirred and moved from her hand.

The door to Quentin's bedroom was open. She navigated care-fully the smooth polished floor and fat rugs until she stood at the bottom of their bed. Their feet were intertwined like a vine and a tree, and at first she could not tell whose leg was where. Ellen's foot was smaller and at the very bottom of the bed, caught in the fold of the sheets and the blankets, her toes discernible, tangible, the arch swelling the blanket. Bending, Deborah felt the outline of her toenails, like seashells in sand.

Ellen's eyes were on her. "Deborah. What's wrong?" No answer possible, and then, "You're frightening me," and movement beneath the covers.

She took her hand from Ellen's foot, and Ellen hid beneath the covers. Quentin rolled onto his back and put his hands behind his head, raising his neck, the better to see her.

Deborah sat on the bed in the bumblebee's light, where their feet had parted. "Did you love her at all?" Deborah asked.

In the dark, it seemed that there was only Deborah and Quentin.

WILLIAM HENRY LEWIS

Shades

I was fourteen that summer. August brought heat I had never known, and during the dreamlike drought of those days, I saw my father for the first time in my life. The tulip poplars had faded to yellow before September came. There was no rain for weeks, and the people's faces along Eleventh Street wore a longing for something cool and wet, something distant, like the promise of a balmy October. Talk of weather was of the heat and the dry taste in their mouths. And they were frustrated, having to notice something other than the weather in their daily pleasantries. Sometimes, in the haven of afternoon porch shade or in the still and cooler places of late night, they drank and laughed, content because they had managed to make it through the day.

What I noticed was the way the skin of my neighbors glistened as they toiled in their backyards, trying to save their gardens or working a few more miles into their cars. My own skin surprised me each morning in the mirror, becoming darker and darker, my hair lightening, dispelling my assumption that it had always been a curly black—the whole of me a new and stranger blend of browns from day after day of basketball on asphalt courts or racing the other boys down the street after the Icee truck each afternoon.

I came to believe that it was the heat that made things happen. It was a summer of empty sidewalks, people I knew drifting in and out of the alleyways where trees gave more shade, the dirt there cooler to walk on than any paved surface. Strangers, appearing lost, would walk through the neighborhood, the dust and sun's glare making that place look like somewhere else they were trying to go. Sitting on our porch, I watched people I'd never seen before walk by seemingly drawn to those rippling pools of heat glistening above the asphalt, as if something must be happening just beyond where that warmth quivered down the street. And at night I'd look out from the porch of our house, a few blocks off Eleventh, and scan the neighborhood, wanting to see some change, something besides the nearby rumble of freight trains and the monotony of heat, something refreshing and new. In heat like that, everyone sat on their porches, looking out into the night and hoping for something better to come up with the sun.

It was during such a summer, my mother told me, that my father got home from the third shift at the bottling plant, waked her with his naked body already on top of her, entered her before she was able to say no, sweat on her through moments of whiskey breath and indolent thrusting, came without saying a word, and walked back out of our house forever. He never uttered a word, she said, for it was not his way to speak much when it was hot.

My mother told me he left with the rumble of the trains. She was a wise woman and spoke almost as beautifully as she sang. She spoke to me with a smooth, distant voice, as if it were the story of someone else, and it was strange to me that she might have wanted to cry at something like that but didn't, as if there were no need anymore.

She said she lay still after he left, certain only of his sweat, the work shirt he left behind, and her body calming itself from the silent insistence of his thrusts. She lay still for at least an hour, aware of two things: feeling the semen her body wouldn't hold slowly leaving her and dripping onto the sheets, and knowing that some part of what her body did hold would fight and form itself into what became me nine months later.

I was ten years old when she told me this. After she sat me down and said, *This is how you came to me,* I knew that I would never feel like I was ten for the rest of that year. She told me what it was to love someone, what it was to make love to someone, and what it took to make someone. *Sometimes,* she said, *all three don't happen at once.* When she said that, I didn't quite know what it meant, but I felt her need to tell me. She seemed determined not to hold it from me. It seemed as if somehow she was pushing me ahead of my growing. And I felt uncomfortable with it, the way secondhand shoes are at first comfortless. Soon the pain wasn't greater, just hard to wear.

After that, she filled my home life with lessons, stories, and observations that had a tone of insistence in them, each one told in a way that dared me to let it drift from my mind. By the end of my eleventh year, I learned of her sister Alva, who cut off two of her husband's fingers, one for each of his mistresses. At twelve, I had no misunderstanding of why, someday soon, for nothing more than a few dollars, I might be stabbed by one of the same boys that I played basketball with at the rec center. At thirteen, I came to know that my cousin Dexter hadn't become sick and been hospitalized in St. Louis, but had gotten a young white girl pregnant and was rumored to be someone's yardman in Hyde Park. And when I was fourteen, through the tree-withering heat of August, during the Watertown Blues Festival, in throngs of sweaty, wide-smiling people, my mother pointed out to me my father.

For the annual festival, they closed off Eleventh Street from the downtown square all the way up to where the freight railway cuts through the city, where our neighborhood ends and the land rises up to the surrounding hills, dotted with houses the wealthy built to avoid flooding and neighbors with low incomes. Amidst the summer heat was the sizzle of barbecue at every corner, steamy blues from performance stages erected in the many empty lots up and down the street, and, of course, the scores of people, crammed together, wearing the lightest clothing they could without looking loose. By early evening the street would be completely filled with people and the blues would have dominion over the crowd.

The sad, slow blues songs my mother loved the most. The Watertown Festival was her favorite social event of the year. She had a tight-skinned sort of pride through most days of the year, countered by the softer, bare-shouldered self of the blues festival, where she wore yellow or fiery orange outfits and deep, brownish-red lipstick against the chestnut shine of her cheeks. More men took the time to risk getting to know her, and every year it was a different man; the summer suitors from past years learned quickly that although she wore that lipstick and although an orange skirt never looked better on another pair of hips, never again would she have a man leave his work shirt hanging on her bedpost. With that kind of poise, she swayed through the crowds of people, smiling at many, hugging some, and stopping at times to dance with no one in particular.

When I was younger than fourteen, I had no choice but to go.

Early in the afternoon, she'd make me shower and put on a fresh cotton shirt. *You need to hear the blues, boy, a body needs something to tell itself what's good and what's not.* At fourteen, my mother approached me differently. She simply came out to the yard where I was watering her garden and said, *You going?* and waited for me to turn to her, and say yes. I didn't know if I liked the blues or not.

We started at the top of Eleventh Street and worked our way downtown over the few hours of the festival. We passed neighbors and friends from church, my mother's boss from Mills Dry Goods, and Reverend Riggins, who was drinking beer from a paper cup instead of a can. Midway down Eleventh, in front of Macky's Mellow Tone Grill, I bumped into my cousin Wilbert, who had sneaked a tallboy of Miller High Life from a cooler somewhere up the street. A Zydeco band was warming up for Etta James. We stood as still as we could in the intense heat and shared sips of that beer while we watched my mother, with her own beer, swaying with a man twice her age to the zip and smack of the washboard.

Etta James had already captured the crowd when Wilbert brought back a large plate of ribs and another beer. My mother came over to share our ribs, and Wilbert was silent after deftly dropping the can of beer behind his back. I stood there listening, taking in the heat, the music, the hint of beer on my mother's breath. The crowd had a pulse to it, still moving up and down the street but stopping to hear the growl of Etta James's voice. The sense of closeness was almost too much. My mother was swaying back and forth on her heels, giving a little dip to her pelvis every so often and mouthing the words to the songs. At any given moment, one or two men would be looking at her, seemingly oblivious and lost in the music.

But she, too, must have felt the closeness of the people. She was looking away from the stage, focusing on a commotion of laughter in front of Macky's where voices were hooting above the music. She took hold of my shoulders and turned me towards the front of Macky's. In a circle of loud men, all holding beer, all howling in laughter—some shirtless and others in work clothes— stood a large man in a worn gray suit, tugging his tie jokingly like a noose, pushing the men into new waves of laughter each moment. His hair was nappy like he had just risen from bed. But he smiled as if that was never his main concern anyway, and he held a presence in that circle of people which made me think he had worn that suit for just such an appearance. My mother held my shoulders tightly for a moment, not tense or angry or anxious, just firm, and then let go.

"There's your father," she said, and turned away, drifting back into the music and dancing people. Watching her glide towards the stage, I felt obligated not to follow her. When I could see her no longer, I looked back to the circle of men and the man that my mother had pointed out. From the way he was laughing, he looked like a man who didn't care who he might have bothered with his noise. Certainly his friends didn't seem to mind. Their group commanded a large space of sidewalk in front of the bar. People made looping detours into the crowd instead of walking straight through that wide-open circle of drunken activity. The men stamped their feet, hit each other in the arms, and howled as if this afternoon were their own party. I turned to tell Wilbert, but he had gone. I watched the man who was my father slapping his friends' hands, bent over in laughter, sweat soaking his shirt under that suit.

He was a very passionate-looking man, large with his laugh, expressively confident in his gestures, and as I watched him, I was thinking of that night fourteen years ago and the lazy thrust of his which my mother told me had no passion in it at all. I wondered where he must have been all those years and realized how shocked I was to see the real man to fill the image my mother had made. She had made him up for me, but never whole, never fully able to grasp. I was thinking of his silence, the voice I'd never heard. And wanting nothing else at that moment but to be closer, I walked towards that circle of men. I walked as if I were headed into Macky's Mellow Tone, and they stopped laughing as I split their gathering. The smell of liquor, cheap cologne, and musky sweat hit my nostrils, and I was immediately aware not only that I had no reason for going or chance of getting into Macky's, but that I was also passing through of a circle of strangers. I stopped a few feet from the entrance and focused on the quilted fake leather covering the door's surface. It was red faded fabric, and I looked at that for what seemed a long time, because I was afraid to turn back into laughter. The men had started talking again, slowly working themselves back into their own good time. But they weren't laughing at me. I turned to face them, and they seemed to have forgotten that I was there.

I looked up at my father, who was turned slightly away from me. His mouth was open and primed to laugh, but no sound was coming out. His teeth were large, and I could see where sometime before he had lost two of them. Watching him from the street, I had only seen his mouth move and had to imagine what he was saying. Now, so close to him, close enough to smell him, to touch him, I could hear nothing. But I could feel the closeness of the crowd, those unfamiliar men, my father. Then he looked down at me. His mouth closed, and suddenly he wasn't grinning. He reached out his hand, and I straightened up as my mother might have told me to do. I arced my hand out to slide across his palm, but he pulled his hand back, smiling—a jokester, like he was too slick for my eagerness.

He reached in his suit jacket and pulled out a pair of sunglasses. Watertown is a small town, and when he put those glasses on, he looked like he had come from somewhere else. I know I hadn't seen him before that day. I wondered when in the past few days he must have drifted into town. On what wave of early morning heat had he arrived?

I looked at myself in the reflection of the mirrored lenses and thought, *So this is me.*

"Them's slick basketball sneakers you got," he said. "You a bad brother on the court?"

I could only see the edge of one eye behind those glasses, but I decided that he was interested.

"Yeah, I am! I'm gonna be like George Gervin, you just watch." And I was sure we'd go inside Macky's and talk after that. We'd talk about basketball, and then he'd ask me if I was doing well in school, and I'd say not too hot, and he'd get on me about that as if he'd always been keeping tabs on me. Then we would toast to something big, something we could share in the loving of it, like Bill Russell's finger-roll lay-up or the pulled pork sandwich at

Round Belly Ribs or the fact that I had grown two inches that year, even though he wouldn't have known that. We might pause for a moment, both of us quiet, both of us knowing what that silence was about, and he'd look real serious and anxious at the same time, a man like him having too hard a face to explain anything that had happened or hadn't happened. But he'd be trying. He'd say, *Hey, brother, cut me the slack, you know how it goes...* and I might say, *It's cool,* or I might say nothing at all but know that sometime later on, we would spend hours shooting hoop together up at the rec center, and when I'd beaten him two out of three at twenty-one, he'd hug me like he'd always known what it was like to love me.

My father took off his sunglasses and looked down at me for a long silent moment. He was a large man with a square jaw and a wide, shiny forehead, but his skin looked soft—a gentle, light brown. My mother must have believed in his eyes. They were gray-blue, calm and yet fierce, like the eyes of kinfolk down in Baton Rouge. His mouth was slightly open; he was going to speak, and I noticed that his teeth were yellow when I saw him face to face. He wouldn't stop smiling. A thought struck me right then that he might not know who I was.

One of his friends grabbed at his jacket. "Let's roll, bro, Tyree's leavin'!"

He jerked free and threw his friend a look that made me stiffen.

The man read his face and then laughed nervously. "Be cool, nigger, break bad someplace else. We got ladies waitin'."

"I'm cool, brother. I'm cool..." My father looked back at me. In the mix of the music and the crowd, which I'd almost forgotten about, I could barely hear him. "I'm cold solid." He crouched down, wiped his sunglasses on a shirttail, and put them in my pocket. His crouch was close. Close enough for me to smell the liquor on his breath. Enough for him to hug me. Close enough for me to know that he wouldn't. But I didn't turn away. I told myself that I didn't care that he was not perfect.

He rose without saying anything else, turned from me, and walked to the corner of Eleventh Street and the alleyway where his friends were waiting. They were insistent on him hurrying, and once they were sure that he was going to join them, they turned down the alley. I didn't cry, although I wouldn't have been embarrassed if I had. I watched them leave, and the only thing I felt was a wish that my father, on this one day, had never known those men. He started to follow them, but before he left, he stopped to look over the scene there on Eleventh Street. He looked way up the street, to where the crowd thinned out, and then beyond that, maybe to where the city was split by the train tracks, running on a loose curve around our neighborhood to the river; or maybe not as far as that, just a few blocks before the tracks and two streets off Eleventh where, sometime earlier than fourteen years ago, he might have heard the train's early morning rumble when he stepped from our back porch.

Aftermath

The outer Cape in mid-October. A new tilt to the earth and its altered angle to the sun make for a suffusing clarity. Hopper's light. With the tourists gone, the beaches have been reclaimed by gulls, and the road that traverses the peninsula is bare. At this time of year, delays occur behind school buses.

Telephone to his ear, Bernardin looks at the evolving geometry of the painting on the easel in his studio, and, filled with dread and sadness at what he is hearing, conjures up the face of Malcolm, who, according to a tearful Jocelyn, has just been pried dead from the wreckage of a head-on at the blinking yellow on Route 6 by something called the Jaws of Life. The woman who was Malcolm's passenger has been taken to the hospital in Hyannis. The driver of the truck that crossed the center dividing line and struck them is unhurt.

"D'you know this woman?" Jocelyn asks.

"Yes," Bernardin says.

"None of the rest of us do."

Malcolm's secret, Bernardin thinks.

"The hospital's calling her Jane Doe."

"I'd better call the hospital," Bernardin says. This enables him to hang up without answering further questions.

A nurse in the emergency room tells him that the Jane Doe brought in by the rescue squad is in serious but stable condition with head injuries.

"Her name is Ingrid Torquist," Bernardin says. "She lives in Oregon."

"Are you by chance a relative?"

"A friend," says Bernardin, going back two hours in time, when Malcolm and Ingrid stopped by his place on their way to Malcolm's house to pick up her luggage before driving up to Boston, so she could take a plane to Portland and tell her husband that she was leaving him and coming back to live with Malcolm, whom she has always loved. They imparted this intention to Bernardin in breathless confidence. Like a couple of kids who were planning to elope. Even Ingrid's daughter, who is at college in Connecticut, and whom she just visited on the occasion of parents' weekend, doesn't know what's afoot.

"Is Mrs. Torquist conscious?" Bernardin inquires.

"Off and on. She's been asking for someone named Malcolm."

Malcolm of the grand, impulsive gesture, Bernardin thinks. "Tell her that Harry called," he says. "Tell her I'm going to contact her daughter and bring her to the hospital."

A few minutes later, Bernardin finds himself talking to a dean of women, whose suspicions have been honed by the feminist times and the fact that Bernardin has forgotten Ingrid's daughter's Christian name. This is not an altogether surprising lapse, since he has only met her once, during the spring, when she and her mother spent a weekend at Malcolm's while visiting various colleges in New England to which the daughter had been accepted.

"We're very careful when granting permission for our freshmen women to visit strangers," the dean explains.

Bernardin wonders if he should offer to supply some character references. The only names that come to mind, however, are those of his art dealer in New York and some gallery owners in Provincetown—none of whom are likely to inspire trust and confidence in the dean, whom he imagines to be thin-lipped. "Miss Torquist will remember me," he says. "She and her mother and I had dinner last April at Malcolm Prescott's house."

His own memory of that improbably romantic evening—he will learn later that it was the first meeting between Malcolm and Ingrid in twenty years—remains vivid: Malcolm getting sloshed on bourbon while steaming lobsters in the kitchen; Ingrid, languid as a cat in sunshine, watching from the table; the daughter beside her absorbed in her impending choice of schools; Bernardin unaware of having been invited for the same reason that Gatsby invited Carraway to tea with Daisy, but sensing that the occasion is momentous because of Malcolm's elaborate attempts to appear at ease. Men of their age (past fifty) seldom confide in one another about women, and when they do they tend to leave out the details—even when they're as close to each other as Bernardin and Malcolm considered themselves to be.

Bernardin decides not to tell the dean that Malcolm has been killed in the car crash. There's no point in upsetting Maria any more than necessary.

"Maria!" he exclaims. "Maria Torquist."

The dean does not respond to this evidence of recovered memory. She asks Bernardin for his telephone number and that of the hospital, and says that she'll call back. When she does, an hour later, it is to tell him that everything has been arranged. Maria has contacted her father, who will fly east tomorrow. Meanwhile, she and her roommate are packing. They will arrive at the airport in Hyannis on a chartered plane at about seven o'clock that evening.

"I'll be on hand to meet them," Bernardin says.

"We are much obliged," the dean replies.

There is windshield glass in the roadway at the blinking yellow, but the wreckage of Malcolm's car and the truck that struck it have been towed away. The glass glitters in the flat trajectory of late afternoon light. Bernardin turns off the highway and drives out over Sansquit Neck to Malcolm's house. Malcolm's son, Ryan, who cooks at a restaurant in Chatham, opens the door and steps into Bernardin's consoling hug. Beyond the young man's shoulder, Bernardin sees two women whom he vaguely recognizes as neighbors, sitting on a sofa in the living room, beneath a wall on which one of his own watercolors and some of Malcolm's photographs are hanging. Among the photographs are a battle scene taken at Pleiku and a female nude taken from behind. There are other people in the room Bernardin does not know. He does not see Malcolm's wife, Helena, who suffers from schizophrenia and is in an institution.

"Has your mother been told?" he asks.

"They're driving her down from Boston. She'll be here soon."

"I'm on my way to the airport to meet Ingrid's daughter," Bernardin says. "I came by to pick up her bags. They're probably upstairs," he adds, aware that even if Ryan has figured out about his father and Ingrid, grief may have prevented him from considering the delicate problem that the presence of her luggage might now present.

As they are putting Ingrid's suitcases into Bernardin's car, Ryan tells him that the police have called about her purse. A garageman found it in the wreck, after it was towed away. They're holding it at the station.

The plane that taxis up to the chain-link fence in front of the terminal is small and improbably sleek. Maria smiles and waves at Bernardin as she alights. She is taller and more heavily boned and not as delicate as her mother, whose chiseled features and pale complexion remind Bernardin of a European actress, whose name, like Maria's earlier, he has managed to misplace. Her roommate is a solemn-looking redhead, who appears to have been crying. While the pilot is pulling their bags from the nose compartment, Bernardin tells Maria that a staff neurologist has been notified of her arrival and is waiting at the hospital. He suggests that she inquire about the advisability of transferring her mother up to Massachusetts General so she can be examined by specialists there.

The neurologist says that Ingrid is suffering from a severe concussion, a broken nose, and a dislocated knee. When Maria asks about the specialists at Mass. General, he says that he expects Ingrid to pull through without complications and that it would be unwise to move her now. Happily, a CAT scan has not revealed any dangerous swelling of the brain.

When a nurse takes Maria in to see her mother, Bernardin is left in the waiting room with the roommate, whose name is Alison.

"She's been terrific about all of this," Alison says. "I've been more scared than she is."

"It's a scary business," Bernardin replies. He is thinking of how Malcolm would have hated the idea of people watching as he was being extracted from the wreckage by the Jaws of Life.

When Maria returns, she describes how Ingrid looks. "Both her eyes are black, and her whole face is black and blue and swollen, and she keeps crying out for Malcolm. The nurse and I tried to tell her he was dead, but she won't listen. She just keeps crying out his name."

"She's in shock," Bernardin says, putting an arm around Maria's shoulder. "It'll wear off gradually."

"But the way she keeps crying out his name. It's so hysterical."

"She's in shock," Bernardin explains again.

"I didn't even know she was coming here. I thought she was flying home from Boston."

"The Cape's only an hour or two out of the way. She probably wanted to see it in the fall."

"She talks a lot about the Cape," Maria says. "She loved it here."

She loved Malcolm here, Bernardin thinks. During the summer, twenty years ago... "The police have your mother's purse for safekeeping," he tells Maria. "We'll pick it up on the way to my place."

The duty officer at the station, who sits at a desk that is bathed in glare, seems uncertain about his authority to release the purse. He telephones the chief, who lives close by. The chief—short, stout, and in uniform—arrives a few minutes later. Bernardin knows that to Malcolm's mortification he and his men were called to the house on several occasions, when Helena got out of hand. He asks Maria a number of questions about her mother—maiden name, date of birth, that kind of thing—which means that he has probably examined the contents of the purse. In the end, he seems reluctant to hand it over.

"Is there a problem?" Bernardin asks.

"Only that we prefer to return personal effects to an adult relative."

"This young lady's in college," Bernardin says. "Her father won't arrive until late tomorrow, and when he does he'll want to be with his wife."

The chief gives a nod of understanding and instructs the duty officer to make out a property transfer slip for Maria to sign. While this is being done, he draws Bernardin aside.

"Rotten shame about Prescott," he says.

"A sad business," Bernardin agrees.

"Quite a photographer, wasn't he?"

Of war and women, Bernardin thinks.

"How's the girl's mother?"

"In a state of shock."

"Conscious?"

"Pretty much."

"You'll see *she* gets the purse and not the husband?" The chief has put unmistakable emphasis upon the feminine pronoun.

"If you think it's best."

"I think it's vital," the chief tells him.

Malcolm's house is ablaze with a false festivity of light. Cars have been parked every which way in the wild rose and bearberry that line the dirt drive leading to it. Inside, Bernardin introduces Maria and Alison to Helena and Ryan, who are sitting on the sofa in the living room. Maria offers words of sympathy to Helena, who blinks like a child struggling to stay alert at a party. "Shouldn't I know you?" she inquires.

"Maria's mother was a friend of Malcolm's," Bernardin explains. "She was hurt in the accident but she's going to be all right."

"Well, *that's* good news," Helena says. She pats the sofa cushion beside her that Ryan has vacated in order to take Maria and Alison off for something to drink. "Harry. Dear old Harry."

Bernardin sits and takes her hand. "Helena, I'm so terribly sorry."

"Well, Harry, it's a time to be sorry."

"Can I get you anything?"

"I'm not allowed to drink, you know. On account of my medication. Tell me about the girl you brought."

"She goes to college in Connecticut. She and her roommate flew in this evening to visit her mother in the hospital. They're going to spend the night at my place."

"Guess what," Helena says brightly. "It's not her I thought I should know. It's her mother. Did you ever hear about the first time she took a ride with Malcolm?"

"That was a long time ago," Bernardin tells her.

"Yes, it was," Helena says. "Dear old Harry."

When it seems right to leave, Bernardin fetches Alison and goes to look for Maria, whom he finds with Ryan in Malcolm's study at the rear of the house. They are sitting in chairs, face to face and hands in hands, elbows on their knees.

"She's going to feel a lot better when she sees your father," Ryan is saying.

"Right now, she's terribly upset about *your* father, Ryan. She knows something awful has happened, but she can't remember what."

"When you see her tomorrow, tell her we're pulling for her."

When Bernardin arrives at his house, he shepherds Maria and Alison inside and shows them the guest room in which they'll be sleeping. Then he sits them down at a counter in the kitchen, puts a kettle on for tea, and goes out to fetch their bags, which are sitting in the car trunk next to Ingrid's. Best for everyone to have gotten Ingrid's bags out of Malcolm's house, he tells himself, knowing that he has at least managed to spare Helena, Ingrid, and Maria some unnecessary pain, not to mention Maria's father, who will have enough on his hands without having to confront head-on a truth there is no longer any reason for him to have to face. A matter of avoiding collisions when you can, Bernardin thinks grimly, as he reaches up to close the hatch. But just then he remembers what the chief has said about Ingrid's purse.

Bernardin carries all the luggage into the house and sets it down in the guest room. Then he goes into the kitchen and makes tea for the two young women, whose faces reflect the fatigue he feels in himself. The three of them need to get some sleep, he says. Tomorrow will be a long and busy day.

Maria agrees, for she is anxious to return to the hospital early so she can be with Ingrid. Also, she must remember to get rooms for herself and Alison and her father at a motel near the hospital, and arrange for her father to speak with the neurologist and his colleagues.

Bernardin has been trying to think of how best to say what he has decided he should say. "I brought your mother's bags inside," he tells Maria. "You ought to go through them at some point. And her purse as well. Just to make sure everything's in order."

Maria gives him a look of puzzlement that is quickly canceled by a shrug. "If you think I should..."

"In the morning will be fine," Bernardin says.

He awakens to the sound of weeping, which is overlapped from time to time by a comforting voice, and, lying still in his bed, hopes it is a letter Maria has found and not—as he suspects from what the chief has said—a photograph. When the weeping shows no sign of abating, he climbs out of bed, pulls on his clothes, and goes into the kitchen to make some coffee. Alison joins him a few minutes later.

"I take it there was something in Ingrid's purse," he says.

"Yes," Alison replies. "You knew all along, didn't you?"

"I only guessed."

"I don't see why Maria had to find it."

"What if her father found it while Ingrid was lying half-conscious in the hospital?"

"Whatever it was, was pretty explicit. Maria's devastated."

"That's sex for you," Bernardin tells her. "It's always explicit, often devastating, but almost never tragic."

"Aren't you being kind of cynical?"

"I'm trying to keep things in perspective," Bernardin replies. Good old Malcolm, he thinks. Plying his profession to the end... "Why don't you go get Maria so we can cheer her up?"

When Maria comes into the kitchen, her eyes are red, but she has managed to compose herself.

Bernardin hands her a cup of coffee. "It must be a relief to find out your mother's not a saint," he says.

Maria laughs and starts to cry.

"Just think," Bernardin tells her, "how much easier she'll be to live with now."

Maria wipes her eyes with a napkin and drinks some coffee.

Once they arrive at the hospital, Bernardin arranges for the motel rooms, keeps Alison company, fetches soft drinks, does what he can. In the evening, he goes out to the airport to pick up Maria's father, who flies in from Boston on a commuter plane. Hervold Torquist is a slender man in his early forties, with deep blue eyes and an earnest Swedish accent. As might be expected, he has some questions.

"Have I understood correctly from Maria that Ingrid has been a passenger in this car that crashed?"

"That's right," Bernardin says.

"Which has been driven by a friend of hers named Malcolm?"

"Malcolm Prescott. A friend of hers and mine, and a fine photographer to boot."

"I'm sorry to hear he's dead," Torquist says. "Was he by any chance an older man?"

"My age," Bernardin replies. "Middle fifties."

"Ingrid has often been friends with older men."

"Is that so?"

"Oh, yes. And something similar to this has happened once before, when Ingrid was friends with a composer of music, a man in his sixties, who took her all the time to see foreign films, until one day while they were watching one together, he dropped dead, just like that, of a heart attack."

During the rest of the way to the hospital, Torquist informs Bernardin that he is a cabinetmaker and that things are hard on the West Coast because the recession there has lingered. When they arrive at the hospital, he thanks Bernardin for picking him up at the airport and for his kindness to Maria.

Three days later, Bernardin is standing before Helena and Ryan and several dozen mourners on a cliff above the Great Outer Beach. It is an unseasonably cold day with a brisk northwest wind—the kind that migratory birds wait for at this time of year, before launching themselves toward the South Atlantic. The wind makes everything seem impermanent. Once it stops blowing, Helena will be taken back to the hospital, Maria will return to college, Ingrid Torquist will fly home with the sun, and Malcolm's ashes will have mingled with the sand.

Bernardin waits as some elderly latecomers are helped across the dunes and listens to Malcolm's voice, not as it came to him over the telephone the day after the dinner party in April, when he first met Ingrid, but as if it is being carried on the wind. "You won't believe what's happened," Malcolm says. "D'you remember the woman I once told you about, the one in the bikini down by the pier that time, twenty years ago, when I came by in the Buick convertible and called out to her how beautiful she was, who slid herself onto the hood and sat there like some figurehead on the prow of a ship while I drove slowly through the whole damn town and out to the beach? Well..."

The wind is blowing past Bernardin toward the sea. He will have to shout if he is to be heard above it.

Some Other Angel

Daniel was already home. "Hi," he yelled from the kitchen as Em wrestled her overcoat onto a hanger in the overfull front closet. What the hell was he doing? Breaking rocks on the counter? "Hi," she yelled back, unwinding her scarf. "Annie call?"

Wham. Wham. Wham. "No," Daniel called back. Wham.

"What are you *doing*?" She draped the scarf over a peg inside the closet door.

Daniel appeared in the kitchen doorway in a paint-ticked maroon T-shirt and gray sweat pants, barefoot, one of her French kitchen towels, damp and dark and knotted around something, hanging from his hand. "Cracking ice."

"Daniel!" She went in to deprive him of the good towel, leaving her laptop and briefcase against the wall by the open closet door. In the kitchen, cracked ice glistened in a red plastic bowl—a mound of it. Daniel leaned against the wall as she hunted an appropriate rag from the upper cupboard above the fridge. "It's just a kitchen towel," he said, clearly baffled.

"It's an expensive kitchen towel."

"Who makes expensive kitchen towels?"

She hadn't changed from her work clothes; she hadn't had a glass of wine yet; she wasn't particularly in the mood for Daniel's offhand inclination to dispute everything in the universe. "Just use this instead? Okay?"

"Sure," he said. He twisted a plastic ice tray, dumped the cubes onto the rag, then leaned across to kiss her hello. He seemed in good spirits. She was wary of that.

"I'm going to change," she said, heading out of the kitchen. "Do we have enough wine?"

"What, change now and then change again?"

Em turned at the door to regard her husband with a momentary but intense dislike. His back was to her; she watched as he folded the rag around the ice, aligning the points, then picked it up, hefted it once, muttered under his breath, "Now, Mr. Leung, you pay the *big* price," and started slamming it against the metal counter. Her irritation shaded into a bemused affection; she might have slipped into a scene from their life three years ago. But the repeated banging was too loud, too harsh. Daniel's broad shoulders rolled as he slammed the ice down, over and over, no joke, blow after blow.

Their bedroom was quiet. It felt sealed off, except for the thump and whine of the December wind off the Hudson against the window. Sealed off, removed from the world, but the bed was unmade, the flowered sheets and blue-striped duvet kicked down at the end, her grandmother's quilt draped across the director's chair they'd bought that summer. If it's a chair, and we can't sit in it, then, um, Em—why own it? Because I want it, she'd said. The chair was from the fifties, the green cloth back and seat sun-faded and frayed, the wood as seasoned as driftwood. She loved its indications. It summoned her childhood: Cape Cod summers, her parents desperate to appear as casually well-to-do as practically everyone around them. And why was that nostalgic?

Daniel had come home early and taken a nap, she thought. Not the best sign. Em made the bed before hanging her blazer, stepping out of her skirt, peeling off wretched hose—why, if you dealt with money, did you have to wear hose? Curators could bop around *sans* hose. Social mystery. She tucked the limp vestiges of the corporate side of museum work into a net hosiery bag, tossed it into the laundry basket, and then, because the task of becoming herself had overwhelmed her, sighed. She began to unbutton her blouse. People would be here soon. They were going to need more wine.

"We have six bottles of red and six of that Argentinean chardonnay that was okay," Daniel said, suddenly there, leaning against the doorway. He liked to lean against things. Once, she had thought of him as the kind of person who could walk through one of those askew, tilted-floor funhouses casually upright. But the world wasn't a funhouse. "Whoa, check it out," he added as she unhooked her bra. "Red-hot mama. Ouch."

"What's with you?" she asked, lightly.

"What can I say? Just full of love. Oh, and Max called. He

claims he's going to be here, believe it or not."

"No summer cold?"

"No summer cold."

He came over and put his arms around her from behind, nestling his rough chin into the hollow of her collarbone.

"No business trip to Erie? Car wasn't stolen?"

"No business trips, no stolen cars."

"You should shave."

"I know. Never got around to it this morning." Had he been out of the apartment at all? His arms were warm against her belly, but she laid a hand on his bony wrist, half holding him at bay. "Hi," he whispered into the tangle of her hair, the whorl of her ear, a real greeting, saying *home* with breath, *home*.

"Mm," Em said, almost seduced; but the air in the room was cold. "You're warm, but I'm freezing. I'm all nipply."

"Yes, I see that." He let her go, going to stand in front of the window, then sitting on the far side of the bed as she buttoned her blue shirt. A comfort shirt, she'd had it for years. "Spooky wind," he said.

Thump. A gust against the window. The air in the room tightened. They were high enough that they got the hard wind right off the river. Thump. Daniel reached forward and put his palm to the cold glass, and when he sat back a ghost of his hand remained, then dissolved. Was gone. Past his familiar back, nothing but night and the floodlights on the Jersey shore and the wind whining. Daniel murmured, "Let us in, human child..."

"Jesus, Daniel, you're giving me the creeps."

"That's my talent for eerie hokum."

He had his legs drawn up and was looking out the window.

"What did Max say?" she asked.

"Just that he's not bringing some woman named Lisette. Another two-week special, from what he said."

She wasn't surprised. Max flickered in and out of women's lives the same way he flickered in and out of her and Daniel's life; but in romance there was only one flicker, and then Max was gone. In friendship there were repeated sightings. Max the mirage. Em brought her duck boots over to the bed and sat down on the edge, then leaned closer to Daniel, reaching out to smooth the unruly hair on the back of his head. "Hey, funny guy," she said. "Bad day?"

"Strange how you never see anyone down in that courtyard down there," he said.

Snow had started to sift down. Eduardo held the door for her, saying, "I got that feeling, bad winter, you know?" He was sniffing and arching his brows, too, giving a good deal of credence to Daniel's theory that he spent his breaks coking up in the boiler room. Had she ever imagined a time in her life when she would be positively grateful for a sweetheart Dominican cokehead for a doorman? They sometimes let Eduardo use their phone to order Chinese food for his dinner break; they were younger than most of the couples in the building.

Down on the street, the wind wasn't as bad, and the first faint snow had stuck to the sidewalks, miraculously polished and white, settling at intervals into the fine, dark lines of the squares of pavement. A city paved in enormous kitchen tiles, New York looking clean for once. Give it five minutes. The blowing snow stung Em's face. She walked briskly under the arched streetlights up 104th Street towards West End, avoiding the brooding silence of Riverside. Though it was a Friday evening, the streets were comparatively desolate. There was a kind of Indian summer on Fridays in New York, after work and before people went out for the night—a time of dressing and making phone calls, or of looking out the window and wishing someone would call, she thought. As she passed the quiet, sheathed cars, hatless, with the snow caught and pointed with light in her hair, an awareness that she still loved Daniel curled up through her unexpectedly; and at that moment, as she hurried forward, she could feel an almost perfect forgiveness for his furies and depressions, the kind of forgiveness she could never quite seem to summon while she was with him. Maybe the cost was too high in terms of selflessness. Why, when she was with him, did giving feel like giving *up* something—precious grains of her own life, which he needed. Their life, her life, his life, our life, your life, my life—what did you own except loss? Nothing. She wished she could click her heels together three times and go back to when they'd been happy more often.

When Em crossed 106th, she realized someone was pacing her, and she glanced over just as a voice sang, in a kind of softshoe rhythm, "You don't have to be a Rockefellah to help a little fellah..."

The homeless man was tiny: he barely came up to her shoulder, scuttling along, a wizened, black-bearded figure, with a ridiculous felt thing like a medieval monk's cap yanked down almost over his eyes. A brown corduroy coat, too light for the weather, the nap flattened with grease, trailed sleeves that came down past his thumbs. He showed her fingertips, chapped but with pale, almost polished nails. "When you're down, you get around—"

She tried to ignore him. Past the used bookstore on the corner of 105th, crossing the street. Her shadow, following, sang at her. Her boots rutched against wet gravel in the street where the snow had melted. In the middle of the intersection, he stopped, she sensed his presence fall away. She was generous. She gave to several shelters, to several liberal political organizations; she paid her New York tithe of conscience. She could walk past. "Hey!" his voice brayed out behind her. "Hey! You *nothing*! You *less* than me! Hey!" She was at the liquor store door. "Hey!"

An older man, coming out, caught the tail end of the beggar's harangue. An extinguished cigar like the root of some small shrub nestled in the corner of his mouth, above a wet and liverish and distended lower lip; he held the door for her, enormous in gray cashmere, and winked as she stepped past. "Tell 'em to go to hell," he muttered, "fuckin' charity cases," his manner so foul she almost said something sharp in response. But then the door was closed, and what would she have said, anyway? That she *would* give, that she *had* given, but that she simply couldn't afford to give anymore?

"Guess who's here?" Daniel yelled as she let the door slam shut behind her.

Max poked his head out from the kitchen. Deep-set dark eyes; hair cut short, revealing a bony forehead; his shadowed jutting jaw.

"This is a surprise," she said. He was early.

Daniel emerged from the kitchen behind Max, wiping his

hands—to hell with it, she gave up—on the other of the French kitchen towels. He tossed the cloth on the couch as he went by, and took the bag from her arms. The bottles clanked together. He peered in. "What, are they cutting down on cardboard?"

"What's a surprise?" said Max. "That I'm here? I'm always here."

"They should put those little cardboard strips in," Daniel said, vanishing into the kitchen.

"That you're on time," Em said, accepting Max's broad, one-armed hug. Max was six-four, long-armed, long-legged, his huge hands delicate, his tapering long fingers sparsely stroked with black hair.

"Time," said Max, making a gesture as if flicking water from his fingertips. "Pfff. Overrated."

He looks like an undertaker for movie stars, Daniel had observed the first time he'd met Max, at their wedding. She laughed, because he was right, also because they were giddy in love; but she had always thought Max looked more like a concert pianist, a Russian one.

"You go to the place on 104th?" Daniel yelled from the kitchen. "Or the 106th place?"

"Hundred sixth," Em said, picking up the French towel from the couch, folding it without thought. That little fingertip gesture—Max was an encyclopedia of studied gestures. They all worked.

"That boy in there is a finicky bastard, for an artist," Max observed.

"I like *things*," Daniel yelled, overhearing. "And I like them to be right."

"Your coat?" Max held out his hands as she shrugged it off.

"What happened to—?"

"Lisette," he said. She walked with him to the closet. He found a space on the bar that hadn't existed when she left, hung the old coat—she really hated it, she needed a new one—with a deft gesture. He didn't answer the question she'd asked until he had picked up his drink from the coffee table, dipped a long finger in it, stirred the cubes, sucked the tip of his finger. "I am a man who can't give her what she wants," he said finally.

"That's such crap, Max."

He shrugged. "Fidelity. Love. Affection. Plans. Tomorrow as opposed to today. *Der kinder.*"

"You only went out with her for two weeks."

"Past thirty, the chicks move fast, Emsworth."

They regarded each other. Then she reached forward and peeled back his suit jacket, whose blue was a slightly unusual shade, whose weave drew a hint of attention to itself. Glancing at the label, she said, "My, my."

A rare thing: Max blushed. It made him look blotchy. He never looked blotchy. She felt pleased with herself.

"Well, fuck me," he said, "it's all appearances, right?"

Daniel emerged from the kitchen with two glasses of white wine. "Max the knife."

"Are you changing?" she asked him. He had. Into jeans, a sweatshirt.

"Hadn't planned on it."

"All right." She gave her attention to Max.

"Okay," Daniel said. "Fine, fine. I'll change."

"Thanks, sweetie," she said, touching his arm as he moved past.

When Daniel was gone, there was a momentary silence. Max studied Daniel's paintings. One above the couch; one above the black chair. One in the entry hall. Blocks of text—from letters Daniel's grandfather had sent Daniel's mother, not the pseudo-cryptic artsy-political sloganeering hanging in every gallery these days—and hints of landscape under the words, gray and umber: if Anselm Kiefer painted moors. Not uplifting; not that she wanted art to be uplifting. Grim—but actually good, Em thought. She liked the one above the couch most, one haunting little statement, "Last night my dream life opened up for me. Ask me about it." Marry a painter with a family history of chronic depression and paranoid schizophrenia, bright move, sweetheart. Love was always such a bright move.

Em tried to read whatever reactions were under the reactions Max was letting her see. It was hard. He probably liked them. *Like them,* she commanded silently.

Max nodded after a moment. "That one over the chair's new, isn't it?"

She nodded. Then she changed her mind and said, "Actually I think he reworked it."

"I like it."

"I wish someone who mattered would."

Max chuckled. "Thank you ever so much."

Em took a long drink from her wine. When had she turned into someone who *needed* a glass of wine? Well, since starting work at the museum; not everything dissolved into the tension she felt here. Home: the painting over the chair, blacks, blues, purples, hard-edged words, history of love and family, all the heavy paint. It was hard, arduous, carrying someone else's belief in himself, as well as your own. Daniel went to the studio three days a week, doggedly, impatient with himself and less and less sure of his work, and the other four days sat in a small room producing computer images of cancerous cells and graphs having to do with the deaths of rats for a medical journal out of Columbia Presbyterian. As he had said, sharply joking, "It's some kind of ur-level of artistic misery—about six steps *below* prostituting your talent." He was thirty-two, and she remembered so clearly from six years ago his enthusiasm, his unquestioning confidence, and a kind of optimism in his anger, joyful outrage rather than bitterness—bitterness was hard. For two weeks this past summer, there had been construction in the curatorial offices at the museum. They had worked through it, drywall dust in the air, so much that it felt caked in her lungs, and she would escape at the end of the day into the August heat feeling as though she couldn't draw a full breath. Bitterness did that, too.

Strange to be tied to someone by marriage—by love—and feel your own life moving forward, successfully, in a series of promising little explosions like cream poured into coffee—and see the other person getting darker. Last winter Daniel had spent days in bed. She would come home and find him lying in the dark despite doctors, despite prescriptions, despite her—and she was good at making people happy. She was.

"So," Max said. "How's money at the museum?"

Em laughed. "What money? It's like trying to pull rabbits out of hats, but we don't have any hats, and we don't have any rabbits."

He smiled. One day Max would be rich; he might be already.

Max's many secrets. He was in bankruptcy law—"Yes," he had once remarked, "you're having dinner with one of the city's foremost rising eaters of the dead."

Max in his beautiful suit turned to face Daniel's black painting again. "So," he said, voice pitched a little lower. "Also curious. How are—?"

"Things?"

"Things."

Em decided not to answer that question. "I'll tell you later. You?"

"Me?" Max said. "Well, Emswell—"

The doorbell rang, then rang again, a long jangling insistent ring.

"Shit," she said, "people."

"They're all people from Hoboken Lou *grew up* with or something," Annie said. "Was I supposed to know they'd all turn up at the bar?" A long black sweater revealed her right shoulder, the fall of the cloth in line with the swoop of Annie's curly, bronzish hair. She had her feet, in a pair of small fleeced boots, up on Em's coffee table and was explaining the presence of the five stoned but belligerent *Star Trek* fans, who had arrived with her and Lou. Lou was the *Star Trek* editor at the publishing house where Annie worked, though he wanted to move into espionage novels. Annie was having a not-quite involvement with him. "Apparently there's some sort of 'new' season which is completely different from the *old* season—except that the new season is already old, too, or something—so I made about six kinds of terrible *Star Trek* faux pas, if you can believe that." Annie, smoking, adjusted her sweater, considering Lou from hooded eyes as she spoke. She was higher up than Lou where they worked; it was a sticking point. "Anyway," Annie said, "I was sitting there, drunk off my ass, thinking, Why do I feel like an idiot? *These* people are *clearly* the idiots. It's so insidious when idiots act as if they aren't idiots. But they brought all that vodka. And they get very good weed. I guess that makes up for something."

"Estonian vodka," Em noted. She was sitting on the arm of the couch next to her friend.

"Maybe that's a *good* thing." Annie hugged her black-tighted legs to her chest. "He's fucking that chick in the yellow boob-top, by the way."

"She looks like a ferret."

"Tell me about it. Maybe you could have Daniel push her out the window by accident later or something." Annie sucked down a large portion of her drink. "Of course the problem is he thinks if he goes out with me then I'll work some kind of successful-woman emasculation voodoo on him or something." She leaned forward, pitched her cigarette into a discarded beer, reached for the pack on the cushion, shook one out. "I mean, it's pitiful," she added. "I have no idea why I'm attracted to him."

Across the room people laughed: Daniel with his gnome face on, fingers clutched into claws, spinning dire stories about the life of the artist. His studio was in the West Twenties near the highway. Amazonian dyed blondes in lace teddies patrolled the block on Sunday morning, getting in and out of Hondas with New Jersey plates. Transvestite hookers picked up by bridge-and-tunnel *Star Trek* fans? Why not? Annie, following her gaze, nodded, blew out smoke.

In another direction, Max held court. Such grace. Like an emissary you'd expect to see walking down a glass staircase from heaven, white tux, white roses in his hand. Em looked back at her husband. He seemed manic, almost desperate, and possibly drunk.

"How's the shrinkage?" Annie asked.

"I don't know. He says he likes the woman he's seeing."

"Well, anything has to be better than the last one. I mean, an anorexic ex-actress from Queens? Who decides who gets to be therapists anyway?"

"You're funny."

"I'm trying to be, dummy."

"I know," Em said.

"Hey, come on—you sad?"

Em shook her head, though she was. Exhausted, suddenly, too. Why were they having this party?

Annie nudged her. "Tomorrow we can talk a lot, right?"

"No, that'll be good," Em said.

"Hey," said Annie, "look at you. You're doing that totally-negative-there's-no-hope-and-it's-all-completely-doomed thing."

She watched his hand reach for his drink, groping blindly for it, as he continued his story. "You're right," she said. "Sorry."

"Oh, look at that," Annie said then. "Look, look, look. It's *so* embarrassing. I mean, yes, everyone *knows* you have breasts, darling."

She and Daniel rendezvoused outside the back door, on the dark landing of the back stairwell. Her husband's hair was sticking out; he wasn't wearing his glasses anymore. "Those friends of Lou's were getting stoned in the bedroom. I figured you'd rather they didn't. I beat 'em with sticks until they got out. Good dope, though."

The landing smelled of cigarettes, which meant they'd get complaints from their next door neighbor, the man-whose-nose-ran, in the morning. Daniel finished the drink in his hand, looked at the glass appraisingly, licked his lips several times. "This vodka's very strange—tastes like it's got wood chips in it or something."

She touched his arm. "Hey—maybe you should take it easy?" She knew this pattern: he wasn't a drinker except when he was depressed. So she'd been right not to trust his good mood, his easy affection, his arms around her—now she would give, and he would take. She didn't want to come home to two weeks of silence.

"People who take it easy don't get very far," Daniel said flatly.

"That wasn't what I meant."

He smiled at her. "I know."

Rather than take up the challenge, Em stepped over and opened the stairwell window, under the sign that said "These windows must stay closed at all times." She wanted air. It was too close.

Daniel came up behind her. "Hey, Em? Sweetie?"

"What?"

When she turned, he stepped back and shrugged, his little boy's what-did-I-do-wrong expression on his face. It was exasperating. She felt like giving him lessons: number one, acting innocently wronged when you are deliberately pissing me off is a stupid tactic. "Daniel?"

"Mm?"

"Do you think tomorrow could we set aside some time, to talk—a specific time? Have a plan? In the morning?" The counselor they'd been to a few months before had suggested this as a good idea, proactive, set aside time, blah blah blah. Em had felt vindicated: Of *course* it was a good idea.

"Talking," Daniel said, as if it were something he'd heard about, a new fad. "Thought I'd go to the studio in the morning."

"The whole morning?"

"Yeah. Most of it. I wanted to get started early."

"Okay, fine, forget it."

"No—look—what about after?"

"I'm meeting Annie downtown. Then there's that reception. The donor thing. That's at five. Forget it. It's pointless. Never mind." The real problem was that after being at the studio, he would be in a terrible mood, and they would fight. Em was certain that the anger she felt at that moment could only be half towards Daniel— the other half simply rose out of frustration at the resistance and clutter of their lives. But here he was, the sullen, half-drunk target. She wasn't going to give up Annie, and the reception was work and couldn't be dropped, and she wasn't going to back down, even to make him stop her, to prove that what was between them mattered to him. No: she would wait him out. And as far as she was concerned, they could wait until the next Ice Age. In this one instance, he could be the one to compromise.

He was staring intently at his shoulder.

She waited. Hello, Ice Age. Okay. Screw it. She gave up. "Dan? Are we still having a conversation?"

He nodded, then reached up and, between thumb and forefinger, delicately trapped a long hair, lifting it from the weave of his sweater. The pale filament trembled in the air between them, caught in a plane of light from the partly open kitchen door.

"Yours," he said.

She sighed. "Is that significant?"

Now he looked at her, an intensity she recognized and loved in his face, overlaid with a sliding lack of focus. Self-pity and vodka and resentment. It was horrible. "Hey," he said. "What do you mean? Of *course* it's significant. It's *yours*. I *love* you."

. . .

It was midnight. "Like taking your fucking ego to the fucking shooting gallery," Daniel was saying, some anecdote about taking slides to galleries. "Bing bing bing bing bing, down you go."

Annie laughed, clearly drunk.

When Max came up, Daniel rounded on him, too mockingly friendly to be taken as anything but antagonistic. "Max! Secret Max! What secrets lurk in the dark heart of Max, fucking shadow knows—"

Max rubbed the corner of his mouth, decided to smile. "No secrets, Daniel. You know me. Perfectly transparent."

For a moment, Em hated his composure. It felt unfair somehow.

"You're not in Pennsylvania. Pennsylvania. In fucking Gary, Indiana, or something."

"Not tonight. We're busy cleaning up a department store."

" 'Cleaning up,' " her husband said. "I love you, Max. What the fuck does that mean?"

"It's like 'collateral damage,' " Em said, trying to make a joke. "Soft targets."

"Thank you very much. I'm a lawyer, not an animal." Max was unruffled. He loved attention in any circumstance.

"What do you lawyer?" one of the stoned friends of Lou demanded.

"Bankruptcies. Fiscal carrion. I'm the grave digger. I hold the widows' hands and comfort them after the man in the suit takes the long dive. All that," Max said. "I'm good at it."

"Max the *knife*," Daniel said. He was leaning against a table. Then his face changed, and he turned and walked off, towards the bedroom.

When Em went back, she found Daniel on the bed, on his stomach but draped off the edge, with one hand on the floor to support himself. He was sweating, and his hair was matted against his forehead. The lights were off. Em shut the door behind her. "Sweetie?" she said. "You okay?"

"I'm sorry."

"Are you sick?"

"Yeah. I'm sorry."

She came and knelt and stroked the back of his head. With his hand on the hardwood floor, he seemed to be bracing himself against the downward pull of his own weight. "Do you want to get all the way on the bed?"

"Nope. Too drunk."

"Okay," she said, standing up.

He swallowed, licked his lips. "You need help? Cleaning up?"

"Shhh. People are still here. Annie's here. She'll help. Max, too." Part of her felt such despair, she couldn't even understand where to place it.

"I didn't get any work done today. I can't work."

"Yes, you can," she told him. An exchange that had become ritual. She wondered if she should get a towel. There was still the world, after all: he was lying on her side of the bed.

"I'm a fuck," he said. "I can't. I can't work. Fuck, I feel sick."

After a moment he added, "I feel like you used to be happy, and then I came along and fucked it up. I'm so frightened."

He rolled away from her, curling up on the bed. She got on the bed and lay next to him and held him as he cried.

Her exhaustion made the party feel as if it had moved underwater. A number of people had left as well, and the wreckage—the cups scattered here and there, the chips ground into the floor, the empty bottles in the kitchen—seemed all the sharper. Annie came up to her. "I'm floozled. It's a new word. I made it up. Like it?"

"Just don't you be sick, too," Em said—what was she, mother to the world?

"Is Danny sick?" Annie twisted a ringlet with her forefinger. "Poor guy."

She was carrying a nested stack of sticky cups into the kitchen when Max materialized.

"You need more wine. We'll take a walk. I'll buy it."

A walk sounded like a gift. Even five minutes. At the closet, she suggested to Annie that she might—God knew how, since Annie could barely stand—keep an eye on things. Annie seemed pleased with her new authority. "Max is going to buy me a yacht, and I'm going to sail to Bora Bora," Em told her. "I'll be back in six months or so."

Then they were in the hall.

"Take the stairs?" Max suggested. "I need to get my blood flowing."

"Max, eight floors?"

"Pff," he said, his adopted French mannerism, and held the heavy black door to the stairwell for her. It boomed behind them as they set off.

Outside, the snow was falling harder. "Didn't I tell you?" Eduardo said at the door. He held it open after them—the flowery iron grillwork swinging easily and silently on oiled hinges— then stood rubbing his hands, a concerned expression on his face.

"Take Riverside," Max said, steering her by the elbow.

Inexplicably the wind wasn't as sharp against the high silent buildings as on West End. On the lower street, traffic rushed hissing; a pale fog, luminous from within, was fingering in off the Hudson; above them snow spiraled down, whirling in cones of light.

"So fucking peaceful," Max said.

Em said, "I think it's spooky. Look, can we not talk about anything about my life and just talk about yours, okay?"

"Of course. I love talking about my life. The interpretations are so various."

She was relieved. "Good."

But he didn't say anything for a moment, striding silently along. His black shoes impressed the snow without sound.

"Well, I've decided that I'm in love with you," Max said finally.

"Oh, Max, not again. Jesus. I mean, this is without question absolutely the worst possible time, you know?"

"Ah, but this time I've thought about it," he said lightly.

"Max," she said.

" 'Max,' " he repeated, walking a little ahead of her, gallant, as if the buildings might fail abruptly and open to Russian fields.

Riverside on nights like this always made her think of Jack the Ripper—she wished Max would walk next to her, but just *walk*. Not talk, not push. Not ask for anything. And not be charming. In her sadness, she didn't have the energy to play a good game.

"Max," she said, "listen. We're just getting wine. Then we're going back to my apartment."

"Pfff."

"Please stop pfff-ing? Okay?"

Max came to an abrupt halt. He turned to face her. "As far as I can tell—and I did think about this—anything I feel for you has nothing to do with Daniel. Right?"

"Wrong," she said, and walked past him, brushing against his coat as she did, against his presence. In her life again. They'd slept together, once—after she was married, but a long time ago, the first time Daniel had been seriously depressed. The sex, Em had always felt, had not been a betrayal but an escape, into the clarity of Max's flat confidence and playfully grave desire. Like taking a shower so you could have privacy to think. She had never told Daniel. It would have upset him beyond what the infidelity had meant: He wouldn't have understood that sleeping with Max had been about their marriage, not about Max. But Max had understood; and vanished. A hint of self-protection? She'd always thought so. Five years—any physical memory of that afternoon was far outweighed by how long she and Max had been friends. By the complexity and weight of her life with Daniel.

They walked together silently up to 106th Street, and by some mutual consent, crossed it and kept walking up Riverside. I should not be doing this, Em thought. But she did feel her exhaustion lift in the freezing air. At least she could play, flirt. Lighten up.

"I mean, Max," she said, "how many women have you slept with? Just this year, all right?"

"Emswiggle," Max said, "believe me. There's only you."

She laughed, and then glanced at him. "You are joking, aren't you?"

"Of course," Max said, utterly unknowable.

Several city buses, their fluorescent interior lights stark on rows of desolate seats, hurtled by under the trees, down below on Riverside.

"Em," he said, his breath smoking out, his black coat swirling around his legs as they walked, "think about some things. You've tried. You're such a giver. Right? But look at Daniel. He's falling. Some other angel's going to have to catch him this time."

"Stop it," she said. "Do you want me to hate you?"

"I'm such a creation," Max replied after a moment. "It's funny. I finally managed to perfect myself." The night air was empty and quiet. "You're wonderful," he said. "We'd have fun. It's not a proposition, it's an invitation, understand?"

"And you'd vanish, and my marriage would be over."

Max turned and grabbed her hands. He said, "That's right."

The Excitement Begins

On the day before his fiftieth birthday, Bill Lander received a letter from a woman he had never heard of—Amber Harding—saying she'd be pleased to come to Wallace to meet him and be his birthday date. She noted the time she'd arrive on the train and said she'd have no trouble recognizing him. "I'll just look for a tall, silent type," she wrote, but warned that she had modified her appearance some since her ad ran in *Soulmates*. "I took the plunge," she said, "and had my hair cut and permed. The color's the same." She closed by saying she looked forward to meeting a real cowboy and seeing Wyoming. Her letter was mailed from What Cheer, Iowa, and Bill read it again, certain there had been a mistake. He called Directory Assistance, then Amber Harding, hearing her answering machine playing a musical selection—something that sounded like "Yesterday."

"There's been a mistake," he told the machine. "This is Bill Lander leaving this message." He noted the time and date, and left his phone number.

He was outside, spreading hay, when it came to him that someone was playing a birthday trick on him, someone's idea of a gag. He flung the hay, hitting a heifer, her big eyes regarding him stupidly, her tail flicking at a halo of flies.

He had a long list of culprits to choose from. He had lived in Wallace all his life, the townspeople knowing all the particulars about him. He was a bachelor, and friends were always trying to hook him up with someone. They were the ones who were going all out for his birthday. They had rented the Union Hall and hired a local band, promising him he'd have a night to remember.

He got in his pickup and went to the barbershop in town. Ned Jencks grinned broadly at him, saying, "The birthday boy. The big five-oh. I passed that milestone a ways back myself. Bet you're here for a haircut."

"No," Bill told him. "I'm here on other business." He saw *Soul-*

mates on top of a stack of magazines and picked it up.

"That's an interesting publication," Ned said.

"I'll return it shortly," Bill said, and prepared to leave.

"This isn't a lending library," Ned shouted.

"It's a joke is what it is," Bill said, and went to the Busy Bee café, knowing he was making matters worse, walking in with the magazine and seeing men sitting at the counter, their heads rising from their breakfast plates to look at him.

"Going through the change of life already?" one of them shouted. "Don't recollect ever seeing you here on a weekday morning."

"Had business in town," Bill said and sat at a booth.

It was the spring issue of the magazine, and hearts and flowers were drawn along the border. On the cover was a picture of a woman named Roxanne in a red blouse, short hair arranged stiffly like a helmet. Roxanne was smiling, holding the collar of a stonewashed denim jacket over her right shoulder. The caption beneath her photo said "The happiest woman alive."

The publication was printed in Montana and boasted an ever-growing readership. In the Editor's Comments column, someone named the "Love 'a Ranger" talked about time moseying on, waiting for no one. "Choices are a lot better than what you have been seeking every day around you in your town or even the country you happen to be in. Hey, that old system went out the window a long time ago! Most everyone travels these days and is willing to go the distance. Now, roads are good. Who says you can't have it all just like on television?"

Bill skimmed the ads and pictures, annoyed greatly that people meddled in his life and in this pathetic way. Did they think he was desperate?

There was no picture of Amber Harding, but her ad was longer than anyone else's. She started off with a brief description of herself, saying she was petite—five foot three—and had maintained a desirable weight for years. She had shoulder-length brown hair and was forty, born and bred in the Midwest.

"I'm not afraid to take on projects of considerable magnitude and complexity. Friends describe me as intelligent, witty, mysterious, a deep thinker, compassionate, gentle, fun-loving, and somewhat guarded. I have an interest in good nutrition, reading labels and taking supplements. I wouldn't mind meeting a man who cooks and bakes on a regular basis and who is humorous by nature. I like riding horses who don't offer to buck without advanced warning. I love surprises, not shocks! Am hoping to hear from interested parties. Only, no inmates, please."

Unlike the other ads, Amber Harding's listed no occupation, just a box number at the magazine. Someone had chosen to write to her, he assumed, because the ad seemed silly. He looked at the men in the café, every one of them married to local women, as if it were they who were afraid of surprises, or afraid of him because he had chosen to remain single and had no complaints. He watched them leave the café, one of them giving him the thumbs-up sign and saying, "Looking forward to the party, Bill. Wait till you see the hall. Folks went all out. Yes, sir, they went the distance this time."

He could pull off a surprise on all of them by not showing up, getting out of town, but he'd have to live with them for the rest of his life. He wanted to collar someone and say, "It's no big deal turning fifty," but cards had been appearing in his mailbox, reminding him that it was a big deal. His own father had died at fifty-two, old and spent, brittle toward the end, as if finally heeling under the strain of living in a punishing land. And here was this Amber Harding, entertaining romantic notions about Wyoming and cowboys.

He glanced at the rest of the ads, seeing photographs of women dressed as if they were to step out for an evening on the town, the men wearing old-fashioned western outfits, their ads insistent on transformations and the desire to settle down and have a second chance after divorces and drinking. These men described themselves as being reborn, finding real values and a longing to live in wide-open places, preferably with like-minded women.

Bill distrusted everything the writers said, but continued reading.

"Middle-aged man, tall, silent type. Filled with common sense. Has spread. No dependents. Can be outgoing. Realistic, all-around nice guy, average-looking. Been doing the solo act for years. Something's missing. Desperate to fill other half of team harness I've been dragging around. In mind, have no one particular."

He saw the name Bill underneath and "Big Horn country, Wallace, WY."

"Jesus," he muttered, imagining friends and neighbors sitting down to compose such an ad and a letter to Amber Harding.

On his way home, he passed the railroad station, a squat, cement building, its outside benches and plaster defaced with crude hearts, names and dates. "If you lived here," someone had spray-painted, stopping the message at that.

Beyond the station was the Union Hall, a few cars in the lot. He sped off, raising a plume of gravel and dust.

Even though he had neglected most of his daily chores, he went into his house, threw *Soulmates* in the trash, but couldn't shake the portrait of himself depicted in the magazine. He wasn't aware of ever telling anyone that something was missing in his life; most likely, it was their projection. If he had to describe his feelings, it might come out as a kind of contentment, along with the conviction that something dramatic—possibly awful—was in store. The day he broke his leg, three years ago, he came close to pinning down that feeling. It was in the spring, the first fine day after a hard winter, and he had decided on a horseback ride in the high country. He could've sworn he heard a woman crying, moaning luxuriously, somewhere behind the rocks. He spurred his horse, and the old bay, resentful and spooked, bucked him, then ran off. He knew some damage had been done to his leg, but he was afraid to look, afraid to move. Then a mountain lion emerged, making that female crying noise. The lion took possession of a boulder, sitting regally on it, its flanks still and chaired, its eyes observing him lying in the damp grass as if patient to watch the spectacle. Bill would long recall the sight of the lion stretching itself on the rock to sleep, a thin white cloud sailing by indifferently, and his own disbelief at the stillness of it all.

A sheepman found him, nudged him with the toe of a muddy boot, then hefted him upon his shoulders like a bum lamb. During his hospital stay, friends and neighbors visited, signed his cast, and assured him they were seeing to things on his ranch. They brought flowers, homemade food, and get-well cards full of jokes about pretty nurses and goldbricking. Bill forced smiles at the cards, and for the people who seemed to want a tale, he described the accident. "Thought I was a goner," he'd say, never mentioning the curious emotion, almost like elation, that had seized him that day. "Figured it was a matter of time before that lion sprang on me." The visitors would shake their heads and tell him he was one lucky fellow.

He had read of people who had brushes with death, their whole outlook changing afterwards, but when he returned home, everything seemed the same. The cattle moved along in deliberate processions, following the same rutted path to the fields and home again. Every two weeks, he went into town for a haircut, getting weary of Ned Jencks talking about the accident to men in the barbershop who seemed to look at him, then themselves in the mirror, as if to confirm their own good fortune.

Sometimes he rode back to the site, stopping always at the place where he had fallen and lying down there to stare at the boulder again, waiting foolishly to see the mountain lion and to feel that solitary excitement.

On his way outside to tend to chores, he saw the clipping he had pinned to his refrigerator from one of his trade journals about an autistic woman who had designed a humane apparatus that hugged cattle on their way to slaughter. The woman had such an apparatus in her own home, and a picture showed her being hugged by the machine. "Can't get close to humans," the woman said, insisting that cattle changed her life. Bill wondered about the cattle, thinking it hard on them to get something good just moments before their end.

He put the clipping in a desk drawer, realizing that he was already imagining Amber Harding coming to his home.

He hardly slept at all, waiting for his phone to ring, and fretting about enduring the next day. Whenever he looked out the window, he worried about snow, even though it was May. It had been known to happen even in June, and on this night, the sky had a low-slung look to it, no stars, and a hazy gibbous moon, flimsy and forlorn like a piece of crust.

When he finally left his bed, it was not yet day. Fog sheathed the grass and crouched in the higher country, lying in the private places, furring over the foothills and Big Horns. He thought himself a fool for the patch of disappointment he felt about Amber Harding being deprived of a proper view of things. He had hours to go before meeting the train at noon and couldn't imagine the other time beyond that when he would have to occupy a stranger until six o'clock, the time of the party.

He completed his chores, then took a long bath, scrubbing himself red and trying to make his hands look clean. He dressed in a white western shirt and Wrangler jeans. He bet this woman was expecting a man in a Stetson and pointed boots, but he wore his old oxblood Ropers and no hat.

He walked to the mailbox, knowing that an assortment of predictable cards awaited him, but there was only one card, a standard thing from his insurance man, reminding him of his age and the need to update life insurance options.

There were no other people at the train station, and he was glad for that. The day was still overcast, but it had warmed up, the sun moving in and out of rags of clouds, as if it couldn't decide whether or not to make an appearance. The train was late, and there was no one at the ticket booth to give him any information. It surprised him to see some battered-looking luggage left for anyone to take. On the distempered walls were pictures of old-fashioned trains, sleek locomotives conveying passengers over scenic mountain passes and silver streams. He occupied himself looking at the posters and a map of the United States. He traced his finger from Northeast Wyoming to Iowa, trying to locate What Cheer, the red and blue road routes, train symbols, and rivers so tangled and close he might be staring at a complicated wiring grid. He was still looking for What Cheer when he heard the train and saw, to his surprise, a teenaged boy rushing out of the men's room, grabbing the luggage, and heading outside. Bill went outside and stood with the boy on the platform. "Train's late," the boy said, "but it's here." He looked at it incredulously and boarded, even though no railroad people appeared.

Bill couldn't see anything in the train windows because the sun had emerged, casting plates of light on the smudged panes. He flirted with the idea of letting Amber Harding stay put, the fault of the busybodies who concocted the scheme, but he stayed where he was, knowing this was another price he was paying, feeling both enraged and paralyzed. It occurred to him that he was experiencing the worst part of the birthday joke, standing there like a lunatic, waiting for a fraudulent date. A hiss of steam from the locomotive startled him, and then the curious sight of a step stool dropping to the dust as if flung there. In time, a boot emerged, a pink western boot, small and unlikely-looking, like a shrimp in the desert.

She wore a salmon-colored dress, bell-shaped at the bottom, stiff and unyielding, as if filled with wire. Bill would not call this woman petite—short, perhaps. As he walked to her, she shaded her eyes, then reached back for a large blue suitcase and a plastic shopping bag.

"Miss Harding?" he said. "Amber?"

"That's right," she said. "Howdy." She shook his hand vigorously. "Hotter than I expected here, but dry, not like home."

"What Cheer," he said.

"Whatcher," she corrected. "Like what's yer poison?" She laughed loudly, and Bill smiled to be polite.

"Welcome to Wallace," he said.

"We both come from places that begin with a *W*," she remarked.

He said nothing as he lifted bags that seemed heavy as hay bales, and he felt silly when she asked him to pose for a picture outside the depot. "Wish there was someone around to take a shot of both of us," she said.

He put her bags into the back of the pickup, hearing the train pull off with a shrill, mocking whistle.

"Did you have a good trip?" he asked her in the truck.

"Worst food in the United States," she said, "and I didn't trust the water supply, either. Good thing I packed my own food to tide me over. Brought my own bottled water. You're just as tall as I pictured."

"Your ad was accurate, too," he lied, surprised to hear her laugh again, slapping her leg, her petticoats making a sound like wrapping paper.

He took the back roads home, avoiding the town entirely, uncertain of what was the greater cause for embarrassment—the sight of the town or of himself and this woman, frocked up in an outfit a mail-order catalogue might describe as old-fashioned country-western.

"It's greener here than I expected," she said.

"We had lots of snow," he told her, "a good spring runoff. Around this time of year, you get late-afternoon thunderstorms." He was certain he sounded like a hired tour guide, conveying a flatlander to a Wyoming dude ranch. "The party's at six. You can rest up first."

"Rest up?" she said. "This is a once-in-a-lifetime opportunity. I want to see things. Later on, I'll kick up my heels."

He was about to ask her why she put an ad in the magazine and why she picked him, but she piped in by telling him she had never done anything like this before, going off to meet a perfect stranger, even placing an ad. "I'm not a lonely woman," she said. "I turned forty in January. I have studied two-step dancing and spend my spare time reading travel books."

"What do you do in your other time?"

"Well, Bill," she said, "I practice self-improvement. What about you?"

"I'm a little short on spare time," he said, "but I like movies and reading my trade journals, and tinkering with things, gadgets and the like. Sometimes I'll take an appliance apart, for instance, clean it and reassemble it."

She looked at him quizzically. "Do you go to rodeos, dances?"

"Sure, and livestock shows and auctions."

"It's always something, huh?"

"You bet," he said. "I can hardly keep track of the time."

"I haven't seen a single ranch," she remarked.

"We kind of keep to ourselves out here," he said. "My father bought the land, and I've been running things on my own ever since my folks died. My mother was an Easterner, not used to this kind of country." He looked over and saw that she was asleep, her head plastered against the window, ruining a hairdo he suspected she got expressly for this trip, a kind of windswept thing, short on the sides, the wings of the hair above fanning out severely. He brought his hand quietly up to her head, touching the brown hair and finding it softer than he expected.

He nudged her awake at the ranch, and she rubbed her eyes,

casting them over the property and him with a look of disbelief. "I was dreaming," she said. "They say you can go right back into dreams if you concentrate. Never worked for me, though. So, this is the spread. Does it have a name?"

"No. I just call it home."

She grinned. "You have got a sense of humor."

As she looked at the house, the muscular hills flanking it, and the livestock shambling along, he wondered what she might be thinking. "Most everyone around here," he said, "raises cattle or sheep. Not a lot of excitement, I guess you'd say."

"In my dream," she said, "I climbed up a big tree, only it was inside, like a gymnasium, and you know what? There was a polar bear at the bottom of the tree just waiting for me to let go."

"Did you?" he said. "Let go?"

"I woke up. Wish I could go back to it."

"Maybe you ought to rest up before the party," he said. "You've had a long trip."

"But we haven't gotten acquainted, Bill. Wouldn't be right to go to your birthday shindig, hardly knowing a speck about you. That letter of yours piqued my curiosity."

"What part?"

"All of it. Here's a sincere man, I said to myself, but guarded, like me."

"You and me are alike," he said, "in a partial way."

"I'm in the Big Horns," she exclaimed, as she got out of the truck.

He gave her a short tour of the property, and as soon as he led her inside, she moved about the place deliberately, as if it were one she had known all her life. In the kitchen, she admired the gas range and ran her hand over the table. "I'll bet you and your folks had some fine times at this table," she said.

"Yes," Bill lied, knowing it was a place where his mother gazed out the window, and his father, a good man, but unable to fathom his wife and son, tried hard to bring them happiness, buying them presents all the time, TVs, household gadgets, and toys, saying after every offering, "Just the ticket, huh? This'll make a difference."

He watched Amber removing food items from her plastic

bag—oat cakes, cashews, raisins, apples, peaches, carrots. "I'll fix us something light, a nice fruit salad. You've got a big night ahead of you," she said.

He had the odd sensation of being displaced and cosseted, as if he had stepped into another's childhood. He felt sleepy. Curtains ghosted in and out the window near the sink where Amber stood, washing fruit, cutting it, the delicate taps sounding like a code.

"I'll put your suitcase upstairs," he said.

"Sure. Then we'll sit down and eat. The bag's heavy because I couldn't decide what to bring and what to leave behind."

As he lifted it, lumbering up the stairs, he figured the what-to-leave-behind part lost out. He placed it on the bed in the spare room and heard her humming downstairs.

He deliberated a few minutes, then opened her suitcase. She had packed as if guided by traveling how-tos: sweaters rolled neatly underneath folded blouses, shoes in plastic bags, along with cosmetics, dry-skin creams, and makeup said to contain no animal fats or petroleum products. In a clear plastic bag, he saw a red dress, a ruffled thing, its pleats reminding him of an accordion. He cringed at the thought of her showing up in that dress at the party. A white lacy nightgown was on top, still bearing the store tags and surrounded by lavender sachet packets. It had a plunging neckline. He looked up immediately, feeling a rush of shame. But he continued anyway, examining her things, until he found *Soulmates* and a letter inside.

> Dear Amber,
>
> Sure liked your ad. I am about to turn fifty and would like it if we could hook up. I am a bachelor and have an ad in the very same magazine you're featured in (p. 23). Don't have a lot to say about myself, except I am average-looking, nothing to write home about. Those others in the magazine are certain of their likes and pet peeves. I am not. Generally, I take things as they come, but I have been known to wonder what's around the corner. I run my own household. I can cook. I have cattle. It is pretty here. Would like to show it to you. It'd be enough if you could just come for my birthday, as I do not have any close person. I promise no shocks. (The birthday date is May 10.)

She was, he was certain, going to be on the lookout for signs of his desperation. He glanced at himself in the mirror. Well, she was nothing to write home about, either. She wasn't homely, but if he'd had any selection in the matter, he would've discouraged her from getting that hairdo. It made her face seem broad and looming, like one a person might see if he sat up too close to a movie screen.

When he went downstairs, he felt sheepish, half expecting her to know what he had been up to. She was sitting at the table, vials of vitamin pills near two place settings.

"I've got a confession to make," she said. "I poked around in your fridge and kitchen cabinets. You're partial to nitrates. Hooh, the bacon and hamburger meat. I found Cheetos."

"Amber, I've got a confession, too."

"No shocks, remember?"

"I remember," he said and looked over at her. She had almond-shaped green eyes. He had not noticed them before, and she seemed scared, or was it his projection? The table showed signs of her efforts: a bowl of fruit salad, water glasses with slices of lemon, and a loaf of bread, a large, miraculous-looking thing studded with nuts and raisins. "My ad and letter," he said, "weren't entirely true."

"Bill," she said, "I guessed as much right off. You do not pay strict attention to diet, and you like things just the way they are."

"I'd call that a fair assessment," he said.

She served him his food, and as she went at hers, he noticed she had a good appetite.

"I left out the occupation part in my ad," she suddenly announced, "because I don't have one, not at the moment any-how. I was employed at the senior center as a cook. Of course, I couldn't really exercise my skills because they had set menus, bulky stuff, packaged pudding mixes, and so forth. Lost the job because of budget cuts. Isn't that a sad thing, Bill, scrimping on old folks? Some of them are lucky to get one meal a day."

"It is sad," he said, helping himself to more bread.

"Hey," she said, "today's your birthday, and I'm telling you sad-sack stories."

"I like listening to you. How long have you been out of work?"

"Five months," she said. "I've been exploring options. I check out books from the library all the time about significant life changes. I wasn't always on top of my nutrition. Seeing those senior citizens every day, well, it scared me. I'm afraid of old age."

"Shoot," he said, "you're only forty. You look good."

"A lie, Bill. I'm forty-six."

"You look good, Amber."

"And you look like you could use some personal attention, if you don't mind me saying so. Are you afraid of ending up alone, maybe having to go to a home?"

"No, I never pictured that happening to me."

"That's the spirit. I like a man with a positive attitude."

They remained silent for a moment. Bill looked up at the clock, surprised at how quickly time had passed. They had an hour before the party.

"Holy smokes!" she exclaimed. "We leveled off this food, didn't we? Must be the mountain air. We can work it off on the dance floor."

He wanted to remain in the house with Amber Harding, as if the moment might come, as it had minutes ago when he felt expansive, hearing her talk about her life and fears, hearing himself say he wasn't afraid of the same things as she.

"I'm a little rusty," he said. "Haven't kicked up my heels in a while." As soon as he spoke, he felt deflated, wishing he had tried to tell her something significant.

"Back home," she said, "we got a television program that shows people two-stepping. Looks like fun to me, but most of the dancers could stand to lose weight. They dress in western wear and have themselves a real good time."

"We've got a band and everything tonight," he said.

She looked at her watch. "Guess we better change."

Her petticoats made a noisy sound as she went up the stairs. He followed meekly, regretting going through her suitcase.

"What a pretty room," she said. "I plan to get up bright and early tomorrow to watch you with the cattle. I've been picturing it."

"Big difference sometimes," he said, "between what you picture and the way things really are."

He closed her door and went to his room. He had not planned on changing his outfit, but he went to the closet, deciding to wear the fancy blue and red striped shirt an aunt had mailed him. He took off his Ropers and put on black shiny boots and his good black Stetson. He tried various poses in the mirror, considering himself from all angles. He recalled the photographs in *Soulmates,* the men trying too hard to look like something made up. He removed the hat, and went downstairs.

She was taking her time, it seemed, and his impatience and resentment surprised him. He could hear no sounds upstairs and imagined that she had dozed off again, or, worse, had discovered his luggage excavation and was pouting. He would have a prepared story to tell her, he decided, and would divulge that the entire thing had been someone's idea of a gag. He would give her some money for her troubles and see to it that she returned to Iowa in the morning.

"Close your eyes," he heard her say at the landing.

Obediently and without hesitation, he did as she said, hearing his heart beating frankly, and the rasping sound of her clothing as she came down the stairs.

She was upon him suddenly, smelling of lavender, her warm breath on his face. "Surprise," she said and gave him a peck on his cheek.

He opened his eyes and saw her in the red pleated dress, her feet encased in uncomfortable-looking new boots, also red, and, of all things, rattlesnake-tail earrings that trembled with warnings. She held a gift-wrapped package, which she offered to him, her hands cupped as if she might be presenting a drink of water. "Hold on," she said. "I want a picture of you. Don't you look nice."

He smiled, his eyes startled by the flash. "You went all out," he said.

"I got the dress in Cedar Rapids," she said. "Go on, open your present."

He removed the wrapping paper, handing it to her, and feeling like a boy again. Inside a jewelry store box was a gift card that said: "Happy Birthday, Bill. Mighty glad I could hitch my wagon to yours on this special night. Hope you like this little token of appreciation."

It was a gold key chain of a bull's head. On either horn was an initial, *W* and *L.*

"I know you go by Bill," she said, "but I figured your proper name was William. Besides, we've got those *W*'s in common, remember?"

"It's a great gift," he said. "Gold. Monogrammed and everything. Thank you, thank you."

"Soon as I saw it, I said, Girl, this man is taking the bull by the horns. This is the gift for him."

"You're the one who's taking the bull by the horns. I'll think of you every day when I see the gift."

She laughed loudly. "You're a riot, Bill."

He saw his hands shake as he put his keys on the new ring, Amber helping him. "I got big, clumsy hands," he said.

She put her hand on his and said nothing for a moment. "You're a cattleman, a gentleman, too, I can tell."

"You don't know me at all," he said.

"It's part of the attraction, Bill. I like a sense of mystery."

"No shocks, though. Amber," he said, after a pause, "something of a shocking nature might just happen tonight. You see—"

"Let's just pretend, okay? Would that be all right? I'll know when I see a certain woman what's going on. By the way, you might want to lay off the caffeine. That's what makes you shake."

But it was she who was shaking, the snake earrings confirming it. It was all an act, he realized. This woman was guarded, as her ad claimed, putting on a big outward show for him or because she might've assumed she could be someone else. When he told her he liked her the way she was, she looked at him as if she had missed something.

He helped her into the truck, her dress covering most of the seat. They said little on the ride into town, except for her comments about the views. "Is this the road we came in on earlier?" she asked. "Seems different to me."

"No, I took you home on a different road this afternoon."

"And I ended up falling asleep. I missed the sights."

"When I was a boy," he said, "I went on a trip with my folks and saw a crop-dusting plane fall right out of the sky. I kept waiting for it to hit. It was a yellow plane, and we were headed right toward it."

"What happened?"

"This is the funny part," he said. "My parents claimed I was asleep and had dreamed up the whole thing."

"If you have a falling dream," she said, "you always awake before hitting the ground. That's what they say. It happens to me all the time."

"Me, too," he said. He had not thought about the plane in a long time and was certain, even now, that he had seen black numbers on the wings and breath-colored streams of smoke in the tail section. "I had something happen once," he said and went on to tell her of the mountain lion incident, describing the rich smell of spring grass and the dampness he felt through his clothing as he lay on the ground. "A mountain lion sounds like a female in distress. This one had my number, all right, but she chose not to pounce on me. She wasn't even skittish. She gawked at me, then fell right to sleep. I've never told this to anyone, Amber, but for some reason, things seemed harder after that."

"So, Bill," she said, "you reckon your friends will wonder about me at the party?"

"They'll be happy for me, I reckon."

It might have been a used-car lot for the number of vehicles at the Union Hall and for the banners someone had ringed around the parking area. The hall was lit up, and the band was playing an unrecognizable tune, something that sounded like it needed a faster tempo. Bill got out of the truck and opened the door for Amber, but she seemed reluctant to step out. He assured her she'd be looked after. Just as she had emerged from the train, her boot appeared first, and the sight of it suspended there moved him. He put his hands on her waist and lifted her from the cab. She seemed suddenly and surprisingly light.

"You're crying," he said, seeing her trying to conceal it.

"Tears of fulfillment, Bill. Let's go."

The townspeople had decorated the hall lavishly with balloons, crepe paper, and an enormous banner that said: "Happy Birthday, Bill. Just because the corral's in sight don't mean you can't enjoy the pasture. Watch out for cowpies, though." Friends had signed the banner with good-luck wishes for many birthdays to come. When a cheer went up, Amber held his hand tightly. People approached, standing to look at him as if they couldn't recognize him.

Then they returned to the buffet table and the dance floor. He led Amber to the food, pointing out the Rocky Mountain oysters, and watching her trying some and seeming to enjoy them. She ladled potato salad on her plate and helped herself to chips and dip and hot dogs. People nodded when he introduced her to them, making little show of any surprise, as if they had known her a long time.

"You've got lots of good friends," she said when they finally sat down. "You're lucky."

"Yeah," he said. "I am lucky."

In a short time, the band stopped, and Ned Jencks stood in the center of the floor, making jokes. He was followed by others also making jokes about birthdays and Bill, like TV celebrity roasts. Bill laughed along, but knew he'd never remember a single one of their lines. Ned Jencks called to him, and Bill reached for Amber's hand, but she declined. "It's your night," she said.

He felt embarrassed standing there, and he dreaded the spectacle of a surprise announcement. A drum roll began, and people quieted down. "The grand finale," Ned said. Bill looked over at Amber. She was sitting primly by herself at a long table. Then the lights dimmed.

Someone was making his way from the back door toward the center of the room, carrying a saddle. It was the sheepman, Bill realized, the one who had rescued him three years ago. The sheepman slowed at Amber's table. "Please," Bill muttered to himself. "Don't tell her people cooked up a scheme." He closed his eyes and waited.

"For you," the man said, startling him, coming suddenly upon him. He leaned towards Bill's ear and whispered, "I did it, picked Miss Harding out special. This here saddle was someone else's idea." He placed the saddle at Bill's feet.

Bill thanked him profusely and saw him retreat, walking uncertainly for a moment, until the lights came back on.

Instead of the "Happy Birthday" song, the band played a waltz. They were out of tune, and the selection they chose eluded Bill. People swarmed on the floor, their boots clacking loudly as if they were running instead of dancing. Without hesitation, Bill joined the fray, having no trouble at all finding Amber Harding for himself.

Creatures

Elna had once said that beautifying was nothing more than grabbing Mother Nature by the throat and showing her who was boss. When Shelly arrived for her appointment, her friend was vigorously at work on an alabaster-complexioned teenager. Testimonies of terse, coiled ringlets spiraled downward at the girl's ears and the back of her neck.

"Hey there!" Elna called as Shelly settled into a chair across from what they laughingly called "the hot seat."

"Where's your cat population?" Shelly asked. She unbuttoned her coat and slipped it onto the back of the chair. Elna's cats had become a quick barometer for the household's travail since Elna's marriage had been in trouble. No matter in what state she arrived, Shelly always felt strangely cheered by the prospect of Elna's troubles—maybe because they were harder to solve than her own.

When Elna and Eugene had tried to split up the previous year, the clients had commiserated with Elna, said she was "doing the right thing." That Eugene was "only along for the ride," etc. But in the end, Elna had let him stay, and her clients now kept their opinions to themselves.

This time around, Eugene was calling the shots. The day after New Year's, he'd announced he was moving out, but not until spring, when an apartment he wanted would come available. Elna had complained so bitterly about the marriage earlier that her friends were astonished she'd agreed to this. But theory had it Eugene might settle more congenially if she did things his way. Shelly knew it was harder for Elna to let the marriage go, now that Eugene was the one heading for the door. Still, things had been building up.

In the months prior to their current situation, Eugene had been giving all the signs of a man having an affair—late nights, strange excuses. Once, he'd even called Elna to say the gold cap on his front tooth had fallen into a load of gravel. It would be a while. Another time, he'd phoned from a training session in a nearby town. He'd been learning to install a new kind of insulation. The afternoon meeting was supposed to allow him to come home that night, but he'd called Elna with a change of plans. He said his hemorrhoids were bothering him. They were so bad, he couldn't make the two-hour drive home. He'd have to spend the night there alone, in pain. He was sorry. He was having to stand up while making this very call, he said, an odd catch in his voice. Elna's friends said it didn't sound like your regular excuse. He'd also started bringing home single rosebuds wrapped in cellophane from the supermarket. Out of the blue, he'd call Elna from a pay phone to say, "Hi, honey, just wanted you to know I love you."

It had been hard for Elna to believe Eugene had somebody on the side—even harder to admit it, once she believed it. Shelly had been all too willing to confirm the diagnosis. She'd had her own experiences with cheating men. She'd been glad to share with Elna an article in a women's magazine that told all the signs. "Constant irritability and fault-finding"—those were two they'd agreed especially fit Eugene.

As she settled herself in her chair, Shelly continued to scan the shop for the cats. When she didn't see them, she called to them by name. Elna, who'd been methodically swiveling the curling rod to the teenager's head, withdrew it and stepped over to Shelly. She bent and, in a confidential tone, said, "Honey—Lucky and Lightning are no longer with us. They've gone where all good, but sadly flawed creatures go." Then she retreated to her client, having seemingly dispensed with a very unpleasant matter.

Shelly tried to absorb what she'd heard. Clearly things had taken a desperate turn. She consoled herself, noticing that the remaining young black cat, Veronica, was basking in the last rays of afternoon sunlight. She nudged the cat with the toe of her shoe, and its eyes blinked open and shut several times, as if completing some coded message from a dream-filled interior, then shut them.

"I wish I could have gone with them, straight to Kitty Heaven," Elna was saying. "Do not pass Safeway or Twelve-Star Video. One minute the needle, then poof! Heaven."

The idea of heaven had always eluded Shelly, and, linked to "kitty," the word only revived images of the two missing cats, stranded in some lonely outpost of the mind. They had been fixtures the ten years she'd been coming to the shop, always curled in one chair or another. Each time a client uprooted them, they would tolerantly re-situate themselves.

Lightning, a huge white cat with a streak of black down one side, was forever inviting himself into a client's lap and having to be scolded down. The other, Lucky, a tea-colored part Siamese, was like the sleep of the world. She had once crawled into the clothes dryer for a nap and managed to endure several minutes on Knits/Gentle/Low with a load of bikini panties. "If she'd been on Cottons, she'd be looking *up* to the mice," Elna had quipped. She'd been affectionate about even the failures of her cats. It was hard to believe she'd had them put to sleep.

Recently Shelly had heard on a talk show that willful deaths or injuries to innocent pets often signaled a worsening of relationships between their owners. Elna leaned against the mirror that ran the length of the room and appraised the rather glum-looking teenager undergoing transformation. "Lucky, with her own little motorized tongue, licked down an entire cube of butter, then did her job in my yarn basket. *One* of the clinchers," Elna said. "They just got too old." Shelly didn't contradict her friend, though she suspected age had nothing to do with it.

"Veronica, you lucky devil," Shelly said conspiratorially to the remaining cat, "to be young and in control of your functions—house-trained like the rest of us."

Shelly had been feeling the closest thing to joy in a long time when she'd entered the shop. She hadn't been prepared to hear about the disposal of Elna's cats, and was dismayed at how suddenly any relief in life could be so quickly burdened again with sadness. Her eighty-year-old mother had gone through a diagnostic test that afternoon which had taken longer than expected. During the test, Shelly had sat with a magazine on her lap, imagining the long thin probe being worked into her mother's stomach and upper intestines while the doctor's eye searched for the reason she had been bleeding. Shelly had mentally entered that darkness as a small wink of light grazing and scraping the deep interior. The trouble with the imagination, she thought, was that the mind could go anywhere, so you could never tell from one moment to the next where you might end up.

The doctor had prepared Shelly and her mother to deal with stomach cancer or ulcers, but miraculously nothing had been found. She had come to her hair appointment prepared to celebrate her mother's good fortune. But the deaths of the cats had changed all that.

"Oh, honey, we were just bawling our eyes out after I took them to the vet's. My clients sat in their chairs and cried, and I blubbered right along with them," Elna said, bending to the teenager. "Cousin Flo came over on her lunch break to say goodbye to them. Then I closed those poor babies into the same cardboard carrier and drove them to the clinic."

To be shut into a small dark space against your will was one of the most frightening things Shelly could imagine. Her mind veered out of the box with its doomed cats and back toward her friend. Shelly could see Elna didn't know at all how to represent what she'd done. She was alternately hot and cold over it—pitying the cats while trying to justify her part in their fate.

The bells on the shop door jangled, and Gretchen, Elna's daughter, entered with her two children. Her face looked puffy to Shelly, like a person who'd been either hit in the face or crying, or both. "I need some of your magic hair spray, Mom," Gretchen announced. She picked peppermint candies for her children from the fishbowl which had been converted to a candy dish when the fish were found floating belly-up one morning. "Hey, it's like a funeral in here."

"If you only knew, dear," Elna said.

"She *off-ed* Lucky and Lightning," said the teenager, like the surviving member of a Greek chorus.

Gretchen made a sound deep in her throat—an eruption that sprang from the unpredictability of human utterance itself.

"I can't believe you did that, Mom," Gretchen said, holding her children by their jacket collars to keep them from taking another step toward their grandmother.

"I suppose I could have just let them scramble for it outside," Elna said, ignoring her. "But I would have been worrying all the time.

Besides, it's cold out there, and if something chased them—"

"My cat sleeps with me," said the teenager, a beacon of ruthless insinuation.

"Lightning slept with me, too," Elna said quietly, making clear that no amount of intimacy could have staved off the inevitable. "The last straw was him spraying down the floor vent. We breathed cat piss for a week. I dumped cologne, Purex, baby powder, a bottle of cedar scent down it—even got back into my hippie days and burned incense."

With the cats gone, the shop felt larger, less cozy. Shelly noticed Veronica had moved to the back of a chair at the window, one paw V-ing the Venetian blind where she gazed into the yard. "She's looking for them," Elna said. "She can't imagine what's keeping them, thank God. Lucky and Lightning," she mused, "forever expected in Veronica's cat mind."

"We didn't even have a funeral," Gretchen said, plaintively.

"Flo and I thought about going sentimental, burying them in the backyard with two little stone markers from one of those catalogues, but I chickened out," Elna said. "No—they just went into the incinerator. 'Cremate them,' I told the vet, 'and do whatever you do—I mean, when no one takes whatever's left.'"

At the mention of the backyard, Gretchen's children wriggled from her and eased out the shop entrance. Shelly wished, for a moment, she could go with them. She knew Elna made light of things when she felt them most, that she would be cryptic with bursts of admission until she had eroded some kind of invisible barrier between her actions and her feelings.

"Honestly," Elna said, "Lucky would sashay in from the great outdoors, stand right up against the door she'd just walked through, lift her leg, and spray, right in front of me!"

"I didn't know female cats lifted their legs," Shelly said.

"This one did. Lifted it just like a Tom, smart as you please, and shot her tank. Then she'd prance off like she'd accomplished something."

"Little did she know," Gretchen said.

"You bet," Elna said, with muscle in her voice. "The Kevorkian of cats had called her number." It was five o'clock. Elna walked over and closed the Venetian blinds. "Open them, shut them.

Who cares?" Elna said. She returned to the girl in the swivel chair and rotated her toward the mirror.

Elna's swirling of the chair, then stopping it, steadied everything for a moment. With the blinds closed, the eyes of the shop seemed closed, and Shelly felt the particular intimacy of women alone in a room, talking, trading confidences, speaking their minds.

"Kimberly's wearing forest green to the prom," Elna said, her voice rubbing the consonants in "forest green." The ebony of trees at dusk entered Shelly's mind—a pungent, under-boughs' darkness that overpowered the smell of hair spray mingled with cat urine. She imagined night falling in the forests on the mountains behind the town, the creatures alive there, able for nights and days in snow and rain, searching for food, for shelter.

A strong draft ran through the shop as Gretchen's children burst into the room again. "Stay inside, please, children, or stay out," Elna said. Shelly realized eerily that Elna was using the same tone with the children she'd used with the missing cats. The children had just dropped to their knees in the middle of the floor with the black cat when the shop door suddenly opened and Eugene entered. He veered around the children and, without a glance, shot past everyone into the kitchen.

"Brace yourself," Elna said, with a knowing look.

"Mom, okay if I make a long distance call?" Gretchen asked, seizing the moment. "It's about a job. They shut off my phone." Shelly saw Elna go into her stoic helpful-against-the-odds mode.

"Use the kitchen phone," Elna said, "but make it snappy."

Shelly could feel how stretched beyond limits Elna was because of Gretchen, yet she knew Elna would likely do a lifetime of setting aside boundaries for her daughter. Shelly hated her friend's helplessness, but she also took pity and even admired her, because at least helplessness meant you were out there in the deep water, risking things. Her friend lived somehow beyond the prudent, fix-it mentality of others she knew. For Elna, things were patently wrong, and they were going further in that direction, no matter what Shelly or anyone wished for her. She tried to imagine a life where Elna wouldn't be burdened and ensnared, but no matter what she considered, no likely solution occurred to her.

Soon Gretchen could be heard laughing and exclaiming through the open door to the kitchen. She was always "looking for a job" or "about to get a job." In this, it struck Shelly, she wasn't so different from Eugene. After a few minutes, the register of her voice shifted, and she could be heard talking to Eugene. Her tone was placating, the way someone who is used to calamity tries to soothe away consequences.

"All that room out there!" Eugene suddenly blurted. "All that ocean and forest, and she has to ram a goddamn California lawyer with two kids in a goddamn camper." On the way into the house, Eugene had spotted a dent Gretchen had left in his pickup. Elna stopped what she was doing to listen.

"Why not ram the ocean? Something with a little give and take," Eugene cried at the top of his voice. "Aim for an oil tanker, be ambitious—a raft of logs, a fishing trawler. Give chaos a chance!" he ranted.

"Eugene's off his spool again," Elna said, a high ripple in her voice meant to counter his tirade by seeming to indicate the malfunction of an ordinary household appliance. Eugene had always claimed that Gretchen's problems, her sudden incursions on his and Elna's lives, her bad choices in men, two children by an absent father—these ongoing pressures had made it impossible for him and Elna. To a certain extent, Shelly thought he was right. Whatever faults Eugene had, no one could dispute the fact that he'd been an absolute natural, a veritable blue ribbon champion, at living with things in a mess. He reentered the beauty shop now, drawn backwards by some invisible force centered in Elna.

"You never asked *me*," he said to the company at large, his back to Elna. "The queen of demolition derbies, and you loan her my truck like loaning a can opener."

"My God, Gene, it's only a dent," Elna said, hardly grazing his attention.

"I can't get over it," he said. "Snuff the cats. Ram the truck. I guess I'm lucky to have a door to walk through." He hitched his jeans and ducked to look at himself in the mirror. His black hair roiled in a glistening wave he pushed back from his forehead.

Shelly noticed Eugene had dark circles under his eyes and he'd lost weight. So had Elna, for that matter. She'd always been wasp-waisted, but now her skin seemed oddly transparent, as if everything inside, the entire circuitry of her body, were visible to whoever came within her parameters. Eugene disappeared into the kitchen.

Elna spun the prom girl toward her and gave her a hand mirror so she could see the back of her head. "Mister Righteous," Elna said. " 'Honey, honey,' he'd say—'there's a mess in here. You might want to check it out.' Well, I checked it out all right!"

The prom girl stared into the mirror, adrift on the small bright raft of her face in a shark-infested sea. She bobbed her head, and the drooling curls danced briefly.

Meanwhile Gretchen's children had forced the surviving cat under the nail-polishing table. Shelly had the all-encompassing sensation that places of refuge were thinning out across the face of the planet. Soon enough, if a human impulse fixed its mark on a creature, it would be found and destroyed. There could be delay, but no lasting retreat. Maybe it had always been this way, and she was just now realizing it.

"You're going to look amazing in that forest green," Elna said to the teenager. "If that boy was shy before, he's going to be speechless now." The girl pulled at the neck of her T-shirt and frowned. It was clear the shirt wouldn't lift easily over her hairdo.

"Is that expendable?" Elna asked.

"I guess so," the girl said, vaguely.

"Darlin', you'd be surprised what's expendable by the time you get my age." Elna reached into a drawer and took out a pair of scissors.

"I still don't see how you did what you did, Mom," Gretchen said, reentering from the kitchen. She was speaking to her mother in the mirror. "Just because you and Gene aren't making it. We had those cats fifteen years," she said. "You're mean. Just plain mean!" Shelly could tell her friend was carefully not letting herself be provoked.

Elna took the scissors and began a vertical cut from the girl's neckline between the hints of her breasts. The scissors snipped viciously in the silence of the beauty shop. When she finished, she dropped them into the drawer, then slid it shut with a decisive thud.

From the kitchen, a loud cascading of pans sounded. Eugene swore, and Shelly looked up to see him pace past the doorway. He returned to stare briefly at the women in the shop, then broke away into the kitchen again, having evidently collected fresh energy from just glancing at them.

Child voices murmured from under the table. Shelly felt an undercurrent in the room, as when messages and secrets are being exchanged. She remembered what it was to be a child, crawling into the musky darkness under beds and tables, able to hear everything that went on; being there, yet not there. Once a pan of grease on the stove had caught fire while she'd been exploring the space under her parents' bed. Her mother had run through the rooms, carrying the flaming pan, yelling, "Fire!" and calling for her in a tone of ultimate panic, which changed to fury when she'd eventually discovered her under the bed. Even to this day, Shelly instinctually connected certain states of anxiety and threat with fire.

"Things are going to change around here," Elna said. "I see to everything else, and I'm seeing to that. There you go, dear," she said to the girl. Elna helped the prom girl lift the T-shirt over her head through the rough slit. The girl sat uneasily a moment in her bra until Gretchen reached into the little side room where her mother mixed hair colors and handed her a flannel shirt. The girl slipped into it quickly, shyly.

"Kimberly's going to dress in my bedroom," Elna said. "I told her I'd do her hair for free just to see her in her dress."

A mournful howl came from the cat, then giggling from the children. Their legs spidered from under the frilly table. "Jo-Jo, come out!" Gretchen called to her son. When he didn't appear, she pulled him forth like a wheelbarrow by his legs.

"After what she did, I'm scared to leave my kids with her," Gretchen said. She took up a comb from the counter and raked it across her son's scalp. Gretchen's daughter approached Elna's work area clutching the glaring cat by its middle.

Shelly was used to the charade of Gretchen and her mother fighting over the children. She'd been in the shop once when Elna had called the Children's Protective Services, threatening to take them away. But since Gretchen left her children with Elna most of the time anyway, the threat was empty.

"When I was pregnant with her," Elna had told Shelly, "if I'd known the trouble I was in for, I'd have climbed onto the roof and dashed myself to the pavement like a watermelon."

The prom girl slowly eased into the doorway. Everyone had turned to look. Eugene was visible over one bare shoulder in the fluorescent kitchen light. Gretchen pulled at one of the small gold rings in her nose and, with her eyes on the girl, sat down under a dryer that was cocked open near Shelly.

The girl rustled forward, leaving a cool tracing of air in her wake. The taffeta sheen of the dress dimpled with dark whispering pools as she glided to the center of the room and turned, her arms lightly at her sides. Like a calm fir tree in their clearing, she stood for a moment, then began again to turn, slowly, like someone at the center of a dream who did not see them, or if she did, saw them from far away.

Suddenly the black cat let out a long, involuntary moan. It struggled free of the child's grasp and leaped precariously onto the swivel chair. Before they realized what was happening, the cat was midair in a short unwieldy arc toward the girl's bare shoulders. Its claws sank into the pure fleshy center of the room. The girl gave a raw cry of pain. If an eagle had dropped onto her shoulder to lift her from earth, she would have given such a cry. Poised, electric, the cat stared violently at them from its human perch.

Elna rushed forward with her face turned away, like a woman about to handle fire. She caught the cat by its fur and flung it from the girl's shoulders against the mirror. For a moment, the animal appeared to be leaping out of itself, multiplied, quenched and resurrected at once as it rippled along the counter, then became airborne again, clearing the fishbowl before it dropped to the floor and streaked past their ankles. The girl began to shudder, then to sob openly, holding herself.

When Shelly moved, it was to Elna. She caught her friend firmly by the shoulders and held her. "There," Shelly said. "There." She took Elna's helpless blows against her back until they subsided. The cat had made its escape through the kitchen. Shelly imagined it tunneling into the farthest recesses of the house.

When Elna broke free and turned to the others, it was clear she'd crossed some boundary, from which she looked back at them like one who holds territory and holds it beyond challenge. Everyone else in the room balanced unsteadily on the rim of the moment. A switch had somehow been thrown in all their heads at once. Night had fallen suddenly in their clearing. Each of them gazed warily out of the darkness at the others with the lime-green eyes of the young black cat, a creature forced to its limits and past.

There was unearthly calm and stillness in the space they now inhabited. They seemed suspended in the close chemical smell of the room, but elsewhere in the house, they heard things falling, glassware shattering—the racing, desperate plunge of an animal seeking its full measure of darkness.

Shelly stared at her friend and realized she didn't know what Elna might do next—that everything, and everyone, had somehow been reduced to their simplest, most destructible element. She was aware that her childhood dread of fire was unreasonably and wildly alive in her. Whatever was flammable in the room rose to make itself known all at once—the nylon flounce along the mirror, cans of hair spray, raw clumps of hair at the base of the swivel chair, cellophane glinting from a wastebasket, hair again, the very hair on her head. The hair on all their heads. A woman with a pan of fire seemed to be running through her mind, fanning oxygen into flames, igniting whatever she passed. Shelly knew she and the others had arrived at some precarious boundary between what was human and what was not—where, despite their strongest instincts, they seemed to have agreed that no one would run from this room.

Dear Nicole

They grew up playing hockey on Everett Pond, long after supper, after homework and *Bonanza* or *Laugh-In* or *My Three Sons,* after they said good night and went to their rooms yawning as if headed to sleep. The grown-ups pretended not to know about the rendezvous at the rink, but some of the fathers had, as boys, given birth to the midnight game, a raucous winter lullaby for the far end of the street.

Allie Sprinkle was one of five or six girls who listened for their parents to fall quiet behind their bedroom doors before they padded downstairs in their nighties, tucked hems into leggings, pulled on boots and big jackets and mittens but left their hats behind, and went out to the cold where their friends were waiting. They gathered at the top of King's Hill and locked arms for the descent on snow to the edge of the pond, where there was an extra goal box turned over for them to sit on.

When they saw them coming, the boys halted their game so the girls could settle. They paused to lean on their sticks, glad for the excuse to catch up on their breathing, then resumed darting and slapping with a louder, sharper energy because they were being watched. The game was dottily lighted by the moon and stars, and by four bulbs strung on a parade of extension cords around the rink. The girls clapped their mittens together and gave soft shouts of "Way to go, Burkie," and "Guard that goal!" When someone scored, a cheer rose from the players and their crowd, and Allie turned her face straight up to the black sky, closing her eyes, tasting a love and safety she knew would never be duplicated, that certainty a sweet stab in her heart.

The winter most of them were twelve, the season came to an end without warning on a crinkly December night. Nicole Rueger was sitting on the goal bench, next to Allie, coughing into her gloves, when Gerald Burke hit the puck with such force that Allie Sprinkle swallowed the ball of Beech-Nut wedged in her cheek.

There was a moment during which they all lost time—they knew the puck was flying somewhere, but they couldn't see it—and then Allie felt the cold whish of it by her face. She turned her head to follow the puck and watched Nicole fall from the bench beside her, headfirst into the hard bank, making a cracking sound as she landed. The boys skated over and stood in a bigger circle behind the one the girls formed around Nicole.

"Get her up," Gerald Burke said. He was wobbling on his blades.

Allie bent over to touch Nicole. There was no blood, but they all knew she was knocked out.

"Don't move her," said Michael Usiak, whose father drove an ambulance for Memorial.

"Well, what are we supposed to do?"

"I say we carry her up the hill. She'll probably wake up by the time we get there."

"Everybody wait a minute," Michael said. He was unfastening his skates, and the laces flashed in the moonlight. He began to run up the hill in his sock feet. "I'll get my dad," he told them, tripping as he turned to call over his shoulder. "Somebody take off their jacket and cover her up."

It was so cold they shivered just listening to his words. They all knew he was right, but not one of them, facing the wind, could imagine undressing in it.

"It was Gerald who hit her," Dickie Domermuth said after the silence. "He should be the one."

Even as Dickie spoke, Gerald was unzipping his jacket, flinging his body out of it like a wrestler escaping a hold. He stuck the toe of his blade into the bank to stay steady as he lowered the jacket across Nicole. He went to take off his sweater, too, but Dickie caught his arm and said, "That's enough." For a moment the wind stopped above them, and they heard peace in the trees.

Then came the sound of grown-ups running, out of the houses and down the slick hill. It was more than just Michael and his father; most of the other parents came, too. Allie could see her mother's nightie flapping under her coat, and her father's robe belt dragging across snow. It looked like a scattered army closing in for the kill.

"I didn't mean it," Gerald confessed to them, as he fell on his knees to the ground.

It turned out that Nicole had a concussion, which sent her to the hospital through the rest of the night and then gave her headaches for the next sixteen years, until she had her first child, when the pain seemed to leak out of her with the milk. After she and Gerald were married, she never mentioned the headaches to him in private, but if they had guests over and there was a light-hearted feel to the room, she sometimes went into a little routine to recreate what had happened back then.

"I was sitting on the goal bench, next to Allie Sprinkle the nerd," she began, tapping a salt shaker against the tablecloth to place her listeners at the scene. "It was one of those frosty nights where you can feel your nose hairs, and all of a sudden this puck comes whizzing through the air."

At this point Nicole usually chose the wine cork to simulate the puck's route. She aimed it at the salt shaker and let fly. Even when she hit the mark, there wasn't enough weight to push the shaker over, so she flicked at it with her fingernail, and salt scattered across the cloth. The guests laughed at this unlikely representation of Nicole knocked flat in the snow, but anyone who looked carefully through the candlelight could see Gerald wincing behind his smile. Someone always asked how the two of them ended up together, after that, but Gerald and Nicole always said they had no idea.

Usually, it was the accident itself that caught the guests' attention. But on a Friday night when they had some people from Gerald's office over for crab cakes and beer, one of the men said, "Allie Sprinkle. That sounds familiar. Would I know that name?"

"I don't see how," Nicole said, twirling her wineglass by the stem in a circle beside her plate. "This was a little town called Oxbow, up near Buffalo. By a butchery. They had the best barbecued wings you could ask for, but the air smelled like blood."

"Do you ever get back there?" someone asked.

"Not if we can help it," Nicole said. "Gerald's parents are dead, and we make mine fly if they want to see us." She was looking deep into her glass. Then she gave one of her famous smiles, as if to indicate she was only kidding, and swiveled in her chair to face Gerald. Ever since the headaches had left her, she found she couldn't resist making sudden movements with her neck. Sometimes Gerald caught her doing it, and asked her why, but she said she didn't know. She knew she would never have the courage to tell him she missed the pain he had given her, if this turned out to be the truth.

Nicole looked around the room at her guests, at their confident and capable faces; at the solid and pretty furniture she owned, and the silver tableware; at the ceiling above which her sleeping children dreamed of things they had yet to learn would never happen on this unmagical earth. She felt filled and blessed, and knew she should wonder what she had done to deserve any of it.

"Coffee?" she said brightly to the other end of the table, as she felt the mood of the party sliding toward the floor.

Across from her, Gerald looked up. He smiled at the woman he had nearly killed once, then come to believe he loved.

"I'll get it," he told her. Before he left the room, he reached over to set the salt shaker back on its bottom, and he brushed the spilled crystals from the tablecloth.

The man who had asked at the party about Allie Sprinkle remembered, on his way home, where he had heard her name before. "It's the woman who took Laura's picture," he said to his wife, who was driving. "That woman Nicole was talking about, from their hometown? Allie Sprinkle. That's the name on the portrait we had done of Laura, when we lived in Rochester."

"How do you remember these things? Besides, that's too much of a coincidence," his wife said. "It could be a whole different person with the same name. Besides, who cares?"

"Well, I do," her husband said. "I like things like this. I like it when it turns out that people knew each other somewhere before. It always makes me feel better, like the whole world is connected somehow. Just think about it," he continued, holding the dashboard as she cut a corner too fast. "If you believe in the Bible, we're all descended from Adam and Eve. If you go with the Big Bang, we all exploded from the same star, or crawled up from the same batch of ooze. Doesn't that make you feel better about the world? To imagine everybody's related to everyone else?"

"It doesn't really make me feel anything," his wife told him. "Besides, you've been drinking."

"It always makes me feel better," he said again. They were home.

He remembered bringing his daughter to have her photograph taken by Allie Sprinkle. Allie worked where she lived, a house on a side street in a town whose name he could not recall, although Nicole's "Oxbow" seemed to ring some bell. *A. Sprinkle* was bolted in black above the mailbox.

When she came to the door, Allie looked small against the shadows of the foyer behind her, like a child herself. But once they were in the studio, which had been converted from an upstairs bedroom, she inhabited twice as much space as her body required. The air around her was charged with movement, not only of her arms, which flew around Laura's face and hair, but also of an energy that was almost visible in itself, like the confettied light thrown off by sparklers on the Fourth of July.

The portrait they ordered of Laura resembled a piece of art from an earlier century. Her eyes were locked in the camera's hold, and they contained a cast of—could it be mercy?—that neither he nor his wife recognized from before the photograph, and that they hadn't witnessed since. His wife went so far as to suggest that the negatives had been altered. They loved the picture for the beauty that was their child, but they were each secretly afraid of it, and they each learned a way of walking through the living room without looking into those eyes.

He became intrigued by the idea of the Burkes and Allie Sprinkle having known each other as children, and by his role as their connection later in life. In the strongbox that held the family's papers, he found the sheet of contact proofs Allie had given them, and he ordered an extra print of Laura's photograph. With the order he enclosed a note to Allie, telling her of how her name had come up at a dinner party in Maryland. She sent the picture but did not respond to the note, and as the years passed, as Laura grew up to look less and less like the wise child watching him from above the piano, he found it easier to look at the face in the filigreed frame. Soon after the dinner party, he left the firm where

Gerald Burke worked, and so he had no way of knowing that in the month following his message to western New York, a letter arrived at the Burkes' home in Silver Spring, addressed to Nicole (Rueger) Burke. In the return address corner of the envelope was a design logo composed of a camera, the name Sprinkle, and the legend *Please let me shoot your kids.*

The letter had been tucked, under the load of the day's mail, into a newsmagazine; Gerald found it that night as he turned the pages. He was in bed, and Nicole was in the bathroom. When he heard the bathroom door opening, he stuck the envelope back in the magazine, feeling his heart beat beneath his Orioles shirt. Nicole was damp from the shower, and she leaned over to kiss him, smelling of shampoo and cream. "Just a minute, honey," he told her, and he carried the magazine into the bathroom.

He held the letter up over the sink, reached for the nail file in the toothbrush cup, and slit the seal with a sweep.

"Dear Nicole," the letter started. *"It's been a long time, but I don't believe any of us could ever forget Everett Street. Or each other.*

"I understand you have a son and daughter. Congratulations. Although I'm still amazed that you would marry Gerald, when that puck was meant for me."

As he read this, Gerald felt a chill on the backs of his hands, but when he looked beyond the paper into the mirror, he saw that he was smiling. With relief he noted that Allie had added a postscript—*"Just kidding"*—in the margin of that sinister line.

"The next time you're in Oxbow, I'd be happy to photograph your children. My work is taking pictures, and kids are my specialty. Enclosed is my card. In the meantime, my best to Gerald, and I hope the headaches have gone away.

"Sincerely, Allie S."

Gerald studied the signature closely, the way the *S* towered over the other letters, the way the *A* of *Allie* resembled a star. He put it back in the magazine and hid the whole surreptitious package in the basket of periodicals by the toilet. He returned to bed and made love to his wife with such attention and energy that when it was over and they looked at each other before turning out the light, he was not surprised to see suspicion in the face she turned to him.

. . .

That was November. At the beginning of December, Gerald took Allie Sprinkle's note and business card out of his briefcase, where he had been keeping the envelope since the day after it arrived. Answering the phone, she did not seem to hesitate when he said who he was, and for a moment he was afraid they might have had some contact in the past twenty years that he had forgotten since. "I intercepted your letter to Nicole," he told Allie, "by accident. But then I didn't give it to her, because I wanted to make it a surprise. The photograph. We're coming there for Christmas, and I was wondering if you could take a picture of our kids." Whenever he lied, his throat closed up and he had to keep clearing it, but he figured Allie would just think it was habit.

Allie's voice did not sound familiar, yet Gerald could, as they spoke, envision her clearly at the other end of the line. But then he realized he was picturing the small, sharp face in a stained snowsuit hood, turned up to the winter sky while the other girls watched hockey and called boys' names to the stars.

He remembered the time his father, who owned a Chevrolet dealership, sold Mr. Sprinkle a new car. It happened fast: one Sunday the two men met at the sidewalk, taking a break from cutting their lawns, and Gerald's father followed Mr. Sprinkle to the Plymouth Fury in the Sprinkles' garage, popped the hood, and started talking as he pointed. Gerald, who was watching from a tree, saw that Mr. Sprinkle, who was a packer at the Feible Meat Company, didn't understand what Gerald's father was saying. Mr. Sprinkle had an accent, and he gave little smiles of embarrassment as Gerald's father tried to explain things, gesturing at the motor with his cigarette.

After dinner that night, Gerald heard his father telling his mother about the conversation with Mr. Sprinkle. His father used the word *chump*. "Too bad the flocus valve had to blow like that," his father was saying, and Gerald could tell that he was helping himself to the last piece of pie, eating it straight out of the pie dish in forkfuls. "That flocus valve will sure do it every time." Then Gerald heard the sound of his father's laughter blending with blueberry swallows. Gerald had not yet learned very much about cars, but he knew there was no such thing, in any model ever made, as a flocus valve. The next weekend, the Fury was gone, and Mr. Sprinkle was driving a new Nova from Burke Chevrolet. In the tree, Gerald watched Allie and her parents pull out of their driveway. Allie was in the back seat, and she saw Gerald and smiled and pointed at his name ornamenting the trunk, *Burke* in shiny chrome across the backside, and he knew that she meant with the gesture to thank his father for taking care of hers.

On the phone, Gerald and Allie arranged a date and time for Gerald to bring the children to be photographed. "I live in the Tartaglias' old house now," Allie told him. "Remember? Behind the middle school."

He thought of the house with the long backyard where they sometimes had to chase home-run balls during kickball games. Mrs. Tartaglia used to sit on her back porch, sewing, and when a ball came rolling from the field onto her property, she acted as if she were about to have a heart attack. Nobody was ever willing to go get those balls except Allie, so they always let her play.

Two days before Christmas, Gerald set out with his family for Oxbow early in the morning. Because of the holiday traffic, the trip took most of a day. The kids spent the time fighting, snacking, and sleeping in the back seat, and Nicole napped for much of the ride, too, so Gerald was alone with the radio and the road. In Pennsylvania, when he rolled down his window for the toll ticket, he let in the cold air from outside, and his family woke up to complain. His son spit gum out the window, and his daughter performed a marriage ceremony between two of her dolls. "Do you, Jason, take her, Margo, to be your awfully wedded wife?"

Finally, they came to the exit for Oxbow and headed into town. All around them was the swill of exhaust and gravel, and ahead they could see the old stockyard from Feible's drawing near. When they came to Four Corners, Gerald was both dismayed and thrilled to realize how little had changed since they'd last been here—could it be six years? Yes, because their daughter had been in her infant seat, crying at the cold. As it had then and as far back as Gerald could remember, Costa's Snack Shoppe stood between the beauty parlor and the bank. Across the street, lights on the Christmas tree in front of Grace Lutheran blinked pastels across the snow.

From the back seat, their daughter asked, "Why did you guys get married?"

Nicole murmured over her shoulder, "Because we love each other, honey," and, rolling up the window, looking in the mirror, Gerald saw with pride and pain that the baby knew better. They wound their way down their old street, which curved like an arm around Everett Pond. The afternoon had simmered into dusk, and teenagers were skating, girls in pairs or triples beside the banks, boys gliding in dreamy circles as they patted their pucks. It had snowed only a few times so far this year, and the pond's shoreline was congested with slush and weeds. The ice itself was ragged; they could see bumps in the gray surface, even from the car.

Still, though it was not as beautiful as they remembered, Nicole and Gerald held their breath together when they saw it, as if they had come too suddenly on a scene from a mutual dream.

That night Gerald didn't wake up to hear the hockey game, but Nicole told him about it in the morning. It had gone on past one o'clock, because there was no school. Christmas Eve, the rink was quiet, and most of Everett Street went to midnight Mass. On Christmas night, the game started up again, and this time Gerald heard the familiar sounds through his sleep, the scrape of blades and the rings of laughter looping the empty trees.

He got out of bed and went to the window. Ice glittered on telephone wires. The flickery bulbs suspended above the pond had been replaced by floodlights which illuminated the whole rink, even the corners, where it used to be you could hide, if you wanted to leave the game for a few minutes to be alone with your heartbeat and stars. The girls didn't sit on a goal bench to watch anymore, but stood in a circle, some of them smoking cigarettes with their backs to the boys, all of them talking while the action passed by. They wore their daytime clothes under their coats and jackets, instead of pajamas and gowns. Occasionally they said something to one of the players, or admired a shot with a flirty hoot, but it was a tired admiration, and Gerald saw that the girls might just as well have been hanging out at Costa's, laughing over pop and french fries, for all they cared about the game. He closed the curtain with a sick sensation and the feeling that he had been fooled.

The appointment he had made with Allie Sprinkle was for the

next morning at ten o'clock. After breakfast, Nicole's parents went out on errands, and Gerald stretched and said he thought he would go over to the Hello Dolly, to see if anybody was around. The Hello Dolly was the diner next to the Oxbow branch of the public library, which was so small that the smell of books clung to you when you left it, like cigarette smoke in a bar.

"The day after Christmas?" Nicole said. She was arranging herself beneath the afghan on the sofa, and Gerald knew there was no danger of her wanting to join him at the diner. Whenever they were in Oxbow and she saw someone she recognized, she crossed the street or aimed her eyes straight ahead with the look of a woman who had too much to think about.

"Some of the guys used to hang out for coffee," Gerald said. "Like Usiak and Dickie and Bob Kelliher. Maybe they won't be there, and either way, I'll only be a while. Hey, how about I swing by Costa's on the way home, and pick up some wings for lunch? The old recipe."

"Yuck," said the children in unison. Nicole's smirk turned into a smile. She would never admit how much she craved the tart tang of her childhood, but he knew he had offered exactly what she missed most.

He kissed them all goodbye, which surprised everyone including himself. Then he went out. As he drove, everything felt smaller and darker than the way he remembered it, and the air held more weight, as if he were climbing too high. On the stoop of the house he still thought of as Mrs. Tartaglia's, he raised the knocker next to Allie Sprinkle's name. When she answered, he had to squint into the light she brought with her to the door, and he felt the panic that comes from being seen clearly and not being able to see back.

"You're here," she said, reaching her arm out, and he stepped forward to hug the warm shadow before he realized she had only meant to shake hands across the distance between them. But by then it was too late to check his momentum, so he followed through, drawing her shoulders toward his coat and giving a kiss to the hair by her ear.

"Where are your kids?" she said, leaning to look beyond him at the empty stoop.

"They couldn't come," Gerald said. He stamped his feet on the mat and watched his lie take physical shape in the form of white breath. "They got sick at the last minute. I figured I'd keep the appointment, anyway." He had not yet lifted his eyes entirely to meet hers. "I'll pay for it, don't worry. Like when you have to pay the doctor for not canceling in time."

Allie's smile was stronger now—he could feel it, touching him—and he allowed himself, at last, to look at her. Her skin was darker and appeared slightly tough, the way it would be if life were a sun she had been exposed to in amounts that weren't good for her. For the first time, he understood what it meant for someone's features to *grow into themselves;* her eyes were the right size, finally, for all the sorrow she stored in them, and her mouth was worn to a fine crease by laughter and—who knew?—perhaps love.

"Well, surprise," she said, reading all of this in his face. "Come on in."

She took his coat and hung it on the banister knob. "I hope you don't want me to take *your* picture," Allie said, as she led him down the hallway to the kitchen, where water was whistling. "Because I should warn you, something bizarre happens when I put grown-ups in front of my camera. They all come out looking like Richard Nixon."

"Even the women?"

"*Especially* the women." She laughed, inviting him to join her in it. It was the sound he associated with winter nights at the pond, but before he could even realize this completely, Allie set a cup of tea down in front of him and said, "You know, I drove home by way of our old street the other day. It was before supper, just getting dark, and the little kids were still out on their double-runners. They all kept falling and then trying to stand, and they'd lose their balance and fall again, till their moms came over to help them back up." She smiled at the memory of what she had seen. "I know we all learned how to skate together when we were their age, but mostly when I remember growing up on Everett Street, I think about that night."

He knew right away, of course, which night she meant. She was talking about the accident: about those moments when he sent the puck with a clean crack into the shadows, lost it, then heard

JESSICA TREADWAY

and saw the hard black circle knocking Nicole Rueger in the side
of her pretty head. In the months that followed, he had watched
the scene often behind closed eyes. He began with receiving the
pass flat at the edge of his stick from Michael Usiak, feeling the
puck sit there on the wood for a few seconds before he hauled off
and slapped it, no holding back. Then came the images of Nicole
lying on the ice, her long hair splayed out beneath her, one leg
bent behind her at the knee; Nicole coming home from the hospital, using her parents as crutches, a white bandage where she used
to have bangs.

But what was most vivid to Gerald about that night was not
anything about his victim, or what happened after she fell, but
what it felt like to hit the puck the way he had, as hard as he
could, one solid stroke and a single motion, letting everything go.
Afterward he asked himself, when he could stand to, if he had
known it was possible he might hit one of the girls. The puck had
not gone anywhere near the goal he would have scored in. Was
there a wish involved? Had he—God help him—even aimed? He
didn't think so, but he couldn't be sure, and the not being sure
was what kept him awake so many nights when he should have
been sleeping.

Of course, he would never tell Nicole that. When, because his
mother made him, he went to visit her at her bedside the day after
she came home, he kept his head lowered, and he even, briefly,
touched her hand, a gesture unusual for any twelve-year-old boy,
but remarkable in him. By the time she was well enough to go
back to school, he began picking her up in the mornings so they
could walk together, apart from the other Everett Street kids.
Before then he had always walked with Michael and Dickie, and
they had plenty of things to say to him, none kind or clever, about
his new habit of walking with a girl.

When they kissed for the first time, one January afternoon on
the way home—they'd stayed late, he for detention and she for
cheerleading, and it was already dark as they came to the pond—
it felt to both of them like what was supposed to happen next. It
was a quick kiss, little more than lips overlapping, but they both
knew what it meant. They were officially a couple; he had con-
sented to his fate. Nicole snipped her face and Gerald's from the

old class photograph of Miss Huberty's second grade, and she taped the pictures to each side of the locket her parents had given her on her hospital homecoming.

"Me, too," he said to Allie now, referring to that night. He could feel, in his chest and throat, the desire to tell her about the joke Nicole had made out of the accident over the years, knocking over the salt shaker with her fingertips. But before his voice found the first word, he discovered that he did *not* want to tell her. Instead, he turned the impulse into a cough.

Allie nodded as if she understood. "I always wondered what would have happened, if I had been the one," she said, and Gerald believed he heard a tremble in her voice. "Instead of Nicole. You know?"

He did know, perhaps more than she did; but he also knew that he shouldn't admit it. He closed his eyes at the thought of the puck having taken a different route, fallen to gravity sooner, found Allie Sprinkle as its mark. The vision stirred a sweet wailing in his gut as he heard the apocalyptic approach of a town truck coming through to spread salt on the street. Before he could open his eyes again, the backs of Allie's warm fingers were laid against his forehead, the way a mother checks for fever in a child. He had never been touched by her before, and he knew he should be startled, but it felt—what was the word he wanted?—more *ancient,* or *familiar*—than Nicole's touch ever had.

Allie took her hand away from his face when he looked at her, and recklessly Gerald reached out to cover her fingers with his own. But she retreated, pulling away a loose fist from the question in his clasp. "I haven't seen you since the night of graduation," she said. "Remember how hot it was, under those rented robes? When we all walked into the gym by homerooms, it was the best feeling of my life. It was like those nights at the pond, before the accident. I could sit there and close my eyes, and feel love floating around in the air like snow."

Gerald watched as he listened, resisting the temptation to touch her lips with his fingers. She seemed to be saying something he had always known, but which he had never heard before, in his own voice or any other. "Remember when Emil Marsh brought in those cocoa cookies his mother made for the bake sale, and everybody made fun of them because they looked like turds? Emil was trying to laugh, but I could see him swallowing. It made me so sad, I felt like screaming. Same with Karen Harder, the time she wore that skirt with the dog her grandmother sewed on it. Girls used to wear poodles like that. Her grandmother just didn't know they didn't anymore. And we were too old to think a dog on a dress was the best thing. By then, we all knew it was queer.

"The only time nobody ever made fun of anyone was during the hockey games. Then we were all just out there together, laughing in the cold." Allie was staring into her teacup. Steam slithered from the surface, and Gerald imagined it was this warmth flushing her face. When she said, "Come upstairs," he stood hastily, banging his knee on the table. On the steps, he made sure not to follow too closely, in case she stopped without warning and he could not keep himself from reaching up to begin an embrace.

She opened a door at the top of the hallway and led him inside. Again, there was too much light coming in through a wide window, and he beat his eyes fast a few times to adjust to the snow-blink and sun. It was not a bedroom. On the far side of the room was a rolled backdrop, with sitting stools of various heights anchoring the canvas where the roll met the floor. In the center of the room, a collection of cameras and other equipment—umbrellas and meters, flash fixtures and lights—surrounded a tripod that looked almost like a human figure, tall and skinny, beckoning to them as Gerald and Allie stepped through the door.

Allie went to the window and covered it with a cloth screen. It was then, as the room became dim enough to examine, that Gerald saw the children looking out at him from the walls. They were black-and-white photographs of faces, all with eyes focused straight at the camera. Some were smiling; others only stared. Even the faces of the unbeautiful children riveted him with a force far more powerful than beauty. All of them knew who they were, but they did not yet know who they *would* be, and it was this freedom that Allie had embalmed on her film.

Gerald went toward the faces and touched some of the frames. Allie was watching him, and when he drew in his breath and held it, she moved closer. But when he reached to take her face in his fingers, and brought his lips near hers, she pulled away.

"Go home, Gerald," she whispered. Outside, the salt truck screeched, sounding like the duck-and-cover drills they'd learned as children.

"Bob Kelliher's father still driving that thing?" Gerald moved to the window to lift the screen and look out, though his vision was blurred.

"No," Allie said from behind him, still whispering. "Bob is."

Gerald turned to her again, showing a smile which he knew must look as foolish as it felt. "Would you take my picture?" he said, already knowing the answer but trying to sound as if he believed she might change her mind.

She smiled back, her lips rising to the corners of well-worn grooves. "No."

"Please? I'll pay you. I mean it. I want you to." He knew that both of them could hear the urgency in his voice, and though it embarrassed him, he was helpless to hide. "Allie—" He reached out again to pull her to him. The lust he felt was not for her body, or even for her. It was the desire to have that night and his life back, and it was the fiercest love he had ever felt.

"Gerald, no." Allie moved to the wall to straighten one of the frames he had slanted without realizing, then motioned for Gerald to precede her out of the studio. Behind her, she shut the door.

"Could I stay a little longer, then? To talk?" he asked, when they reached the bottom of the stairs. But he saw that Allie was pretending she hadn't heard him as she handed him his coat.

They went outside. The morning had turned warm, windy, and he felt too hot in his heavy sleeves. The sky and the snow seemed the same shade of gray; in her front yard, Gerald bent over to pick up a handful of slush, and he tried to shape it into a ball, but it fell apart in his fingers. Still, he tried to toss it so that the melting fragments would shower around Allie in a festive rain. When this didn't work, he gave the stupid smile again, and winked streaks of wetness from the edges of his eyes.

He took out his billfold, but before he could open it, Allie reached over to press his fingers closed around the leather. "Don't, Gerald," she told him. "I won't take it."

He started to answer her, but then he knew not to, and he got in his car and began backing out of the driveway. In the cold, watching him, Allie tried hugging herself, but as he pulled away, he could see that it wasn't enough.

He had not been about to give her money. He only wanted to show her pictures of his kids.

He drove the streets without steering, back through Four Corners, past the Hello Dolly and the Feible Meat Company, past the funeral home. Though it had turned brighter outside, the air still felt heavy, as if something not in the forecast was headed his way.

When they were in junior high, the girls all had to wear gym suits, which they bought from the Little Folks Shop. Mr. Neander, Sue Neander's father and the man who would, a few years later, back out of his driveway on a foggy October morning in his Impala and hit and kill Craig Domermuth, Dickie's little brother, who was riding his bike to school, ordered the suits specially at the beginning of every year. The boys got to wear whatever they wanted in the way of gym shirts and shorts, and the classes were boys and girls together, so half of the court or field was always in uniform and the other half wasn't.

What was it that happened to Mr. Neander after Craig Domermuth died? Of course Gerald remembered hearing everything about it, how Sue's father, when he realized what he had done, tried to drive the car off the boy's body; later, they said this was probably what killed him. After school that day, all the kids went by Sue's house to see if they could tell anything. Mrs. Neander was out at the end of the driveway, running a hose on the street. She must have been standing there for a long time already, because the pavement was soaked and the water reached as far down as two houses on either side. When she saw them all watching her, she lifted the hose a little, without seeming to mean to, and the spray came toward them, making them all stumble backward to avoid getting wet.

Their retreat made Mrs. Neander cry. "Please," she said to them across the stream that sounded like summer, "please." But none of them knew what she meant. Mr. Neander never went to jail or even had charges pressed against him, because it had been so

227

foggy that morning, and there were reports that Craig had been riding his bicycle very fast. Sue came back to school the following week, and everybody held their breath the first time she and Dickie Domermuth passed in the hall. But they were all disappointed. There were no screams or slaps between them, no apologies and no truce. Maybe these had been exchanged when nobody was looking. More likely, though, it was easier just not to admit it in any way. It was over and done with, was what the sermon at the funeral seemed to say.

But this was all still ahead of them, after they learned to drink beer in the stockyard, after the first girl in their class got pregnant and had the baby, after nobody could force them to wear gym suits anymore. The girls' outfits were blue on the bottom and white on the top, one-piece cotton suits that zipped up the back and showed every burgeoning bump of soft bodies coming to the fore.

One hot afternoon in April, they were playing softball. Gerald was playing right field, and Allie Sprinkle was in center. When the bell rang and they began to go in, Allie walked ahead of him, and Gerald squinted at the slow shape in front of him, to make sure of what he saw. A brown-red stain spread from between her legs and up the seat of her gym suit, which clung and gathered in the clenched place between her thighs. He did not perceive what it was at first, and when he did—in that sudden way things make sense so that we can never, after that moment, remember what it was like *not* to understand them—he wanted to catch up to her and hand her his windbreaker and tell her not to ask any questions, just tie this around your waist.

But he didn't. It was impossible to translate what he knew he should do into an action, the same way it had been impossible to hold back on that sitting puck. Instead, when he saw Nicole coming in from left field, he called her over. "Do something," he said, pointing forward at Allie with his eyes. Nicole looked, and he saw a cruel smile take hold of her lips.

"*Do* something," he said again, as Allie kept walking, oblivious, wearing her womanhood for everyone to see. She was getting close to the rest of the class, the girls in their gym suits with their secrets and smiles, and the boys throwing the softball back and forth between mitts, except for the one boy who always carried the bats and bases to and from the equipment room, balancing the wood on one shoulder with the rubber mats in his other hand. Gerald always wondered why this boy was responsible for it all, why they didn't each take a piece of the game back with them to make it fair; but nobody ever offered to help, and Mr. Carmody didn't make them, so it was always the same boy who carried everything, and he never complained.

Allie Sprinkle kept walking, passing some of the pack. Gerald watched as first the boy with the bats noticed the menstrual stain and looked immediately down at the ground, as if he wanted to give back what he'd seen. Then some of the girls caught on, and the gasps and laughter made the whole class look, and Nicole ran ahead of Gerald to find her friends, and he saw Allie come to understand what must be happening and to feel the wet shame widening between her legs.

Somebody said, *She must've fell on the floor at Feible's,* which caused a fresh wave of hilarity to float across the field.

Come here, Alice, Mr. Carmody said, but she wouldn't. *I said come HERE,* he said, and instead she walked sideways across the field and through the bushes by Mrs. Tartaglia's house. After lunch she came back to school wearing the gym suit blouse tucked into a long, old-lady skirt that had been cinched at the waist with a velveteen sash. The mocking started all over again when she appeared in this costume, tardy to Earth Science, and as she moved to take her seat, Allie kept her gaze fixed on Gerald's face. He tried not to look back, but he couldn't help it. Now, he remembered what he had known in the moment their eyes met, and in the next—because he was not ready to know it—forgotten: Although she looked like nobody they would ever admit wanting to be, Allie's face held a peace that they had all lost without realizing, and that they would spent the rest of their lives seeking and failing to retrieve.

As he stepped into the house, scraping his shoes on the stoop to get the slush from Allie's yard out of his shoes, Gerald could tell that everyone was home. The children were playing a new electronic video game. Nicole's parents had returned from the pharmacy and the salon. He could hear them all in the living room, talking at the same time. Nicole was still on the sofa, a thumb holding her place in her book while she watched what the children were doing.

She raised her eyes as Gerald came to the doorway, and from the angle of her brow, he saw that he had let her down again in the way only he could, without even knowing. It was the look she used to get along with the headaches, halfway between accusation and an appeal. He shrugged his coat off and threw it across a chair, and only then did he realize that his hands were empty, and he knew even before she did what his wife was going to say.

"Well?" she asked, and everyone else in the room stopped to listen for his answer. "I thought you were going to bring me back some wings."

ABOUT ANN BEATTIE

A Profile by Don Lee

Myth has it that Ann Beattie published her first short story in *The New Yorker* when she was twenty-five years old, signed a first-read contract with them, and thereafter made five to seven annual appearances in the venerable magazine—with stories she would write in one sitting, in one afternoon.

As myths go, this one is pretty accurate. In the early seventies, Beattie was a Ph.D. candidate in literature at the University of Connecticut, and a professor, J. D. O'Hara, who was a mentor of sorts, began sticking stamps on envelopes and submitting Beattie's stories for her. After a couple of acceptances at literary quarterlies, O'Hara suggested she try *The New Yorker.* Her story came back with an encouraging note from one of the editors, Roger Angell, so Beattie tried again. And again. A total of twenty-two stories before *The New Yorker* finally took one. A seemingly arduous road, except for the fact that all the stories were written in a little over a year, each of them banged out in—yes, it's true—a few hours.

In 1976, the simultaneous publication of a collection of short stories, *Distortions,* and a novel, *Chilly Scenes of Winter* (for which the rough draft was written in three weeks), quickly and permanently vaulted Beattie into literary stardom. Her work drew comparisons to Salinger, Cheever, and Updike, and the eight books that followed—all written under contract—confirmed her ranking among the best writers in the country: the story collections *Secrets and Surprises, The Burning House, Where You'll Find Me and Other Stories,* and *What Was Mine,* and the novels *Falling in Place, Love Always, Picturing Will,* and *Another You,* which will be released this fall.

Beattie resides for the moment in Maine with her husband, the painter Lincoln Perry. They live modestly, a large studio for Perry on the top floor of the house their single extravagance. Without children, without fixed job commitments—Beattie taught at UConn, the University of Virginia, and Harvard for eight straight

years, but hasn't had a regular teaching position for the last eighteen—she and Perry can afford to be peripatetic, and they will
likely take off soon to other favored locales: principally Key West
and Charlottesville.

At turns animated and circumspect, Beattie is always witty, self-
possessed, and forthright. She looks much like she did in her
twenties, and often displays a youthful mischief. She is, for
instance, a famous practical joker. Once, she called Rust Hills,
Esquire's fiction editor, before visiting him, and said she would be
accompanied by her personal trainer; then watched his jaw drop
as he opened the door to Beattie and her obese friend, with whom
Hills had to be stutteringly polite. But Beattie has also developed
a territorial distance over the years, wary of intrusions to her privacy. No doubt, much of this guardedness comes from her early
celebrity, which created as many burdens of expectation and envy
as occasions for privilege. Beattie will readily admit, however, that
she was extremely lucky, particularly since writing fiction was
something she just fell into.

Born in 1947 in Washington, D.C., she grew up as an only child—
introverted, but generally happy and bright, until she became a
teenager. The public schools she attended were terrible—academ-
ically indifferent—and Beattie responded accordingly. "I became
self-destructive," she admits. She graduated with a D- average, and
without a providential connection of her father's, she would not
have been able to enroll at American University, much less any
college. Lacking any real plans or ambition, she chose to study journalism. After a few years, though, a boyfriend convinced her that
journalism was "totally uncool," that it was a bourgeois trade. He
told her she should really be more like an artist and consider being
an English major. She switched on the same day.

Not knowing what else to do after graduating, she assumed she
would probably end up teaching literature for a living and
entered the Ph.D. program at the University of Connecticut. Certainly, she never thought writing could be anything but a hobby.
There were M.F.A. programs then, but no one she knew went to
one. Writing short stories didn't seem to be a viable career choice.
To her good fortune, however, J. D. O'Hara heard about her fiction from some other graduate students, and took an interest in

PHOTO: ROLLIE McKENNA

her. "He really became my official editor," Beattie recalls. "He taught me more about writing than I could have imagined learning elsewhere. He did it all by writing comments in the margins of my manuscripts. We never once sat down and talked about things. I would put a story in his faculty mailbox, and he would return it, usually the next day, in my student teaching assistant mailbox."

She didn't—and still doesn't—begin her stories with any idea of where she might go, never charting out a plot or outline. "My feeling is that physically I couldn't," she says. "If there isn't that moment of surprise for me, I don't think that I could stay in the material." Likewise, she did not set out to be a chronicler of the sixties and the baby boomer generation—a label she finds reductive, dismissive. She simply wrote about the people who surrounded her: educated New Englanders, some who'd participated in the counterculture of the sixties, languishing now in the ennui of the seventies, fighting vague disappointments and failures with impulsive acts and eccentric obsessions. Especially regarding relationships, Beattie was fascinated with examining people's passivity—"this whole Beckettian thing—I can't stay and I can't go"—but she chose not to excuse the circumstances in which her characters found themselves, or explicate how they got there. Instead, she adopted the deadpan, stark style about which critics made such a fuss. "I think I was kind of a sponge," Beattie says. "I soaked up all of the obvious weirdness that was around me, and I tended to be nonjudgmental. That tone, apparently, superimposed with the more outlandish things, was surprising to people."

Yet, as she has matured and accrued experiences, it has become increasingly difficult for her to remain objective and open. "I do think I've figured some things out, and it's a disadvantage in a way, because you can pigeonhole people too quickly. You can say, 'This person is only crazy.' In graduate school, I knew this guy who was a genius in mathematics and whose best friend was his dog, and he said, 'Fuck it,' and went to work in a factory making axe handles. I thought, 'Huh.' Now, I wouldn't really think, 'Huh.' Before, I would be surprised in point of fact. Now I'm more surprised that I'm surprised. In a way, it's fighting against what time has taught me."

Stylistically and structurally, her work has changed as well, becoming more complex and sophisticated. "I'm much more interested in formal issues now," she says, "in how things are put together, and what I might do on that level to get a trajectory that is more clearly the author's. I know ten ways to move through time, and my interest is in finding the eleventh. I want to do something that I haven't done before. I'm not so pleased to have written a bright sentence, because even if it's, let's say, very bright, so have others been."

Consequently, she doesn't write with the rapidity or frequency she once used to. A novel like *Picturing Will* will take up to three years to finish, and she'll work in spurts between projects, sometimes idle for as long as six weeks. In recent years, she has also become frustrated with the vagaries of the publishing world, particularly with the magazine market for her short stories, which she has more and more difficulty placing. Despite having a terrific agent, Lynn Nesbit, and being able to choose her book editors, Beattie finds the business disheartening at times. "Any notion that this gets easier, or that people treat me nicer—it's exactly the opposite of what really is the case," she says. "People think that things are progressive, that when you get to hurdle number three, you've won the race. Only to find out that the terrain has changed after hurdle number five, or that your editor is fired after hurdle number eight. The same contingencies, the same contradictions and problems, exist as you're going along. It's not just an obstacle course that you can do correctly and win. The ground rules are always changed by those in control, the people who own the publishing houses."

Those external forces, however, did not, at least directly, lead to the crisis Beattie experienced when working on her new novel, *Another You*. After amassing three hundred fifty pages, she scrapped the book. Pretty much all of it—the entire plot, most of the characters. Less than ten percent of the original version remains in the final manuscript. Why did it take her so long to realize that the novel wasn't working? Part of the problem was that she was writing adequate prose. "Moment to moment, there was no reason to say, 'Oh, I'm really off today.'" But eventually, she recognized that there was no momentum to the novel, and she didn't care deeply about the characters.

No one ever saw a word of the original book—not her husband, not the few trusted friends who usually critique her initial drafts. Somehow, Beattie still managed to get *Another You* to her publisher, Knopf, on time, but she has resolved she will never write another novel on contract, and she will concentrate for a while on her preferred medium—stories and novellas.

The anxiety of *Another You*'s false start still haunts Beattie. It took her five long months to recover and begin anew, and during that period, she found little to reassure her. "I was thinking that really I had to admit to myself that there was no other skill I had, and that I couldn't just get into a snit and change careers, because it just wasn't going to happen. I mean, you just hope that there's mercy."

BLUE SPRUCE *Stories by David Long. Scribner, $20.00 cloth. Reviewed by Don Lee.*

The twelve stories in David Long's third collection, *Blue Spruce*, are distinctive for many reasons, but mostly they are marked by place—namely, Montana and other points Northwest. Restless, lonely, the people in Long's stories are inheritors of the American West, frequently on the run, jumping into their cars for the expanse of the road, for the release of the contemporary frontier. What impels them, though, is vague, and, when pressed to name a destination of preference, they are at an even greater loss.

In "Eggarine," the teenaged Jay McCauley ruminates: "I pictured myself running outdoors and fleeing in the car again, but the thought filled me with desperation. What good was it, where could I go that was not still the earth?" He grows up to be a moody, unmarried man with a dead-end job, and he reproaches himself for failing to meet his parents' expectations. But his mother calmly says to him one night, "There's nothing wrong with you, honey. It's not a race."

Such moments are typical for Long. His stories are rangy, complex, wry, and unpredictable, moving toward what one would expect to be a significant revelation, only to present an ironic and opposite pronouncement—an anti-epiphany. For instance, "Attraction," a stunning, beautiful story, begins when Marly Wilcox is fifteen, shyly in love with Charles, who has been dumped by another classmate, Cynthia. Flamboyant and somewhat crude, Cynthia has an affair with a much older man, whose daughter coolly gouges out Cynthia's eye with a key. Years later, after Marly's mother, Jeanette, has squandered her college fund, Marly waits tables at the same restaurant where Cynthia is employed. She becomes Cynthia's confidant, even babysitting her daughter, Cher, while Cynthia cheats on her husband with Charles. Marly intercedes with her own seduction, however, and, very briefly, contemplates the weight of what she has done. But then she denies herself this indulgence in melodrama, in self-importance: "Hours before, hurrying out of the truck—exhausted, mortified—she'd been hit by the absurd intuition that all their lives depended on her now, even Cher's. By daylight, the momentousness of the night before had washed off, the nervous glitter. It was just true, as Jeanette would say, a fact she'd have to live with."

Time and time again, the characters in *Blue Spruce* dismiss the possibility of solving imponderables. "Who's to say?" a woman sighs. "You can find a reason for anything, reasons are nothing, reasons are common as flies." In another story, a man thinks, "None of it was a mystery, just what happens."

With no answers available, there are only two choices in Long's world: become cloistered in bitterness—"mean" and "constricted"—or move on. Forget, accept, surrender, forgive—whatever the case, just move on. In "Cooperstown," Robert Isham, a former major-league pitcher, goes to visit Andy Hewitt, the phenom he had intentionally beaned twelve years ago, ending what promised to be a Hall of Fame career. Isham, now selling sports equipment, thrice divorced, is looking for absolution, but Hewitt and his wife are beyond recriminations. They have a family now, own a marina. "You don't have to think the same way all your life," the wife says to Isham. In the final story, "The New World," the owner of a hardware business abandons his noisome, alcoholic daughter, buys a new DeSoto, and ends up in Oregon, where he falls in love with a woman and begins an entirely new life. What amazes him is "his own amazement. That the man he'd become, so late in the game, could wonder at things, his mind bright, not swamped and close."

David Long is gifted, often outright brilliant, in bringing this capacity for wonder to his readers. *Blue Spruce,* with Long's sumptuous prose and languid narrative, is a substantial, wise book—and a thoroughly satisfying one.

THE ONLY WORLD *Poems by Lynda Hull. HarperCollins, $22.00 cloth, $12.00 paper. Reviewed by Diann Blakely Shoaf.*

The term *mimesis,* unfortunately having come to be redolent of tweeds and pipe smoke, seems wildly inapplicable to a poet as inspired by the exhaust-fumed ether of today's cities and the musky glamour of their earlier incarnations as Lynda Hull. Yet the classical scholar Gilbert Murray reminds us that the term we usually translate as "imitation" originally implied not a mirror held up to nature, but a fracturing of that mirror—indeed, of all borders between the self and the objective world that urges song. The notion of mimesis, having evolved from the ritualistic chants and dances from which Greek poetry sprang, takes a quantum and very contemporary leap in Hull's work, becoming a raw, even savage means of breaking down the "I" into otherness, into points of view that are "multiplying and dazzling," as she writes in "The Window," the shattering but finally redemptive poem that concludes her posthumous collection, *The Only World*.

Hull loses herself again and again in *The Only World*'s coruscating but gritty panoply of subjects. Junkies and whores, the imprisoned, the beggared homeless of our urban landscapes, those dying or dead from AIDS, do not merely "appear" in these poems, they become past or future selves, alternate selves, feared selves. Hull's poems serve as vessels for human stories that constitute, as she says in "Suite for Emily," "doors you (I?) might fall through to the underworld / of bars and bus stations, private rooms of / dancing girls numb-sick & cursing the wilderness / of men's round blank faces. Spinning demons."

Such doors imply the psychological and spiritual brinks Hull writes about in "Lost Fugue for Chet," one of the tours de force of her second book, *Star Ledger*, which won the 1990 Edwin Ford Piper Award. "Why court the brink & then step back? / / After surviving, what arrives?" she asks there, and these questions, grand rhetorical flourishes with a stern moral fervor at their core, are asked and answered with even greater artistry and more stringent self-examination in *The Only World*. The various brinks that ecstasy—religious, sexual, chemical—leads toward in Hull's poems are always alluring, even as their sirening whispers sometimes smell sourly of death. The survivor of such brinks arrives only and always at other occasions for survival, but such occasions can provide the burden and opportunity of witness.

"Street of Crocodiles," the swirlingly cinematic poem written after Hull's 1991 trip to Poland, a trip made with her mother in hopes of locating what fragments of family remained there, provides one of *The Only World*'s most exemplary moments of reckoning with the personal and historical past, giving voice to those otherwise choked and silenced. Some of Hull's forebears were "to be dealt the yellow cards of the murdered, to know / / the must of between-the-secret-convent-walls." Such fates were suffered during the era of Auschwitz, with its "shorn hair / of 40,000 women turned gray by Zyklon B, / the piled canisters and shoes."

How to sing in such a world? How do we make songs of the notes history jams down our throats, songs that are "crucial and exacting" but not despairing? Mark Doty, whose afterword provides a clear-eyed benediction, also provides an answer to these questions. "Glamour," says Doty, "is a way of making history bearable." And in the songs of Lynda Hull, the term glamour, like mimesis, skyrockets beyond the usual definitions, becoming an ethical force, a survivor's gaiety, and a poetic imperative. In *The Only World*, artifice is not to be confused with frippery; it is at those moments when we try most ardently to be something or someone else that we are sometimes fortunate enough to be launched hardest into the process of becoming our own multifaceted selves. As Hull writes in "The Window," "If each of us / contains, within, humankind's totality, each possibility / then I have been so fractured, so multiple and dazzling / stepping toward myself."

The word fractured indicates the risk involved in such willing transformations, and it became a word with more than metaphoric implications in Hull's life after a December 1992 accident: a taxi slammed into her car, smashing both her feet and ankles. The conversation with Lynda—whom I am blessed to remember as mentor and "girlfriend," as we called each other when feeling silly—that I remember best during her long convalescence took place on a humid, rainy summer evening in 1993, approximately nine months before her death. Though trips outside her Chicago apartment continued to be painful and limited, I'd called to urge her to see *What's Love Got to Do with It?*, the lurid but somehow dignified biopic of Tina Turner, like Lynda a steel-backboned survivor and singer of brinks. Lynda loved being compared to makers of music like Tina, like Billie. Or Chet Baker. Or Bird, whose grave Lynda and fellow pilgrims visited on another humid evening, that one spent in St. Louis and retold in the poem "Ornithology," originally published in *Ploughshares* and ending with a line that represents one of Lynda's many shining legacies: "If you don't live it, it won't come out your horn."

The Only World contains both that life and that horn's sweet, sad, ancient note riffing from praise songs to prayers for mercy to dirges. Its harmonies drift in the direction of God, certainly, but mainly toward this world, on it "each fugitive moment the heaven we choose to make."

Diann Blakely Shoaf is a regular reviewer for the "Bookshelf." Her collection of poems, Hurricane Walk, *was published by BOA Editions in 1992.*

PLAYING OUT OF THE DEEP WOODS *Stories by G. W. Hawkes. Univ. of Missouri Press, $14.95 paper. Reviewed by Fred Leebron.*

A conventional wisdom about short story collections these days is that they must feature stories that are linked in some way—collections that focus on a particular series of characters, or a particular place, or a particular vision. But in G. W. Hawkes's second book of stories, *Playing Out of the Deep Woods,* each story is its own world, unlinked to any other, and organic in its elegantly and originally revealed truths. In one story, a high-tech entity conducts global research on the unexplained emergence of blue triangles. In another, a nineteenth-century drifter faces down the superstitious inhabitants of Killisburne, Scotland.

In the title fiction, a foursome at the Married Couples Best Ball Tournament at Hollow Hills Country Club all lose their balls in the deep woods of the first hole. When each of the golfers ventures in after them, they discover strange and mysterious happenings—the artifacts of a lost childhood, a dead mother, passion, tranquility, and the possibility of pregnancy. The woods contain "a darkness so complete it's romantic," and the three golfers who manage to play their way out are forever changed by their journey into them.

"Peeper" follows fifty years in the career of a peeping Tom, and Hawkes's accomplishment is to somehow make this character likable. We meet him as a fourth-grader, "a boy prophet, a boy spy, a boy soldier; he's a boy the world is going to have to reckon with." But by the end of this particular evening, "by the time it is full light, he has peeped three bedrooms, and he has found out already this early in his career that he likes to watch women dressing or undressing, but not naked." Ten years later, his peeping leads him out of the Korean War, and within the next twenty years, he is arrested one hundred fourteen times. In this story and in others, Hawkes never shies from excess, from exploring extremes in characters and in situations, and yet he is a subtle writer who paints his portraits with broad brush strokes and never appears to be exploiting such material for the sake of shock value.

Quieter stories, like "Mutiny," feature dramas of consciousness, where on the backdrop of a calm setting, the past rattles around in a character's head like "bells in the old brainbox," until a crucial truth rings out. Sir Quentin is a World War II hero who believes he has sired a coward for a son, until forty years later he learns that his own courage in the war was a product of a "doctor's lie, or ignorance, and that he was a brave man by mistake." This revelation cripples him, and he is faced with the first real test of his own courage. In most of Hawkes's stories, characters are tested with more than one crisis, and our intimacy with them is enriched.

Some of the stories function best as allegories. Told in a folksy voice, "Always Cold" occurs in Oracle, Kansas, a place so flat that "the sunlight skips across the town like a thrown rock." Ruth Montgomery is a victim of a vague accident, almost a curse. She becomes so shunned because of this suspicion that she grows invisible to the superstitious town, and eventually, by their will of wanting it so, she disappears altogether from the canvas of life. "The Moveable Hazard," one of three golf stories in this collection, follows a fearless American abroad to Scotland, where he seeks to ignore all the warnings and overcome a mythically dangerous par-five fourteenth hole. In a driving rainstorm, his caddie warns him that the hole's moving marsh "is to remind men of the border 'tween water an' land. Ye'll land in the muck o' the shore of it. Ye can nae miss it." The golfer's adventures are funny and mysterious, and you don't need to know anything about golf to enjoy reading them.

Throughout the collection, the stories are marked by deft, imagistic writing, and a voice filled with authority and humor. *Playing*

Out of the Deep Woods offers a rich range of storytelling, evidence of an author who repeats nothing, and holds nothing back.

Fred Leebron directs the Fine Arts Work Center in Provincetown. His fiction has appeared in TriQuarterly, Grand Street, Ploughshares, *and elsewhere.*

DESIRING FLIGHT *Poems by Christianne Balk. Purdue Univ. Press, $12.95 paper. Reviewed by David Daniel.*

Among the many pleasures of Christianne Balk's *Desiring Flight,* two stand out. First, Balk has—as she showed in her Walt Whitman Award–winning *Bindweed*—a biologist's precise knowledge of the natural world, and consequently her poems convey, at times, the comforting authority of a field guide. But there is much more than that: It is as if Balk has held all the objects of her world, turned them over, and spoken their names until they have transcended the scientific into the poetic. A few lines from "Dusk Sea Walk" may show something of this incantatory magic: "This sea / wants everything—the black cod's eye, phalarope, / green fucus, milky clouds of milt, the otter's coat, / . . . halibut, coho, chum, the small gray tail / slipping from the belly slit, screaming cliffs / of kittiwakes, tide marshes filled with snipe, / cranes, grebes, scaup, duck, forty-pound swans, / even the eagle sitting in the dead spruce, waiting / for the red and silver rivers to flow upstream."

Balk consistently places the people in her poems at the mercy of nature, and the effects of this humility are powerful. Often the narrators seem isolated, incidental participants in the world around them. Their solace seems to come, if at all, from their ability to pay attention to—and sometimes to allegorize—what they find in nature. In a very beautiful poem, "Kantishna Terns," the narrator and a loved one are camping along the banks of the river: " 'Will you?' you asked. / I was too tired to know, but secretly / I asked *forever? What is that?* / All night I heard the sounds / I'd heard all day—/ water meeting wood . . ." Then, as they look out on the river, at trees snagged on its surface, the narrator sees "one branch break free of rock / and begin / to float downstream."

Our ability, perhaps, to surrender our ego to the world—for all its horrors and its beauties—to *read* nature, looking not for answers but simply for understanding, may be the fundamental trope of this fine book.

STYGO *A novel by Laura Hendrie. MacMurray & Beck, $16.95 cloth. Reviewed by Jessica Dineen.*

Although Laura Hendrie's first novel, *Stygo*, focuses on the tiny beet growers' town of Stygo, Colorado, it is in no way limited by its narrow geographic boundaries. To the contrary, Hendrie's brilliantly precise writing offers an organic view of her characters' peculiar isolation, so that their predicaments seem as rich as the soil.

Hendrie's Stygo is sugar beet and cornfields, the Red Spot refinery, the Rockeroy bar, a gas station, and the Funtown fairground. Each chapter of the novel features a different group of characters, and the town's facts and incidents become historied as the chapters accumulate. The people in Stygo feel trapped in the narrow particulars of their lives, but are also rebelliously settled; they look hard at their surroundings not for a way to leave, but for a way out of *wanting* to leave. Tom-Go, the young manager of the Rockeroy, has bragged all his life about getting out of Stygo, but when he wins enough lottery money for a ticket to Alaska, he dawdles on the day of his departure, mopping the Rockeroy barroom floor one last time, hoping someone will ask him to stay.

Two girls who live in the shadow of their brother, a murderer on death row, work locked in a glass ticket booth at Funtown. Frightened by pranksters, they keep the lights off in the booth, but then devise a game to taunt their customers mercilessly, an attempt to make the world outside—not their own lives—the real place of ridicule and danger.

Reba is another of Hendrie's characters who finds a way to transcend the small meanness of her surroundings. Living in a dusty gas station, Reba is usually found under the porch, hiding from her hard-edged father, taking refuge in her love for a pet armadillo, Jubilee. Sent away for a time after her mother abandons the family, Reba returns to find that Jubilee has been run over. Her father has Jubilee stuffed, with a pink plastic tongue, marbles for eyes, and its feet nailed to a board. Reba's fear of the stuffed armadillo is palpable. But, eventually, she forges a fondness for the "new" Jubilee, because it's what she has left.

Another girl, Ruth, searches the "dark green wall of corn around the house" for her mother, who exhibits early signs of

Alzheimer's and has wandered away from a cookout. Ruth stumbles blindly in the rows, seeing "nothing but heat ghosts rising from the fields," then is sent by her father to the top of the silo. There, we expect perspective, relief. But Ruth sees only her father, "his shadow a black crowbar following his feet. Over in the side yard, the coals from the barbecue look like a little piece of sunset fell out of the sky. For every direction the corn is still." Later, after her mother is found, Ruth tries to think of worse things that could happen than her mother's fading. She thinks of her own death, and her feeling of isolation is apocalyptic; she imagines their house "at the end of time, with everyone gone and all the windows and doors blown out and the corn growing wild...and reaching inside."

The last pages of *Stygo* are a cold-hearted inventory from the Red Spot Employee Availability Statistics, including "employability by present company standards." The list reinforces the feeling that these stories are unearthings, each gritty fact revealed myopically, hard evidence, showing a Stygo made up of separate, lonely people who are also integrally tied together by wisdom about the circumstances they share. Laura Hendrie's genius is that *Stygo* describes this bleak town and its inhabitants with astoundingly beautiful clarity.

*Books Recommended by
Our Advisory Editors*

Maxine Kumin and **Joyce Peseroff** recommend *The Moon Reflected Fire,* poems by Doug Anderson (Alice James). Kumin: "These are war poems—war poems and beyond. Vivid, compelling, controlled, and often wildly lyrical." Peseroff: "Not just about Vietnam but resonant with the history of warriors from the backyard to *The Iliad* to the Bible, Doug Anderson's first book burns with compassion, rage, tenderness, and pain. The intimate voice of these poems insinuates their author's images of Americans and Vietnamese into our own memory, as *The Moon Reflected Fire* unrolls 'the carpet we have woven with the hair of the dead.'"

Gail Mazur recommends *Two Cities,* essays by Adam Zagajewski (Farrar, Straus & Giroux): "Zagajewski's a fine poet, one of the best, and this second collection of prose pieces—memoir/essays/prose poems—is the mature work of an ecstatic ironist: cosmopolitan, sweet, philosophical, and revealing. Born in Lvov, Poland, in 1945, Zagajewski is the voice of his generation, everywhere in exile, even at 'home.'"

M. L. Rosenthal recommends *Winter Channels,* poems by James Schevill (Floating Island): "A rare collection of brief lyric pieces, full of gentle feeling, humane wisdom, *and* sharp political and social thrusts, by one of America's most serious—and seriously neglected—poets."

Charles Simic recommends *The Tunnel: Selected Poems* by Russell Edson (Field Poetry Series): "If you wish to know what the prose poem can do, read Edson. He is one of the most original poets we have, widely translated and almost unknown at home."

Gary Soto recommends *Limbo,* a novel by Dixie Salazar (White Pine): "Dixie Salazar is the Kaye Gibbons of Fresno, California. Wealth of detail, attitude, and a sorrowful story."

Richard Tillinghast recommends *Another Person,* a memoir by James Merrill (Knopf): "The late James Merrill turns out to have been a perfect memoirist. The life, the sensibility, the writing style, are perfectly of a piece. A past master in his use of metaphor, Merrill brings that gift to his prose."

Chase Twichell recommends *Where I Stopped: Remembering Rape at Thirteen,* a memoir by Martha Ramsey (Putnam): "This is a remarkably lucid, emotionally gutsy book. Its language is quiet, never sensational, yet Ramsey manages to peel back the layers of memory with real power."

Dan Wakefield recommends *Playing the Game,* a novel by Alan Lelchuk (Baskerville): "This novel has been neglected and deserves to be read. A wonderful and entertaining insight into U.S. sports, with a coach who uses Thoreau, Whitman, and Francis Parkman as inspirational reading for halftime pep talks."

Rita Dove: *Mother Love,* a series of poems that recasts the ancient Greek story of Demeter and Persephone, mainly in sonnets, exploring the cycle of betrayal and regeneration that is at the heart of the classic mother-daughter myth. (Norton)

Donald Hall: *Principal Products of Portugal,* a collection of essays that serves as a tribute to the arts, from sports and poetry to sculpture and trees. (Beacon)

Alberto Alvaro Ríos: *Pig Cookies and Other Stories,* thirteen interrelated tales of a small village in northern Mexico over the course of several decades earlier in this century. (Chronicle)

Chase Twichell: *The Ghost of Eden,* Twichell's fourth book of poems, a visionary sequence of interlocking meditations on the death of nature as we know it. The "ghost" is both the shadow of the paradise we have so carelessly ruined, and the poet herself. (Ontario Review Press)

Ellen Bryant Voigt: *Kyrie,* a mosaic of sonnets that conjures up the influenza pandemic of 1918–19, which killed half a million people in the U.S. Voigt first focuses on a family and then branches out to separate voices. (Norton)

Dan Wakefield: *Expect a Miracle,* a nonfiction book that examines the everyday miracles Wakefield himself has experienced, interleaved with accounts of extraordinary events in the lives of his friends and acquaintances. (HarperCollins San Francisco)

POSTSCRIPTS

COHEN AWARDS Each volume year, we honor the best poem, short story, and essay published in *Ploughshares* with the Cohen Awards, which are wholly sponsored by our longtime patrons Denise and Mel Cohen. Finalists are nominated by staff editors, and the winners are selected by our advisory editors. Each winner receives a cash prize of $400. The 1995 Cohen Awards for work published in *Ploughshares* Vol. 20 go to:

PETER CRABTREE

MARY RUEFLE *for her poem "Glory" in Winter 1994–95, edited by Don Lee and David Daniel.*

Mary Ruefle was born outside of Pittsburgh in 1952. The daughter of a military officer, she spent the first twenty years of her life moving around the U.S. and Europe, and graduated from Bennington College in 1974 with a degree in literature. She attended the writing program at Hollins College, but admits that for many years she was a drifter, holding a variety of jobs in different places. "Nothing led me to writing but *reading*," says Ruefle, "and since I began to write poems as soon as I could read them, it never occurred to me to take anything else seriously— which later turned out to be sad."

Her work has appeared in numerous magazines and journals, and she is the author of three books, *Memling's Veil, Life Without Speaking,* and *The Adamant,* which co-won the 1988 Iowa Poetry Prize. Ruefle has received grants from the Vermont Council on the Arts, the National Endowment for the Arts, and awards from *The Black Warrior Review, The Southern Humanities Review,* and *The Kenyon Review.* She has taught at Bennington College, Colby College, the University of Michigan, and in China. Currently, she lives in Vermont and teaches in the M.F.A. program at Vermont College.

Of her poem "Glory," Ruefle writes: "I don't know what inspires a poem, but 'Glory' was informed by a general self-loathing (and its opposite), a gorgeous autumn, and the bit about the psychic is true. I met a wonderful woman living in one of those awful surfing towns on the Australian coast. She was a psychic and wanted to serve me a kind of candy called Violet Crumble, which I was anxious to try because I believed it was made from real violets. But she couldn't remember where she had hidden it, though she spoke of the events of the next millennium with ease. Later, I found the Violet Crumbles in a drugstore. They were not made out of violets and were regrettable, but that whole glorious afternoon came back to me while I was writing the poem, though not before—I never know what I am going to write about until I write it. I think there's a certain amount of poetic denial in all my work, in so far as writing poems sometimes appears to be in direct opposition to *living,* though in fairness I must admit there are times writing poems appears to be intense living indeed. The tension between the two keeps me working hard at both, complicated by a natural laziness."

MARSHALL N. KLIMASEWISKI *for his story "Snowfield" in the Spring 1994 issue, edited by James Welch.*

Marshall N. Klimasewiski was born in Hartford, Connecticut, in 1966 and grew up in the rural northwest corner of the state. He received his B.A. in English literature from Carnegie Mellon University, an M.F.A. in creative writing from Bowling Green State University, and a second master's in writing from Boston University. During and between his studies, he worked as a short-order cook, an electrical technician, an office temp, and a special projects coordinator for the public television station WGBH, assisting with *This Old House, The Victory Garden,* and *The New Yankee Workshop.* He has also taught creative writing at Bowling Green State University and the University of Hartford.

In 1988, his first story publication appeared in *Ploughshares.* Since then, he has published stories in such magazines and journals as *The New Yorker, The Antioch Review, Quarterly West,* and

ANNA KEESEY

ONTHEBUS. A story entitled "JunHee" was included in *The Best American Short Stories 1992,* edited by Robert Stone, and in an anthology of American fiction edited by the U.S. Information Agency for use among their English teachers abroad. This past winter, he was a writing fellow at the Fine Arts Work Center in Provincetown. He currently lives in Seattle and hopes to return to teaching soon.

About "Snowfield," Klimasewiski writes: "Although the bulk of the story takes place during a single train ride, I originally intended that to be only the initial, brief scene of a longer story. The scene stretched out as I wrote it, and when it was almost finished, it came to seem self-sustaining and complete. But it suggested a great deal more to me, and for about six months I attempted to write a novel for which 'Snowfield' would be the first chapter. I eventually recognized that I wasn't up to the task; the historic and international settings, in 1940's New York and 1920's Poland, were particularly daunting and probably ill-conceived. But Stanley, the narrator, and both of his parents remain interesting to me, and I'll likely make another pass at them in the future. By the way, the Bergsonites were a real and fairly remarkable group of activists during the war. Their efforts are probably detailed most comprehensively by David S. Wyman in *The Abandonment of the Jews.*"

CHARLES BAXTER *for his essay "Dysfunctional Narratives" in Fall 1994, edited by Rosellen Brown.*

Charles Baxter was born in Minneapolis in 1947 and grew up in a town west of Minneapolis called Excelsior. (Baxter remarks: "An even smaller town on the outskirts of Excelsior was named Eureka—exclamatory town names seemed to have been the rule there.") His first job during high school was at Abbott Hospital in Minneapolis, where he once wheeled John Berryman down to the physical therapy unit. He attended the Mound, Minnesota, public schools, received his B.A. from Macalester College, and then taught public school in rural Michigan. He received his Ph.D. from the State University of New York at Buffalo, and since 1974, he has lived in Ann Arbor with his wife and son, and has taught at Wayne State University, the University of Michigan, and Warren Wilson College.

He is the author of three books of stories, *Harmony of the World* (1984), *Through the Safety Net* (1985), and *A Relative Stranger* (1990); two novels, *First Light* (1987) and *Shadow Play* (1993); and a book of poetry, *Imaginary Paintings* (1990). His stories have appeared in most of the major magazines and have been widely anthologized. He has received fellowships from the Guggenheim Foundation, the National Endowment for the Arts, and the Lila Wallace–Reader's Digest Fund. A companion essay to "Dysfunctional Narratives" called "Fiction and the Inner Life of Objects" recently received *The Gettysburg Review* award for best essay printed in that journal during 1993.

About "Dysfunctional Narratives," Baxter writes: "The essay began its life as a talk to the students in the M.F.A. program at Warren Wilson College. For some time, I had noticed (or *thought* I had noticed) that fiction writers in writing programs often refuse to let their characters make mistakes of any kind. They don't mind letting events happen *to* those characters, but they avoid situations in which characters initiate actions and indulge in interestingly adult bad behavior. I wondered why. Richard Nixon was in the hospital during the time I began to think about the essay, and on a whim, I began to read his memoir, *RN*. (I took it out of the library; I refused to buy it, and my wife wanted to get it out of the house as quickly as possible.) It was a rich and strange experience, reading that book, and I am the only person I know who has done so, although I don't recommend it. At about the same time, I began to watch *Geraldo* while I ate lunch. I did this for about two weeks. After I ran across C. K. Williams's phrase about 'dysfunctional narratives,' the pieces of the argument began to fit themselves together, and the essay pretty much wrote itself."

BEST AMERICANS Rafael Campo's poem "The Battle Hymn of the Republic," which appeared in the Spring 1994 issue, edited by James Welch, was selected for inclusion in *The Best American Poetry 1995*, edited by Richard Howard. Two stories from the staff-edited Winter 1994–95 issue, Stephen Dobyns's "So I Guess

You Know What I Told Him" and Gish Jen's "Birthmates," were picked for *The Best American Short Stories 1995,* edited by Jane Smiley.

PUSHCARTS Four works from *Ploughshares* were selected for the 1995–96 edition of *The Pushcart Prize XX:* Eileen Pollack's story "Milk," which appeared in the Spring 1994 issue, edited by James Welch; Frederick Busch's essay "Bad" and Debra Spark's essay "Last Things," both of which appeared in the Fall 1994 issue, edited by Rosellen Brown; and Marilyn Chin's poem "The Barbarians Are Coming," which appeared in an earlier edition of *Ploughshares* edited by Rita Dove and Fred Viebahn.

POETRY SOCIETY Two collections of poems by former *Ploughshares* contributors were recently honored by the Poetry Society of America: Cyrus Cassells won the William Carlos Williams Award for *Soul Make a Path Through Shouting* (Copper Canyon), and Sophie Cabot Black won the Norma Farber First Book Award for *The Misunderstanding of Nature* (Graywolf).

CONTRIBUTORS' NOTES

Ploughshares · Fall 1995

FREDERICK BARTHELME is author of nine books, including *Moon Deluxe, Second Marriage, Tracer, The Brothers,* and the forthcoming novel *Painted Desert* (Viking, October 1995), from which "The Big Room" was adapted. His short fiction has been published in *Esquire, The New Yorker, Epoch,* and elsewhere. He directs the Center for Writers at the University of Southern Mississippi and edits *The Mississippi Review.*

LESLEE BECKER grew up in the Adirondacks. She was a James Michener Writing Fellow at the University of Iowa and a Wallace Stegner Writing Fellow at Stanford University. Her work has appeared in *The Atlantic Monthly, The Iowa Review, The Gettysburg Review, Nimrod, New Letters, Sonora Review,* and elsewhere. She currently teaches at Colorado State University and is working on a collection of stories.

PAUL BRODEUR has been a staff writer at *The New Yorker* for many years. His short stories have appeared in *The New Yorker, Saturday Evening Post, Seventeen, Show, Michigan Quarterly Review,* and *The Antioch Review.* He is the author of a collection of stories, *Downstream* (Atheneum); two novels, *The Sick Fox* (Atlantic Monthly Press) and *The Stunt Man* (Atheneum); and seven books of nonfiction.

TONY EPRILE is the author of *Temporary Sojourner & Other South African Stories.* He received a fellowship from the National Endowment for the Arts in 1994 and is a visiting writer at Northwestern University.

LAURA FURMAN was born in New York in 1945. She is the author of the novels *The Shadow Line* and *Tuxedo Park* and the story collections *The Glass House* and *Watch Time Fly.* Her fiction has been published in *The New Yorker* and *Southwest Review,* and her nonfiction has appeared in *Mirabella* and elsewhere. She lives in Austin, Texas, with her husband and son, and teaches at the University of Texas.

TESS GALLAGHER's most recent work is a book of poetry, *Portable Kisses Expanded* (Capra Press, 1994). Her collection of short stories, *The Lover of Horses,* was reissued by Graywolf Press in 1992. "Creatures" will appear in a collection in progress entitled *Dig Two Graves: Stories of Revenge.* The book title comes from a proverb on the subject of anger: "If you contemplate revenge, dig two graves." Another story, "A Box of Rocks," appeared recently in *Story.*

RAY ISLE is currently a Wallace Stegner Fellow at Stanford University. His work has appeared in *Agni* and *The Carolina Quarterly.* Born and raised in Houston, Texas, he now lives in Palo Alto, where he is at work on a novel.

TOM JENKS is the author of a novel, *Our Happiness*. His fiction and nonfiction have appeared in *Esquire, Vanity Fair, The Los Angeles Times,* and *Story*. With Raymond Carver, he edited the anthology *American Short Story Masterpieces*, and with his wife, the novelist Carol Edgarian, he is currently editing *The Writer's Life in Notebooks, Journals, and Diaries*, to be published next year by Random House.

DEVON JERSILD has published her short stories in *The Kenyon Review, The North American Review,* and *Prize Stories 1990: The O. Henry Awards*. She lives in Weybridge, Vermont, where she is the administrative director of the Bread Loaf Writers' Conference. She has just completed a novel.

CAROLINE A. LANGSTON was born in 1968 in Yazoo City, Mississippi, the youngest of six children. Her stories have been included in *The Gettysburg Review, Sonora Review,* and *New Stories from the American South,* which is forthcoming from Algonquin Press in the fall of 1995. The recipient of an M.F.A. from the University of Houston, she has been an instructor of literature and is currently a Milton Center post-graduate fellow for 1995–96.

WILLIAM HENRY LEWIS was born in Denver in 1967 and grew up in Tennessee and Washington, D.C. He is an assistant professor of English at Mary Washington College, where he teaches creative writing, and he co-directs the Reynolds Young Writers Workshops, a summer program for high school writers, at Denison University. His collection of stories, *In the Arms of Our Elders*, was published in early 1995 by Carolina Wren Press, and his short fiction is forthcoming in *Speak My Name: An Anthology of Writings About Black Men's Identity and Legacy*, to be released by Beacon Press in late 1995.

JAMES LILLIEFORS is a longtime journalist and former newspaper editor. He has been a frequent contributor to *The Washington Post* and other publications, and is the author of the book *Highway 50*. He was educated at the University of Iowa and the University of Virginia, and he currently lives in Naples, Florida, where he is concentrating on fiction writing. "Fugitives" is adapted from a novel in progress.

LINCOLN PERRY, a nationally known artist, has shown his work at the Tatistcheff gallery at 50 West 57th St. in New York since 1979. A number of large commissioned paintings are on permanent display around the country. The cover painting, *Balance* (oil on canvas), measures 7′ x 10′ and was completed in 1988. (Note: The edges of the painting were cropped slightly for the purpose of reproduction.)

STEVEN RINEHART divides his time between Fayetteville, Georgia, and New York City. His short fiction has appeared recently in *Story* and *GQ*, and is forthcoming in *Harper's*. He is a 1995 recipient of a fellowship from the National Endowment for the Arts.

JESSICA TREADWAY's collection of short stories, *Absent Without Leave* (Delphinium Books), received the John C. Zacharis First Book Award from *Ploughshares* in 1993. She is at work on a novel and teaches creative writing at Emerson College and Tufts University.

MARC VASSALLO received a degree in architecture from Cornell University and worked as an architect, a farmer, and an editor before completing an M.F.A. in fiction at the University of Virginia. He lives in Connecticut with his wife, Linda, and their two-year-old son, Nicholas. A story of his appeared recently in *Southern Exposure*, and he is at work on a novel called *Adam's Garden*.

DAVID WIEGAND is an arts editor and book critic for *The San Francisco Chronicle*, where he also writes a weekly column on the Bay Area arts and entertainment scene.

~

SUBMISSION POLICIES *Ploughshares* is published three times a year: usually mixed issues of poetry and fiction in the Winter and Spring and a fiction issue in the Fall, with each guest-edited by a different writer. We welcome unsolicited manuscripts from August 1 to March 31 (postmark dates). All submissions sent from April to July are returned unread. In the past, guest editors often announced specific themes for issues, but we have revised our editorial policies and no longer restrict submissions to thematic topics. Submit your work at anytime during our reading period; if a manuscript is not timely for one issue, it will be considered for another. Send one prose piece and/or one to three poems at a time (mail genres separately). Poems should be individually typed either single- or double-spaced on one side of the page. Prose should be typed double-spaced on one side and be no longer than thirty pages. Although we look primarily for short stories, we occasionally publish personal essays/memoirs. Novel excerpts are acceptable if self-contained. Unsolicited book reviews and criticism are not considered. Please do not send multiple submissions of the same genre, and do not send another manuscript until you hear about the first. Additional submissions will be returned unread. Mail your manuscript in a page-sized manila envelope, your full name and address written on the outside, to the "Fiction Editor," "Poetry Editor," or "Nonfiction Editor." (Unsolicited work sent directly to a guest editor's home or office will be discarded.) All manuscripts and correspondence regarding submissions should be accompanied by a self-addressed, stamped envelope (S.A.S.E.) for a response. Expect three to five months for a decision. Do not query us until five months have passed, and if you do, please write to us, including an S.A.S.E. and indicating the postmark date of submission, instead of calling. Simultaneous submissions are amenable as long as they are indicated as such and we are notified immediately upon acceptance elsewhere. We cannot accommodate revisions, changes of return address, or forgotten S.A.S.E.'s after the fact. We do not reprint previously published work. Translations are welcome if permission has been granted. We cannot be responsible for delay, loss, or damage.

BENNINGTON WRITING SEMINARS
AT BENNINGTON COLLEGE

*MA/MFA in Writing and Literature
Two-year low-residency program*

A. BLAKE GARDNER

CORE FACULTY:

Douglas Bauer, Sven Birkerts, Susan Cheever, Susan Dodd, Maria Flook, Lynn Freed,
Amy Hempel, Verlyn Klinkenborg, David Lehman, Jill McCorkle, Reginald McKnight,
Liam Rector, Stephen Sandy, Bob Shacochis, Anne Winters

RECENT ASSOCIATE FACULTY:

Lucie Brock-Broido, Robert Creeley, Bruce Duffy, Donald Hall, Edward Hoagland,
Jane Kenyon, Bret Lott, E. Ethelbert Miller, Sue Miller,
Robert Pinsky, Katha Pollitt, Tree Swenson

FICTION ◆ NONFICTION ◆ POETRY

For more information contact:
Writing Seminars, Box PL, Bennington College
Bennington, Vermont 05201 ◆ 802-442-5401, ext. 160

AGNI

236 Bay State Road   Boston, MA 02215
Subscriptions:
$18/ year for individuals
$36/ year for institutions